Praise for

"As you get to know the characters, the author ... creates a rivalry between them and a game of one-upmanship that really add some fun to the story. They are both strong and determined and really make a good match once they are willing to open their eyes and hearts to love."
—TheRomanceReviews.com

"Olivia has great sense of romance writing. There is also a bit of humor in unexpected scenes that one does not see coming."
—Amazon Review

"His Viking Bride is certainly one of the more memorable historical romances I've read, both for its authenticity and its characters' undeniable chemistry. I'd dive right into watching Veleif's men meet their matches or just about anything else in this vein that Norem writes."
—FicCentral.com

"A very well written Viking romance book... lots of exciting scenarios... and never a dull moment."
—Goodreads Review

"There are lots of characters, action, adventure, and more... one determined princess who wanted to go home... an equally determined prince... many things here to ensnare the senses and captivate the imagination."
—TheBookJunkieReads.com

"The story was great, characters were all believable and likeable, very well done! ...brutal and gritty in a way that Viking stories should be..."
—L Jones, Author

"*His Viking Bride* (Olivia Norem) is hot, hot, hot! ... endearing to see Æstrid's camaraderie with Veileif's men, and how she used her wits to win them over to do her bidding. Loved it!"
—JaneKelsey.com Diary of a Book Addict

## Also by Olivia Norem

Firewater: A Brothers in Justice Novel, Volume One

Wicked Wicked Passage

Copyright © 2017, 2016 by Olivia Norem
Cover design by StephenSimonArt
Cover image: Getty Images
Back Cover image: periodimages.com

SECOND EDITION
ISBN-13: 978-1541395947

For Stephen
My incomparable hero

# Chapter One

"Stop splashing me, Leidolf!"

"You wanted me here, Æstrid. Now prepare for war." Her brother growled with mock ferocity and a devilish grin.

Leidolf sliced his oar across the surface of the glacial waters, and drenched her full across the back.

"Arghhh!" Æstrid squealed, her shrieks echoed around the mountain lake. A crisp breeze of waning summer gusted suddenly, making her arch and shiver against the icy splatters that soaked her gown.

Æstrid spun and balled her fist, ready to launch an attack as their canoe tipped precariously. She hesitated when she saw the mischievous expression of victory on her brother's face. Bracing her footing, she gripped her oar tighter and drenched him back, erupting into peals of laughter as Leidolf's eyes rounded in shock.

"There brat, that should teach you," Æstrid laughed, and sliced her oar again with determined vengeance.

Æstrid had taunted him mercilessly until he agreed to sneak off with her to the forbidden lake. She boasted she would catch more fish, and they would be able to return before their father Gunnalf, was any wiser.

So far, the only thing they'd caught all afternoon was a good soaking from each other's oars.

Leidolf sputtered and pushed his dripping, strawberry locks from his forehead. At fourteen he was already a head taller than she. While he favored their father's looks, Leidolf's face held none of the fierce, battle-hardened manner of their sire.

Æstrid sighed wistfully and wished Leidolf would stay as he was, but their father was already grooming him to take his place. Earlier this year in fact, Gunnalf gifted him with the silver band on his arm. A mark of Leidolf's princely responsibilities as the future ruler of Karissonholdt.

Leidolf had been required to spend his days practicing with axes, swords, and shields. He was accompanying the men on shorter seafaring raids, and making Æstrid sick with worry until he returned safely home.

The opportunities to steal away with him were becoming increasingly rare, until, Æstrid feared one day too soon, they would not come at all.

"Father will likely beat us if he returns and finds us gone." Leidolf glanced at the sky to gauge the afternoon light. At best, the pair faced a full hour's trek east across the mountain path to return to Karissonholdt.

"Well if we taste his whip, it will be your fault." Æstrid chided with a giggle.

"How will it be my fault?"

Æstrid rolled her eyes. "Oh, Leidolf, if grandmother was in this boat instead of you, I'd have reached shore by now."

"Ha! No fault of mine, sister. Your arms are too puny," Leidolf chuckled.

"Puny? Why you—" Æstrid shrieked and lunged again. Leidolf propelled the canoe with a hearty shove, his laughter buoyant as she tumbled backward landing hard on her bottom.

"You were saying, Æstrid?" Leidolf laughed and paddled them harder into a swift glide. When the canoe slid closer to shore, they were both breathless and laughing. Tucking her skirts up into her belt, Æstrid stepped from the bow of the boat as water sloshed around her boots.

She frowned at Leidolf, puzzled that he remained in the canoe with a strange look on his face. His mouth dropped open and his eyes suddenly narrowed in anger. Why he was still sitting in the boat was beyond her. When did he become such a lazy lout, too delicate to get his feet wet?

"Leidolf? Out of the boat with you, boy. What's the matter with you?" Æstrid insisted. Her bewilderment increased as she saw his hand close over the hilt of the small sword belted to his waist.

"Æstrid, don't move," Leidolf whispered.

"What in the god's names are you talking about?" Æstrid spun around to follow his gaze. Her whole body stiffened in terror. Not thirty feet from her stood two large men at the forest's edge. Their long hair was pulled back and stained inky black. The top halves of their faces were also painted black, making it look as if they wore masks. A riot of scrolls and bands covered their naked chests and arms in strange, undulating patterns of blue woad. Woad was a noxious, staining concoction. Its specific making was unknown to Æstrid, but she knew of the one tribe who did.

Picts!

The bloody Picts were mortal enemies to everyone at Karissonholdt. Truth be told they were enemies of all Norse people. Æstrid's head snapped to the right as two more of the savages emerged from the trees. Their bare chests and arms were decorated in equally grotesque markings of blue and black. Their hands gripped crude axes and menacing wooden clubs.

"Æstrid, get back in the boat now," Leidolf warned. His tone low and sharp.

The strange patterns on their skin undulated as the Picts crossed into the dappled sunlight of the clearing. The designs were hypnotic, rendering her motionless. Yet the enchantment gave way to a growing shaft of fear that seeped into the marrow of her bones. Her voice hitched in a wordless cry frozen in her throat, as she watched two of the giants move toward them.

"Move, Æstrid!" Leidolf growled. It was enough to piece the veil of fear. As she lifted a foot to step into the canoe, one of the men barked a command in their strange language.

The Picts rushed forward.

Leidolf alighted from the canoe, knee-deep in water. As he charged forward her brother shoved the canoe so hard, Æstrid fell backward into the hull. Leidolf heaved it away from the shore and drew his blade at the same time.

"No!" Æstrid screamed, struggling to right herself. "No, Leidolf!"

She blinked in horror as her brother rushed the savages. He ducked the swing of a great stone axe of the nearest Pict. He thrust his sword upward into the abdomen of the next attacker. Æstrid screamed again as entrails erupted from the Pict's stomach. Leidolf stumbled, dropping to one knee. He scrambled to regain his footing on the slippery shoreline.

She tipped sideways in the canoe, screaming at him to rise, swim, *get back!* The second Pict charged before he could right himself. The great brute swung his club without mercy. The sickening thud of the weapon connected with Leidolf's head and her brother instantly crumpled to the ground.

"Leidolf!" Æstrid cried in agony. He wasn't dead! He couldn't be!

Her brother's body lay crumpled on the shoreline, very, very still. With tears streaming down her face, Æstrid screamed over and over for him to get up, but a second ugly thud to her brother's head saw his skull split before her eyes.

A cry of anguish wrenched her. He was dead. Leidolf was dead!

Numb and shocked, Æstrid couldn't bear to look at the motionless form that was her beloved brother. Turning her head aside she squeezed her eyes tight. The world plummeted inward to a cavern of silence and it felt as if hours passed until she could open them again.

Icy tendrils of fear tingled across her body, awakening her from her stupor. She saw the edge of Leidolf's brown tunic lift and wave in the breeze. Moments later that same breeze reached across the lake and turned the twin trails of her tears bitter cold. For Æstrid it was like a delicate slap, but it was enough. She was in danger. Grave danger!

Three Picts mused and gestured over Leidolf's body. From the strange language exchanged between them, it appeared they were congratulating themselves on the slaughter.

Her body was leaden in the canoe and Æstrid could barely feel the wood of the oar, or the knife hilt as she closed around her fingers around it. The shore seemed to move closer as if she were drifting slowly forward in a tunnel. She began rowing in a frenzy as the Picts waded into the water toward her.

One savage's face split into a feral smile, revealing broken, yellow teeth as he gripped the bow of the canoe. Another scream tore from her throat as she struck out at him with the oar. Another Pict quickly came alongside and Æstrid whirled to fight him off. Her hands and arms vibrated with pain as she landed a blow to the side of his head. Momentarily stunned she plunged her knife in a downward stroke of rage aimed for the savage's throat.

Her eyes locked with the man and she saw the light fade from the white orbs in his head. His head leaned back just before his body slipped into the water. A red cloud of blood bloomed around him and Æstrid fought down the bile that rose in her stomach, sickened at what she'd just done.

The hesitation cost her, and her knife. Two Picts, enraged at the death of their fallen brother swooped upon her. One wrenched the oar from her grasp as another plucked her from the canoe.

Æstrid screamed and thrashed, fighting for her life to escape, but the savages ignored her futile fight. She clawed at her captor, leaving trails of blood on his cheek as her nails raked his face. With a wounded growl, he let his hand fly connecting to her mouth. Æstrid tasted blood and blinked hard, trying to clear her foggy vision from the force of the blow. Kicking and cursing, she was pinned against the giant brute who carried her to the shore.

Æstrid fought kicking and cursing. She screamed at Leidolf to get up, shouting out over and over as she glimpsed his face beyond the frame of her terror and rage. His motionless eyes gaped open to the sky and his mouth hung open in a wordless plea. Æstrid's anguish renewed in fury as sobs wracked from her chest.

She felt hands close around her throat as she clawed and spit and cursed. The fists squeezed tighter and slowly everything turned soft and warm. Æstrid looked weakly at her young brother's face, lying motionless on the bank.

"Leidolf..." she sobbed as her world turned black.

### 

A pinprick of yellow light glowed in the distance and Æstrid floated toward it. She drifted closer, hazily thinking it was important to reach it. She willed herself to move to the brightness amid the swirling dark of her vision. Awareness came in slow degrees as a small fire coalesced into view. Long, eerie shapes moved all about the small fire and the ground, hard and unyielding, rushed up to meet her.

Her mouth tasted like she had swallowed a pile of crushed rock. Her nostrils pinched with the char of firewood and the damp, dusky tang of earth. Then the dawning came. She was in a cave and lying on her side. Her limbs were cramped and securely tied behind her back. The eerie shapes surrounding her were long shadows of two Pict women as they moved back and forth in front of the fire.

One's head snapped in her direction and Æstrid could only see the white of her eyes amid the painted stripe on her face. Her hair was raven black and her arms were covered in the dark blue scrolls and bands – the same as the men who had snatched her from the lake. The same as the men who had murdered her brother.

One woman bent toward the fire, then shuffled to Æstrid's side, holding a crude cup. She bent and wrenched Æstrid's head back and the woman dribbled some noxious, warm liquid into her mouth. Æstrid choked against the bitter brew. It tasted faintly of earthy roots and unknown herbs. She coughed and gagged in protest. The woman clucked then murmured to her in her strange tongue, and Æstrid could only guess at the disapproval in her tone.

The other woman joined them, her dark eyes flared behind the painted black stripe on her face. She squatted beside her, arranging makeshift trenchers of withered bark. Æstrid followed her fingers as the woman scooped out the blue mixture and traced a swirl on her upper arm. Æstrid shrank back from her touch and began to struggle against the bonds. The first woman snapped something to the other and they both peered at her curiously.

Then the women's faces began to swim before her. The fire light shifted and danced and bathed the whole cave in a growing glow of orange. Suddenly everything was brighter, hotter and a queer numbness coursed through her. The ground beneath her seemed to shift and grow unsteady, almost as if she were drunk with wine.

She felt four hands upon her, the cool rush of air against her skin as the women tore away her clothes. Somewhere in the back of her mind Æstrid thought that was a curious thing to do, but she couldn't struggle anymore. It took a great effort to do nothing else but turn her head.

She was floating now. Her whole body seemed to hover a few feet above the hard clay floor as the women worked. She felt their fingertips upon her skin, like a soft summer wind, circling, painting her with their blue scrolls, covering her neck and arms, her legs and belly with the feather light touches.

She felt her eyes roll back in her head and she begged for water to quench the sudden burning in her throat. She could smell the woad. It was heady and strong, an offensive mix of bitter herbs and earth and rotted berries.

Suddenly she was back in time and four years old again. Æstrid was home, the room swelled with soft breezes and the perfumed flowers she hung on the top of Leidolf's cradle. She tucked her brother in his wooden crib and slowly rocked it, peering over the edge into his cherubic face. Æstrid broke out in a singsong voice, canting softly the lullaby she used to sing to him.

The swirling orange light grew bright and hot and Æstrid convulsed against the bonds. She felt beads of sweat form on the sections of her skin left bereft of decorations of the strange blue markings. Æstrid focused on her arm. The circles and scrolls seemed to twist and writhe across her skin of their own accord, snaking their way up her arms, tightening over her.

Æstrid screamed but she made no sound and the Pict woman scrutinized her closely. Æstrid saw the woman's face orbiting around her as twin heads, swirling, twirling until they gently circled again and became one.

A shred of clarity returned before the cup was placed to her lips again. Æstrid wrinkled her nose. The cup smelled bitter and in the vestiges of her mind, her body rebelled. She would not drink! Her captors wrenched her cruelly back and spilled the offensive brew into choking, sputtering mouth.

Every color of the universe swam together. The campfire flowed onto the floor in a blazing trail of liquid fire, melding with the blue-black paint of the women, until their faces grew long and distorted once more. Blackness hovered at the vestiges of her vision and Æstrid heard a distant scuffling before oblivion took her once again.

She faded in and out of consciousness, barely aware her arms and legs were pulled and contorted. She could taste the pungent smell of dung and charcoal as hands gathered her hair, pulled it, stretched it.

Æstrid thought she was fighting with infamous Viking resistance, but in truth, she lay on the earthen floor, moaning weakly in protest.

A great, white cloth waved over her as her head lolled from side to side. Her vision was spinning and the singsong lullaby broke once again from her lips.

The shadows of the cave grew smaller and her breath left her. She was lifting, up and up moving against something hard and the ceiling of the cave transformed, flowing like a river of molten clay. Then the clay widened into a huge, black mass covered with tiny, sparkling orbs too far away to reach.

Were those stars?

The awareness was brief as a shiver of night air caressed her skin. She was mercifully outside, but her hands and legs were bound behind her to a rough length of wood. She was being carried somewhere in the dark of night, somewhere beyond the cave.

Her eyes rolled in drugged confusion and she coughed through a thick, black wave of smoke that threatened to choke her. The distant pounding of drums grew louder and the rhythm pulsed in her blood, waking her from her stupor. Her skin turned hot as if she stood in the sun too long. As her head lolled to her right shoulder, Æstrid's world tilted, up and up, then halted with a jolt.

The horror seized her.

Æstrid was surrounded by dozens upon dozens of Picts.

All around, in every direction, their painted bodies writhed in front of the great circle of light. A thin awareness niggled her brain. She was staked and bound, and set before their blazing bonfire.

The bodies moved and danced as their strange patterns snaked across their skin in the hellish light. The drums beat louder and Æstrid struggled to keep conscious, slipping back and forth between blackness and this languid nightmare.

The Picts grew frenzied. Their black hair flying behind them as they twisted, swirled and rushed around her. A big monster of a savage dashed in front of her, then paused and bellowed some strange chant. His entire face and shoulders were painted solid in the blackish-blue woad, and Æstrid could only see the white flare of his eyes, glittering at her like quartz.

The glint of a blade flashed in the corner of her eye, then she felt something warm and wet rolling down her arm. The blackened devil roared a devilish cry, with arms raised and stretched to the moon. He darted past her again and disappeared into the fiery hell of night and drumbeats.

As quickly as the first one departed, a second one appeared. Another quick flash of a blade and Æstrid felt her other arm grow wet and sticky, as her head lolled to the side.

The drums throbbed louder and faster until she felt sickened trying to follow their dizzying dance. Her eyes rolled back again and she inhaled the mingled scents of sweat, woad, and the sharp tang of burning wood. She turned her head gasping, knowing somewhere beyond this hideous revelry, lay the cool, cleansing air of the night.

"Cursed savages!" Veleif whispered harshly to Arnor, who lay in the brush at his right.

"Ah, but what's another Pict woman more or less?" The great Viking whispered back, watching the beastly ritual unfold.

The savages were drumming and dancing all about their great bonfire. They were spinning past their sacrifice and taking turns nicking the female with crude blades. When the red trails appeared on her arms and chest, they roared great whoops of victory, tossing their demon heads back as they shouted to the sky.

Veleif reined in his anger.

He hated these marauders beyond reason. He also knew to fly into their midst in a blinding rage without a plan of attack, would neither serve him nor his men.

"By my count I make fourteen of the savages, Veleif," Halfdan whispered eagerly in his left ear. The man absently toyed with the long, red braids of his beard as he broke out into a huge grin beneath his helm. "With eight of us, 'twill hardly be a fair fight. For them," he chuckled.

Veleif peered sidelong at Halfdan, his lips curled in a wry smile. "Perhaps four of us should stay back then? And give the bastards a chance?"

All three men chuckled softly.

"Kill the men. We'll take the women back as slaves. 'Tis unthinkable to leave them here to survive the winter alone," Veleif ordered.

"Veleif! Better to kill them all. You'd risk taking Pict women back to Kollsveinholdt? They'll slit your throat in your sleep," Halfdan protested.

"Since when have any of us lived in fear of a female?" Veleif scoffed. "We'll keep them until we sail to Novgorod in the spring. We will trade them there."

"By the looks of the bound one, we'd be lucky to get six pieces of silver for her," Arnor muttered and spat to the side.

"You want Pict woman to warm your bed through the winter, Arnor?" Veleif grinned.

"That wench is too slight for him, Veleif. She'd barely last one night beneath that great beast," Halfdan snickered.

"I'd surely break the maid," Arnor admitted. He winced internally as he saw the woman snagged with another cut. "Let us be about this task, before they carve her up, and leave us nothing left to trade at the markets."

Veleif nodded up and down the row, and then raised his hand in signal. Four broke off to the right beneath the underbrush, and he and three others headed left.

The attack came quick and hard.

The Picts were so engaged in their ritual, four of them were cut down silently before they became aware of the attack. They broke out into fierce screeches of rage, grabbing their short blades and stone axes having been snapped from the mesmerizing rhythms of their vicious dance.

Æstrid barely recognized the bewildering scene as it unfolded in front of her. The helms of Norsemen glinted in the firelight between pauses of heavy smoke from the bonfire. Her head swerved side to side, like a doll who had lost its stuffing, as she tried to determine if she had been tossed into another lurid dream.

Banshees, perhaps?

Or gods, come to swallow up these savages in their clouds of charring smoke which waxed and waned in this dizzying dream.

Thuds of stone meeting wooden shields and the anguished cries of screaming blue and black painted men filled the night. She saw a body topple right before her, his head severed clean with the arc of a Viking axe.

Æstrid tried to cry out against the horror of hacking limbs, and writhing men, turning and twisting under the relentless blades. Her mouth opened, but her throat was locked and dry.

Without warning, a large, vengeful god coalesced through the gray, smoldering air. Æstrid's eyes widened in terror. Through the undulating shadows of night and fire, a man's shape began to form. He was broad and powerful, silhouetted against the flames. His face was wreathed in shadows but his armor bore bright streaks of blood and gore.

When the god turned to her she found her voice. A scream of pure terror ripped from her throat. His face glowed large and angry and his eyes pierced her soul. Twin blue orbs flared in rage as a large serpent stretched and crawled upon his helm, finally settling to rest right between his glowing eyes.

Æstrid let loose a second blood-curdling scream.

The orbs narrowed to shimmering slits, then disappeared in a waft of billowing, black smoke.

Veleif cursed at the distraction and spun around in time to ward off the blow from the crazed Pict behind.

The man's arm raised high, poised with a knife. Veleif hesitated in surprise at the glint of silver on his arm. A mere second to recover, he spun his axe, and with a mighty roar cleaved the man's chest with a fatal blow. The Pict's eyes swelled white beneath the black paint on his face. Toe to toe Veleif shoved deeper with his blade and watched the Pict hover on the edge of surprise and death. Then his pupils darkened, and he collapsed dead before he hit the ground.

Arnor rushed to his side, crimson spatters covered his face and chest. His axe and sword dripped red. With a warrior's heat still upon him, Arnor let out a triumphant cry as Veleif wrenched his axe clear from the Pict's chest. He dropped down to one knee and inspected the silver cuff.

"This is no Pict silver. 'Tis Norse," he said, as his finger traced the intricate pattern on the band.

"Probably taken from that lad we found on the shore," Arnor frowned in speculation.

"I agree. But may I rot before I leave a Pict with any gift from our kind. Other than a taste of our blades." Veleif tugged the silver cuff, but it wouldn't come loose. In a growl of vengeance, he raised his axe and cleaved the limb with one clean blow.

"You should have done that before you killed him," Arnor smiled. Veleif shot him a debatable glare. "So the cursed savage could feel the loss of his arm," Arnor shrugged, amiably.

"Good enough he felt the sting of my axe in his chest," Veleif snorted.

He wrenched the bracelet loose and tossed the limb aside. Beyond the blustering waves of smoke, Veleif surveyed the wreckage of the camp. His men were kicking and turning the heathen bodies, looking for anything of value. A few knives were secured but little else could be found among them.

The warriors of Kollsveinholdt, much like their prince, had little regard for anything belonging to the Picts.

Halfdan and Ingor carried out two screaming women, wrestling them from their hiding place in the cave above. Veleif turned to the woman behind him, still bound to the crude stake. Grabbing a fistful of hair, he lifted her face up toward him. The wench's eyes were closed. Mercifully, she had fainted. From the look of her, she'd been drugged or poisoned, and was obviously in no condition to walk.

He went behind the stake and slit her bonds with a quick flick of his sword. The wench crumpled to the ground like a sack of grain before he could catch her.

"Careful, Veleif. She's already abused." Arnor frowned, as he gathered the woman in his arms and slung her over his shoulder. Veleif watched the maid's head roll listlessly against the big Viking's back. Just as well, he thought, at least this one was quiet and not shrieking like the others.

Veleif pursed his lips and sheathed his sword. "I've never seen you so taken with a maid, my friend. She's skinny. *And* a Pict!"

"I am taken," Arnor snapped. "Taken a care you don't damage my spoils."

"Ha! Lie to the maid, not to me. After we ride out the winter, if you're a mind to release her from your bed, Arnor, consider your blessings."

"What say you?"

Veleif grinned and slapped Arnor's shoulder as they headed toward the ship. "The wench may fetch you eight pieces of silver instead of six. She appears to be a bit more rounded up close."

# Chapter Two

By the time Veleif and his men reached their longship, they had already lost one prisoner.

The Pict woman in Ingor's care, managed to wrest a long knife from his scabbard. Before he could snatch it back, she muttered something resembling a curse, and plunged Ingor's knife into her heart.

Halfdan quickly bound his prisoner, lest she snatch his sword and embarrass him as well. Amidst mutterings of 'cursed luck' and 'heathen savages' the men clambered onto their ship.

Arnor laid his wench down onto a thick pelt on the deck. The woman was pale and still in faint. He'd leave her unbound as she was certainly no match for a man his size. Besides, where could she go? Turning his attention to other duties, Arnor put her from his mind.

Veleif took his place at the helm, shouting briskly to the men to take their oars. He wanted nothing more than to hasten home and leave this heathen memory behind. The winds were favorable and the sails quickly filled. When the land behind them began to fade, a shout near the stern caught his attention. Halfdan cursed and shouted, both fists waving furiously to the heavens.

"What troubles you, Halfdan?" Veleif asked, quickly reaching the man's side. He followed the man's line of sight and saw the source of Halfdan's rage. The Pict woman was overboard, her head bobbing in the freezing waves. Then another wave crashed over her and she was not seen again.

"Fool bitch!" Halfdan raged and spat. "Bound and drowned. 'Tis my cursed luck."

"No curse, Halfdan," Veleif assured him and clapped him on the shoulder. "It was the gods saving you from her. As you said, she'd slit your throat while you slept."

Both men turned together and eyed Arnor's wench suspiciously. She lay unconscious on the pelt, yet they exchanged worried glances.

Veleif shouted to the men nearby. "Bind that slave. Better yet, put her in chains. I'll risk no more treachery on this voyage."

Damned cursed Picts!

Arnor threw a questioning look toward Veleif, but seeing the fierce set of his jaw, he knew well enough Veleif's mind was made up. Arnor's mouth set in a grim line as he watched the men put his slave in an iron collar, and secured the thing with a heavy chain.

Arnor had never been one to question an order from Veleif, but this seemed unduly heavy-handed. The wench was all but lifeless. Arnor doubted when she finally woke, she would have the strength to hurl herself overboard, let alone lift a blade. Chiding his protective nature, Arnor bent closely to inspect her wounds.

Despite his terrifying size and skill with both axe and sword, Arnor was a healer. He tended every lamb and every calf at Kollsveinholdt who needed mending. Even the village children would bring him the occasional woodland animal or tiny bird to mend with his gentle care. While his reputation as a warrior was well-earned, no one ever suspected the real motivation why he killed his enemies swiftly.

Arnor hated to see anything suffer.

The wounds on her arms were not deep and would heal well. He blew out a grateful breath and studied her face. The wench was a mystery. Why her own people had chosen her as a sacrifice made no more sense than the dead boy found along the shore.

He tore some linen into strips and dampened them with salt water. Cleaning away the caked blood from her arms, he cleaned her wounds as best as he could. He paid particular attention to removing as much of the blue woad from her skin. He didn't want the stain to seep beneath the cuts as they healed, or the wench would be permanently marked–like the natives he'd seen once on a voyage to the east. They were fierce beasts of men, tattooed in outlandish markings.

The woman barely moved, only now and then opening her eyes to stare blankly up at him, before they closed again. Arnor wound clean strips around her arms, tying them securely. Considering he had nothing on board to properly tend the wounds, it was all he could do until they reached Kollsveinholdt.

"Why do you bother, Arnor? She's a Pict. They deserve no kindness from us," Halfdan queried impatiently. Arnor knew the man's pride chafed at the loss of his own slave. Looking over his shoulder at Halfdan, Arnor smiled. "Scarred slaves did not fetch so high a price, my friend."

Arnor tucked his own cloak about her, encasing her against the fierce chill of the North Sea wind. No use having the wench freeze to death before he could put proper wrappings and shoes on her feet.

Arnor crouched down beside her on the deck and reached into his pouch, chewing thoughtfully on a strip of dried meat. He couldn't wait to return to Kollsveinholdt and dine on better fare.

*Two more days.*

Two more days and he'd sip hearty ale beside the great hearth, and fill his belly with fresh-roasted meats and fish.

Lost in his musings, his head turned as the chain rattled beside him. The wench turned stiffly and moaned. She opened her eyes and stared straight at him.

Puzzlement warred with the confusion on her face, though her eyes sparkled with a feral gleam. Her gaze wandered down, her brows drawn together at the bandages on her arms. He watched her hands go to the chain, climbing upward until she fingered the collar around her neck.

Her scowl turned fierce and a low growl erupted from her throat.

Arnor felt an unfamiliar warning prick of fear along the edge of his spine. His reaction caught him by surprise. He'd never once in his life regarded a woman as a threat, but there was something in her eyes that made him pause.

This wench was dangerous.

Halfdan had been correct. It was best to quell her now than find his throat slit some night at the hand of this treacherous Pict. He pulled the chain hard enough to sit her upright. She whimpered weakly, her eyes flooding with sudden distress.

"I care not if you understand me, wench," he warned, "a slave you are and you'll earn your keep these winter months until I sell you in the spring."

The Pict woman blinked with slow deliberation.

Not an ounce of recognition of what he'd threatened showed on her face. She glanced down at the chain he held in his hands then raised her gaze level with his. With a low hiss in her throat, the bloody wench spat full in his face.

Arnor's hand raised to strike, but he paused. A space of moments passed between them as the boat lurched over a swell.

The wench paled.

A hoarse yelp born of suffering, then she doubled over and promptly wretched all over the deck.

"By the gods!" Arnor cursed and scrambled to his feet, putting a good distance between them.

"More troubles, Arnor?" Veleif growled with irritation. His feet braced wide with his hands on his hips, as he looked down at the heaving lump of female. Seeing the mess he stepped back a pace. "Is this one sick?"

"No, Veleif. I think either the poisons are coming out, or the voyage disagrees with her," Arnor replied plaintively.

*Veleif?*

Did Æstrid hear this correctly?

*Veleif?* Veleif *Kollsvein?*

She risked a sideways glance up to the man towering over her, careful to mask her panic. She'd heard of Veleif Kollsvein. By the gods, every man, woman and child at Karissonholdt, had heard of Veleif Kollsvein.

He was the blood-sworn enemy of her father, hence the enemy to all the Karissons! Though Æstrid had never been privy to the details of her sire's feud, she had heard enough rumblings through the halls of her home since she could remember.

Veleif Kollsvein was a despicable barbarian who possessed neither honor nor honesty. He was a man to be avoided at all costs. The mention of his name was enough to send her father into a blind fury. To think she'd been spared from Picts, only to be captured by the Kollsveins?

Surely life could not get any worse.

Coughing and clutching the deck to steady her reeling world, Æstrid looked up at him. She recognized him now. He was the man from her dream, when she had been bound at the bonfire.

But he wasn't the warrior god, or the beast she had envisioned, with a snake crawling between his great, glowing eyes. His eyes were blue—piercing and icy blue to be certain—but there was no supernatural light coming from them now. And the live snake she had imagined was simply the carved noseguard of his helm.

Oh, how those Picts had drugged her!

Æstrid's mind quickly formed a plan. No doubt these men believed she was a Pict. She was painted as one. Better to remain that way than let them know who she really was. Better to play false of knowing their speech, as who knew what secrets they would reveal? Secrets she could surely use to soften her father's wrath, if, and when, she returned home.

"Keep her away from us," Veleif growled. "If she doesn't improve by morning, toss her over the side. I'll have no Pict diseases brought to Kollsveinholdt."

He stalked away, leaving Arnor to peer down at her sadly. The giant Viking looked like a lad who had just lost his puppy. Finally, wordlessly, he turned away and left her crouching beneath his cloak.

Some hours later, Arnor pressed a skin in her hands. Æstrid grabbed at it greedily and raised it to her lips. She couldn't have cared if the contents were wine, or ale, but sighed in pleasure as the water quenched her burning throat.

She shoved it back to him, but the great Viking shook his head no and thrust it in her hands. If she was contagious, he obviously wasn't about to share a skin with her.

Good.

It was better for them to think she was sick than have them try to ravage her.

Æstrid shrank beneath the cloak and huddled, desperate for warmth. She was sick and cold and if she ever felt her fingers again…

Fraught with misery, she willed herself to a place of comfort, away from the salt spray and the choking odors of the men. She prayed to Odin that this wretched journey would be over soon and she would find herself on land again. Then she would figure out a way to make the long trek back to Karissonholdt.

Another night passed, and thankfully, Æstrid was all but forgotten. The men kept a wary distance, in fear she bore a sickness.

And sick she was. Not from the lingering poisons of the Picts, but from the rolling waves of the deck. The constant motion of the churling seas brought back up every bit of what Æstrid was certain she'd ever consumed in her life.

The prince of Kollsvein passed her once, with little more acknowledgement than an angry glare. Arnor, the giant Norse whose face she spat in, tossed her a few strips of dried meat at dawn. Æstrid slept and retched and retched and slept. When twilight descended upon them, Arnor appeared once more, his face oddly compassionate.

Æstrid tried to steady the nausea threatening to undo her, nibbling at the humble fare. No sooner did she swallow it, then she had to turn her head aside, and heaved pitifully upon the deck. She huddled down in the pelts and moaned in grief. By Odin's mercy, maybe meeting death in the icy waters of the sea would be better than this immeasurable suffering.

With an arm flung over her eyes, Æstrid peeked up to judge the stars. She knew they were moving west, farther and farther from her beloved Karissonholdt, her father, and her people. She groaned into a ball of deep despair, remembering Leidolf's body, lying on the shore beside that lake.

If only they had stayed home, she wouldn't be chained as a Pict slave, carried farther and farther away on this nauseous journey. If only they had stayed home, her brother would still be alive.

If only...

Another long day passed as the ship rolled and lurched across the brutal sea. Oars were pulled up as the sounds of cracking ice hit the hull. The motions grew worse and Æstrid heard the distant commands of Veleif's booming voice, guiding them through the treacherous breakers.

The boat surged high, only to crash down over and over. Great waves of salt water spewed over the deck. The ship's bow lifted skyward, then plummeted down again.

Higher.

Faster.

Æstrid frantically clutched a small protrusion of wood on the hull.

The shouts of the men grew louder, the ride more frenzied as she desperately clung to the ship, her lips moving over and over in prayer as the freezing salt water soaked her to the bone.

Then it stopped.

The ship came to rest, but the lingering effects of motion left Æstrid in the throes of ocean's waves. She heard more shuffling feet and dared to glance from beneath the cloak.

Veleif Kollsvein stood over her. His legs planted firmly apart, his face twisted in a dark scowl. There was something about her he didn't trust. Perhaps her presence was an evil charm, for their landing at Kollsveinholdt had not been a smooth one.

"Arnor!" he bellowed. "Get this slave from my sight, then come back and help unload this boat. And quickly, man! All of us have a need to seek the warmth of the great hall."

Arnor spoke in soothing tones as he pried her hands away from the death grip she had on the ship. Lifting her easily, he tossed her over his shoulder and jumped down into ankle-deep icy waters. Thankfully, he pulled the cloak about her, sodden as it was, and carried her to the beach.

As Arnor turned back to speak with Veleif, Æstrid stifled her gasp. The much-rumored Kollsveinholdt loomed above her. Seeing it in person, quelled any gossips that had ever reached her ears. It took her breath away.

The stronghold was a marvel.

A great mountain of dark rock soared upward to meet the leaden sky. Beneath the towering keep, darkened caves dotted the shoreline. Beneath the towering keep, dark caves dotted the shoreline. In was in that direction, the men hauled the longship with heavy strains and thick ropes.

Up and up her eyes travelled, making out a curving path where Æstrid saw the outlines of small structures lying beyond the mammoth keep. But these were no earthen huts like the ones found at Karissonholdt; these were stone, one and all.

Arnor carried her up the winding path and Æstrid saw the thick cakes of ice bobbing on the shifting sea. She stifled a shudder. It had to be a god's blessing or devil's miracle they had crossed the frozen mass without their boat being ripped apart.

Veleif's men were unloading their cargo, passing barrels, ropes, and sacks in a continuous line. Some spoils were headed to the caves, while others were sorted into piles along the shore. Æstrid assumed those would be carried up later, to the village. The village where Arnor was taking her.

The great Viking seemed to be under no strain as he ascended the path. The brute wasn't even out of breath from the steep trek up the mountainside. Arnor spun around calling out a greeting to a woman who appeared in the doorway of her stone cottage, watching the steady line of warriors return to the village.

Æstrid gasped out loud this time.

The full grandeur of the stone fortress was the largest stronghold Æstrid had ever seen. At least two dozen steps led up to the intricately-carved doors of the keep. The stronghold itself stretched as far as she could see, running along the side of the mountain. Great beams of wood, carved with dragon heads, scowled fiercely at the churning rush of tides beneath. Small breaks in the stones of the colossal structure were covered with glass.

Glass!

That was a wonder. Even as prosperous as her father was, no one had glass windows. Karissonholdt had oiled clothes to filter the light, covering the defensive slits in the keep.

More and more people filtered from the village, until they surrounded Arnor and his curious prize, like ants drawn to a mound of honey. Æstrid's fingers clutched desperately into the thick pelt on the Viking's shoulder as he swung about with dizzying spins.

He hailed greetings to some and orders to others, sending them down to help unload the ship. Their faces thankfully, neither resembled the Pict nor the brutish prince of Kollsvein, but reminded Æstrid of her own people.

However, instead of warm welcomes, she was greeted with expressions of puzzlement, even outright hostility. One woman stepped close and boldly pinched her arm before she spat her disapproval in the snow.

"Berra!" Arnor growled. "Find clothes for this one. And boots as well."

"A Pict, Arnor? You've brought a *Pict* to us! I cannot believe Veleif would allow such a heathen to dwell here," the woman scowled.

"She's my prize, Berra. Now bring her clothes. I'll not have her freeze to death. A dead slave is worth nothing to me in the markets at Novgorod."

The woman left him with a stout humpf and Æstrid felt Arnor's chest rumble in laughter. No doubt despite her protests, Arnor seemed content the woman would obey his wishes.

The snow crunched beneath his great boots, as Arnor made his way along the twisting path to the outer edge of the village. A thick copse of evergreens, interspersed with black trees, stretched in foreboding against the graying sky. Æstrid shuddered.

The forest beyond the village was an unwelcoming place.

If she could make it to the forest, it would be the perfect place to escape. If she could cover her snowy tracks and gather clothing to fight the oncoming winter. If she could carry enough food to sustain her and avoid any lurking predators.

If, if, if…

Even *if* she managed to gather the supplies she needed and escape, Æstrid had no inkling exactly which direction her home was, or how long it would take to reach it.

She shuddered once more. Her future looked as bleak as the forest.

Arnor pushed open the door of a low, stone barn. The raw scents of dung and straw assaulted her nose and sheep bleated in a loud crescendo at the disturbance of the pair. Arnor laid her down gently in a far corner onto a pile of straw.

Æstrid scrambled to cover herself with the sodden cloak, and although the barn was some protection from the frigid clime, it was still cold and drafty. Arnor grunted as he squatted down beside her.

Æstrid shrank away but he merely laughed. His meaty hands grasped the chain about her neck and secured it to an iron ring attached to a beam of wood.

"You'll stay here until I know you do not bring some disease upon us," he pointed.

Æstrid kept her gaze carefully blank.

For a captor, his tone sounded rather gentle. She had seen the way her father had treated prisoners. Gunnalf would have never considered providing his slaves with warm clothing, let alone anything beyond threadbare covering for their feet.

Berra, the woman Arnor had spoken to in the village, pushed open the stable door. Though she still sported a deep frown, the armful of dry clothing she carried was a welcome sight. Peering past Arnor, she huffed in disgust and shoved the clothes in his arms.

"Have a care, Arnor. That Pict will slit your throat the first chance she gets."

"As if a woman could harm me, Berra," Arnor chortled, as he stroked his thick beard in contemplation. Chuckling and shaking his head, he tossed the bundle on the straw next to Æstrid.

"A blind crone could stick you, Arnor. You're too big a target to miss," she taunted dryly, and flounced toward the door.

The huge Viking tossed his head back and laughed. Stifling his mirth, he took a last glance at Æstrid.

"Dress yourself." Arnor pointed to the clothes. "You'll have food later."

Then he quit the barn, leaving Æstrid among the wandering sheep, the smell of manure and the enclosing darkness.

Life, she thought, had just gotten worse.

# Chapter Three

The days and nights that followed in the solitude of the barn, made Æstrid doubt her sanity. She'd dressed in the clothes Berra grudgingly provided. While the tunics and the overdress were plain, the clothes were warm, and fit surprisingly well. There were even wrappings for her feet and a pair of crude, hide boots. With Arnor's dried cloak and burrowing into piles of straw, Æstrid managed to stay reasonably warm.

At night, when the village was asleep and the only sounds were the sleeping livestock, Æstrid would whisper to herself out loud. She thought if she didn't use her voice she would lose her ability to speak. She took comfort in these nights, often speaking to Leidolf, as if he were with her and the two had embarked on another grand adventure.

The only respite Æstrid had, arrived in the afternoons. A thin, fair-haired boy, who she guessed had seen no more than ten winters, would creep quietly into the barn. He would place a meager trencher of food as close to her as he dared, before backing away and gazing at her curiously.

At first, Æstrid growled at him, hoping to scare the boy. She didn't know how long the blue scrolls marking her as a Pict would last. And until she formed a plan to escape, it was better to be regarded as a lowly Pict, than reveal she was the daughter of Veleif Kollsvein's worst enemy.

Although the boy was slight in stature, he was brave in spirit. By the third day, he was no longer dissuaded by her ruse. The boy smiled as she scowled, laying a hand on his chest and saying repeatedly, "Nar. I am called Nar."

Æstrid inwardly softened to his cheery nature. The boy reminded her so much of Leidolf it hurt. She longed to speak with him and take the boy into her confidence, but knew the risk would be too great. Instead, she tried to ignore him and bent her attention to the food, but the boy rattled on about the comings and goings of the village.

While there wasn't one clue of finding a way to escape that Æstrid could glean from Nar's ramblings, after a few more days, she began to welcome the break of the long boredom of the stable. Her time alone was spent trying to pry to iron ring from the wood. After scraping at the fastening for several unsuccessful days, she finally gave up. She had practically lost track of the days and nights that passed. How many had it been now? Six? Seven?

Just as she was resigned to spending the bitter winter in the barn with the cold iron around her neck, the door was thrown wide open, followed by a male groan. Arnor's considerable frame darkened the doorway, and Nar was close at his heels.

The great Viking was richly dressed with a fine pelt of red fox draped about his shoulders. He studied her for a long moment and seemed to approve of her dress, as well as her health. All traces of the Pict poisons and the seasickness had subsided, though Æstrid had no control over the grumbling in her belly. For such a rich keep as Kollsveinholdt, Æstrid found the food very poor. But then again, she was a slave, and she was certain the richer fare was not to be found in the measly trenchers given to slaves.

Arnor spoke to her, and much to his credit, he added demonstration to make his point. Æstrid went wide-eyed as he uncoiled a long whip from his belt. She cringed and shrank back against the wall. Surely after all this time and care, he wasn't here to beat her.

His other hand held a wineskin and he smirked as she crouched in apparent terror. Æstrid could have jumped up, secured his knife and stabbed him before he was wiser, but she was weak from lack of food. Besides, it would be unwise to attempt such an act alone. If she failed, no doubt his meaty fist would close upon her throat and snuff the life from her without a second thought.

"You have a choice," Arnor spoke in a low growl. He extended the wineskin and nodded to it. "Serve in the hall," then he extended the whip and inclined his head toward it, "or I'll beat you until you beg to serve."

His thick, red brows raised in question. Æstrid eyed both objects in his hands, gave him the barest of nods, and she reached for the wineskin.

Arnor smiled her choice and she clutched it to her chest protectively. He unfastened the chain from the wall and pulled her along behind him. Æstrid gritted her teeth against her protesting legs and stumbled to keep pace with his enormous strides.

Once outside, she gulped the frosty air hungrily, but Arnor gave her no time to pause. Pushing open the doors, Arnor thrust her forward with a gentle shove into the great hall of Kollsveinholdt. Blinking to adjust to the shadowy hall, the scene assaulted her eyes as well as her nose.

Fat, soapy candles illuminated very little. Most of the light in the hall was coming from the great hearth at the far end of the room. Low tables, benches and chairs were tossed about in a haphazard mess. Every surface was squeezed with the great hoary men, some ripped meat from the bone, and others sloshed more ale and vessels of wine they they appeared to consume.

Arnor said something and gestured with his chin. Æstrid watched the big Viking weave his way through the hall, leaving her where she stood. He was impossible to hear anyway over this unmelodious chaos.

Men howled in raucous laughter from crude jests, and children shouted and scampered between the tables. Women cackled and squealed and Æstrid jumped with a start as two dogs rushed forward and barked and fought over a piece of discarded fish.

Platters were passed and picked and bones were tossed to the floor in greasy piles. Any thoughts Æstrid had of satisfying her hunger fled faster than a deer in flight. The sickening stench of sweat and men, burned meat and charred fish, mixed with smoldering peat. The reek of the place made Æstrid's stomach flop upside down several times, and the smoke watered her eyes. While Kollsveinholdt was easily thrice the size of her own hall, it sorely lacked any refinement.

Or cleanliness.

"Hold! Bring that wine!" Two broad hands jerked the skin from her hands and the bearded face opened as the man squeezed a liberal draught into his mouth. Apparently, this brute had no patience to use a drinking horn.

Æstrid shuddered as he wiped his hands, slick with grease, across his lips, then shared some hearty laughter with an equally odious companion to his right. She kept her eyes diverted, hoping to pass unnoticed as a simple slave and clung to the shadows. She avoided the large table set on a carved dais at the far end of the room, close to the stone hearth.

She caught a glimpse of the looming figures who occupied it and recognized Veleif Kollsvein, along with a few others from the ship. Keeping her eyes downcast, Æstrid moved warily along the wall, picking her way through the rowdy bunch, and pausing when necessary, to refill a goblet or horn.

Veleif looked over his hall and surveyed his people. His chest swelled with pride. Their final trades of the season had yielded rich furs, new tools, and enough food and exotic spices to fill the cellars of Kollsveinholdt to bursting. His people would survive the upcoming winter in warmth and comfort. The hearth was blazing and the trenchers were piled high with roasted meats and vegetables.

Veleif leaned back, content.

Ingor regaled them with an outlandish tale, and as Veleif exchanged laughter with his men, a furtive shadow caught the corner of his eye. His hand paused as he raised his horn to his lips.

Squinting toward the shadows, he followed the woman's movement. It was the Pict woman Arnor had taken. Considering she had been wracked with sickness aboard had been in on the ship, he hadn't thought to see her so soon. But it wasn't her presence that pricked the hairs on the back of his neck in warning, it was her demeanor.

The wench was suspiciously cautious… or carefully plotting…

Scanning the hall, he saw Arnor disappear to the kitchen. He'd question him as soon as he returned, but Veleif kept a watchful eye on the woman as Halfdan's warning resounded in his mind. A Pict slave would slit their throats.

His hand instinctively toyed with the knife on his belt, and his keen, blue eyes examined the subtle interactions of the female newcomer. A male servant, an old and withered man captured a few years ago during a skirmish with Gunnalf Karisson, halted abruptly when he spied the wench.

Veleif straightened in his chair, his senses on high-alert as he watched the curious exchange. The servant's hand stretched out to the Pict woman, his mouth agape. If Veleif hadn't been observing the pair so closely, he would have missed her barely perceptible glare and the slight shake of her head.

The old man obviously recognized her.

Veleif's suspicions grew, and he stole a glance at his drinking horn. How much ale had he consumed today? Not enough to cloud his reason, or make him imagine he had mistakenly witnessed the exchange. As Veleif watched the girl fill a goblet, his eyes narrowed to slits.

This was no manner of a slave, or even a servant. Her hand appeared duly unpracticed at service. Veleif braced his arms to rise from his chair as the girl passed close to Blotha.

The blonde Viking spied the curve of the Pict woman's backside and slapped her soundly. Uproarious laughter followed as she jolted forward across the table, spilling wine everywhere.

Blotha and several men roared in merriment. Her eyes shot wide in alarm as she scrambled back from the table. The big Viking stood up and regarded the darkening patch on trousers. Grabbing her about her waist, he pinned the woman to the table with one hand and boldly announced, "If you wanted me out of my breeches, you didn't have to waste good wine to do it, wench."

Ingor, Thorliek and Halfdan watched the sport, elbowing each other in hearty laughter. Veleif remained silent and guarded.

Everyone broke into laughter and Blotha loomed over her. He wrenched her head back and placed a sloppy kiss on her mouth. His hands ran up, pulling her dress to reveal a bare thigh. The Pict woman's hand scuttled frantically on the table.

Æstrid's screams were muffled against the assault. The Norseman's wretched breath stunk of putrid ale and his beard was slimy from oily fish.

Desperately fighting him with her unpinned hand, Æstrid grasped a bone knife Blotha had left on the table. Her fingers clamped around the weapon.

She couldn't breathe beneath his weight and she couldn't see beyond the tangle of his matted hair. And Æstrid would be damned if she'd die this way, suffocating under a stinking member of Kollsvein's tribe!

With a feral howl of desperation, she drove the knife into his shoulder. Blotha arched back in pain as blood gushed from his arm, the knife sticking out of his bare skin. With a snarling growl, he yanked the knife from his shoulder and reached for her throat with murder in his eyes.

Veleif slammed both fists on the table and bellowed across the hall. "Enough! Bring that one here!"

Æstrid coughed as the pressure was released from her neck. In the next instant, she was seized between two men. Her wineskin fell to the ground unheeded, as she was dragged to the front of the dais.

Her captors shoved her to her knees roughly and the chain about her neck clanged to the floor. The hall fell silent as every eye turned to Veleif and the kneeling slave.

Æstrid kept her eyes down and saw a pair of fur boots stop in front of her. Still shaking from the aftermath of the attack, she rocked nervously trying to keep her anger in check. Heaving a few gulps of calming breath, she kept her eyes fixed on his boots, refusing to raise them any further. She could hear the beating of her own heart and stared at the blood dripping from her hand.

What cruel joke had the gods played? Had they kept her alive this far in some twisted game of cat and mouse, only to see her head separate from her neck in Kollsvein's hall? Her lips moved faintly in prayer.

Please gods, make the blow quick and merciful.

Veleif looked down at the slave, observing her closely. The firelight on her hair was odd. Her hair glinted dark red among the blackened strands. There was not a single Pict he had ever seen who had reddish hair. He picked up a horn of ale and lifted a fistful of her hair. Startled, Æstrid's shoulders twitched.

He poured the ale over a length of curls and watched as it changed beneath his hand, leaving an inky, black puddle on the floor. Inquisitive murmurs floated up around the room.

"Who are you?" he thundered.

The wench remained silent. With a nod to his men, they lifted her upright between them, holding her in a painful wrench until her feet barely skimmed the floor. He grabbed her chin roughly, forcing her to raise her eyes to his.

Veleif suppressed a flinch of astonishment. The pair of piercing, violet eyes that met him weren't cowed with a single drop of fear, but instead, glittered with sparks of unchecked defiance.

This wench had pure venom in her eyes!

The challenge was inimitable as the woman met his appraisal bold. Audacious. A fair face alone had never captured Veleif's attention for long, but spirit – oh, spirit was another thing entirely.

The fortitude she displayed was overwhelming. His eyes scanned her face, and then moved lower to the heaving bosom, lower still over the indentation of her waist, the arch of her hip. Veleif's jaw tightened convulsively. She was a curvaceous, provocative female who submerged his senses into exquisite, raw arousal – an arousal uncalled-for *and* untimely.

Sensing the course his inspection headed, Æstrid struggled against her captors, but they held her fast to endure Kollsvein's scrutiny. She'd seen him from afar on the ship, through hazy bouts of lingering poison and seasickness. But up close... up close she'd never seen a man the likes of Veleif Kollsvein before.

He was magnificent.

She could feel the heat radiating from the man, an intimidating seductive heat. It rolled off his wide shoulders in waves. His chiseled, warrior's face must have been created in defiance of the gods themselves.

The contrast of the glacial eyes against his dark hair and beard stirred her to some foreign, inky depth she couldn't fathom. His lips, those sinful lips curled back in a maelstrom of masculine fury.

Or was that pleasure?

Reminding herself to take a breath, Æstrid refused to be daunted by him, or the obnoxious pair of men who held her.

Veleif had rarely seen such a fearless display from men he faced down – let alone from a female. His mouth lifted in a smile that quickly faded when the audacious vixen spat full in his face.

He wiped the spittle with the back of his hand and smiled again, a dangerous smile. He should have seen that coming. In the next instant his hand hauled back and slapped her face hard enough to snap the wench's head to the side.

"You're no slave," he sneered.

Her only response was a slight narrowing of her eyes.

He seized her hand roughly to inspect her palm. He ran his thumb over her fingers. They were smooth and absent of any evidence of toil. These were hands that looked as if they lifted nothing heavier than a comb.

"And you're no Pict. Where do you come from?" he prodded testily, leaning in close to her face.

She glared back at him in rebellious silence. The wench hadn't even flinched! Curious dins rose in the crowd. Veleif snapped and pointed to the shriveled, old man who had passed her earlier.

"That one! From Karissonholdt! Bring him here," he commanded.

Another big Norseman grabbed the slave behind his back and pinned him with his forearm around the neck. The old man was dragged forward, barely protesting in incoherent whimpers. Veleif smiled at the man's distress, and noted beads of sweat glistening on the wrinkled forehead.

Veleif pulled a long knife from the scabbard on his belt with one swift hum. He forced the tip of his blade against the man's throat, and looked back at the wench. Her chin rose slightly. Veleif's lips curled in a cruel smile. She wouldn't remain defiant for long.

"Who are you?" he thundered again.

She still glared at him, but he read the hint of disquiet in her eyes. The old man shook his head from side to side, trying to escape the pointed blade. Veleif turned on him with a roar, "Why do you protect this wench?"

The man blubbered incoherently as Veleif grabbed his nose. He slid the blade beneath the nostrils and nicked him with a tiny flick. He knew if wasn't enough to damage the old man, but tiny cut gave him the effect he wanted. Blood poured out and the wench hastily jerked her face away.

"You will tell me who you are, woman. Or would you prefer I carve him up piece by piece? First his nose, then his ears, then I'll cut out his tongue."

Veleif's blade flashed in the light as he swished his knife about the old man's head. He grabbed the man's nose again, who let loose a high-pitched scream. The old man now begged with whines of mercy, as Veleif made a dramatic show, raising his knife.

An authoritative voice rose behind him and Veleif turned in awe of the sound. The wench's face was crimson with rage.

"I am Æstrid Karisson, first daughter of Gunnalf Karisson, ruler of all the land from Karissonholdt Mountain to the Asvarund Sea.

"Now turn him loose, you diseased excuse for a dog! And unhand me as well!"

# Chapter Four

Veleif stared at her in silent astonishment, as inquisitive murmurs broke the stunned silence of the crowd. He grabbed her face again to peruse her more closely. Æstrid jerked her head tetchily from his grasp. Looking past the black-dyed tresses and the hideous scrolls painted on her, he could see it now.

She bore a striking resemblance to Gunnalf Karisson. He cursed himself not seeing it before. Not when he cut her free from the stake, or even as she was lying in a miserable heap on the deck of his ship. The evidence of the dead Norseman on the shore, her unexplained presence being used as a Pict sacrifice – he should have known!

Veleif could only speculate whether it was a fortune or a curse that brought Æstrid Karisson, from the royal house of Karisson, within his hall. He sheathed his knife and nodded to the bloodied man.

"Take him away from my sight!"

"My lord, you won't kill him." Æstrid declared imperiously and jerked against the men who held her.

Veleif peered at her askance. It was her tone that made him pause.

She dared to issue a command rather than a plea?

Roiling with conflicting emotions, Veleif quickly conceded the pragmatic solution was to discuss her presence – and more importantly, what *exactly* he should do with her – away from the audience of the hall. He grabbed the chain around her neck in his fist, and with a nod to his men, they released her.

"He's none of your concern. Come!" He pulled her roughly toward him. Her body slammed into his hard chest and Æstrid recoiled backward as if she'd been bitten. She gripped the chain with both hands and stubbornly planted her feet firmly to the floor.

"I'm not going anywhere until you remove this revolting thing from my neck," she protested.

Veleif stifled the smile which threatened his lips. By the gods, how the crude lout Gunnalf Karisson had managed to sire such a tempestuous beauty, he didn't know.

"You are hardly in a position to demand anything, Æstrid Karisson. Look around you. You have no alliances here," he mocked.

"And neither am I a prisoner of war. There has been no war. You didn't capture me," Æstrid challenged, tossed her head back slightly. Murmurs of agreement resounded around the hall.

Veleif wound the chain around his hand pulling her close. He leaned down until his face was inches from hers. His words came measured, and dangerous.

"As I recall, we rescued you from those savage Picts. I should think that calls for a bit of... gratitude." His gaze dipped to her lips, then rose back to her eyes.

"Gratitude?" Æstrid exclaimed in outrage. She watched his brows draw together in a dark scowl as she adopted a regal pose. Then she dipped to a mocking curtsey, as far as his hold on her chain would allow. Her arms spread gracefully, like a humble supplicant.

"Of course, Veleif Kollsvein. I am but a modest visitor and as yet, unacquainted with the customs here at Kollsveinholdt. I've been so used to the comfort and hospitality of your stables, I did not realize your hall didn't measure to the same."

Loud roars of laughter spilled up around them. Æstrid winced as Veleif cut off her insults, jerking her upright to face him. How dare a Karisson insult him? And a Karisson *woman* no less?

"You dare impugn Kollsveinholdt?" His eyes turned murderous. A tiny flicker of fear pricked her spine, as Æstrid wondered if she had pushed the overbearing warlord too far. Considering his reputation, it probably wasn't prudent to antagonize the brute; but her nerves were stretched to the apex of vexation, and she was tired, cold, filthy and weak. Standing nose to nose with the angry Viking was easy compared to the atrocities she'd suffered in the past several days. At least here was someone to vent her rage and anguish upon.

A quick glance left and right, Æstrid observed the sea of faces surrounding them. Everyone was smiling, enjoying the entertainment of their discourse. A few faces even seemed expectant, eager for the next bout of verbal thrust and parry. Crushing down her apprehension, she plunged headlong into the fray.

"I'm surprised that dogs see fit to dine here… among this filth." She looked at him pointedly from head to toe.

A blood-red haze clouded his vision, as howls of laughter crescendoed to the rafters. He had the sudden urge to break her and bed her all at once. While her beauty and spirit fueled his lust, her biting insults pricked his pride.

Not trusting himself to speak, Veleif turned and pulled her roughly behind him. His angry stride didn't lessen as he reached a wide set of stairs beside the hearth. Triumphant shouts and worried whispers echoed behind the pair as they quit the hall.

"Where are you taking me?" Æstrid choked out behind him.

Veleif's only answer was an indignant snort. She tried to dig in her feet at the base of the staircase, but Veleif growled and jerked the chain again. Æstrid stumbled up the steps behind him, struggling to match his rapid pace.

Torches flickered and danced on the keep's stone walls, casting the upward flight in hellish, glowing pools. Shadows of red-orange light played against his back as they ascended. Æstrid thought Veleif Kollsvein must be the devils own incarnate, leading her straight to the gates of hell.

The hall opened to a large landing with another hallway on the right, and a narrower staircase to the left. He pulled her roughly again and yelled.

"Rafa! Thorgrima!"

Æstrid heard the rushing feet, and seemingly out of nowhere, two women appeared. They weren't overtly beautiful, but they were striking women, just the same.

"Bring water to my chamber for bathing and clothes for this one." He jerked on her neck again to emphasize his command.

"Stop it, you unsightly brute," Æstrid slapped at the chain he held.

Both women gasped at her outburst. Veleif pinned her with an icy glare. Æstrid felt her insides churn, as the cold flood of fear coursed through her.

The women bowed their heads, not daring to move in the terse silence. Veleif finally looked past her and spoke gruffly to the women. "And bring more ale!"

He ascended the stairs quickly, passing two doors, finally stopping at the end of the hall before a wooden door so large, it rivaled the pair at the keep's entrance. Any other time, Æstrid would have admired the intricate carvings, the heavy decorations of inlaid silver – but this was the door leading her straight to doom.

He opened the heavy portal, and pulled her into the largest, most ornate bedchamber Æstrid had ever seen. Without stopping until they reached the other side, Veleif hauled the chain with such force; Æstrid propelled forward and fell straight into a massive, carved bed.

Her gown hitched up, exposing the blue swirled stains on her legs. Veleif grimaced when he spied them. Æstrid darted across the bed, clawing to cover herself with the rich furs surrounding her. She sneered; angry sparks in her eyes dared him to come near.

"I see the rumors of you are true, Kollsvein," Æstrid goaded.

Veleif lifted a single brow.

Was that a smirk playing about his lips?

The fiery wench all but dared him. Her hair hung loosely about her shoulders and seeing her in the middle of his bed was doing strange things to his gut. Twisting him like a ship tossed on stormy waters. Had he been a lesser man, the fact the lady was marked as a Pict, and seething with anger, had nothing to do with his ratcheting lust, which was growing with each rise of her heaving bosom. Had he been a lesser man he would have already claimed her lips...

Veleif swore he'd never witnessed such a display of passion and fearlessness in a woman – let alone one as strikingly beautiful as Æstrid Karisson. He crossed his arms and stared down at her, his legs braced wide apart.

As if seeing him for the first time, Æstrid noticed the thick cords of muscle along his forearms and the wide, twin cuffs of silver at his wrists. While his regard betrayed his ire, his face remained impassive.

"And what rumors have you heard, my lady?" Veleif challenged evenly.

"You are an uncivilized barbarian. Chieftain of an unholy lot. A thief and a torturer. A stealer of women's virtues. Unwilling women," she spat. Veleif leaned forward slightly, holding her eyes with a threatening gaze.

"I'd hold your tongue, woman, unless you want *this barbarian* to prove those tales true," he warned and waved a dismissive hand.

Veleif crossed to the fireplace and added a few more logs to the fire. While his back was turned, Æstrid's fingers stole beneath her gown, threading through the wrappings on her legs. Her hand closed around the tiny dirk Nar had unthinkingly left one night when he brought her food.

She gripped the hilt and quickly assessed the chamber for any means to escape. There was one other door, but from its distance to the wall, it could only lead to an adjoining chamber. The only way out, was through the ornate door from which they'd entered.

The fire blazed brighter in the hearth chasing the shadows from the corners of the chamber. The mammoth bed looked like a hull from one of Kollsvein's cursed ships. It curved upward, with dragon heads adorning heavy, carved posts. The stone floor was strewn with soft sheepskins and fur pelts, as was the bed. A tall, carved chair of exotic, black wood, worked with intricate silver sat next to the hearth. A wide stool, draped in wolf pelts, was placed near the chair, if one wanted to rest their feet. She spied no weapons anywhere, only wooden chests against one wall, and a few scattered chairs.

Æstrid's eyes roved upward. Heavy beams crossed the ceiling. They were carved and painted red and blue. A riot of golden scrollwork reflected off of them in the rising firelight. Rich tapestries woven with silvered threads hung on the stone walls to stave off the chill.

Above the bed a line of glass-paned windows overlooked the cliffs. Even in the faded light, Æstrid could make out wispy whitecaps of the churning sea below.

For a coarse barbarian, the prince of Kollsveinholdt lived in luxurious comfort.

Æstrid clutched the knife covertly. She was resolved. She would stab him in the heart if the warrior prince moved to touch her.

He turned to face her, his eyes wandered leisurely from her head to her feet. His face was unreadable as he unpinned his cloak and loosened his scabbard. When he crossed close to the bed, she mistook him putting his garments away for an attack.

Æstrid sprang from the bed in a snarling rage, the knife poised high in her fist. She lunged and swept the blade with a downward thrust.

With reflexes honed on the fields of combat, Veleif spun quickly and cursed. In the next instant, her arm was captured and Æstrid was pinned against the immovable wall of his body. Æstrid kicked and writhed within his iron-thewed embrace. With a low-warning growl, Veleif squeezed her wrist with increasing pressure until she thought the bones would crush beneath his fingers. The little dagger clattered uselessly to the floor.

He scowled in annoyance and shoved the clawing she-cat back roughly onto the bed. He was stronger, faster, and they both knew there was no way she could win, but Æstrid surprised him with her display of determination. She'd fight to her last breath rather than surrender. As she moved to rebound an attack, Veleif quelled her with a lightning-fast response. He vaulted to the bed and pinned Æstrid's legs beneath his knees. Trapping her hands in one fist, he imprisoned them above her head.

"Cease this foolishness, wench," he snarled.

"Turn me loose you brute!" she demanded, with equal vehemence.

He caught the scent of her and his nostrils flared. A potent mix of furious and female, combined with the soft curves that grappled beneath him, threatened his composure. He was no defiler of women, but he did need to subdue her.

"Any more weapons, my little assassin?" His question was tinged with mirth. Without waiting for an answer, Veleif grabbed the neck of her gown, and in one sweeping pull, ripped it completely from her.

"You... you... barbarian!" Her eyes widened in shock as she tried to wrench. Veleif held fast.

"If I'm so accused," Veleif replied sardonically. Tears of anger and humiliation sprang up as his gaze grew heated, wandering over her nakedness. Æstrid tried to roll away as his palm glided leisurely between her heaving breasts and lower to the flat of her stomach. He brushed over the curve of her hip and dipped lower still, to her thigh.

His touch left a trail of icy terror across her skin and Æstrid trembled helplessly.

His hand closed roughly over her jaw, forcing her to look at him. His blue eyes glittered dark with lust, as his head dipped lower, and paused. Veleif's hair curtained around her, until her world diminished to nothing more than the chiseled line of his cheekbone that glowed amber in the firelight.

The soft fabric of his tunic abraded her bare breasts, making them swell and harden against the broad plane of his chest. Any trace of alarming chill fled, as a shock of warmth swept across her skin. Suddenly, she was hot, enflamed, as if her very bones melted beneath him. His lips hovered a mere breath above hers, promising what Æstrid imagined would be the most searing kiss of her life.

There would be no coming back from such a kiss...

A space of heartbeats passed between them. Veleif's gaze gentled, his eyes roamed everywhere, memorizing each detail of her creamy skin, the shape of her face, the curve of her neck. A knife-slash of lust twisted inside her as the pad of his thumb brushed the swell of her lower lip.

Her mind screamed *this is Veleif Kollsvein, sworn enemy of your father, a ruthless killer...* Æstrid called upon her own ancestors for strength. She had the blood of generations of fierce warriors coursing through her veins. She would not succumb so easily.

"You've had ample time to look your fill, Kollsvein. I have no other weapons. Now get off of me," Æstrid choked out tightly.

The blue eyes narrowed at her and his biceps tightened. The generous lips curved upward, and then his whole face lit up in a dazzling smile.

"Your beauty allows you to get away with much, I think." His voice was smoky with an inexplicable mix of need and warning, and then his smile dimmed. "But the next time you try to kill me, Æstrid Karisson, I suggest you bring a bigger blade."

# Chapter Five

Several brisk knocks on the door made Veleif groan with pure male frustration.

"Come!" He barked as he released her hands and levered away from her. Æstrid quickly snatched up a wolf pelt to cover herself as the door opened. A parade of servants, including the two maids he'd ordered in the hallway, streamed into the room.

Vessels of steaming water, trays of soaps and scented oils were followed by two stout men wheeling in a large copper tray. At Veleif's nod, they wrestled it before the hearth and the women began filling it with the water.

The savory scent of meats and bread and roasted vegetables teased her nose and Æstrid's mouth watered with hunger. Chests were dragged close to Veleif's chair, where he promptly settled, stretching out his legs on the footstool. The feast was arranged on the chests, even a cask of ale was carried in.

Æstrid sat stunned on the bed, watching the steady bustle. Even though her father commanded a rich holding, she had never witnessed so many people attend one man so quickly, or present such large amounts of food. Veleif seemed to take no more interest in her, as he lifted a horn of ale to his lips and speared a roasted potato with his knife.

Rafa approached the bed timidly and offered a hand. "Please, my lady."

Æstrid impaled her with a glare. Though most of the servants had left the chamber, surely they didn't expect her to bathe with all these people about? And not with Veleif perched a mere three paces from the impromptu bath?

"You bathe willing or no, it makes no difference to me." Veleif raised his eyes over the rim of his horn. He straightened taller in his chair, and pointed to the copper tray. "Unless you wish to be carried to the sea and scrubbed raw with sand, I suggest you come. Now!"

His voice thundered through the room.

Æstrid flinched at his outburst. Holding the pelt in front of her, she rose from the bed and tipped her nose upward. No matter what these barbarians chose to do, Æstrid swore she would bear it with the dignity of a princess of Karisson.

Veleif watched her quietly. Touching her curves had been exquisite and her futile disobedience bristled his pride, though strangely, he wasn't entirely displeased. He was slightly angered, in the way a man who was used to having his orders obeyed without question would be. But on a deeper, male level, he wasn't displeased.

Veleif snapped his fingers and the remaining servants fled, leaving only Rafa and Thorgrima in attendance. The pelt was pried from her fingers and Thorgrima raised an urn, pouring water over her hair.

Æstrid shielded her nakedness with both arms as the water flowed over her. Black trails swirled into the basin as the women began lathering her long locks. Her body gleamed in the firelight as all evidence of the blue markings were scrubbed away. Rafa's hands moved over her, gently but with purpose, and Veleif chafed inwardly.

He mistakenly thought himself immune to the shrewish wench. Everything about her was distasteful. She was marked as a Pict, dirty and unkempt. She was a Karisson. And the offspring of Gunnalf no less. Veleif hated both the Picts and Gunnalf with equal fervor, and any evidence of their savage ways should have quelled his ardor. But it did not.

She hadn't given one inkling she desired him in any way – Veleif preferred his women willing. He had never wasted time on females who displayed no desire for him; and forcing his attentions on any woman was unthinkable. Yet moments ago she was lying beneath him, hating him; at the same time arousing him. Her surprising combination of uncommon beauty and a sizzling temper had almost catapulted him over the edge of control. He thought a bit of distance would lessen the lust she inspired, but seeing her so attended, only heightened his desire. He scowled at his lack of judgment.

He'd thought to make her cower in humility, to make her suffer for attempting to stab him with her pitiful knife, but how quickly the tables had turned. In fact, the saucy wench didn't appear to be suffering at all! She stood proudly in the copper tray, refusing to meet his deliberate stare. She chose instead, to focus on some spot on the wall behind him.

What madness had him thinking he could remain a dispassionate observer to her bath? Æstrid's body would tempt Odin himself. Grimacing deeper into his ale, he shifted in his chair, trying to ease the strain of his swollen member.

Quickly refilling his horn, he gulped down another draught. Despite the quantity of ale he drank, the sharp edge of his desire refused to dull. A bead of sweat broke on his upper lip, and his hand squeezed the arm of his chair until his knuckles turned white.

He groaned inwardly as two pairs of hands gently circled Æstrid's arms, her thighs, her skin now glistening as they rubbed scented oils on her shoulders.

The picture became unbearable as Æstrid lifted her arms, speaking in murmured tones to Rafa and Thorgrima, who applied gentle linens to dry her. A wedge of light parted between her thighs and the tinkling sounds of the women's hushed laughter wove a strange spell in his brain.

Despite the soothing ale, Veleif was anything but placated. His mouth turned dry, as guided by the women's hands, they turned her, angling away so the silhouetted curve of her breast glowed from the light of the hearth. She had kept her expression hidden from him, but there was something in her manner Veleif found as intriguing as her beauty.

She managed to maintain refined movements, even when she displayed a fiery tempest, or was it a willful pride? And now, she appeared to be the very source of grace. Veleif caught her profile smiling at his servants.

Was she *thanking* them? By Odin, she was.

And from the faces of the women, beaming under her praises, Æstrid was enchanting them as well. Despite the events that brought her to his chamber, despite the fact she still wore a slave's collar and chain, she was thanking his women, with all the graciousness of a queen. This glimpse of her genteel manner captivated him all the more.

Æstrid shivered under the attention. The heat of the fire warmed her skin on one side, but the chain that hung to the floor was cold and wet. She shrank back as it touched her skin. Rafa applied cloth after cloth to take the water from her hair, as Thorgrima rubbed more oil on her legs.

She stepped from the makeshift tub and lifted her arms as they pulled a soft linen tunic over her. Lying just beyond her reach, Æstrid spied a blue woolen dress with impatience. The cloth was fine, embroidered with silvered threads at the bottom and along the sleeves. She turned closer to the fire, shaking the ends of her wet locks, now drying to shades of light and dark red-brown curls in the firelight.

Thorgrima threaded the damp chain up through the tunic. Æstrid realized she may be bathed and perfumed, but Veleif had no intention of releasing her from this hideous collar. He seemed content to simply fill his belly and sit and stare with an arrogant smirk.

Veleif tossed back an entire horn of ale, cursing the fact it only seemed to sharpen his desire, not ease them. The translucent veil covering her body was more erotic than seeing her naked.

He reached inside his tunic to retrieve the locking key for the collar around her neck. As Rafa was reaching for the dress, Veleif waved her off. He was so adrift in watching the women tend her, he'd forgotten to remove the iron collar.

"Is it your intention I freeze to death?" Æstrid snarled, as she clutched the clinging tunic which dipped low across her bosom.

Veleif chafed at the sting of her words. His hand inside his tunic paused. Rafa and Thorgrima inhaled sharply. All evidence of the graceful maiden he witnessed had vanished, and the irascible shrew returned.

Veleif snorted. And she dared to accuse *him* of being uncivilized? He decided the best way to meet her outburst, was with indifference.

"It is my intention," he rumbled darkly, "to see you clothed, or not – as suits my pleasure."

He took an unhurried sip from his horn, enjoying the fact her mouth gaped open. Æstrid appeared to be at a loss for a waspish retort, and Veleif savored the small victory. He set the drinking horn on the chest, kicked aside the footstool and rose to his feet. It was time the Karisson maid received a lesson in who was the master of this keep.

All three women flinched at the clatter. While Rafa and Thorgrima dropped to their knees, and bowed their heads when he stood; Æstrid, predictably, did not. She arched a single brow and met his gaze with an imperious stare.

Veleif's chest rumbled in a low chuckle at the beauty's countenance of complete defiance. He moved in slow, predatory steps toward her.

"You have a lot to learn, Æstrid Karisson." His voice was low. His smile ruthless. Her pulse raced and Æstrid backed up a step. Veleif pressed deliberately forward. She backed up two more steps, willing herself not to trip in fear at his stalking presence.

He was so close; she could feel the heat radiating from his powerful body as he obliterated the room with his massive shoulders. By the gods, up close if he wasn't the most breathtaking man she'd ever seen.

Veleif continued stalking her, maneuvering her backward trek as he shouldered his movements, carefully countering her own. Before she realized what had happened, Veleif had positioned her less than a dozen steps from his dragon bed. Real fear coursed through her. Gathering her remaining bravado, she struck as only she knew how – with a viper's fury.

"You may make me serve in your hall, chain me, strip me bare, but I'll never bow to you, Kollsvein," Æstrid stammered and halted her retreat.

Rafa and Thorgrima exchanged worried glances.

In a sharp display of pure dominance, Veleif pulled his tunic overhead, balled the garment in his fists, and tossed it aside.

Her eyes widened in shock.

Ah, he was finally getting through to her, but fear was not his goal. She may be smaller and currently helpless, but the wench retained the ferocity of a warrior. Veleif's respect for her increased ten-fold.

Æstrid swallowed hard. She hadn't seen a lot of men, but she swore the Kollsvein prince had no equal. He was a living ode to the gods themselves. His sculpted chest was covered with hard slabs of muscles, and although his skin bore witness to the scars of battle, they did nothing to detract from the sheer male beauty of him. To her utter astonishment, Veleif threw his head back and laughed.

"No, I don't believe you would bow to me, Æstrid Karisson. But I swear if a man could make you do so willingly, it would be a moment for that man to treasure."

She frowned up at him. What a strange thing for him to say.

"Now get to my bed!" he pointed. The blue eyes smoldered down at her. His mouth turned up in a slight grin. He saw her mask the fear behind her eyes and stiffen defiantly.

"I'll kill myself before I share a bed with you." She grabbed the chain in both hands.

Rafa and Thorgrima cried out as Æstrid wound the chain around her neck.

Veleif moved quicker than a bolt of lightning, pinning her to him so swiftly, her breath left her lungs in a huff. This was the final insult he would tolerate from her tonight, and his patience dealing with this shrew was at the end. He snatched the chain in one fist, and his arm squeezed her waist like a band of iron. She could feel the reverberation in his chest as he spoke. His voice angry, as his words tumbled forth with measured strain.

"While I'd not suffer your loss, wench, I think a night in those adornments would suit you better. Or maybe a week? A month? What say you, Æstrid Karisson?"

"If you think I'll beg for mercy, you're sorely mistaken," Æstrid gritted in protest. She squirmed violently, trying to break his hold. Veleif only pinned her tighter.

"Mercy?" he questioned brusquely. Leaning closer he growled in her ear. "Did you think you'd find mercy within the chamber of an uncivilized barbarian?"

Her only reply was a yelp of fury as Veleif lifted her easily. With her toes barely skimming the floor, he advanced to the edge of his bed. Æstrid struck his shins with her foot. While she knew it would pain him, her action only seemed to infuriate him more.

"Cease you vixen!" He gave her a little shake, his eyes crackling with anger.

Æstrid slapped at him in vain as he forced her to the floor. Ignoring her flailing hands, Veleif secured the chain in a shortened length to the foot of his bed, ensuring it would be impossible for her to strangle herself.

Æstrid thrashed in indignation as he moved away. "How dare you?" she seethed, "how dare you do this to me."

Veleif's anger and unrequited lust, knotted together in a lethal combination. He surrendered to the warrior's need pumping through his veins, flexing his fists, and screaming for relief. Right now he could fight, or fuck, and with the half cask of ale he'd consumed, he didn't care which he chose. He tossed a jerky nod toward the bed, and stepped back as his eyes raked her body.

"You think I would taint the pelts on my bed with the arrogant stench of a Karisson?"

A gasp of outrage escaped at his insult.

"The creature Nɸkk must seek your council for advice on cruelty," she countered.

His body pitched toward her menacingly. "Nightly, my lady," he ground out between clenched teeth. Thinking it better to slake his lust than stoke his rage, Veleif straightened.

"Rafa! Thorgrima! Attend your lord!"

All three women jumped at the harsh command. He stretched out his arm and Rafa came to him immediately. He curled her roughly to him and took her mouth in a crushing kiss.

Without breaking Rafa's kiss, Veleif snapped his fingers. Thorgrima rushed to his side and Æstrid cringed back against the bed's hard frame. She crouched down and snatched a sheepskin from the floor.

His mouth moved from one to the other, trading moaning kisses between the women. His hands soon had their garments freed to their waists, and his head dipped over Rafa's full, rounded breasts. As Veleif drank his fill of her, Æstrid watched in disbelief, but she couldn't draw her eyes away either.

This *was* wrong, *wasn't it?*

Seeing Rafa's head draped backward as moans of pleasure escaped her, stoked pinpricks of yearnings deep within her.

What would it be like to be in Rafa's place?

Æstrid grimaced, hating the thought. She loathed Veleif, yet those tiny flames of need sparked along her limbs, and fanned into a full-blown blaze until her skin was hot, and her breathing ragged.

*No!*

Her mind screamed as her traitorous body shivered. The man was overbearing, cruel and her sworn enemy; yet Veleif's hands—very skilled and capable hands by the looks of them—roamed the woman's bodies in tender reverence.

Thorgrima knelt before him as her dainty fingers began to peel down his trousers. She gasped as the woman freed his massive lance, erect and hard.

Veleif caught Æstrid's eyes briefly and he laughed.

Æstrid hastily turned away. She shrank back as far as the chain would allow, squeezing her eyes tight.

"It seems your tender prisoner is unaccustomed to such sights, my prince." Rafa's voice reverberated in a husky laugh across the chamber.

Veleif chortled in kind, and lifted her clear from the floor with one arm. He pulled Thorgrima up from her lavish attendance with the other. He glanced down at Æstrid, huddled tightly in a ball on the floor and couldn't help but admire the curve of her buttocks.

"Then let's to bed my beauties, lest we further disturb her virgin eyes."

As the women tittered at his jest, he glanced down at Æstrid, who was huddled tightly in a ball. Despite the lusty promise of his double burden, Veleif couldn't help but admire the curve of her buttocks.

Æstrid covered her ears with both hands, trying to muffle the squeals and moans coming from the bed. The commotions became louder. Feverish.

Æstrid chanced a look upward.

The shadows on the wall behind the bed melded and lengthened. As their bodies mingled, the silhouettes twisted into contorted shapes, undulating to their own melody of sighs and groans of passion.

Æstrid jumped and froze as Thorgrima's head popped over the edge of the bed. Her unbraided hair fell in a clouded tangle around her face. Her cheeks were rosy and her eyes sparkled with unabashed pleasure.

The two women locked eyes. Thorgrima's mouth parted as she released a stunned gasp, and then dissolved into a peal of giggles.

"Pardon, my lady," Thorgrima whispered breathlessly between her laughter.

"No need." Æstrid shook her head. Before any more words could be exchanged, Veleif's voice rasped above them.

"This night is far from over, maid. Come." His voice was thick and graveled.

Æstrid's eyes went wide as moons, and Thorgrima's wider still, as she was dragged backward, disappearing beyond the edge of the bed in a wake of tinkling laughter. The soft moans soon gave way to commingling shrieks of both women and the hard slapping sounds of skin against skin.

Æstrid tossed uncomfortably, cursing the man's lust. The games on the bed above her lasted well into the night. Was he never sated? Veleif's deep moans joined the women. His hearty cries rumbled across the chamber not once, not twice, but thrice before it seemed their passions cooled.

Before sleep could take her, she heard Veleif croon in low, soothing tones. Æstrid couldn't make out the words; but judging from the soft sighs of the women, he was lavishing tender compliments upon the pair.

Æstrid's brows knitted in confusion. Veleif Kollsvein, the vile barbarian who had chained her to the bed, was capable of gentle speech?

She held her breath, catching scant phrases of 'pleasing' and 'beautiful' amid faint rustling of the pelts. It felt like hours passed until the tender groans and sighs of spent pleasure finally gave way to deep breathing.

Only the occasional crackling of the logs in the fireplace sounded in the chamber. Æstrid exhaled an inaudible sigh of relief. She dared to unwind her limbs from their tensed pose, and holding the chain in both hands for fear it would rattle them awake, she rose up and stole a look over the edge of the bed.

Veleif lay upon his back, his limbs stretched wide across the furs. His broad chest rose and fell in peaceful slumber, partially covered with the tangled manes of the women tucked beneath each arm.

The firelight played upon their milky curves draped across his hips and thighs, contrasting to the smooth bronze of his skin. Even while sleeping, the man was exuded power.

Æstrid swallowed hard and shivered. It was the cold she told herself, and drew the furs tighter around her. It certainly wasn't from a desire to be tucked protectively under his arm, or lying with her own leg draped across him. It *was* something else. Something she couldn't quite name.

# Chapter Six

A hazy dawn broke across the horizon of the sea when Veleif entered the hall. He halted abruptly. Considering the early hour, he thought to find it empty. Instead, Halfdan, Arnor and Thorliek all turned at his approach. It appeared none of them had sought their pallets.

This, he thought, could not bode well.

"What's amiss?" Veleif asked cautiously, his eyes bounced from one man to the next. All three men smiled in unison at his query.

No, this definitely did not bode well.

"My prince, we must discuss a most important matter." Thorliek urged him to take a chair.

"Concerning the lady Æstrid," Halfdan piped in. Thorliek raised a hand to silence the man. Veleif's eyebrows rose.

"The lady is well," he answered gruffly.

"She remains... untouched?" Thorliek asked warily.

Veleif shot him a sharp look. Only Thorliek's sage wisdom and elder status allowed him to dare such a question. Veleif glanced sidelong at the expectant faces of the other men.

"Yes, but I hardly think it is a concern of yours," Veleif snapped.

All three shoulders sagged collectively in relief. Veleif filled a horn of ale, and grabbed a few loaves of bread from their untouched platter, as he patiently waited his men's game.

"Arnor and Halfdan told me how she came to be in our keeping. They said you had found another before engaging the Picts in the fray. A boy. He lay dead not far from where you took the lady Æstrid?" Thorliek prompted.

"The armband you took from the Pict, Veleif. It bore the royal symbol of Karisson," Arnor explained flatly.

"When I checked the boy, his arm was marked from the sun. As if he wore that same band," Halfdan speculated.

Veleif broke off a piece of bread and drenched it in honey. The hall was uncomfortably quiet and he felt the weight three pairs of eyes boring into him. Lifting his attention from his trencher, his hand paused mid-air as he waited for the three grinning fools to continue.

"And?" Veleif prodded impatiently.

"Then one would assume the boy was Leidolf Karisson, the lady Æstrid's brother. Gunnalf's only heir," Thorliek paused. Seeing Veleif's attention focused on his food rather than their conversation, he leaned forward to emphasize his words. "Only *male* heir, that is."

Veleif shrugged. He could not disagree with the logic. After all, Æstrid had identified herself as a Karisson. He made a mental note to question her about her brother later, and swallowed another large hunk of the bread. His mouth turned downward in a scowl. He needed more than bread to stave his hunger after a vigorous night of bed play.

"Why are there no meats this morning?" Veleif asked with annoyance.

"This leaves Gunnalf without succession to his kingdom, other than the lady in your chamber, that is," Arnor said, ignoring his question.

"It stands to reason the lady Æstrid will inherit the entire of Karissonholdt. Gunnalf's lands, his people, the fleet of longships…" Thorliek mused aloud, ostensibly to himself. He templed his fingers and was stared at the beams crisscrossing the ceiling.

"More than thirty ships by my count last summer," Halfdan interrupted. He earned a second warning glare from Thorliek.

"The fleet is valued to be sure," Thorliek ventured, "but Gunnalf's position even more so. The lands at Karissonholdt are fertile. The herds of sheep and cattle thrive there, making for rich trade."

"I don't dispute anything you're saying. But these details are well known to us. What is not known to me, however, is why my own high counsel, and my two most trusted commanders have stayed up all night, discussing these obvious truths?" Veleif pointed to them with his ale, taking a hearty pull before he continued. "It can't be the ale, for it tastes no more special now, than it did yesterday, or the day before that."

"There is no love lost with Gunnalf to be certain. But you have to see the lady's presence as opportune, my lord," Thorliek insisted.

"Opportune?" Veleif asked perplexed.

"An alliance, forged between the house of Kollsvein and the house of Karisson," Thorliek urged.

"An alliance? Gunnalf would never agree to an alliance. No more than I would with him," Veleif scoffed.

"A deeper alliance," Thorliek hinted.

"A bond between the houses," Halfdan added.

Veleif gave his men a blank look and tipped the horn back again.

"A marriage, Veleif," Arnor stated, with a grunt.

"A marriage?" Veleif thundered.

He shot forward in his chair, ale spewing from his mouth. Coughing and choking on the brew, he wiped his lips with the back of his hand and shook his head. It was too early in the day for them to play such mischief. He wondered at the size of the wager they made between them, getting him to spray ale from his mouth like an untried lad.

Veleif looked closely studied the three faces. There was no evidence of jest, even Arnor looked serious.

"Veleif, you have no heir to rule Kollsveinholdt. Would you leave your people stranded?" Thorliek frowned accusingly.

"No, but…" Veleif sputtered. Thorliek rushed headlong into his explanation before Veleif could finish his protest.

"The lady Æstrid is more than suitable. Take her as your bride and the riches of Karissonholdt come under your control. You merge the kingdoms and make it the largest and most powerful holdings of all the Norse lands. Without bloodshed on either side."

"Without bloodshed," Halfdan parroted.

"No bloodshed?" Veleif protested indignantly. "None but my own you mean. If not from Gunnalf's hand, then from his cursed daughter. Just this night past she tried to stab me."

"Ah, so that's why you chained her?" Halfdan's brows raised in question, as he pointed to Veleif with his drinking horn.

Veleif frowned and slapped his palm loudly on his thigh. "Rafa and Thorgrima sorely need to be reminded not to gossip about my hall. But back to Gunnalf. He'd run me through on the spot for even the suggestion. We are not exactly on the best of terms."

"There is naught to disagree if the wedding is already done," Arnor smiled.

Veleif regarded him stunned silence. Arnor shrugged and sipped his ale.

"The lady *is* already here, Veleif. *Conveniently* here."

Veleif threw his head back and laughed.

"Your faces… so serious," he stammered between his chuckles. "I admit, you had me," he managed between loud hoots of laughter. "What a lavish prank... played out… for my benefit." Veleif's hearty chuckles filled the hall as he managed to spill out the words. He laughed even louder.

"A marriage…" he laughed louder still, "with a Karisson," he cackled, until he felt tears spring to his eyes. As Veleif's shaking shoulders diminished into quiet guffaws, he noticed none of the others, unfortunately, shared his mirth.

"Oh? This is *not* a jest?" Veleif dulled.

All three shook their heads no, and the remnants of Veleif's laughter faded abruptly.

"You three are *serious?*" Veleif sobered.

"Veleif, you are a man of reason, but you are also a man of duty. You cannot disagree this is a fortunate path for Kollsveinholdt *and* for an heir," Thorliek said quietly.

"A Kollsvein will control the largest holding in the North Seas," Arnor stated dispassionately.

"Gunnalf won't live forever," Halfdan stated triumphantly.

Veleif frowned at Halfdan. Sometimes the man's penchant to state the obvious was maddening.

Veleif had to admit, the thought of passing on an even more powerful holding to his offspring, and leave a legacy held merit. While the wench was comely enough, the thought of her in his bed was far from distasteful.

Hadn't he needed two maids last night to expel the passion she aroused in him?

Thinking himself rid of the lustful demons, he'd been plagued through the night dreaming of her in his arms. But being saddled with that spitfire for a wife, and a queen, was another consideration entirely.

Æstrid was challenging. Provoking. Her eyes beheld an intelligence and spirit he knew he wouldn't tire of, but her everlasting baiting… would she treat his people with the same insensitivity she'd shown to him?

But the whole idea tweaked his sense of honor…

"For Kollsveinholdt, no, I cannot disagree," Veleif said, as he stroked his beard thoughtfully.

"Then what plagues you?" Halfdan coaxed.

"It reeks of treachery," Veleif began. He pushed back to balance on the back legs of his chair. He ticked off his reasons on his fingers.

"First, Gunnalf has no knowledge of this union, so he has not given his blessing. Second, the lady Æstrid, in case you haven't noticed, does not seem inclined to agree to *any* type of suggestion. And third…" Veleif brought his chair forward on the floor with a loud thump. "While the three of you were conspiring to broaden the holdings of Kollsveinholdt, did any of you consider I may not *want* a wife?"

Halfdan opened his mouth to dispute Veleif, but paused as Thorliek laid a staying hand on his arm.

"Did you not give his son a proper burial?" Thorliek elaborated, not really expecting an answer.

"Well, yes. To leave any Norse lying unattended at the hands of those murdering Pict, to become nothing more than food for carrion—" Veleif retorted harshly.

"That deed in itself deserves some gratitude," Thorliek interrupted. "To let Gunnalf know his son's murderers have paid with their lives. I think he would be grateful."

Veleif inhaled deeply. If he himself hadn't taken the lives of the Picts who had slain his wife, Tofa, he would have laid the weight of silver and gold at the feet of the man who had.

Thorliek leaned forward, his tone hushed low in his familiar role as a practiced advisor. "Send Gunnalf a tribute to soften the news. It is well known Gunnalf loves silver more than life itself, more so even… than his own people."

"Deliver to him your intention with the Lady Æstrid, and let him know his son has been avenged," Arnor said. He leaned back and looked over to Halfdan, giving him an almost imperceptible nod as a cue.

"I will go to Karissonholdt, Veleif. While you take your bride, I will deliver your message," Halfdan announced, sitting up straighter. Veleif and Thorliek stared at him.

"A voyage to Gunnalf's lands at this time of year would be unwise," Arnor smiled at him proudly.

Halfdan only shrugged and turned to Veleif.

"My prince, if you are willing to take the lady Karisson as bride, I am willing to secure her father's blessing. It is for the good of us all, is it not?"

Veleif shook his head. "The passage is one you will not likely survive, Halfdan. It is best to wait until the ocean is not so treacherous."

Thorliek shook his head. "No it is not. I agree there is some deception, but we must use the time wisely. If Gunnalf doesn't accept this tribute and decides to lead a full attack, he will have to wait months until the weather allows it. I believe he will be agreeable when he finds his daughter expectant with an heir, instead of newly wed. Especially after the loss of his own son."

Veleif ran a hand over his beard and shook his head in disbelief. "Your assumptions are as innocent as they are astonishing, Thorliek. Let's *assume* what you say is true, I'm anxious to hear how you've solved the second problem of this scheme..."

"I do not believe the lady Æstrid will agree to this union willingly..." Thorliek shifted nervously in his chair.

"No? Now I know you jest," Veleif drawled sarcastically.

"We hold the wedding at winter solstice. The ceremony can be conducted using the old ways, one she will not recognize. Meanwhile, we send Halfdan to Karissonholdt with news of the marriage. By the time he returns, Gunnalf's blessing will not matter," Thorliek said persuasively.

"This is complete treachery," Veleif reprimanded.

"Then we war anyway, and take Karissonholdt in the spring," Arnor chuckled, slapping his palms on the table. "Either way, you will have a wife, and quite possibly, an heir on the way."

"Perhaps we should let the lady Æstrid know her fate beforehand?" Halfdan mused.

"No!" Thorliek and Arnor shouted in unison.

"I don't see her as a creature of reason. Duty perhaps, but not reason. Besides, her answer is of little importance. There is more at stake here than the lady's… feelings," Veleif contemplated.

"Maybe it won't be so bad, Veleif. If the lady would grow fond of you first, the task of wedding her may be easier," Arnor encouraged.

"I agree. The lady needs to be treated well, Veleif. She needs to become familiar with our ways. She's no prisoner here. She's your future queen." Thorliek hurriedly sipped his ale as Veleif glowered at him over the rim of his cup.

"Treated well? So that's the way of it then?" Veleif slammed his fist on the table and growled at them. "What would you have me do that I'm already not?"

Arnor, Halfdan and Thorliek all laughed at his outburst.

"I hardly think keeping the lady chained to your bed is considered a gentle act," Arnor chuckled.

Thorliek leaned forward and patted Veleif's arm. "Woo the lady, Veleif. Woo the lady."

"That is if you haven't forgotten how," Arnor chided with laughter.

Veleif shot him a withering look.

"You have to admit, Veleif, you could do worse. A comely wench to warm your bed is not exactly a terrible way to spend a harsh winter."

"Winter solstice is a month away. I'll leave in the morning for Karissonholdt. Though having glimpsed the lady's temper, I vow my ride may be gentler than yours," Halfdan sniggered.

Arnor hooted with laughter.

"Somehow I think your journey will be far less perilous than my own, Halfdan," Veleif mumbled.

He envisioned Æstrid's blue eyes sparking to violet, the moment she realized she was married. To him. Veleif exhaled in a deep groan and shoved his chair back from the table. Rising quickly to his feet, he tossed his empty horn noisily on the table.

"I have much to think about," Veleif announced, and turned away.

"We don't have the luxury of time, Veleif. If Halfdan is to be underway, we need to know before sundown," Thorliek called out.

Veleif regarded the elder with an unblinking stare.

"You'll have my answer before sundown," Veleif agreed.

### 

Æstrid sat on the large dragon bed contemplating her fate. Rafa and Thorgrima had unfastened the chain and seen her warmly clothed and fed before they quit the chamber. At least some of the Kollsveins demonstrated a modicum of kindness.

She sat up on her knees and looked out the window to the rocky beach below. Huge plates of ice shifted and crested on the sea, and a heavy sleet fell from a pewter-tinged sky. She sighed morosely. Even if she could get to a longboat, she couldn't manage it by herself across the hazardous seas. With the heavy onslaught of snow and rain, passing overland to reach her home would also prove an impossible task. The mountain passes would be closed. Even in the best of weather, she knew Karissonholdt lay several weeks journey to the east.

Æstrid sighed dejectedly and threw herself prostrate on the bed. She stared up at the painted ceiling and grudgingly accepted the fact her escape would have to wait until spring. There had to be something she could do to relieve this endless tedium, and there *must* be some way to shed this horrid chain and collar.

Her hands stroked the soft fur pelts and she rolled to her side, inhaling deeply. The bed smelled of him. Of Veleif, the warrior, who ruled his tribe and cut down the horrid Picts. Veleif, with his threatening ways and blustering curses and piercing eyes. He was the same man who whispered tender endearments to the two women who shared his bed hours before.

She lay back and squeezed her eyes shut. She bent her legs up and rested one ankle upon her knee, trying to blot of the vision of the three shadows dancing on the wall last night. She exhaled deeply and ran her hands along her thighs.

What would it be like to be touched by him?

Her hands curled into fists and she pounded the bed in frustration. How could her mind stray to such thoughts when she'd just witnessed her brother's murder?

The memory of Leidolf lying motionless of the shore, came flooding back with haunting clarity. If only she hadn't persuaded him, no, *goaded him* into joining her—her precious brother would still be alive. They would be home, at Karissonholdt. They would be busily avoiding their heartless father, but they would be home.

Veleif paused outside his door.

Thorliek's words preoccupied his thoughts, but the argument was such that Veleif could not argue with reason. He had planned to quit the hall and let the crisp air clear his mind. He had planned to take a walk along the cliffs and consider everything the men had proposed. He had *planned* to form a series of solid contentions against their idea – what he had *not planned* was finding where his duplicitous feet had led him.

He was standing outside his own chamber.

He didn't remember the walk up the stairs, and when he found himself staring at the portal to his chamber, he frowned. He needed a cloak. A warm cloak to stave off the chill for his walk. That was what led him here, he reasoned. It wasn't because *she* was on the other side of the door.

His hand paused on the latch. If only he were stepping on the deck of his warship, or venturing out across the sea to raid. Those would be easier tasks than maintaining iron control over the fervency rushing through him. Æstrid Karisson inflamed both his lust and his intellect.

Given time he could foresee her as a potential mate. But to take her as a wife with deception? This trickery left a sour taste in his mouth.

Curse the gods, why did Tofa have to die? Why had his wife been slain while carrying his unborn son? He squeezed his eyes tightly to quell the vision of her, lying murdered upon the sands. Instead, he chose to remember Tofa, with eyes brimming with love whenever their gazes met—not glittering in hatred like the lady currently in his chamber.

Tofa, who had thrown her arms around his neck, smothering him with kisses when she became his wife, eager and willing to share his bed.

As much as he swore he'd never marry again, a small part of him always believed if he *did* take another wife, it would be one who at least wanted him as a husband. Not one who cursed him to hell, or saw him as nothing more than a savage.

Thorliek's counsel, though debatable at first, was well-founded.

An alliance with Gunnar Karisson would forge both holdings to be the greatest power in the North Seas, as well as the Baltics. And to achieve such an alliance with no loss of life for either side? Well, it was certainly worth conquering one wench.

Veleif growled as he pushed open the door and steeled himself against whatever lay ahead. The best way he knew to explore uncharted oceans, was to first test the waters.

# Chapter Seven

Æstrid clambered upright, and pushed down the hem of her gown when she saw Veleif's broad shoulders fill the doorway.

Her breath hitched in a gasp and her face flushed red with embarrassment at having been caught in such a position. Although he'd seen her completely exposed when he'd ordered his women to bathe her, this was different. She hadn't bathed lying supine in the middle of his bed.

Veleif's mouth went dry as he struggled to form a coherent thought. Her creamy thighs, bare to his gaze, sent his pulse pounding. Of all the places to find her, lying on her back with her gown hiked up was unprepared.

Veleif was never unprepared.

He watched her slide off the bed without a word. She moved with a natural grace, one that complemented her beauty. He swore silently. In all his days, he'd never seen a more captivating female. She leaned back against the massive post waiting, as if she dared him to speak first.

"You didn't have to move on my account. I'm not opposed to sharing my bed with you," he crooned, a hint of a smile in his tone.

"I was only in the bed because you were not," Æstrid informed him stiffly.

And there it was.

The blazing fire of hatred rekindled in her eyes. Veleif muttered a curse beneath his breath. He was fool to assume would be simple. His hand stroked his beard as he contemplated the best approach. A gentle tone went a long way to soothe a frightened creature.

"Not because you find the floor unsuitable?" Veleif smiled playfully.

Æstrid snorted and placed her hands on her hips. He watched her mouth part, ready to hurl a string of oaths at him and likewise his parentage.

He raised a hand to halt her tirade. "I came to see to your comfort."

"Comfort?" she grunted skeptically. Veleif stepped toward her and Æstrid darted behind the bed.

"Surely, Æstrid, you're not frightened of me?" Veleif cajoled softly.

"No. I am not. It is you who are afraid of me, Kollsvein." She lifted her chin proudly and stared him straight in the eye. "Answer me true. Didn't you sleep more soundly, knowing I was chained? Well out of reach to inflict harm?"

This time it was Veleif's turn to snort.

"Come here and so I may free those chains." Veleif beckoned with a wave of his fingers. He smiled as a look of surprise crossed her face.

She took a tremulous step toward him and stopped. It was clear he had no intention of moving toward her. If she wanted to be free of the wretched weight around her neck, she would have to come to him. It was a dominant move and he knew it. The arrogance of the man!

*Show no fear*, she told herself. Æstrid boldly stepped right in front of him. Refusing to meet his eyes, she kept her gaze fixed on the wall beyond his shoulder. Wordlessly, Veleif extracted a crooked iron key from his tunic. She gasped as his warm fingers touched the skin of her neck.

The sound didn't escape his detection, but neither did the smooth texture of her skin. For a brief moment their eyes locked on each other. She quickly looked away and saw his smile widen from the corner of her eye.

He inserted the key in the lock on the collar. With a turn, the whole thing loosened and Veleif pulled it carefully away, then tossed the collar and the chain to the floor. Æstrid couldn't suppress a flinch at the clinking thud on the stone.

He placed her hands on her shoulders and waited until she turned her face up to him. His voice was tender when he spoke.

"You're no prisoner here, Æstrid. You are now my guest."

She wrenched away, and shot him a look of pure venom. Ignoring her reaction he continued magnanimously.

"I extend to you all the hospitality Kollsveinholdt has to offer."

"Do you always chain your *guests*, Kollsvein? It would seem you have much to learn in the ways of hospitality," she scoffed, tossing her hair behind her shoulder.

Veleif ran a frustrated hand over his beard. The woman had the gift to test a man's patience. He was here to woo her, not be flayed by her shrewish tongue. He took a portentous step toward her and inwardly admired the way she held her ground.

"Through that door you'll find your own chamber, with clothes and boots you may call your own. You'll have servants to attend you. You may venture anywhere you wish throughout the keep and the village."

Her eyes widened and Veleif preened, congratulating his victory on rendering her speechless.

"There is only one thing I require," he informed her.

Æstrid's eyes narrowed in skepticism. Here it was. What was the barbarian's price for such *freedoms*?

"You will neither abuse, nor speak ill to anyone here, as they too enjoy my protection. To do so will find my patience *and* my hospitality quickly at an end." Then he leaned in so close, his nose almost touched hers, as if daring her to defy him. His blue eyes speared her with icy flares. "Do we have an accord, or should I presume you prefer the chain?"

"Listen well, Kollsvein. I would not harm… your people," Æstrid promised imperiously, and crossed her arms in front of her.

Veleif eyed her warily and considered her words.

The wench thought she was clever with her pledge. The blatant omission, made it quite clear she wouldn't spare *him* an insult, or an attack. She had a lot to learn if she thought she could best him in a spar of words.

"Anyone," he warned, "means *everyone* here."

"I understand," she smiled sweetly. Adopting a submissive pose, she clasped her hands behind her back.

She congratulated herself privately at the crossing of her fingers. It was a habit she used often with her father. Besides, she was offended Veleif thought she would take vengeance upon an innocent. It was *he* who was the target of her rage.

"We're clear?" Veleif prodded suspiciously, with a tilt of his head.

"Clear as crystals," Æstrid flashed him a smile, squeezing her fingers behind her back even tighter.

"All right. Unless there is something else you need, you may go then," he nodded his head stiffly to the door. It was best to keep their first exchange brief, and, he thought, it had gone better than expected.

"My lord, there is something I would know first," Æstrid purred demurely, and laid a tentative hand on his forearm.

Time stopped unexpectedly when she touched him.

Veleif looked down at her delicate, perfect fingers resting on his arm. Beyond his own volition he covered her hand with his own, absently stroking his thumb along the back of her hand, as if he were in awe of her silky skin. Her softening manner was beguiling. Hearing 'my lord' tumble affectionately from her lips caught him completely off-guard.

His touch possessed a gentleness she hadn't thought possible from this overbearing Viking. The infinitesimal strokes shot rivulets of lightning up her arm. Æstrid quickly snatched her hand back. His eyes probed her face, and for a moment, he looked as stunned as she.

*Had he felt that too?*

Quickly recovering her aplomb, Æstrid blinked and turned hopeful eyes to his. "When are you planning to return me to my home?"

Veleif hesitated.

His mind muddled with the warring sentiments roiling in his chest. The woman stirred his desire to paramount heights. Her beauty and spirit were worthy of proper persuasion. If she didn't find him so detestable, he'd lavish her with a lover's attention; but the maid couldn't even bear his briefest touch, pulling away as she had.

She loathed Kollsveinholdt with such abundance, her only thoughts were returning home, and as soon as possible. It was clear she couldn't bear another moment here.

Veleif knew immediately there would be no wooing Æstrid Karisson to become his wife. The thoughts of deceiving her into marriage, forcing her to bear his children, all in the name of duty, forced him to frown in distaste.

He didn't imagine Æstrid would be one to forgive such duplicity readily. She'd hate him and he'd be left with a loveless union. Still… it was a month until the solstice celebration…

He decided to meet her query with indifference. Veleif crossed his arms and considered her with a slight downturn of his lips.

"Truthfully, the thought is not pressing."

"Not pressing? I assure you it is most pressing with me!" Æstrid declared. Her fist clenched over her heart.

Veleif's reply came short and clipped. "In case you haven't noticed, my lady, the seas are almost frozen. The land over the mountains is impassable. No one, not even I, will be going anywhere. Therefore, the only thing *pressing* for now, is we *all* survive the winter.

"I can assure you my concerns are for the protection of *all*, and I'll not waste time thinking about the whims of one. So I suggest you find some occupation of your time."

"So in the spring then? You'll return me in the spring?" Æstrid entreated optimistically.

By Odin's mercy, could a female be more aggravating than this one? Veleif stifled the urge to exhale in frustration. Thorliek's voice echoed a staunch reminder in his mind. *'Woo the lady.'* His eyes sparkled with mischief as he flashed a lazy grin.

"Perhaps I will return you in the spring, if you still wish to go, Æstrid."

Æstrid's eyes narrowed briefly at his softened manner. He moved closer, with his arms still crossed and pitched his body forward.

Æstrid was too stubborn to give him quarter, refusing to let him intimidate her. She lost her breath as the back of his warm knuckle brushed the hollow of her cheek. His eyes burned into hers.

"I'll naught fault you, my lady, should you change your mind." He glanced at her lips.

Ooh, the arrogance and conceit of this man! She hated him with a passion unequalled to anything she had felt before. Her blood was up, a true Viking's fury building within, and when unleashed, she would make certain he'd feel its full impact.

It was time to show him exactly who he was baiting. If Veleif Kollsvein thought to entice her to a dangerous game, Æstrid vowed she would leave him no doubts as to the winner.

Immediately, her arms shot out, swiftly encircling his shoulders. She pulled his head down to hers so quickly, he had no choice but to respond to her impassioned kiss—yet Æstrid was unprepared for the torrential reaction she ignited.

An iron band clamped around her waist as Veleif pulled her tightly along the hard length of his body. With one hand winding up into her hair, he was kissing her back, slowly, thoroughly. Raw male passion demanded an answer, and Æstrid's body responded with every fiber that was female.

Pierced on the horns of a dilemma, Æstrid abruptly pushed away from him, staggering back a step before she yielded to this frenzy. Seeing the startled confusion on Veleif's face, she struck viciously, her voice laced with contempt.

"Well, now that I have experienced *that*, I assure you, Veleif, there is *nothing* here that would keep me from returning to Karissonholdt." Æstrid brushed an invisible speck from her sleeve.

Veleif's temper flared so quickly at the insult he almost struck her. But then his pride reared up. He would give her no indication she'd bested him – this time. Cursing under his breath, Veleif hadn't prepared for the audacity of this woman.

Spinning away brusquely, Æstrid wrenched open the door to the adjoining chamber. The huge blocks of stone seemed to shake as the portal slammed behind her.

Veleif took half a step toward the offending door she'd slammed and stopped himself sharply. Besides, the kiss she initiated had so unnerved her, she mistakenly called him by his given name.

Perhaps there was a flicker of hope with this contentious female?

When she'd flung her arms around his neck, the scales of his decision tipped. When she'd pressed her lips to his, regardless of her motives, she'd sealed her fate.

Willing, or not, Æstrid Karisson was going to wed him at Winter Solstice.

Æstrid leaned back against the door, trembling in stunned silence at what she'd done. A tumult of emotions washed through her, and climaxed with bubbling ire, as she heard Veleif's laughter echoing from the other room.

Stamping her foot in frustration, Æstrid waved her fist at the door and fumed her promise.

"War will *occupy my time*, Veleif Kollsvein. For we are now at war."

# Chapter Eight

Kollsveinholdt was unlike anything she'd ever seen.

While Æstrid's experience of the world had been her home and a few surrounding holdings, she had never seen or heard of any domain anywhere that compared to this.

Kollsveinholdt was a veritable city. Over a thousand families lived within the protective stone wall of the kingdom, with the cliffside fortress centered as the hub of activity.

Æstrid spent the first few days of her newfound freedom wandering the intricate arrangement of stone cottages and buildings.

It was a perfect guise.

Her true purpose was to reconnoiter the terrain, determine potential weaknesses in the holding, and become accustomed to all probable paths for escape.

She didn't trust Veleif to return her in the spring, and the sooner she acquainted herself with the inner workings of Kollsveinholdt, the easier it would be to break away when the weather turned favorable. Besides, it kept her from further exchanges with Veleif.

Word had quickly spread through the Vikings of her identity, and despite the fact Æstrid was a Karisson, she was welcomed among the people. The untrusting and skeptical faces she'd first seen upon her arrival had vanished.

The craftsmen and artisans of Kollsveinholdt were particularly eager to show the fruits of their trades. Æstrid met tanners, weavers, brewers and cooks, along with shepherds, farmers, fishermen and shipbuilders.

Nar, the boy who had tried to befriend her in the stable, became a constant companion by her side. Oftentimes, he would slip his hand in hers and tug impatiently with a cheery smile.

The boy's radiant mien was infectious, and for the first time in weeks, Æstrid enjoyed a respite from her worries.

She'd even found herself skipping alongside him, smiling and giggling at Nar's persistent questions, as he proudly introduced her to the carvers and stonemasons.

Æstrid also discovered Veleif Kollsvein had been grossly underestimated by her father's advisors. The man commanded a formidable fleet, and he was building more. She counted at least fifty longboats secured on the beach below. And though she had yet to visit the construction firsthand, she listened with interest as she learned the caves beneath Kollsveinholdt's stone fortress housed the shipbuilding.

Her contact with Veleif was limited to evening meals, when she was forced to sit beside him at the main table. While Ingor, Thorliek, and Arnor kept her entertained with lavish tales, Veleif remained noticeably quiet, almost pensive in her presence.

Æstrid was secretly pleased to exchange no more than the barest civilities, and Veleif usually took his leave before anyone finished their meal.

Thorliek would readily apologize for the prince's brooding behavior. The wise elder sported long, snowy hair and a beard to match, but his twinkling eyes hinted at the man's proclivity for mischief. With Veleif's unpredictable moods, Thorliek was always ready with a comforting word, followed by a grandfatherly pat on the arm.

"He's usually not so sullen, my lady," Thorliek reassured. His mouth pressed in a disapproving line, as he watched Veleif leave through the massive doors and fade into the night.

"May I speak freely, Thorliek?" Æstrid inquired innocently. The old man waved his hand graciously and bowed his head.

"Of course, my lady."

"I've often found peevish brooding is very much like a bag of apples," Æstrid continued, loud enough to be heard by the others at the table.

"How is that?" Ingor leaned forward, curious.

"A rotten one can spoil the lot." Æstrid twisted her head intentionally toward Veleif's exit. She spread her hands wide and favored them all with a bright smile. "But remove the rotted one, and the rest of the crop remains unspoiled."

The table erupted in merriment.

"I would say only a fool would starve at his own table, when he leaves the tastiest morsels… untasted." Arnor hinted in her direction, joining her mirth. The big Viking earned an affectionate slap on the arm.

The next morning, she broke her fast alone.

Nar usually shared the meal with her, but the news of twin lambs having been born in the wee morning hours, caused the boy to wiggle excitedly in his chair.

He was such a distraction, Æstrid had no choice but to release him before they embarked on their day together. With a promise to return quickly, Æstrid was left alone to ponder life at Kollsveinholdt.

While the workings of the stronghold were similar to her home, there was a marked difference between the two.

The people.

Æstrid had only witnessed shrugs of indifference, or outright dread, in the faces of the people at Karissonholdt. Gunnalf Karisson wasn't a man inspired to rule by reward, but rather by chastisement.

Her father was in no way deemed a tender man.

The people of Kollsveinholdt showed nothing but pride and care in their labors. They were quick to give welcoming smiles or lend an extra hand to each other.

They were… happy.

Æstrid bit thoughtfully into a piece of bread and spat it out immediately. She quickly gulped down a full horn of ale to quell the sour taste.

There was *one* key difference where Kollsveinholdt suffered the disadvantage. Despite the vast stores of foodstuffs, rich grains and exotic spices; the food that made its way to the tables, was simply awful.

"Is it the bread you find distasteful, or would it be my presence?" Veleif asked silkily, behind her shoulder.

Æstrid choked, sputtering the ale at his unexpected arrival.

*Two days!*

Two days with hardly a word spoken between them, and the bane of her existence had to catch her at a most undignified moment. Worse, the hall was almost completely empty. She'd have to face him alone. Æstrid squared her shoulders and eyed him with a look that threatened dire repercussions.

"Just when I thought fortune favored me with your absence," she muttered dryly.

Undaunted, Veleif slid into the chair beside her. He cheerfully broke off a piece of bread and dipped it generously with berry jam.

Æstrid shuddered. She wondered if the jam made the offensive stuff more palatable, but wasn't brave enough to try. Veleif regarded the bread as if in deep thought, then he stuffed the whole thing in his mouth. Æstrid's brows winged up. She fully expected him to choke, but strangely, he did not. The man's stomach must be cast from iron.

"Truthfully, my lady, I've come to make amends," he smiled graciously.

"You're returning me home?" Æstrid rocked forward, hopeful.

"No," he shook his head with a negative gesture and refilled the drinking horn. Taking a swallow of ale, he turned and held her eyes. "I've been remiss as a dutiful host."

"Oh." Her shoulders sank in disappointment. She scooted her chair under the pretense of adjusting her comfort.

Why did he have to sit so close?

Æstrid had the uncanny impression he was regarding more than her facial expressions and twisted to face him slowly.

"It would also seem," Veleif continued leisurely. His interest was dedicated to spreading sticky jam on the bits of hideous bread, rather than meet her eyes. "I've failed in the basic duties as lord of this keep."

"Yes, the food here, and most especially the bread, is miserable," Æstrid sighed.

Veleif's head snapped toward her absently, as if the comment distracted his purpose. "What? What's wrong with the food?"

"Oh, you weren't speaking of... never mind, Kollsvein. You were saying?" Æstrid shook her head in disbelief, as he swallowed another small loaf. She'd witnessed on more than one occasion the dogs in the keep backing away from fallen scraps. Definitely cast from iron.

He leaned so close his shoulder brushed hers. She inhaled the clean scent of man and leather. A slow warmth pooled in her lower belly as his blue eyes smoldered with unspoken promise.

"If you have suffered unduly here these past two days, then I have failed to give you my protection," Veleif admitted. Looking at her askance, he smiled inwardly at her confusion.

Æstrid cleared her throat and sat ram-rod straight in her chair. The man's eyes were hypnotic. She quickly crushed the vision of him lying on top of her in his bed.

"Put your worries to rest, Kollsvein. I assure you, I've been well cared for... *without* your company."

"Have you? Has anything been amiss in your chamber?" Veleif queried lightly.

"Uhm..." Æstrid started to formulate an answer. His hands slammed down on the table before she could finish and Æstrid jolted from his outburst.

"I knew it! I assure you, my lady, that treachery within these walls will not be tolerated," he vowed sternly.

A cold lump of dread bloomed in her stomach.

Veleif was testing her.

So the water vessels in his chamber *might* have smelled suspiciously of sheep urine... and the combs for his beard and hair could have *possibly* been misplaced...

She almost felt a pang of guilt – almost. Veleif had been more than generous with her. The thick fur boots and rich garments which inexplicably appeared in her chamber were nicer than any she had ever seen—worthy of a queen even.

If she hadn't questioned Oresti about the longship leaving Kollsveinholdt headed in an easterly direction, she might have accepted his gifts as a peace offering. But Veleif had been adamant no one would sail. The seas were too risky to return her home. Yet, one of his ships *had* sailed eastward. Upon learning the news, Æstrid's resolve to war with the deceitful prince of Kollsveinholdt renewed with vigor.

If he refused to return her home when he had the ability to do so, she had no choice but to make his life hell.

"Treachery?" Æstrid asked innocently.

"Treachery," he nodded and popped another piece of bread in his mouth.

He studied her intently as he chewed.

Æstrid kept her face carefully guarded.

Veleif swallowed another healthy draught of ale, secretly hiding his amusement at her discomfort. If the maid thought to continue her childish pranks at his expense… well… not only was he going to terminate these tricks, but he was going to turn her mischief to his advantage.

"While you have formed some close bonds within a short space of time, don't think to protect any villainy here, Æstrid." He waved his hand to indicate the hall. Before she could react, he swiftly turned the arms of her chair and spun it to face him. His legs splayed on either side of hers, essentially trapping her between. Under the guise of speaking as a confidant, Veleif's hands closed over her fingers as he inclined his head intimately toward her neck. His breath fanned hot on her ear.

"It would seem, my lady, someone has decided to play me for the fool." His tone was seductive and measured. His fingers squeezed in intimate emphasis and caused ripples of delicious shivers to race up her arms.

"While I vow to take the imp in hand, it would pain me greatly to have any harm befall you before I see the culprit properly punished. Therefore, I must revoke your freedoms."

"What! Why?" Æstrid exclaimed.

"Temporarily," he asserted, and fixed her with a level gaze.

As if on cue, Arnor appeared from the kitchen, absently wiping his hands on the front of his tunic. Judging from the astonished look on Æstrid's face and the smug look on Veleif's, Arnor knew the role he had to play had begun.

"Join us, Arnor," Veleif waved him over.

The chair groaned beneath his weight, as Arnor settled himself in beside Veleif.

"Arnor, the lady's protection is paramount to me." Veleif spoke in low, hushed tones, invoking them as confidants. "Here is my plan. You'll secret the lady Æstrid away to the old cottage. It's well-suited away from prying eyes. Meanwhile, I'll make a display of going off to hunt. You sneak into my chamber and await the culprit. It would appear they like to play their mischief when no one is about.

Thinking my chamber empty for a space, I'm certain we'll be able to catch them red-handed."

"But... but—" Æstrid protested. Veleif's hand tightened over hers as he interrupted.

"This is the safest way, my lady," Veleif assured her. "Now go. Arnor will see to you."

"Come, my lady. I have just the means to slip you to the cottage unnoticed," Arnor urged.

Before Æstrid could protest, the big Viking took her hand and pulled her to her feet. Arnor spirited a dazed Æstrid toward the kitchen.

Veleif crossed his arms behind his head, and he put his feet up on the table. A wide grin split his face as he leaned back in satisfaction.

### 

"I'm *not* going in *that*," Æstrid protested as Arnor held out a large, empty bag. Arnor sighed and patiently held the sack, waiting for Æstrid to step in.

"I assure you, there is no better way."

"This is unnecessary, Arnor."

"The sooner Veleif leaves and I can wait in his chamber, the sooner this whole ugliness can be put to rest. Now come, my lady. Make haste." Arnor inclined his head to the sack.

With a sigh of resignation, Æstrid knew she had to play out this silly charade. She stepped into the sack with a grimace as Arnor pulled it up around her and tied it securely. He hefted her over his shoulder, shaking his head, as he carried her back through the hall. Of all the daft ideas Veleif had, this one was undoubtedly the worst.

Æstrid could hear the muffled din of voices through the sacking, as people started to fill the room. She heard Veleif's question ring out clear and strong.

"Where are you going, Arnor?" Veleif shouted. His mouth dropped open in silent laughter.

Arnor rolled his eyes at the exaggeration.

"Just carrying some worthless pieces to the cottage," he answered dispassionately. The reply answer earned him a sharp knee to his gut.

"I think it is a fine morning for a bit of sport, my friend. Join me to hunt when you've finished," Veleif ordered, harshly. It took everything he had to suppress the laughter that threatened to undo him.

"Very well, *my prince*," Arnor sighed.

*A bit of sport indeed.*

The two men acknowledged each other with a brief nod. Veleif lengthened his stride to match Arnor step for step in the crunching snow. He did not want to alert Æstrid to his presence, but couldn't resist a bit of amusement with his friend.

Veleif shoved him hard, almost knocking them into a corner as Arnor rounded a cottage. Arnor slipped and Æstrid squealed. Veleif clapped his hand over his mouth to stifle his laughter, earning a warning scowl from the bulky Viking.

Æstrid wiggled within his arms and cursed. "Arnor, if you drop me..."

"Ease your worry, Æstrid. It was just a patch of ice."

Arnor shot Veleif a warning glare.

Æstrid shifted uncomfortably against his shoulder. Twice more the big Viking slipped or bumped, and twice more Æstrid yelped and cursed. Her body was stiff and her nerves were frayed, and within the confines of the rough sack, she wondered how everything had quickly spun out of control.

Despite Veleif impeding his progress, they finally reached the last cottage on the far edge of the settlement. The place had long been abandoned with the death of a childless crone the previous winter. The cottage was used primarily for storage of broken furniture, odds and ends of axes and swords waiting to be reforged, and other items anyone in Kollsveinholdt chose to help themselves to, or discard as they needed.

Arnor shouldered open the door and gingerly picked his way through the cottage. It certainly wasn't the place *he* would have chosen for wooing the maid, but Veleif's actions the past few days didn't seem to have much logic attached to them anyway.

"Well done, my lady," Arnor praised, as he set her down on a discarded pallet.

"Arnor, get me out of this sack," Æstrid urged. Veleif looked at the wiggling bag on the bed and bit his lip to keep from laughing. He shook his head negatively at Arnor's questioning gaze.

"In a moment. I want to make certain no one trailed us, then I'll build a fire."

Arnor shrugged his shoulders at Veleif. The dark prince shooed him toward the door with both hands.

"Now," Æstrid wailed, "I can't see a wretched thing."

"Patience, Æstrid," Arnor said calmly. He bumped Veleif's shoulder hard enough to make him stumble. It was a small payback, but worthwhile seeing his startled face. Arnor grinned with a victorious nod.

With a silent exhale of frustration, Veleif placed both hands flat on his chest and forced him backward toward the door. When Arnor was outside he bent his head in a guarded whisper.

"See no one enters here, Arnor. I'll not be disturbed until the lady concedes."

"Until she concedes? That could take a *fortnight*," Arnor whispered back, incredulous.

Veleif's head snapped up. He saw the big Viking's eyes twinkling merry with mischief, and Veleif's mouth pressed into a hard line. Without another word, he shoved the sniggering man backward into the snow, and shut the door.

"Arnor, this has gone far enough," Æstrid complained and squirmed, "build the fire later."

Veleif leisurely watched the writhing sack on the bed. Her steady streams of protests were muffled, but there was no mistaking her patience was coming to an end.

He ignored her, and bent his attention to the small hearth. Tossing in bits of wood and kindling, Veleif struck a flint to iron, and soon had the flame crackling.

"Arnor!" Æstrid wailed in earnest.

Veleif added a few more logs from the wood bin and stood back, leisurely warming his hands. He decided to let her suffer a bit longer for her troublesome deeds. Besides, he reasoned, keeping her bound inside the sacking was a gentler punishment than those he first considered. Somehow he didn't think the maid would appreciate the water in *her* chamber tainted with sheep urine.

"Arnor!" Æstrid threatened. "I swear I'll carve out your eyes and feed them to the dogs if you don't release me at once!"

# Chapter Nine

Veleif turned toward the sack as a taunting smile lifted the corner of his mouth. He couldn't help but admire her resolve.

Weaponless and securely bound, Æstrid was still spouting threats. He sliced the ties from the top of the sack and stepped back. With his fists clenched to his sides, he prepared for her cyclonic rage. Once she realized it was him in the cottage instead of Arnor, he had no doubts her full fury would rival that of an unleashed Kraken.

Æstrid thrashed wildly at the tangled fabric. Her hair had cascaded loose from its braid and she frantically shoved the strands back from her face. Her eyes widened in shock as Veleif gave her a mocking bow of his head.

"You!" she cried.

"Tainting my water isn't enough? Now you wish to carve out my eyes as well?" Veleif tsked.

Æstrid went livid with rage. She sprung forth like a wild beast, forgetting her legs were still trapped inside the sack. She tripped headlong into Veleif. He caught her hard against him, just in time to save her before she crashed to the floor.

"Let me go you whelp of a bastard!" Æstrid screamed, and wormed ineffectively at the twisted sack imprisoning her feet.

"Feed my eyes to the dogs you said," Veleif taunted. He pressed closer, his voice laced with amusement. His arms tightened around her waist as he leaned back, lifting her so her toes skimmed the floor. Between the jollity in his voice and the evidence of his arousal against her thigh, Æstrid's temper crested beyond reason.

She kicked in earnest, trying to free the wicked sack. Stamping the thing out of the way, her knee shot up and accidentally struck him hard in the groin.

Veleif's arms dropped immediately as he doubled over and clutched his manhood in pain.

Æstrid stumbled backward, momentarily stunned she'd gained the upper hand.

"You… hell-bound… vixen," Veleif choked. His eyes narrowed dangerously beneath dark brows. "I warn you, Æstrid. Cease this foolishness."

"Foolishness?" Her voice pitched. "Yes, I was a fool. A fool to believe your lies."

A shriek of frustrated rage escaped her. Seeing him at a disadvantage, Æstrid continued to press the attack. Grasping at anything she could lay her hands on, she seized upon a half-broken shield and chucked it hard in his direction.

Veleif flung his arm upward to ward off the missile. The shield clattered noisily to the floor.

"Lies? What madness has seized you, wench?" he fumed, defensively. Veleif ducked, as a battered pot sailed past his head. A warning growl rumbled in his chest as he crouched low.

Æstrid sprang lightly across the room, grabbing a discarded hilt from a useless short sword.

"You said you had no ship to take me home. Yet at dawn, one sailed East!" she raged.

She drew back her arm with a snarl and let the thing fly. The sword, woefully unbalanced, missed him wide. It clanged and rattled in the hearth behind him, scattering a shower of sparks across the floor.

Veleif jumped to stamp out the glowing embers, lest the place catch fire. Æstrid hurled a second sword, this time catching his shin. With a pained grunt, Veleif bent to rub his leg.

Æstrid glanced about wildly.

The cottage was so crowded there was no clear path to the door. Veleif could easily cut off her escape. He maneuvered toward her and Æstrid launched a clay vessel at him. He dodged it in time to have it splinter behind him.

"Cool your temper, woman! I brought you here to talk," Veleif thundered darkly. Her hand paused above her head, ready to launch another earthen pot.

"Talk?" Æstrid retorted harshly. "You had me stuffed in a *sack!*"

"Ah! A small retaliation for the pranks you've played in my chamber," Veleif smirked and cocked a brow. Æstrid stopped so abruptly, the wake of her skirts swirled around her as she gaped at him. If she didn't know better, the blackguard seemed to be enjoying himself.

"Arghh! I hate you! Liar! Whoreson!" Æstrid shrieked. With renewed rage she let a barrage of pottery fly, accompanied by a long string of every curse she had ever heard.

Shielding his face with his arm, Veleif ducked toward her. Æstrid feinted to her left but Veleif mimicked her movements. Seeing her deception, he spread his hands wide to cage her in. Darting to her right, she grabbed a shelf with strength born of rage and heaved it with all her might.

Veleif took the brunt of the shelf with his shoulder as broken wood, metal bits and earthenware rained down upon him.

Æstrid scrambled past, twisting away, but Veleif's fist snaked out and snatched a handful of her skirt.

Veleif yanked her backward with a growl. Her foot skidded on a broken chair leg, and she fell face first to the ground with a hard *thunk!* A searing pain shot up her leg, and Æstrid yelped a vile oath.

Ignoring her outburst, Veleif leapt on her in an instant, pinning her to the floor with his weight. Æstrid screamed, her fingers desperate to grab hold of anything to use as a weapon.

Outside the cottage, Arnor turned a quizzical eye toward the thunderous commotion and wails coming from within. Judging by the volume of the male groans, it appeared the maid was winning. Just as he was resolved to save his prince, Taar passed close enough to favor him with a puzzled look.

"Problems, Arnor?"

The big Viking's hand paused on the latch. Veleif would never forgive him if anyone were to witness the prince of Kollsveinholdt needing to be rescued from a wench.

Arnor smoothed his beard and shrugged.

"Nothing is amiss, Taar," he assured, and waved him off.

Æstrid's shrill scream pierced the air and both men visibly winced. Taar rushed closer, his face fraught with confusion.

"But, that's a woman's scream," Taar worried, and pointed nervously.

"Be off with you, Taar. It's only Veleif." Arnor leaned in conspiratorially. "He's wooing the lady Æstrid." He gave Taar a knowing wink and smiled as the man stiffened in shock.

Both men's heads snapped toward the door as a loud smash rang out, followed by a male grunt of obvious pain.

"Wooing? The lady Æstrid?"

"Aye." Arnor nodded.

"From the sounds of it, I don't think our prince is wooing… more like warring," Taar joked.

A female scream rent the air once more. Both men shifted uncomfortably.

"How long has he been at it?" Taar's thumb jerked toward the cottage.

Arnor blew out a gusty breath and peered at the door askance. "It can't be too much longer. There's not much furniture left."

Taar nodded in agreement, but his mouth twisted skeptically.

"I could use an ale." Arnor rubbed his neck in diversion.

"I'll bring you one," Taar promised and trudged back the way he came.

"Better make it two, my friend. This wooing is thirsty work."

Veleif straddled her back and grabbed her hair in one fist. "You're rash with madness, wench. Calm yourself before I seek more fleshly pursuits," Veleif panted.

Æstrid's arms windmilled frantically as she tried to loosen Veleif's grip from her hair. The shoulder of her gown caught on a protruding nail. As Æstrid fought to avoid his clutches, the fabric parted with a rending tear, baring her shoulder and leaving the soft linen kirtle beneath her gown exposed.

Veleif exhaled an annoying breath and lifted up just enough to roll her to her back. Seeing her breasts strain against the thin cloth, combined with the sparks shooting from her eyes, he was gripped with lust of an unfathomable depth. The woman was wild, irascible, and utterly bewitching. He craved to experience the full onslaught of her passion without breaking her spirit. This quicksilver realization catapulted him on a headlong course to tame this creature.

Sensing a change as Veleif's gaze wandered, Æstrid let loose a mortified gasp. She shielded her torn bodice with her arm. "You black-hearted pig." She spat, "Brute!"

"You should never allow your anger to cloud your reason, Æstrid. You will lose every battle before you ever begin the fight. That's your first lesson," he rasped.

"Lesson? As if I could learn anything from you, Kollsvein," Æstrid barked.

The flat of her hand thumped his chest, trying to push him away. Veleif snatched the flailing member and enveloped it in his larger one. Ignoring her resistance, he pressed a warm kiss onto her open palm.

Æstrid inhaled sharply at the searing touch of his lips against her flesh. Forgetting the pain in her knee, she strained in earnest. Veleif leaned closer, squeezing her immobile between his powerful thighs. The hand in her hair tilted her back, exposing the creamy column of her throat.

"The second lesson, my lady, if you harnessed your temper and expended a like effort toward passion instead..." he grinned at her rakishly, and trapped her useless hand over his heart. "I vow you will bring the entire kingdom of Kollsveinholdt at your feet."

Æstrid stilled as his soft words permeated her brain. The scent of leather from his trousers, and the pressure of his hard body around hers amplified her fluttering pulse.

Veleif's eyes roamed down her face, her neck. His measured gaze paused leisurely on her heaving bosom. Æstrid felt her cheeks broil under his deliberate perusal. Did he think to keep her as a willing bedmate? Her lips curled back in a sneer.

"You vow?" Æstrid's brows arched in astonishment. "From which side of your mouth do you speak, Kollsvein?"

"I would ask you that question," Veleif replied lazily. The icy eyes locked with hers in a chilling demand.

"Me?"

"Yes. You broke your word," Veleif stated.

"I did not!" Æstrid denied hotly.

"Did you not give me your word you wouldn't harm anyone here?" Veleif chided.

"Didn't you tell me no ships would sail until the spring?" Æstrid countered. Hot tears of frustration sprang to her eyes.

"Did you not say 'clear as crystals' to my request?" Veleif parried.

"And the ship I saw this morning was my imagination? You could have easily—" she argued.

"Enough! You speak of things you do not know," Veleif interrupted. He snatched her hand covering her bosom and pinned it above her head. Veleif leaned down even closer and Æstrid swallowed as she read the flare of hot desire in his eyes.

"You have no right to treat me thus!" Æstrid protested in a croaked whisper.

"As lord and master of Kollsveinholdt, I'll treat you as I see fit. Lesson three, my lady, and this one I encourage you to pay special attention to," Veleif threatened in a low growl. "You're better served to stir my pleasure. Not invoke my ire."

"You dare threaten me?" Æstrid hissed.

Veleif smiled. He held the advantage, yet the vixen still challenged him. His fingers squeezed her hands in warning, until he heard her whimper. Veleif gripped her hands tightly in one fist, and nudged her legs apart, until he was cradled between her thighs. He pressed against her, leaving her no doubts the evidence of his arousal.

Æstrid's eyes went wide with panic, as his free hand plunged into her hair. Her wasted struggles seemed to do nothing more than tempt him.

"I dare more than that, Æstrid Karisson." Veleif's voice was husky with need.

"We are enemies sworn, Veleif Kollsvein," Æstrid reminded.

"By your admission, not mine." His lips hovered above hers and his gaze seemed to drink in every detail. "I cannot remember ever facing an enemy more beautiful, or desiring one so well." He rocked his hips against her to underscore his words.

"Your lust has unbalanced you, barbarian. Until you return me to Karissonholdt, I vow you'll not have a moment's peace." Æstrid promised tightly. Veleif chuckled deeply as his thumb grazed the delicate line of her jaw.

Æstrid stiffened.

"I agree. There wouldn't be a moment's peace around you. You stir a man's blood to boiling," Veleif admitted, twisting her words. Shrouded within the inky curtain of his hair, his lips pressed tiny kisses against her neck, leaving streams of fiery trails in their wake. "Give up this recklessness, Æstrid," Veleif murmured along her skin.

His intention, bringing her to this deserted cottage was to lay down the law to her, even frighten her a bit at first. She was formidable, his warrior princess. Her reactions were instinctive and predictable. She had fought and squabbled and waged a protective front against her fear. After all, she was far from home, and the familiarity of her people.

Veleif wanted to assuage her fears, convince her to relinquish any more conflict between them, and comfort her with his protection. But facing the most tempestuous vixen he'd ever encountered wouldn't be an easy victory. His intention was to turn this battle to his favor, calm her with a reassurance of peace, and gain a degree of her trust.

His *intentions* were rooted in honor, but his body quickly outpaced his mind. He hadn't prepared for the sight of her lips parted with her heaving breath, or her skin flushed with passion.

Veleif reined in his melting control. The storm of his mood was about to be unleashed and he *should* put some distance from her before the torrent of his desire rained unchecked.

Testing his resolve, Veleif considered the alluring swells of her breasts. The gods themselves wouldn't be denied by this tempting bounty – and Veleif knew he was no god.

A quiet sound of resignation died in his throat. Just one more taste, one more touch, and then he'd return to win this game.

His head dipped lower, placing hot kisses along the swelling outline of her curves.

Æstrid tugged at her arms as his hips ground erotically into her. The brush of his silken hair teased her skin. The gods help her, a deep curl of wanting unfurled in her belly.

She could feel the full power of his strength, yet Æstrid knew instinctively Veleif would not harm her.

Threaten her? Most likely.

Chide her? Certainly.

But hurt her? No.

Somewhere deep inside she felt safe and protected in his embrace, and though she may be damned for doing so, she wanted more.

Her body combated against her mind.

This was Veleif Kollsvein, a deceitful barbarian, yet loved by his people. He was reputed for his heinous acts, yet the only evidence she'd seen of his brutality was directed against the Pict.

He was overbearing, unyielding, and a liar, yet he was holding her protectively.

She wanted to hate him, *needed* to hate him; yet her resolve was slipping away under this enchanting assault. Grasping at the remainders of her tattered reason, she had to divert him before she surrendered.

"I thought you brought me here to talk?" Æstrid asked weakly.

"There are many forms of talking..." Veleif whispered. He shifted and fixed her with glittering stare of unbridled heat. "Not all of them involve words."

A tiny whimper escaped her throat as Veleif released her hands and cradled her head. The next instant his lips plunged down on hers.

The kiss was claiming, borderline brutal, as Veleif marked her as his. He gave no quarter, quickly breaching past her forsaken defenses, forcing her lips open to meet his challenge.

Her body arched beneath his as his tongue warred in the silken cavern of her mouth. Swirling, taking, and demanding. To his amazement, her hands locked around his shoulders, not fighting against him as he expected. The maid matched him with equalled fervor, as he swallowed the soft cries in her throat. His fingertips caressed her face and Veleif angled deeper.

Locked against him, suspended in the maelstrom of warmth, Æstrid soared up and up, beyond the hard floor, soaring past her anger, or her reason. She half-heartedly tried to recoil, but Veleif's hand in her hair brooked no withdrawal. He was taking her on his terms, plundering her mouth with commanding insistence, unready to depart.

An unexpected stab of longing lanced through him as he felt her relent. He memorized every purr, every thrust, and every parry of their kiss, until the world around them fell away, like shards of breaking ice melting into a sea of oblivion.

Tampering his bold attack, Veleif withdrew to a leisurely pace, kissing her not only with his lips, but with his heart. He bared his soul to her in the intimate exchange. Everything he was, as a man, a fierce and loyal protector, a lover who could pleasure her thoroughly, would be imprinted on her soul leaving her no doubts words weren't needed to express what was blossoming between them.

When he finally broke the kiss, the only sound in the cottage was the rapid breaths each of them struggled to take. Æstrid stared at him wordlessly, still floating on eddy of his kiss. As the sensual fog he'd woven between them began to clear, Æstrid hesitantly lifted two fingers to her lips, astonished to find them still tingling.

Veleif's eyes followed her fingertips, noting the shape of her mouth, dusky and swollen. A surge of masculine satisfaction coursed through him. He had made her lips look that way. He had put that glazed look in her eyes. He had made certain she was left weak and spent. He'd vanquished her wrath, now it was time to negotiate the terms of her surrender.

Veleif's face darkened as he watched her shaking hands hold together the pieces of her ruined dress. Pulling himself to his feet and extending his hand, Æstrid tentatively clasped his arm with both hands. She looked up at him with a violet plea. Her knees had turned to butter and she could no more bring herself to her feet than if her life depended on it.

Veleif smiled in reassurance, not mocking her predicament, but oddly, compassionate. He quickly pulled her upright, and in an effortless flex of his strength, lifted her clear of the floor until she was cradled against him.

In two fluid strides, he set her easily on the paltry mattress. Cursing her body's reflexive betrayal, Æstrid tilted forward, thinking he would kiss her again. Veleif dipped toward her, but didn't take her lips. Instead, his hands pressed on either side of the mattress, his arms caged her in. His tone was placid, yet oddly strained when he spoke.

"As much as I'd like to keep you near me at all times, Æstrid, I fear it is impractical. So I've assigned Berra with your care."

Æstrid was still adrift, her mind a tiny lost ship, tossed about upon the dark seas of oblivion. Her nostrils were filled with the warm, male scent of him, the span of his shoulders, and the foreign sensation of longing he awakened.

Somewhere in her dazed consciousness, a sound broke across the horizon of her awareness, breeching the waves of confusion… Veleif had been speaking to her. Looking up into his eyes, she saw his expectant gaze, and the words finally registered in her muddled mind.

"I'm sorry… what is… Berra?" Æstrid inquired absently. Veleif's fingers captured her chin and he glanced at her lips before he spoke. Æstrid gasped as he bent, grazing her mouth with a feather light touch.

"Berra is not a what, my lady, but who," Veleif informed her lightly.

Æstrid followed his every movement as he picked up his own cloak and tucked it about her shoulders. Her hands clasped the fabric together tightly and she felt the heat rise to her cheeks. What had just passed between them was earth-shattering, devastating, and beguiling, all the same.

Yet Veleif was standing before her, and tending her with a detachment as if she were nothing more than a stray lamb. The equaled but conflicting emotions of anger and passion that had raged through her in a hands-breadth of time, collided together leaving her exhausted and confused.

"I don't understand," Æstrid said.

"Berra is a woman with less patience than I for idle schemes," Veleif informed her softly as he crossed his arms. The simple action stayed him from touching her before he lost control completely. Seeing the state he'd reduced her to, he could easily coerce her to deeper seduction, but that way not the way to win this war.

"Idle schemes?" Æstrid's brows drew together, perplexed in innocence. The folds of his cloak clung with his scent, and she felt the warmth seeping through her limbs. It was like a memory of being in his embrace.

"I think a week or two in the kitchens under Berra's tutelage should keep you occupied against more maladies. Better to soil your hands with foodstuffs than with sheep urine," Veleif chided as he cocked a brow at her.

"You're sending me to the kitchens?" Æstrid fidgeted in disbelief.

"You have to agree it is a gentler penance than others I could exact from you," he stated, confidently. The hint of a smile tugged at the corners of his mouth.

He predicted his teasing declaration would break the enchantment of his ardor. His warrior princess could leave their dispute vanquished, but with her dignity intact. He wasn't disappointed to see her mood snap and her sauciness return. His maneuver was timed perfectly.

"Why did you kiss me?" Æstrid demanded.

Veleif picked his way through the rubble of the cottage. With his hand on the door, he paused and turned to look at her.

"Arnor will escort you back. There are more gowns in your chamber, Æstrid. Please find one quickly for I'd hate to split a skull over anyone who dares steal a gaze at your state of undress."

Æstrid stood up clutching the cloak tightly around her. "Why did you kiss me, Veleif?" she repeated, her voice rising with her insistence. His eyes held hers for a stretch of time before he shrugged his answer.

"You needed kissing, Æstrid."

Veleif closed the door behind him, concealing his mirth that he'd rendered her speechless. Meeting Arnor's questioning gaze, he simply smiled at the big Viking.

Veleif plucked the horn of ale from the man's hand before he could protest. Swiftly draining the full contents, Veleif wiped his mouth with the back of his hand, and thrust the empty vessel back into Arnor's stunned palm. Arnor's lips pressed into a tight line as he scanned Veleif quickly.

"Well you appear unscathed. But who knew wooing built up such a thirst?" Arnor jested, looking down at the empty horn.

"My friend, you have no idea." Veleif slapped the man's shoulder and gestured his thumb to the door. "See her back to the keep, Arnor. And have a care when you remind her to return the combs she borrowed."

"Combs? What combs?" Arnor called out as Veleif headed through the drifts.

"I want them returned before eventide," Veleif tossed back over his shoulder.

"What combs do you speak of?" Arnor yelled, only to be answered with a wave of Veleif's arm above his head and his retreating form.

"Women!" Arnor grumbled to himself as he contemplated the empty horn.

Eating, drinking, fucking, warring... and more drinking, he thought with a sigh. That is what life used to be.

Life used to be much less complicated, when it didn't involve a bride.

# Chapter Ten

In less than a week since her encounter with Veleif in the cottage, Æstrid assimilated easily into the rhythm of the kitchens at Kollsveinholdt. Where she had first been met with confusion and skepticism when Arnor first announced the position of her new labors, they were rapidly replaced with smiles and camaraderie.

Berra, the jolly cook who controlled everything from measuring out the larders, to overseeing the scrubbing in the scullery, took an instant liking to Æstrid. Despite her state of advanced pregnancy, Berra was tireless. She ushered Æstrid to a stool and bustled around her, showering with compliments on how she'd stabbed the drunken Blotha, and how unfitting it was a princess of Karisson should be reduced to the kitchens.

Æstrid could barely utter a word against the steady stream of the woman's chatter. On the second day of doing nothing more than resting her chin in her hand, she sighed and drummed her fingers idly on the tabletop. Following Berra's endless movements was proving to be exhaustive. Æstrid was determined to do something to alleviate this boredom, and sitting lazily in the kitchens while others toiled, went against her nature.

She quietly observed the workings of the vast kitchen at Kollsveinholdt as Berra droned on. And on. There were long, heavy tables to prepare the food and not one, but three hearths for roasting, boiling and baking. They were so large, even Arnor could have stood inside the rounded arches and never touched his head.

After seeing the bounty of the spices and vegetables, and the smoked fish hanging from the rafters, a wicked idea formed in Æstrid's mind. But this plan would take a bit of time to execute, and involve a modicum of trust.

Berra paused her stories every now and then to issue a sharp command, but never once stopped for air. The woman was unflagging and her hawkish eyes missed nothing.

Æstrid hopped off the stool, her face lit with excitement.

"Berra? If I might…" Æstrid placed a friendly hand on the woman's arm. "I know I'm here until the weather breaks in the spring, yet I long for a taste of home." Æstrid glanced over to the table where two women were busy molding the hideous loaves into long pans. "I would be honored to share some of the recipes of Karissonholdt, but only with your permission…" Æstrid steered.

"Well, I…" Berra hesitated.

"Berra, this is exactly the tonic I needed for my homesickness," Æstrid continued before Berra could protest, and pinned on an apron.

"You miss your home, my lady?" Berra asked, her eyes wide with sympathy.

"Oh yes. I promise I won't get in anyone's way," Æstrid assured her with an airy laugh. Æstrid scurried to gather the supplies she needed and carved out her own place at one of the long tables.

It wasn't long before Berra, and the others surrounded her, intrigued by her methods. Æstrid demonstrated a way to grind the grains into finer flour, and mixed with fermented ale, eggs and milk, she promised to produce bread that was tall and light.

Æstrid was so absorbed in her labors, and the jovial exchanges of laughter with her newfound audience, she completely missed the dark prince of Kollsveinholdt observing from the doorway. Veleif's arms folded across his chest as he scowled. Thinking to find her grouchy and scrubbing the worst of vessels, the last thing he anticipated was the sight before him.

Æstrid was happy, laughing, and had taken full command of the kitchen. Even Berra, who maintained a militant authority over her domain, hung on her every word.

She'd managed to avoid Veleif the past few days. When Veleif sent Nar to inquire why her place beside him was vacant at the evening meals, she sent the boy back with her reply.

She was occupying her time, as he'd suggested.

Was there no end to the wench's disdain? Or her conquests?

The women joked and smiled and the whole air in the room had changed. His own people looked to her for direction and eagerly listened as she answered their questions with patience. She had earned their respect in an extraordinary short amount of time, Veleif noted with pride. He could have relegated her to the stables, knowing Æstrid would probably charm the sheep into shearing themselves, or convince the goats to drop milk into their own pails.

But it was her smile that entranced him. It was heartfelt, and so genuine it chased the frigid chill from the air. He vowed it would be no more than a handful of days before she'd bestow him with that earnest smile.

A hard nudge to his shoulder bumped him from his musings.

Veleif teetered sideways, cursing as he lost his balance. How deep in thought had he been? He hadn't even sensed someone coming up behind him.

"You look like a moonstruck lad," Arnor frowned.

Veleif snorted.

"Merely seeing the wench stays on task, and causes no more trouble," he grumbled.

Now it was Arnor's turn to snort.

But as the big Viking opened his mouth to speak, the rebuke died on his lips. He was interrupted at the sight of the most beautiful breads he'd ever seen.

Arnor's eyes widened as his head followed the delights being carried from the ovens and over to the tables to cool. He smacked his lips as the tantalizing smell wafted toward them. They inhaled as one, appreciatively, and both their mouths watered.

The men took an impulsive step forward, and halted abruptly before they crashed together, like two dogs scrambling for a piece of meat. Arnor grunted.

Forever being ruled by his gargantuan appetites, he was overcome with the tempting aromas. Deference for his prince be damned. Using his sheer size, he pushed past Veleif headlong into the room.

"What is this?" he demanded, and pointed eagerly at the bread.

Pursing her lips into a frown, Berra ignored him. With hands on her hips, she craned her neck past Arnor's bulk and set a hawkish gaze on Veleif.

"The day the prince graces my kitchen, not once, but twice..." Berra chided.

Æstrid's attention snapped up. She quickly masked her startled gaze and smoothed the front of her apron as both men approached.

*Twice? Veleif had been here twice?*

Æstrid felt her face grow hot as Veleif strolled to her side. She had carefully avoided him, not wanting to encourage further confrontation after their disastrous parting in the cottage.

Not yet.

She'd welcomed the distraction that lending her talent in the kitchens provided. Not only did the position afford a keen distance from the handsome, overbearing warlord, but it was the perfect place to covertly architect another revenge.

If Veleif Kollsvein had thought she'd go meek at his command, he If Veleif Kollsvein had thought she'd go meek at his command, he was sorely mistaken. She wanted to go home, and Veleif's arrogance was the only impediment preventing her return. She saw the ship leave Kollsveinholdt with her own eyes, and Æstrid knew her eyes hadn't played her false, even if the prince had.

Æstrid was practically pinned under the intensity of Veleif's gaze. His eyes sparkled to dazzling blue depths as they swept her from head to toe.

Not to be outdone, she raised her chin slightly and matched his perusal. She ran her eyes over him, scrutinizing with the same discretion. When her gaze lifted to his face, he had one dark brow raised and an amused quirk tilted the corner of his lips.

She told herself *he* was not the reason she'd tossed restlessly in her bed these past nights. Æstrid crossed her arms protectively in front to suppress a shiver.

Ignoring her defensive posture, Veleif stood as close as possible without touching her. The manly scent of him wormed into her brain and the room grew uncomfortably warm. It was the nearness of the hearth, she lied to herself, *not* the heat emanating from his body. The body, she knew, that was hard and male. Arms impossibly strong, and lips… those lips.

Her blood skittered wildly in her veins as her face flushed hotter. Cursing where her mind had wandered, she took a calming breath. Æstrid stood taller and kept her gaze straight ahead, refusing to look at him.

"Be off, you great lout! There's nothing here needing a warrior's attention." Berra waved an annoying hand at Arnor, who lingered over the table.

"Ah, but there is," Arnor laughed with unadulterated pleasure. His eyes locked on the tiny tendrils of heat wafting from the bread. As he leaned forward and inhaled deeply, a low moan escaped his throat.

Æstrid thought if he didn't sample one of these rolls soon, the entire kitchen would fall victim to a full Viking's berserker rage. She sidestepped Veleif, broke off a flaky roll, and spread it thickly with butter.

"Here, Arnor. Since you seem so eager," Æstrid giggled.

His face beamed like a child at Candlemas.

Veleif chafed inwardly at her blatant snub. Æstrid laughed and clapped her hands as the Viking's face transformed from one of curiosity to absolute ecstasy.

"Oh! Oh!" Arnor half-roared, half-sighed aloud, as he chewed, unable to stifle his bliss. "This… this is surely what the gods feast upon…"

Æstrid quickly readied another, her smile radiant beneath Arnor's compliments. The women broke into happy dins of tittering laughter as Æstrid passed around more of the tempting delights, her eyes bright with pleasure. The sound rankled Veleif's ears as he watched her attend Arnor and the others.

The sound rankled Veleif's ears as he watched her attend Arnor and the others. Her head was thrown back in laughter, exposing the creamy column of her throat. She was certainly enjoying herself, as much as an evening of dancing and celebration. Æstrid's skirts twirled about her ankles as she hurried to serve up more bread.

When her eyes met his, her smile faded instantly. Veleif's disapproving gaze deepened to a downright scowl. He leveled Æstrid with an arctic stare.

"Everyone out!" Veleif barked. "Except you." Veleif

The kitchen silenced.

All movement ceased, as if everyone were frozen, too petrified to move. Even Arnor's hand poised in mid-air, his face riddled with confusion. Berra was the first one to break the trance. Her voice was low and uncharacteristically gentle.

"Come away everyone." Her hands waved frantically, as she shooed the astonished women toward the door. Berra turned a stern look at Arnor, who wisely decided to retreat, but not before he snatched up an armful of bread.

Æstrid whirled on him, her eyes narrowed to slits. Veleif casually leaned a hip against the table and waited until the last person departed the room. He could feel Æstrid's tension stretch at the forced silence between them. He turned his attention back to her, silently daring her to speak first. He smiled inwardly as the wench didn't disappoint.

"I can't imagine how *efficient* the workings are at Kollsveinholdt, that the prince cannot find anything better to serve his time, other than to check on the workings in the lowly kitchen," Æstrid accused mockingly.

Veleif felt his cock twitch.

Odin help him, he relished her combative tone. Her fiery mode stirred his blood until his fingers ached to run through the silken lengths of her hair. He'd banished her to the kitchen, yet the maid still baited him. He wanted to push her against the wall and taste that spirit of hers again and again until they were both consumed with it.

Veleif straightened and took a step toward her. Æstrid cautiously retreated, matching his movement to maintain an equal distance between them. After all, their encounter in the cottage was still fresh in her mind.

"Frightened doesn't suit you, maid," Veleif taunted.

"I'm not frightened," Æstrid countered quickly.

In truth she was. She was frightened that if Veleif simply crooked his finger, she'd fling herself against his chest. She'd plead with him to take her lips again in those glorious kisses... no. *No!* Her mind screamed at the traitorous thought. That was *not* the solution to assuage the torment of her disrupted nights.

"Come," Veleif commanded softly. His hand waved to beckon her. "I would taste these gifts you've bestowed upon us."

It was a challenge issued in a silken glove. While Æstrid kept her distance, Veleif was pleased she sidled closer to the table without further protest. He noted how her fingers curled in a forceful grip on the edge of the wood. Her nostrils flared slightly. She fixed her stare on the loaves Arnor had left unpillaged.

"And your… desire to taste…" Æstrid parried, "does this require you roar about and clear the room?"

"If I wish it, I'll clear this keep entirely and see to my desires," Veleif answered in a low growl. Æstrid felt the heated blush stain her cheeks and rewarded him a withering look.

"Barbarian," she murmured. Her lips pressed together in a thin line.

"I?" Veleif chortled, and reached for the bread. He tossed it in the air and caught it in one hand, gesturing to her. "You're the one unschooled in civility, Æstrid. I could take offense at your disrespect. You should first seek the lord's approval… before offering such temptations to others." Veleif's eyes flickered briefly on the bun in his hand, then fixed her with deliberate regard. His head tilted to a cocky angle and Æstrid chafed at his backhanded insult.

Ooh he was insufferable! How dare he accuse her! Æstrid bit her lower lip to hold her tongue. Every fiber in her being cried out to slay him in this verbal spar. Leave him cut and bloody, shred to ribbons on the edge of a vocal axeblade. Raising her chin a notch, she squared her shoulders.

"*Your* approval? Considering what's come out of your kitchens before my presence here, I hardly thought your palate to be a worthy judge."

"Worthier than most, Æstrid, if not all." Veleif's face lit up with a wide smile. Without breaking her gaze he bit into the bread. Then he paused and turned his attention to the wonder he held in his hand.

This wasn't bread. This was something else.

A downy bite of warm heaven. The flaky, golden delight rolled in his mouth and teased his tongue. It was delicate, more savory than the sweetest ale. He took another taste, joining the first, savoring the mouth-watering goodness.

Veleif chewed slowly, relishing the soft, yeasty flavors until his eyes closed briefly and a moan of pure pleasure escaped him. Truly, Arnor had described it well.

*Food for the gods* the man had said.

While Veleif appreciated food as well as the next man, in all his days he'd never tasted anything so divine.

Æstrid watched him, with her hands on her hips. Her brow winged up as she waited for his verdict. The hint of a smug smile curved her lips. Veleif swallowed and without thinking, reached for another.

"With food such as this, I could almost ignore your hellish tongue," he muttered, half to himself. He held up the bread reverently, as if regarding it as a precious treasure, before he finished off the piece. Before he could stop himself, Veleif claimed another. He paused, and began to laugh.

Æstrid puzzled at his amusement. Of all the possibilities of his reactions, laughter was not what she'd expected.

"Are you well, Kollsvein?" she snipped. Her smile faded and her brow furrowed. "Stricken with a fever perhaps?"

"I'm quite well, Æstrid. Contrary to your hopes." Veleif nodded, reining in his mirth. "Never could I have imagined your penance in the kitchen would bring such fortune to my people. Or to me."

"You're truly favored by the gods, Kollsvein." Æstrid rolled her eyes.

"Why did you make this?" Veleif ventured curiously, and held the bread aloft. He enjoyed another piece and inched closer to her, his dark brows arched with expectation.

"Why did you clear the room?" Æstrid countered defensively.

Veleif sighed inwardly as he watched her nails tighten on the table. The hellion lashed out predictably when she felt threatened. But Veleif didn't want her defensive, he wanted to gain her trust, and eventually, much more. Winter Solstice was fast approaching and having Æstrid constantly vexed was not conducive to a peaceful future.

Years of warring had taught him surprise went a long way to gaining advantage against a suspicious enemy. Instead of demanding recompense for her insolence as she'd be expecting, he chose surprise instead. Sweep her feet from under her and watch the maid land on her proverbial backside, so to speak.

"I merely wanted to thank you," Veleif admitted. He smiled as he watched her frown dissolve to confusion.

Æstrid eyed him warily.

"Humility doesn't suit you, Kollsvein." Æstrid crossed her arms and leaned a hip against the table.

Veleif laughed again and shook his head.

"I'm not offering my humility, Æstrid, but my gratitude." His eyes sparkled with sincerity. "The people of Kollsveinholdt are already much improved with your contribution." He waved a hand above the table. "Does Berra know how to duplicate this?"

Æstrid nodded. Her jaw went slack. A compliment was the last thing she'd expected from the brash warrior.

"Then you no longer need to spend your time here."

Æstrid's heart plummeted at his words. If she was removed from the kitchen, her carefully prepared revenge would be for naught.

"But...but I don't wish to spend my time anywhere else." Æstrid licked her lips hesitantly as she wringed her hands. She raised her eyes to his and smiled softly. "I like Berra's company, and... and cooking."

"Then do what pleases you, Æstrid." Veleif reached for her hand and it held it gently, curling her fingers over his. For some inexplicable reason, Æstrid couldn't pull it back from his tender grasp. His thumb absently stroked her knuckles.

"You are not my enemy, Æstrid Karisson. While it pains me I am unable to return you quickly to your home, I want you to take advantage of all the comforts Kollsveinholdt provides."

Æstrid was stunned at his speech. Twin pangs of guilt for what she planned for him warred with the solace of his words. He had caught her unprepared. Her notions of him as the uncouth barbarian did not include this... this kindness. Veleif Kollsvein was wearing down her resolve in the worst way possible.

He was being *nice*.

Veleif looked at her hand resting in his, so small and pale against his own. His eyes were warm and his gaze never wavered. With unhurried care, he lifted her hand to his lips and pressed a tender kiss against her flesh.

A surge of warmth coursed up her arm at the brief brush of his lips, coiling, tightening, until it fluttered straight to her core. Suddenly everything around them drifted away, falling off in silent, shattered pieces. There was no bread, no kitchen, and no lingering bodies straining their curious heads at the doorway. There was only the cadence of her racing heartbeats, and Veleif. He cradled her in the soft cocoon of his voice, which turned low and raspy.

"Know with my gratitude, you will always have my full protection, maid." His lips still hovered over her hand as his eyes skimmed her face.

Æstrid opened her mouth to speak, but no words formed. His blue gaze was intense, mesmerizing. His eyes lingered on her lips, breaking the trance, then returned to meet hers once more. A rush of heat lanced through her, and Æstrid knew he was dwelling on their private, passionate exchange in all its vivid glory.

"Why *did* you kiss me, Veleif? In the cottage?" Æstrid asked, her voice barely above a whisper.

Veleif looked at her for a long, hard moment, as if fighting some inner battle. His body stiffened and he took a step back, releasing her hand. He frowned a little before he smiled.

"Perhaps I was thinking of something more than your skills with flour, wench." His voice was so low, she had to strain to hear him. In the next instant, Æstrid flinched as his bark broke the stillness of the room.

"Berra! Return! For I know you've not strayed far," he shouted. He favored Æstrid with a lazy grin. As the barrage of women flooded the room, Veleif gave her nothing more than a brief nod, and then he turned away.

Æstrid watched him go, absently stroking the spot on her hand where his lips had touched.

"*I may have your protection, Veleif,*" she thought, "*but who will protect me from you?*"

# Chapter Eleven

A vicious blizzard descended on Kollsveinholdt, which made routine comings and goings from the keep impossible. Savage north winds tore through the mountain passes, accelerating in downward spirals to the forest's edge. Breaking limbs and branches hurled like deadly javelins across the village. On and on the blinding storm raged, stinging ice and fierce gusts swept everything unsecured into the angry depths of the ocean beyond.

Despite the brutal tempest outside, spirits within the thick walls of Kollsveinholdt soared. Howling gales and the cries of distant, cracking ice didn't push the people huddled together in disquiet groups, as they would have been at Karissonholdt. Veleif's people embraced the storm.

And celebrated.

Æstrid couldn't quite decide if their concerns were wiped away by the copious amounts of hot, mulled ale she'd helped Berra and Asa prepare and always have on hand, or if it was the distractions Veleif himself had organized.

Caught up in their festive mood, Æstrid guided Asa, Berra and others in the kitchen through dish after dish. Their faces turned to delight and they praised, with unabashed honesty, the flavorsome delights Æstrid created. With so many people now ensconced in the keep, the demands on the kitchen grew. Through a wreath of smiles, Berra thanked Æstrid repeatedly for the help.

Gaining the woman's trust had been Æstrid's plan, but she found she genuinely liked Berra. Building camaraderie with the woman who controlled this domain, was easy. Winning her respect through her cooking, had been even easier. Æstrid's brow furrowed in sincere concern when she saw the woman arch, furtively seeking to ease her aching back. Berra didn't protest as Æstrid ushered her to a stool.

"You should be resting, Berra," Æstrid said, kneading another batch of flour. It was almost impossible to keep up with the demand for her baking. Despite the exertion, the lighthearted moods of those surrounding her lifted her own spirits, and kept the dark memories of Leidolf's death at bay.

She was accepted and respected. She joked and teased with the women, as well as the men. More than once today, she had laughingly slapped both Thorliek's and Arnor's hands from stealing away generous fistfuls of fresh bread from the platters. Æstrid realized, in spite of all the trials of late, she'd never been happier.

"And you should not be working so hard, my lady," Berra chided.

"It's hardly work, Berra," Æstrid laughed with a shrug.

The sound of a pronounced *thwump!* followed by loud cheers and guffaws made both women pause.

"What is happening?" Æstrid asked.

"Who knows what amusements those men devise? They look for any excuse to drink and play their games. A storm is as good a reason as any." Berra smiled with a dismissive wave.

Another loud *thwump!* More male shouts and cheers crescendoed from the hall. Nar appeared at her side, tugging her sleeve for attention. His effervescent smile was so innocent, Æstrid couldn't help but giggle at his presence.

"My lady! Come see!" he chuckled and bounced on his toes. His eyes sparkled with excitement. Unable to deny his exuberance, Æstrid wiped her hands from the dough and let Nar tug her into the hall.

Her mouth dropped.

Every table and bench had been shoved to the walls, leaving a long, unbroken space in the center. The men crowded together, laughing and elbowing each other good-naturedly, passing skins and horns of mulled ale between them.

At the far end of the clearing, one of the massive wooden tables had been upended, resting on its shortest side. A hastily painted blue circle marked its center. Embedded in the circle's lower right edge, was an axe.

Veleif stood facing the target, about twenty-five paces away from the table.

"What say you, my prince? Can you best Arnor's aim?" Slothi called out.

"We'd best hope he can, for Arnor's sake," another voice chimed in, followed by raucous laughter.

"Perhaps I should call one of the women to challenge," Veleif tossed out to the crowd, "surely their aim could be no worse." Rowdy laughter circled between the men and Æstrid bristled at his jest.

Veleif pulled a horn from Arnor's grip and tossed back a hefty swig. "Do you want to retrieve your axe, Arnor? Or leave it lie? I'll offer you another round."

"Another round?" Arnor feigned repugnance. "Of axes? Or of ale?" The men howled with merriment as Arnor yanked the horn back from Veleif's grasp.

Æstrid quickly shielded Nar, as four unbalanced sots were so overcome with the cheer, they stumbled and crashed together.

"Ah! You'll leave it lie then." Veleif stripped off his tunic, rolled his bare shoulders and cracked his neck to the side.

Æstrid blinked and her mouth went dry at the sight of Veleif clad only in his trousers. The first time she had seen him unclothed in his chamber was no less of a shock than it was now. His sculpted presence hailed him every inch the Viking warrior that he was. The slabs of muscles rippled with raw power as he shrugged, and stretched. The smooth skin of his back and shoulders were a velvety contrast to the twin silver cuffs which glinted off his forearms, marking him as the prince of Kollsveinholdt. He stood tall, commanding, unequaled to the men surrounding him. A man such as Veleif could easily share a place in Odin's hall, while bards composed tales of his legends...

Nar squeezed her hand in excitement. It was enough to break the scattered shards of her senses, and Æstrid flashed him an encouraging smile.

"Look at the game, my lady. There's none better with throwing an axe than Veleif!" Nar wiggled proudly. Æstrid raised a singular brow skeptically at the boy and wisely bit back a retort.

"Certain you don't need more ale, Veleif?" a slurred voice piped above the din.

"Give the man another horn!" Blotha called out, hefting one in his direction.

"A horn? A prince of his size needs a full skin of courage!" Another voice chimed in. Hoots of laughter followed the banter.

"Back away you mongrels!" Arnor roared in mock anger and cleared a wide berth with sweeping arms. "More ale will only sharpen his aim!"

Through the haze of speculative jests and chortles, Æstrid watched Veleif's profile as he smiled. He picked up an axe and hefted the weight in his hand, testing the balance as he studied the weapon.

Veleif turned his back to the makeshift target. He braced in surprise when he saw Æstrid looking on. He acknowledged her with a slight nod, then gave an audacious wink to Nar. The corners of his lips lifted in a mischievous smile and he held out his empty hand, turning his eyes back to Æstrid.

"More ale!" Veleif called out, never once breaking his intense regard.

Arnor rolled his eyes. Irik hurried forward and shoved a skin into Veleif's outstretched hand. His eyes glittered across the hall as he propped the skin on one shoulder and tipped it back. Æstrid shifted nervously as a few heads turned toward her, following the object of Veleif's stare.

"You're done in, Arnor! A man's aim only sharpens under a lady's regard," Irik shouted above the laughter. Æstrid felt twin stains bloom on her cheeks as the men elbowed each other in approval. Arnor swayed around and when he saw Æstrid looking on, he released an audible groan and rubbed the back of his neck.

"Argh! For certain I'm done in," Arnor mocked, as he snatched the skin away from Veleif. He waved an impatient hand toward the target. "Well. Get on with it, then!"

Veleif picked up a second axe. The noise from the men threatened to wake the dead, as the hoots and shouts escalated toward the beams. He squared off with his back to the target and favored her with a blazing grin. Though Æstrid's heart lurched at the sight of him, his dark bearing of lithe confidence, she awarded him with a skeptical brow.

The hall held a collective breath as Veleif crouched low. Beginning with a low bellow, the sound roared to life in his chest, drowning the room. With an inspiring grace, his body unwound like a coil, as he spun to his right, letting the first axe fly. It hurtled end over end with blinding speed.

Veleif didn't halt his spin, but came full around again, letting the second axe fly, ending with a low bow to one knee. His arm still poised in an open-handed throw. The first axe knocked Arnor's soundly, sending it hurtling to the floor with a clang. The second axe landed dead center in the circle, the handle still vibrating from the impact of the throw.

The cheers were deafening as Veleif slowly drew himself up. The men swarmed him quickly in congratulations and Nar flew from her side, winding his way to Veleif. Arnor accepted conciliatory pats on the back and laughed as well.

Veleif lifted the boy to his shoulders and craned his neck over the crowd, trying to catch the look of admiration he was certain to see on Æstrid's face.

"That display should surely win the lady's heart, Veleif," a drunken voice called out.

Æstrid froze.

She stood mute, yet the aftermath of the words hung in the air like a foul stench. *Win her heart? Is that what Kollsvein intended? Is that why the ship had sailed without her?* The crowd seemed to part by magic and Æstrid searched Veleif's face for any truth to the drunken slur. She needed no further evidence. The candor was plain on his face as he jostled Nar proudly and sent her a look like a hopeful suitor.

Feeling her anger boil within, Æstrid wisely tempered her infuriation. Veleif Kollsvein soared beyond every impressive example of male she had ever witnessed. Certainly a man among men, probably envied by the gods themselves even; and he ruled Kollsveinholdt with the earned respect from his people, not with force and terror like her father.

She understood how a simple maid could easily succumb to such a man as Veleif. A simple maid would ignore his lies, his arrogance, and his turpitude. A simple maid would share his bed, lose her heart, even...

But Æstrid was no simple maid.

He may have distracted her from her purpose with those few sultry kisses, but seeing him now, her resolution resumed. He had changed the game? Well, so would she. If Kollsvein thought to keep her here in whorish dalliance to ply away the winter in his bed, he had sorely underestimated her. *If she wanted to return home in the spring,* echoed in her mind. What outright arrogance! Instead of flying at him in irrational rage, Æstrid took stock of what she had – her skills, her wits, and Veleif as an unsuspecting prey.

She smiled sweetly and bowed her head in courtesy, all the while, cursing him silently. Shouldering her way through the crowd, Æstrid stood near the table where the axes lay.

"Did you see my lady? Did you see?" Nar called out excitedly from his perch on Veleif's shoulder. She rewarded them both a dazzling smile.

"Yes, Nar, it was a most impressive display. Veleif." Her chin dipped in acknowledgement.

"If you have anyone as skilled with an axe at Karissonholdt, Æstrid, I would certainly like to meet him." Veleif preened.

Ooh! that he should look for praise and impugn her home in the same breath! Drawing on every ounce of temperance she could manage, Æstrid waited as the room quieted to a lull. Conversations ceased and heads turned, curious for her answer.

"I have doubts there is any man at my keep *equal* to your skill with these weapons, Kollsvein." Æstrid thoughtfully stroked her fingertip down the handle of an axe. Remarks of praise at Veleif's skill echoed through the crowd.

Veleif's eyes narrowed. His jaw tightened. In a handful of days he'd already learned she had a fondness for ignoring his given name when she was vexed.

"Explain yourself," Veleif frowned.

"A Karisson *woman* can best *your blade!*"

Before he could grasp her full meaning, Æstrid picked up two axes in her fists and hurled them both over her head. In the blink of an eye, both blades landed with hearty thwumps! The wood severed on each side of his own, knocking it to the floor. The reverberating sound of metal striking the floor was the only thing to be heard, as the hall stood in dumbfounded silence.

Dusting her hands triumphantly, Æstrid rewarded him with a proud smirk.

Veleif closed his mouth, which, he realized, was gaping open. It was a near impossibility to strike that target with one axe with no preparation. The fact she'd used two, was nothing short of a miracle.

"Ha! The prince has found a worthy match!" Oresti slurred. He laughed and tripped, breaking the silence. All eyes turned to Veleif as Æstrid glowered at Oresti's staggering form.

*Match indeed!*

Veleif slid Nar slowly to the ground, his eyes never leaving her. Her fiery temperament admittedly stirred him, but this display churned his gut to roiling turbulence. A cauldron of lust and longing, and something else, yet unnamed, boiled together and pumped through his warrior's veins. Oresti's drunken words had never rung more true. *A worthy match.*

His nostrils flared as he probed the depths of her violet eyes. He was spellbound with an overpowering need to claim her, draw her into him and shout to the heavens this woman was *mine!*

The air grew taut with tension. Everyone held their breath waiting to see how the prince of Kollsvein would receive Æstrid's brazen act. The collective nervousness ebbed as a slow smile spread across Veleif's face. He shook his head and began to chuckle. With his hand on his hips he eyed her up and down, not bothering to conceal his desire.

"And to think I'd wondered if this maid's skills lie beyond mere flour and water," Veleif laughed audaciously. His grin turned puckish and his eyes sparkled with mischief.

"May the wonder of my skills plague your nights, Kollsvein," Æstrid quipped.

The men howled with laughter and bawdy jests as Æstrid quit the hall. Thorliek wormed his way to Veleif's side as both men's eyes followed her retreating form.

"I don't know which would benefit that maid more? A good beating or a good fucking?" The elder pondered.

Veleif stroked his beard thoughtfully. In truth, he had almost the same question running through his mind. The former elusive thing joined the chaos within his chest and thundered through him with startling realization.

He was proud of her.

"Will it matter, Thorliek? I'm the man to give her both."

# Chapter Twelve

Æstrid returned to the kitchen prickling between her small triumph and the unnerving stare of Veleif's blatant desire. She'd bested his axes and even left with the last word, but tonight, Veleif would have no doubts to the hardness of her heart. She'd best him again – with her food.

She encouraged the weary Berra to rest for the evening, with a promise to send her a trencher when everything was completed. Looking about with satisfaction, Æstrid had full run of the preparations for this evening's meal.

Dish after dish was brought to her for approval. Asa and the others would hold their faces expectantly, then clap and grin with Æstrid's appraisals as she sampled the roasted meats and fish. She carefully set aside a special portion to be served to Veleif himself. Marking his platter with a thumbprint of flour, Æstrid smiled.

The excitement was palpable in the hall. Every man, woman and child of Kollsveinholdt who had been stranded inside from the blizzard, waited eagerly at the tables. Rumors and truths had spread all day, not only about Æstrid's talents in the kitchen, but also of her skills with the axe.

Veleif descended the stairs to take his usual place among his men. He paused for a moment, seeing the tables and benches filled to overflowing, but there was something markedly different. The table they'd used for target practice had been righted, but there was a strange sense of order to the place.

Twice the number of candles seemed to light the hall, and it was... cleaner.

"What is this?" Veleif frowned at the trencher Nar placed before him. The fish and fowl were recognizable, but Veleif had never been served his meat already torn on his plate, and surrounded by some strange-colored liquid. The other side of his plate was roasted onion, carrots, and potatoes.

"Your supper, my lord." Nar puffed proudly and quickly stepped back. The boy watched as Arnor, Thorliek and everyone else at the main table were served. Other platters were quickly carried to the tables and soon the hall was filled with moans of appreciation at the food. Veleif extended his horn and the boy filled it with ale.

"Berra made this?" Veleif grumbled suspiciously.

"Er, yes my lord, with the lady Æstrid's help." Nar said with a bow and beat a hasty retreat.

"So I'm to be poisoned then?" Veleif muttered dryly to Arnor.

Arnor dug into his plate heartily, not bothering to swallow before he spoke.

"How goes your wooing, Veleif? The wench not only has talent with an axe, but one who cooks like this, I'd fair split your skull over."

All the men laughed heartily and showered complements over the food. When Nar returned with a platter of bread Arnor stood and bellowing a great roar, wrenched it from the boy's hands.

"That'll do, boy. Fetch another so the others may taste these pieces of heaven for themselves," Arnor thundered possessively. Nar stuttered, trying to explain the platter *was* for the table. Seeing Arnor's possessive glare, Nar thought the better of it and hurried off to the kitchen to retrieve another.

"Fortune smiles upon you, Veleif," Thorliek said, stuffing his mouth with the tasty fare. "Not only is the wench beautiful, but she cooks food worthy of Odin himself."

"Aye, and if her beauty fades, your belly will still find pleasure – even if your cock does not," Irik laughed. The table howled with laughter.

When Veleif placed a tentative morsel of Æstrid's food between his lips he thought his men had lost their minds. Despite the juicy liquids swimming on his plate, his meat was rubbery, tasteless and had a most peculiar smell. Veleif frowned and drained half a goblet of ale just to swallow the piece.

Æstrid entered the hall and was greeted to hearty cheers from his people. He speared a piece of fish with his knife and watched as Oresti lifted her high above his head, spinning her around in a victorious dance. Her squeal of happy laughter cut him like a double-edged blade. Veleif was pleased she was enjoying her acceptance among them, yet disheartened it wasn't he, who had brought the joy to her lips.

Entranced at how the maid softened under the attention, her eyes bright in merriment; Veleif absently put the fish in his mouth. The horror choked him. It was so salty and bitter, his eyes watered. Gagging and spitting the offensive morsel, Veleif grimaced and quickly reached for his horn.

"More ale!" he coughed. He watched Æstrid make her way toward their table. Her carriage was poised and graceful, just as it had been when Rafa and Thorgrima had attended her bath. Though her progress was impeded as everyone stopped to shower her with thanks and praise, she accepted their approval with humility. The wench was puzzling – a vindictive hellion, wrapped in a regal shell.

"What say you, Veleif?" Arnor nodded toward him. The man was so lost in his own consumption, he'd missed Veleif's display.

"I've truly never tasted anything like it before." Veleif stabbed the meat mercilessly with his knife. He glanced sideways at his men. He'd never witnessed them so silent before. They were more intent on filling their bellies than their usual talk and routine jests that accompanied their meals.

Veleif tossed a piece of meat to the dog behind him. He watched the beast bound over to the scrap, sniff, then whined and quickly retreated with its tail between his legs.

Veleif frowned as Arnor called out to Nar to bring him another plate of her noxious food. The huge Viking rewarded him with a light growl as Veleif stole the last bit of fowl from Arnor's trencher. The meat from the man's platter was pure, pleasure from heaven. It was flavored with garlic and onion and something else, all roasted to a juicy perfection. He'd never tasted anything so succulent before and his mouth watered for more.

Then the dawning came. Despite his warnings, and whatever progress he thought he'd made with the stubborn princess of Karissonholdt, she obviously hadn't ceased her chicanery. Veleif caught her eyes and held her with an icy stare.

"The lady Æstrid is a cook of unusual talents," Veleif announced to his table as his gaze wandered over her. His men nodded and grunted in agreement. He raised his horn to her in a mock salute, a sly smile played about his lips. She returned his stare coolly and gave him a brief curtsey. Æstrid's attention was quickly torn away, as Blotha of all people, came up and kissed her hand while murmuring his thanks.

Veleif snorted. If the vixen thought to best him with her deviousness, he had a thing or two to show her about who was master in this hall. Veleif pushed back his chair and hastily jumped to his feet. Both Arnor and Thorliek eyed him curiously as his voice rang out over the murmuring din of the meal.

"People of Kollsveinholdt! A toast! Hail to the lady Æstrid!" Veleif shouted and raised his horn high. The hall broke out in echoing cheers and fists pounded in approval on the tables.

Æstrid stood immobile amid the outburst. Her eyes narrowed briefly, then went wide as moons as Veleif leapt up on the table, his arms spread wide. If he hadn't had everyone's attention before, he certainly had it now. Jumping off the other side with a lithe grace that belied a man of his size, Veleif landed with a blazing smile.

Taking up his trencher, he sidled toward her in the center of the hall. She managed to keep a smile plastered on her face as all eyes were upon them. His blue eyes glittered like ice, as he held up a piece of fish between his fingers. Turning slowly, the clamor of voices began to hush as everyone in the hall strained to see what he held, and Veleif began his dramatic oration.

"My lady stirs and cooks and toils," he announced loudly, then lifted the piece to her lips. His eyes narrowed at her and he continued. "And for all her well-laid plans, let my lady share the spoils."

The hall erupted into another round of hearty whoops and shouts at Veleif's toast. Æstrid clenched her fingers into fists at her side. She knew to refuse his gesture outright in front of this audience, could carry repercussions even the prince himself may not be able to curtail.

"Such pretty poetry, Kollsvein," Æstrid gritted. Her eyes snapped sparks behind her smile.

"Inspired by the care you took to prepare this for me," Veleif whispered harshly with his grin plastered on his face.

To everyone watching the pair, it appeared a tender act. Only Veleif and Æstrid were aware how he had to force the odious morsel between her lips. The crowd resumed another hearty cheer as Veleif fed her, his smile unwavered. Veleif chuckled softly as he watched one eye half-close and her body attempt to stifle a cringe against the assault of the bitter meat.

As Æstrid was rendered silent, Veleif pressed his full advantage. She could neither spit nor choke down the sour fare in the midst of the audience. He gripped her elbow in an iron hold and prodded her forward.

"Come. We dine together on this fine fare. As you've *honored* me my lady, it is only fitting I return the favor."

Another chair was quickly squeezed between Arnor's and his own. He half-tossed the trencher onto the table where it landed with a bang and pulled her roughly down into the seat beside him. Æstrid quickly gulped ale from his own horn, not waiting for her own.

"I fear we'll exhaust the winter stores in half the time, if you continue to serve us food like this." Arnor smiled at her. Æstrid blushed at his compliment. She sat ramrod straight as Veleif poised a piece of meat before her lips with the tip of his knife. She turned toward him, pushing his arm away with her hand.

"My lord, I – I fear I'm stuffed so full I could not eat another bite." Æstrid smiled sweetly for the benefit of the table.

"Nonsense, Æstrid," Veleif encouraged and stamped her foot beneath his boot. When her mouth opened in a gasp of pain, he stuffed the meat into her mouth. She stiffened in shock and Veleif leaned in, his breath fanned her cheek.

"Do you concede my lady?" he whispered, gravelly, his voice so low only she could hear. "Or shall I feed you 'til naught remains on this wretched platter?"

The tone of his threat was hardly veiled. Æstrid discreetly spit the meat into her hand then met his challenging gaze. Veleif waited. His broad shoulders penned her to the chair. He appeared as immovable as a wall of blackened stone. Her eyes refused to cower and Veleif felt himself grow as hard as iron. The woman was maddening, fearless, and breathtakingly beautiful.

The storm outside may have begun to wane, but the tempest between them crackled with impending thunder. Veleif, demanding she yield, Æstrid, refusing to acknowledge her defeat. It was all he could do to keep from crushing her in his arms and sear her lips in another soul-stealing kiss.

"I'm not afraid of you, Kollsvein," Æstrid blinked at him stubbornly. Veleif chafed inwardly at her form of address.

"Nor am I afraid of you," he growled low as his boot pressed down in warning. Veleif stabbed another piece of meat and brought it close to her face.

"Do you yield?" His question was tight with restraint. Veleif's free hand tightened over hers, pinning it to her thigh. Æstrid tried to pull away, but was rewarded with a squeeze that didn't falter. His gaze was arctic, yet the press of his fingers were as hot as a forge, searing her skin and burning through the thick fabric of her dress. The masculine scent of him swirled around her, ratcheting her heart to a quickening pace. His nearness was unwanted, obstinate, and helplessly intoxicating.

"You test your boundaries, Kollsvein," Æstrid sneered nervously as her eyes flickered downward to his hand covering hers.

"Ah! You dare accuse me of such?" Veleif questioned with a dangerous chuckle. "You, my lady, could give lessons in peripheries." His eyes darkened from ice to indigo as he licked his bottom lip.

"Better periphery than perfidy," Æstrid snapped back. Veleif's hand tightened down on hers. He admired the clever twist of speech, but couldn't ignore the sting of her accusation. The stubborn wench simply refused to release her claim. He crowded in closer to her ear, his lips a hair's brush away from the nape of her neck.

"Your wit is as sharp as your tongue, Æstrid. Perhaps we should test whose tongue is sharper?" Veleif noted the tiny shiver ripple across her shoulders as he laid the knife on the table. His freed hand covered her other arm. He fixed his stare on her parted lips and cocked a brow before his voice dropped to a husky promise.

"In my chamber perhaps?" Veleif grinned as he heard the soft intake of her breath.

"You're a barbarian, Kollsvein!" Æstrid sputtered. "If you think... argh!" A startled cry interrupted her protests. Quicker than a flash of lightning, Veleif ripped her from her seat and half-dragged, half-carried her to the sheltered alcove of the staircase.

Arnor and Thorliek turned startled heads, following the wake of their furious prince and the billowing skirts of his aggravation. With brows raised, both men traded slack-jawed stares with one another.

"Not exactly gentle wooing," Thorliek finally mused.

"Considering that maid's vexing temper, I'm surprised he hasn't broken before now," Arnor shrugged and turned his attention back to his meal.

Veleif shoved her roughly against the wall, his fingers circled her wrists in an iron grip and pinned them flat against the stone.

"Veleif! You will call me, *Veleif!*" he snarled, as he pushed her wrists stressing his name.

"Because you wish it?" Æstrid's question was laced with sarcasm. Her face flushed hot, from both indignation and embarrassment.

"Because I demand it!" Veleif roared, "You will cease your barbs, your tricks and anything else you're planning. And when you speak to me, you will use my name. Now say it!"

Glaring down at her, the shadows and light cast from the flickering torchlight played wickedly on the swells of her breasts, doing strange things to his mind. Without thinking he leaned in and pressed along the full length of her. His body turned heavy and hard.

Veleif struggled to right his thoughts; a near impossibility as his leg wedged between her parted thighs. The memory of her body lying beneath his still burned, and the urge to sweep her upstairs overrode his waning control. He was rapidly sailing far beyond the horizon of constraint, not even the defiant expression on her face could subdue the rising swells of his desire.

*Curse* this vixen!

Thorliek's council had been ill advised. Veleif was no gentle bard, to coerce a maid to his bed with tender speeches. He was a warrior, fierce, and proud; facing an opponent of equal and furious determination. One didn't emerge victorious battling across tempestuous seas by placing a gentle hand upon the helm.

*Woo this hellion?*

He almost laughed aloud realizing the absurdity of such a strategy.

Æstrid scowled back at him with a look that was anything but yielding. Veleif felt the heat of their impasse surge.

Two opponents, twin adversaries, nose to nose. Both demanding terms, and neither willing to surrender.

Veleif's nostrils flared, his body tensed for combat. One more outburst, one more slight from her lips contrary to his demands, and he'd pillage her so thoroughly, they'd both burn from the ferocity of the attack.

"Tread upon my patience further, Æstrid Karisson and you will find this is no longer a one-sided war. Say. My. Name." Veleif ordered in a voice he usually reserved for enemies.

Despite the powerfully built and *enraged* Veleif who blotted out the world with his dark presence, Æstrid refused to capitulate. She'd pushed him over the precious cliff of his restraint when he'd dragged her from the hall. If he thought to intimidate her with blustering displays of male dominance, he obviously hadn't grown up with Gunnalf Karisson.

"Say it!" Veleif demanded, giving her a little shake. Æstrid speared him with a contemptuous smirk.

"The battle for this *war,* was drawn by you, *Kollsve-!*" Æstrid's insult was cut abruptly, as Veleif covered her mouth with his. His assault was so cruel and reckless, it couldn't be deemed anything close to a kiss. Swallowing her futile cries, Veleif parried her resistance, forcing her lips to open for him. Every grain of anger, every shard of lust, fused together and exploded in a stormy rush of invasion.

Æstrid fought and struggled with renewed vigor, but the battle-hardened warrior pressed his attack, determined to prevail until every shred of her defense was obliterated to a wasteland. His tongue warred with hers, dark, deeper, demanding. He overpowered her mutinous will until the bloodlust descended upon him. He swore he could hear the distant drumbeats of victory pound in his ears, and an almost profound sense of destiny swept through him.

Veleif felt her weaken, yet offered no quarter. Pulling back just long enough to suckle and nip the edges of her lips, he took her mouth again, exploring the honeyed silk of her. The contours of her body surrendered beneath his rigid frame. Her cries of objection turned to soft songs of pleasure.

Veleif guided her hands to his shoulders, and released his hold on her wrists. Mercifully, her hands stayed and a surge of triumph rippled through him as Æstrid's fingers wound and tangled into the sleek length of his hair.

Threading his fingers up the nape of her neck, his other hand settled firmly on the curve of her hip. Angling deeper into her with unrestrained passion, Veleif's intention of subjugation transformed. He was no longer facing her as the Prince of Kollsveinholdt, her father's enemy, or the leader of his people – he was simply Veleif, the man.

Æstrid couldn't pinpoint the moment her defenses collapsed. Veleif shattered through every carefully architected barrier. She was dreaming and drowning at the same time yet could no longer deny the tempting urgency of his kiss. Somehow, her hands found his shoulders, her fingers wound through the dark silk of his hair, pulling him tighter as he swallowed the soft sighs that bloomed in her throat.

The mercurial prince inspired muddled and conflicting instincts, yet his fervidness crushed her contradictory sentiments. She sensed the shift in him as well as herself. Their anger floated away and he was kissing her with a treasured tenderness, lulled on gentle waves of promise and desire.

The world about them fell away as she answered the call across the urgent seas of bliss, soaring up to meet him at the apex of surrender. Veleif, the male, awakened every fiber in her that was thoroughly female. Kissing her as if she was the only woman in the world, desired, protected, and adored.

Veleif moved from her mouth, with low male groans that made her heart flutter and skip in her breast. Guiding her head back, he pressed soft kisses along the exposed column of her neck and her jaw before he returned and rested his forehead to hers. They both rasped for breath, their eyes locked for an extended space of time.

Veleif drifted in her passion-glazed eyes and the curve of her lips, now deep and swollen from his kisses. Æstrid floated, directionless in the depths of his eyes, now sparkling at her, filled with inexplicable emotion.

"Veleif," Æstrid murmured tenderly. The warmth of his gaze flared behind a subtle lift of the corners of his mouth. Æstrid's fingertips stole upward, reveling against the smooth gloss of his beard.

"Veleif," she repeated, in a breathy voice that was both dreamy and reverent. In slow, suspended degrees, Æstrid watched his dusky lashes drift downward. Rivulets of flames sparked across her body as he drew nearer still, then fanned to all-out wildfire as he kissed her again; softly at first, then deeply, imprinting her with his very soul.

Veleif's hand glided up the curve of her waist, then higher still, rounding the feel of her breast against his palm. Æstrid moaned lightly and arched into his hand. He pressed his rigid member against her thigh, drawing out another sigh and answering with one of his own.

They were so lost in the intimate exchange, neither noticed the diminutive presence staring up at them. After what seemed like several minutes, Veleif felt a tug at his sleeve, growing more urgent by the second. Somewhere in the distance, a voice registered in his brain, snapping him from the reverie of the feel of her plaint curves.

Veleif turned and blinked, clearing the fog from his mind as Nar glanced between them with innocent curiosity. Æstrid gasped aloud and hid her face to the side in awkwardness.

"Does this mean you're married now?" Nar chirped hopefully.

Veleif chuckled at both the child's timing and his inquiry. He stole a look at Æstrid who reddened deeply at Nar's question. He gently grasped her chin and turned it toward him, favoring her with another warm gaze.

"Patience, Nar," he smiled confidently. He finally released her from within the circle of his embrace and took half a step back. Æstrid cleared her throat and tried to steady her shaking hands by smoothing the front of her skirt. She stared back at him, as if his words had yet to reach her. Æstrid grasped the boy's hand, then bent her head to his.

"Come with me, Nar. Let's fetch Veleif another platter. I fear his has gone cold."

Æstrid gave him a shy glance over her shoulder as she led Nar away toward the kitchen. Veleif crossed his arms and heaved a sigh of release. He had assuredly won this battle, and he had no doubt he would win this war. But a flicker of uncertainty furrowed his brow as he stroked his beard in contemplation.

Would he be able to obtain what he wanted most of all?

Her heart.

# Chapter Thirteen

The damage of the blizzard slowed the progress of shipbuilding and had taken a toll on some of the outermost houses at Kollsveinholdt. While the men enmeshed themselves making repairs in the bitter cold; Æstrid immersed herself in collecting the fragments of emotion Veleif had scattered in the aftermath of their own tempest.

*It was only a kiss,* her mind protested stubbornly. *Actually it was several kisses,* her heart chided, bringing a blush to her cheeks. The man was skilled, so accomplished in fact, he had planted the seeds of desire within her. It was lust, simply lust, she reasoned, and cursed her inexperience.

But Æstrid couldn't settle the nagging doubt that plagued her, certain something more had passed between them. For the first time, he had appeared raw and genuine, as if she could see into the depths of his soul. *Had that been part of his game?* Æstrid cautioned herself and cursed Veleif's temptation.

*He was used to getting his way,* she reminded herself. He was toying with her to distract her from her resolve. But he was also kind and quick to put the needs of others before his own... and what had he meant when he'd answered Nar with "patience?" And why, could she not stop thinking about him? Why did her heart skitter nervously whenever his name was mentioned or he was nearby?

But why, in Odin's name, had he not spoken to her in the past few days? Other than exchanging the barest civilities over supper, where Veleif would inquire to her health, or compliment the food, they were silent in each other's company. She'd find herself foolishly stumbling for words at his polite inquiries.

Æstrid couldn't sort the answers to the untold questions racing through her mind. It was best to avoid him, as he appeared to be doing with her. Besides, there were plenty of activities to keep her mind from the inscrutable prince of Kollsveinholdt.

With the storm's abatement, and the kitchen functioning efficiently, Æstrid sought relief from her thoughts by wandering the stone cottages of the village. She learned there were five mothers, all expecting babies within another month or two.

Grateful for a new distraction, Æstrid found the women woefully unprepared by her standards. Kollsveinholdt certainly didn't lack for amenities, and Veleif wasn't stingy with his people by any means, so Æstrid threw herself headlong into this new diversion.

She spent her evenings ensconced in her chamber with Rafa and Thorgrima, fashioning stacks of tiny gowns of soft linen and finely woven woolen blankets for the newborns. The women were cheery company and had nothing else to occupy their evenings. It appeared as if Veleif hadn't requested either of them to accompany him in his chamber and if Raga or Thorgrima missed his attention, neither woman spoke of it aloud.

Æstrid sought out Taar, the tanner, and requested pelts of his softest furs, to be cut and used for wraps and lining for the newborn's cribs. When she finished describing her requirements to the Viking's bewildered gaze, the thought dawned on her – cribs. Æstrid hadn't seen one crib in any of the homes she visited.

Securing Taar's promise the furs would be ready by the week's end, Æstrid left his cottage and gritted her teeth against the cold. She lifted the hood in place and pulled her fur cloak tighter against the wind. The garment was a rich gift, unlike anything she'd ever seen. It had appeared in her chamber not two days before. When she questioned Rafa on the appearance of the white fox pelts, beautifully fashioned into the cloak; the woman simply met her with a shrug of her shoulders.

Æstrid trudged across the yard toward the great open canopy where she spotted the now familiar faces of Irik and Oresti and at least a dozen others. They spent their days hewing thick trees into firewood, as well as planks and boards to be taken to the caves beneath Kollsveinholdt's keep.

"Oresti," Æstrid called out. The burly Viking turned to her with a smile and a wave of greeting. The tangy scents of fresh cut wood and honest sweat teased her nose in the crisp breeze as she neared. Boards were loaded onto a contraption that was nothing like Æstrid had ever seen. It was ingenious really. Ropes and pulleys lowered the heavy loads over the cliff's side onto the beaches below, where they were taken to be formed into Kollsveinholdt's great longboats.

"Careful," Oresti's hand grasped her elbow as Æstrid picked her way through the bark and scraps of wood. Æstrid smiled up into his merry face and stopped her hand mid-air to keep from brushing the shavings that dotted his long, thick beard.

"Hardly a fit place for you, my lady Æstrid. What brings you into this chill?" Oresti smiled and bowed his head as he brushed clinging flakes from his tunic.

"I'm in need of some cribs to be built, Oresti. Can you assist me?" Æstrid smiled sweetly and laid her hand on his arm.

"Cribs?" Oresti frowned quizzically.

"Small beds, for the babies who will be arriving soon." Æstrid motioned with her hands.

"I know what cribs are, my lady," Oresti laughed. His ruddy cheeks deepened a shade and his dark eyes sparkled with humor. "But we just cut the wood here. Anything that needs to be fashioned would take place in the caves below Kollsveinholdt."

"Oh," Æstrid sighed with disappointment and glanced over to the path leading down the cliff. "And who there would oversee such a task, Oresti?" Æstrid asked, though as soon as the question left her lips, she dreaded the answer. He patted her arm and leaned in conspiratorially.

"Take your request to my lord Veleif," he said reassuringly and gave her a broad grin. "The man wouldn't deny you anything, I think."

Æstrid cocked a single brow at him as her lips pressed into a thin line. "What of Arnor? Could he help me?"

"Perhaps," Oresti shrugged, "there is only one way to know. Come. I'll escort you there."

"No need," Æstrid waved him off and raised her chin. "I have no issue facing Veleif."

"Not for your sake, my lady, but for his. Your skill with the axe is well known," Oresti boomed with laughter.

Æstrid couldn't help but smile at his jest as she made her way toward the path leading to the caves below. Every icy step steeled her determination, even though the yeast cakes and honey she had for breakfast flipped in her stomach.

Veleif would listen to reason, after all, this was for the benefit of his people. But when had anything between them ever been sensible? Perhaps the best negotiation would be with Arnor, not Veleif.

Æstrid was astounded when she stepped into the cave at the base of the cliffs. The opening was just wider than the breadth of a ship and twice as high, but it was deceptively small to what lay beyond the entrance. The rock angled slightly to the left and provided shelter from the piercing winds and frigid waves of the sea. But once inside, the sheer size of the cave made her breath hitch in her throat.

The entrance gave way to a mammoth cavern stretching up and up and up until it disappeared into blackness. The depth of the cave tunneled deep and dark into the mountain and Æstrid shuddered, suddenly feeling smaller than she ever had in her life. Moving along the rock face, Æstrid carefully avoided the small tide of lapping waves and stepped up onto the wide bridges made of timbers.

Venturing deeper inside, the rich aromas and echoing sounds of shipbuilding greeted her. Cauldrons of hot pitch and raw, cut wood, mixed with the tangy salts of the seawater and damp stone. Everywhere she looked men were bent in their labors, busy amidst the hum of wood cut and smoothed, and the grunts of hammers upon planks. Large stone circles banked the fires and scraps of wood and bark were gathered by a few of the younger boys who constantly fed them into the blazing flames. The fires not only provided light, but also a surprising amount of warmth.

Sitting proudly in the center of the bustling men, was the largest skeleton of a ship Æstrid had ever seen. The ribs of the beast were carefully poised on rough timbers and the hull was half-covered with long planks. Æstrid's mouth gaped open and the hood of her cloak fell back as she followed the line of the bow upward. If three men Arnor's size stood on each other's shoulders, they still wouldn't be able to reach the top of the long warship.

She scanned the faces of the men and exchanged a quick nod of greeting. The air was warmer in the bowels of the cave, and Æstrid unfastened her cloak and carefully laid it over her arm.

Veleif was nowhere to be found, but Æstrid spotted Arnor. The great Viking wore nothing but trousers. His broad back gleamed with sweat as he pulled and strained a long plank of wood, forming it to the side of the hull. She waited in silence, not wanting to disturb his grunting efforts, as two other men fastened the plank in place before Arnor could safely move away.

Æstrid shivered, thinking of the bruises or broken ribs Arnor would have suffered had he not been able to hold the board. With an air of triumph, he lifted a skin of ale to his lips and tossed back a long pull. He paused with his head back and his eyes lit when he saw her. Æstrid smiled with an incline of her head and Arnor broke into a wide grin.

"My lady, it is a surprise to find you here, but a welcome interruption nonetheless," he shouted, then chuckled jovially and wiped the sweat from his forehead. Æstrid wondered why he seemed to speak the greeting up over his shoulder. Arnor stepped forward and taking her hand in his giant palm, he lifted it to his lips and grazed a respectful kiss on her knuckles.

Æstrid tilted her head back to meet his twinkling eyes. Other than her father, he was the biggest man she'd ever seen. But unlike her father, Arnor was infinitely kinder. Though she'd seen him practice fiercely with axes and swords, Æstrid had no doubts the great giant could defeat any enemy with his warrior's skills. Her nose wrinkled slightly at the pungent smells of wood and ocean and male sweat that clung to him.

"I did not come to disturb your work, Arnor. I hoped to plead with you a favor." Her smile widened and she laid a hand on his massive bicep. A hearty laugh echoed from a distance above them.

Æstrid looked up and saw Veleif perched on top of the bones of the hull. His tunic was loose and a wide ribbon of sweat darkened the front. His feet swung nonchalantly, giving him a carefree air. His long hair was tied back from his face and seeing his mischievous expression, Æstrid's smile quickly faded.

"Your conquest must be great, Arnor, to spur this lady to plead *your* favors," he grinned down at them.

"The only plea you'll hear from me, Veleif, is none but innocence." Arnor's laughter rumbled as he raised his hands in mock protest.

Æstrid sighed. Her eyes narrowed as Veleif moved seamlessly to his feet. Balancing on one foot on the precarious beam, his grin widened as he winked at her knavishly. Æstrid's mouth dropped open as he did the unthinkable. Veleif extended his arms out to his sides and Æstrid screamed as he took a bold leap in the air. Her hand flew to her mouth as he landed with bent knees, then straightened gracefully on his feet in front of them. A scandalous grin completed his performance.

"I'm touched with your concern, Æstrid." Veleif put his hands on his hips gave her a deep, mocking bow. A dispassionate week had passed with barely any words between them and now he chose to mock her. *Did this man's taunting never cease?*

"What favor may I grant the princess of Karissonholdt? You've already taken over my kitchens, perhaps you'd like to take over the building of my ships as well?" Veleif swept his hand dramatically behind him. His eyes danced with humor as his gaze swept her from head to toe. He paused briefly at the cloak draped on her arm, and Æstrid thought she caught a flicker of pride cross his face.

Æstrid stiffened, wishing the arrogant brute had snapped his leg when he'd jumped from the hull. Stifling a scathing reply, she thought the better of it and smiled softly up at him. Perhaps gentling her approach would work? It certainly seemed to with Arnor.

"My lord, Veleif," she stressed his name gently, like a caress, "I seek no favors for myself, but for others." Veleif looked at her suspiciously. He was more confused by her tone than by her words, though he did enjoy the way she spoke his name.

"For who?" he asked warily.

"For Asa, Gudney, Berra, Ingulfrid and Skur, my lord. It seems they are ill prepared for the births of their babes and I would like you to see it otherwise."

Arnor shuddered with loud groans. "We're fighting men. I'm afraid we know little of childbirth. Nor do we want to learn." He trembled again and hefted the skin to his mouth. Æstrid was startled by his response; that a man of Arnor's size could be... squeamish at the thought of childbirth. She continued with a melodious laugh.

"I'm not asking for help with *that*, Arnor." She turned to Veleif. "I simply wanted to know how we might have some cribs built, and how long they would take. I... er... you will need five of them, to be exact."

"Cribs?" Veleif frowned at her.

"Yes, small beds to place beside their mother's. Where the babe can sleep and be tended easily," Æstrid pointed out, struggling to keep her irritation at bay.

"I know what cribs are, Æstrid. Why can't they sleep with their mothers?" Veleif asked roughly.

"A crib is far easier for the mother and the babe, Veleif. I would ask you make a simple box about this long and this wide." She pantomimed with her hands. "The sides must be tall, so when the babe begins to crawl, he will not fall out, like he could from a bed."

Veleif thoughtfully stroked his lower lip with his thumb as he regarded her. Putting Kollsveinholdt to right since the storm subsided had given him the excuse to stay away from her. He worked to sheer exhaustion from dawn to dusk and still hadn't successfully curbed the raging desire coursing through him. The scent of her skin when she sat beside him at supper, the mix of lavender and woman... twisted him in knots.

Since their last encounter, Veleif barely trusted himself to speak with her, so as not to provoke the urge to whisk her to his bed and prove himself the barbarian she had often accused him of being. It was regretful enough the scheme to marry her, and the very least he could do was not ravage her before she was his wife in truth.

He felt a burning ache spread through his loins as he watched the fire's glow play off the sheen of her hair and the curve of her neck. Her face was even more beautiful when she spoke in gentle tones. He relished how easily his name tumbled from her lips. The soft, pillowy lips that swelled beneath his, and how they had darkened, as if she'd been eating sweet berries when he kissed her passionately...

"What say you, my lord?" Æstrid asked touchily, snapping him from his musings.

"You want me to suspend the progress of my ships to construct... cribs?" His arms crossed his chest as if finding her request ridiculous. Veleif's eyes sparkled with a teasing light, and his gaze rested on her breasts overlong before he found her eyes again.

"What favor would you offer in return, my lady?" Veleif cocked an arrogant brow at her. Arnor practically spewed ale from his mouth as Æstrid gasped in outrage.

"Favor? Why none, my lord. They are *your* people. I would think aiding in their comfort should be favor enough," Æstrid snapped indignantly. When he simply stared at her and caught his lower lip in his teeth, she let loose a huff of exasperation.

"*Well?*" Æstrid blurted out impatiently.

"I will give the matter some thought, Æstrid." Veleif answered evasively.

"Some thought?" she echoed hotly, her voice rising. "Pray the matter does not *strain* you, Veleif. I've heard it is what happens when a muscle is little used." Æstrid turned and stalked away from them as Arnor roared in laughter.

*Curse the man!* To think she had spared any thoughts these past days *and nights* on his intolerable hide. Could anyone be more self-serving, arrogant, or positively unpredictable than Veleif Kollsvein? With an exaggerated sweep of the cloak around her shoulders, Æstrid clutched it firmly and made her way out of the cave without a backward glance.

# Chapter Fourteen

The weather warmed enough to snow, blanketing the village in thick drifts. Outcrops of rocks and walls lay hidden under bumpy white mounds. The trees in the distant forests were lacy, crystalline blossoms bursting from their darkened trunks. Though the violent winds had abated, Æstrid could not bring herself to venture outside the protective walls of Kollsveinholdt.

She was seated before the crackling hearth in her chamber with Asa and Berra. She'd piled furs beneath their feet as the women both settled comfortably in their chairs, easing the strain of their rounded bellies. All three women were bent in sewing more garments for the impending newborns and chatted happily, laughing over potential names for their babes.

Her thoughts drifted to Veleif, Arnor and a dozen others. Despite the ice-cold blasts of weather, the men remained occupied in their labors, and weren't deterred by the bouts of wet snow and sleet. Æstrid smiled to herself, thinking how baffled they'd first been when she'd stopped them and passed out heated potatoes. When she explained they could place them inside their tunics to keep their hands warm, Veleif thanked her graciously and kissed her cheek.

Æstrid stifled a giggle in her musings, remembering how Arnor had sought her out later in the day. He was especially pleased with her thoughtfulness and told her the roasted potatoes made a wonderful snack. When Æstrid had asked if they warmed his hands sufficiently, he only peered at her with a puzzled frown.

"How is it Veleif has no wife?" Æstrid asked the women innocently. Asa and Berra halted their sewing and exchanged worried glances. Æstrid frowned lightly at their silence, wondering what gave them pause. "What is amiss? I just find it…strange is all." Æstrid wondered aloud with a shrug.

"He did have a wife, Æstrid," Berra confessed in a hushed whisper.

Æstrid shot forward in her chair, the news struck her like a thunderbolt. *Veleif had a wife?* Asa glanced worriedly to the portal to Veleif's room and nodded her head in affirmation. Æstrid grew anxious at their odd behavior. Even in the short time she'd known them, she'd never seen the pair so guarded.

"Oh now you must tell me!" Æstrid's eyes sparkled with curiosity.

"It is an ill-fated thing to speak of, Berra," Asa warned.

"Veleif's wife, Tofa, was murdered two years past," Berra whispered.

"Murdered?" Æstrid's hand flew to her throat. Her mind raced quickly. While she'd seen Veleif rage in tempers, she didn't think he was a man who could murder his wife.

"Tofa was six months gone with child. It was spring and she wandered far along the beach," Asa remembered softly.

"She was with my eldest son Ingor, he had only passed eight winters..." Berra's voice trailed off and her eyes shone with tears. Æstrid placed a comforting hand on her knee.

"A band of Picts stumbled upon them. How they came to be this close to Kollsveinholdt is still unknown. We'd never seen Pict on our shores before, and none since," Asa told her.

Æstrid shuddered. The vivid memory of Leidolf's murder made her own eyes sting with tears. Berra absently rubbed her swollen belly as she continued the story.

"My lord, Veleif, he... he was the first to find them. It is said our prince went into a berserker's rage. Only Arnor could accompany him as Veleif hunted the Picts down. From what little Arnor recanted, there were hardly pieces left of the Picts big enough for the crows to eat, except for one man. Veleif left him alive and sent him in a boat, back to his own shores. Veleif... well Veleif will not speak of it."

Æstrid's heart clenched for them. She knew firsthand the grief and sorrow, seeing someone you loved murdered before your eyes. She squeezed Berra's knee and the woman laid a hand over hers. She wiped her eyes and smiled hopefully at Æstrid.

"But I know I carry a new son. When he is born I will name him Ingor, and he will carry on as my first Ingor did."

Æstrid slid to the floor and placed her head on the woman's knee. Berra stroked her hair soothingly and spoke to her in low tones.

"Ease your fears, my lady. Even now Veleif works to build even bigger ships. This year he'll sail to their cursed island and wreak more vengeance. I think, perhaps, that may help to soothe his hurt."

Æstrid could not speak but sat back on her heels and looked up at both their faces. All three women startled when Veleif threw open the door after barely a knock. Æstrid's heart leapt to her throat. *Had he heard them?* He paused, surprised to find her occupied with the women and cleared his throat with a nod to Berra and Asa.

"My lord, Veleif?" Æstrid prodded, deliberately. This was the first time she had seen him in the past few days, and he had certainly never bothered to come to her chamber before.

"A word, Æstrid," he said gruffly and jerked his head toward his room. Despite what she had just heard about the loss of his wife, it was a bitter excuse for out-and-out rudeness. Æstrid stood fully upright and stubbornly crossed her arms in front of her.

"I don't recall giving you leave to enter my chamber at your will, my lord. But since you're here, you may speak," she sniffed imperiously.

Berra and Asa gasped and Veleif's brow winged up at her audacity. He should have known better! Just when he thought her demeanor overcome, the harridan returned with a vengeance. And to think he was going to ease his conscience tonight and confess the details of his scheme to wed her.

"Your *chamber*, happens to belong to *me*, and I'll enter it anytime it damned well pleases me to do so," Veleif ground out. In two strides he crossed the room and glared down at her. "Come, I want to speak with you," he commanded.

"No need, Æstrid. We were just leaving." Asa and Berra quickly gathered up their sewing and toddled to their feet. Berra blushed and shot Æstrid a sympathetic glance. The women quickly bustled from the room, leaving the pair almost nose to nose, glaring at each other. Æstrid's eyes flashed deep blue, like violets behind her sooty lashes as she frowned at him.

Veleif scrubbed his palm over his beard. What was it about this wench that flared his temper? He couldn't stop his biting tongue or his brutish behavior. Despite his plans and secrets, Veleif wondered if Æstrid would ever come to see he wasn't entirely the savage she believed him to be. So far, he was failing miserably. This contentious female intrigued him with her intellect, and at the same time provoked his pride and his manhood.

"Well speak! Your temper has ensured the privacy you wished." She waved an impatient hand at him. She watched his brows knit together in a brief frown and then his expression softened. Veleif blew out a loud exhale and held up one hand. Damn her for affecting him like this.

"Peace, Æstrid. I didn't come here to fight with you. Do you find this chamber satisfactory?" he began distractedly. Her eyes went wide at his question then narrowed suspiciously. Veleif hadn't burst in to inquire if she liked her room. His eyes followed her as she crossed to stand behind the chair Berra had vacated.

"It is more than satisfactory, Veleif. When I first saw it, I couldn't help but wonder if you treated all your captives to such luxury," she laughed nervously. "But that is not what you came to ask me."

"You're no captive, Æstrid, and you haven't been for some time now." He leveled her with a look so penetrating, Æstrid caught her breath. His words both warmed and disturbed her, and Æstrid crossed her arms to suppress the shiver. She hoped he didn't notice, but in the next moments was certain he did as he cleared his throat and crossed to the hearth to lay more wood on the fire.

"Pour us some wine," he instructed softly over his shoulder. He moved to the chair opposite the blazing fire and stretched his legs out in front of him. Baffled by his behavior, Æstrid studied him covertly as she filled the only cup at hand.

The light flickered across the sharp angles of his face as he stared into the flames. The man was so breathtakingly handsome, yet tonight his face was drawn and she noticed the fatigued slant of his shoulders. As Æstrid quietly poured the wine, her heart tightened with a stab of compassion. She realized Veleif carried a multitude of burdens, and he carried them alone.

Æstrid crossed the room and stood so close the hem of her skirts brushed his chair. She extended the silver cup.

"Where's yours?" he asked.

"I only have one cup here. If you wait, I'll get another," she breathed.

"No need. I'm happy to share." He made no move to take it from her and gestured for her to take the first sip of the sweetened wine. She passed the cup back to him, a bit wary by his curious behavior. Æstrid poised stiffly on the edge of her chair, wishing she could be more at ease. If only Veleif wasn't so... irritating.

"Do you like the cloak?" he asked, finally breaking the silence.

"That was from you?" Her eyes went wide.

"I cannot imagine who else you thought might bestow such a gift?" Veleif chafed behind his cup. A shadow of disappointment crossed his face.

"It, just, I... we... we don't really talk, my lord. I don't even think we like each other," Æstrid confided.

"I've never known a woman to speak to me with such abandonment." Veleif threw his head back and chuckled.

"Perhaps more should," she chided.

"No, it is plain you do not care for me overmuch, Æstrid. But then, there are times you make me think otherwise..." his voice trailed off. He held the cup out to her with a roguish grin and Æstrid snatched it from him a little too hastily. He turned slightly in his chair to give her his full attention.

Æstrid's eyes met his over the rim of the cup. He was intentionally baiting her and she refused to fall victim to his implications.

"For example, why do put so much effort into helping my people?"

"I'm merely doing as you suggested, Veleif, making the best use of my time while I'm here," she answered crisply and extended the goblet back to him. Both his hands closed over the cup, trapping hers within his grasp. His expression turned serious as he searched her eyes.

"Are you certain it is nothing more?" His question flowed over her like warm honey as he slowly released her hand. The warmth of his lingering caress on her bare skin sent tendrils of heat throbbing straight to her heart. Æstrid exhaled her breath in slow degrees, annoyed at how easily his mere presence conjured up erotic remembrances of their intimacy.

"No, Veleif. It is not," she replied, and watched him sip from the cup. If only he would unfurrow the perpetual frown from his brow, and if only she was the one to give him the reason to do so. The gods help her if she ever gave her heart to Veleif Kollsvein.

"Despite whatever conclusions you may have drawn, I do want you to be happy here, Æstrid," Veleif admitted, and handed the cup back to her.

He crossed his ankles and folded his massive arms behind his head, pensively gazing into the fire. Veleif's attempt at civility wasn't lost on her, and hearing the news of his wife and child, Æstrid felt a pang of guilt. She met him halfway and sought to provide some soothing words.

"I realize I've been in error, Veleif. I have been so busy focusing my attention on keeping the war between us, I never thanked you." Æstrid looked down into the goblet and felt the heat rush to her face. She could feel his eyes turn upon her but she couldn't meet his gaze.

"You saved me from certain death. I thank you for that Veleif, for saving me. And the cloak..." her voice faltered. Æstrid smiled wistfully and turned her head behind her where it lay folded neatly over a trunk. "I... I've never had one so fine before."

"Humility doesn't suit you, Æstrid. I think I almost prefer it when you're cursing me at every turn." Veleif shifted to ease the tightening strain in his loins. The sound of her dulcet tones conjured images of Æstrid moving beneath him. He could almost hear her lost in passion's throes as the firelight washed her creamy skin. He wanted to see her eyes languid as he kissed her until she begged him to stop. He could imagine those lips right now, how they would taste softened with this honey wine...

He took back the cup from her and tossed back the last of the wine. A light groan betrayed him as she brought the jug and refilled the cup. Her hair curled softly behind her shoulder and she was standing so close he could drink in the sweet smell of her skin.

"Was there something more you wished, Veleif?" Æstrid asked softly. He looked up at her and felt his pulse quicken and his blood turn to lead. Time between them lengthened and stretched like the shadows in the room. *By Odin's grace, yes there was more he wanted! Her! He wanted her!* Seeing her question was put in all innocence, Veleif cleared his throat and sat up straighter in the chair.

"The day we found you, Æstrid, there was another…" he began gently, "a young man by the shore of the lake. He was not a Pict, but a Norseman." Veleif paused waiting for her to speak.

Æstrid's stomach clenched and she moved to lean on the mantle. He watched a delicate hand raise to wipe her eyes and groaned inwardly. He could face anything this fierce vixen hurled his way except this one. Her tears.

"He was my brother, Leidolf," she whispered into the flames. Veleif felt the weight of her crushing grief. Cursing himself for being seven kinds of fool, he set the cup on the floor and moved swiftly to her side. Veleif enfolded her in his arms he whispered a silent prayer of thanksgiving the maid didn't protest.

Veleif wrapped her tightly to him, resting his chin lightly on the top of her head as he felt her silent sobs release against his chest. He whispered nonsensical words of comfort, lightly stroking her back until he felt her relax against him.

"Please I do not wish to speak of it," Æstrid muttered numbly, wiping her eyes discreetly. The crushing grief that threatened to undo her began to drift within his strong embrace. Never would she have imagined finding comfort within the arms of Veleif Kollsvein, or tender words of comfort flowing unbidden from his lips.

"Æstrid," Veleif's voice broke deeply with emotion unguarded and her knees threatened to turn to liquid. His hold shifted and she looked up at him. Veleif remained quiet for a long space of heartbeats. The only sounds were the crackling logs in the hearth as her senses became acutely aware of the strength pouring from him to her. His eyes gleamed in the firelight with unrestricted feeling. It was the same look he'd given her in the hall; a raw gaze of fathomless promise.

"There is no shame in grief," he said finally. Veleif smiled softly and captured the last tear from her flawless cheek with a gentle thumb. "And if you can take any comfort from my words, know this. Your brother's death was avenged."

"But his body…" Æstrid's voice cracked as her eyes welled with fresh tears.

"Shh," Veleif interrupted gently and shook his head, "your brother was laid to rest properly."

A startling truth struck her. Despite their clash of temperaments, if Veleif and his men hadn't been there, she would have met the same fate as her brother. He deserved some matter of gratitude for that act alone.

"Why are telling me this, Veleif? You could have easily let me suffer to my mind's own wanderings." Æstrid searched his face. Veleif inhaled deeply and put a step of space between them. His fingers twined with hers and he looked at their tangled digits. His confession came so low in his throat she had to strain to hear it.

"Perhaps I've come to care for you more than I would admit?"

A surge of raw longing tumbled through her body as Veleif was successfully ripping away every barrier she had constructed.

"My lord, I…" Æstrid stuttered as the rasp of his beard found her palm.

He pressed a kiss into it and held her eyes.

"It is my turn to thank you, Æstrid." Veleif slowly released her hand. It was time to lighten the mood between them before his raging desires moved past his control. "I never thought Kollsveinholdt could be better, but our food is much improved. And the babes who will arrive soon will want for nothing it seems." He smiled down at the small stack of blankets the women had left in their haste.

"Arnor, I think, will be most disheartened when you return me in the spring," Æstrid demurred as she hugged her arms to her body, hoping her quaking limbs went unnoticed. Veleif winced inwardly at her words. Telling her she would be his bride not two weeks hence would wreck her softened manner. He quickly deflected an affirmation with a question.

"It would seem, Æstrid, you and I are no longer at war?"

"Even though I have not known you overlong, Veleif, I cannot help but think you will find some way to break the peace between us," she smiled.

If the maid only knew sager words had never been spoken. Veleif laughed and sidled close. He looked down and lifted her chin beneath his finger. Æstrid held her breath as she met his eyes. The pad of his thumb reached up and brushed her lower lip. Just as she expected him to bend his head to kiss her, Veleif straightened and moved to the door. With nothing more than a brief nod of his head, he left her in stunned silence.

Æstrid lay in her bed on her side watching the fire for hours. Tumultuous feelings washed over her as she watched the coals burn, dancing from yellow and orange with the occasional fleck of blue. She couldn't shake the vision of Leidolf's face, staring blankly at the sky, no more than she could shake how her pulse beat rapidly when Veleif had merely stroked her lip. She was caught between a chasm of grief and the confusion of unknown desire, and truly, she did not know which one disturbed her more.

Flinging herself from the bed in frustration, she crossed to the hearth and added more wood until the blaze licked to a dangerous height. She drained a full goblet of wine and then another. She poured another, and then one more, until the empty goblet slipped to the floor. Æstrid silently prayed to Odin to rescue her from this tormenting perplexity.

Stumbling to the bed, she crawled beneath the furs. Æstrid stared into the fire until the flames began to swim before her. She hoped sleep or drunkenness would soon claim her. Her eyes went droopy as the shadows around the room lengthened and the fire began to swirl around her.

She drifted toward the flames as they molded and stretched. The haunting pounds of drumbeats claimed her. She saw painted faces of blue and black, writhe and dance before her, as her head tossed side to side trying to escape. Undulating swirls of skin and sweat, poised before her as flashing glimpses of a blade slashed down again and again. Æstrid cried out and struck in vain at the monstrous faces.

An ominous thud snapped her upright. Leidolf crumpled to the ground. He stood up once more and an arm raised beyond a hidden veil, crushing his head beneath the great stone axe. Her shoulders wrenched as she tried in vain to slap them away. Her screams grew louder. Her limbs thrashed and flailed as hundreds of Picts surrounded her and then descended with snarling vengeance.

"Æstrid! Æstrid!" Veleif pinned her thrashing arms in one wrist and shook her shoulders, trying to wake her from her nightmare. The furs of her bed were flung askew when he'd burst into her room hearing her screams. He quickly scanned the shadows, and seeing her alone, he realized she was still asleep.

"Æstrid wake up. You're dreaming, wake up." He shook her gently. She stilled her movements and slowly peered up at him without a measure of recognition. The dark creature listed forward, defying the tilting edges of her room. The firelight danced and swayed until the broad form of a man began to take shape. Æstrid shrieked in terror, kicking and fighting his grasp.

"Stop Æstrid! It's me, Veleif." His voice was laced with concern. Snapping out of the lingering nightmare, she froze and stared up at him like a stranger. The recognition returned in slow degrees. She was in her room, and in her bed, though the bed continued to rock and spin precariously. Æstrid tried to gather the scattered splinters of reality, then remembered the wine. She'd had cup after cup of the stuff and silently cursed. Why had she drank so much?

"Veleif?" she rasped, her voice hoarse from screaming.

"Hush, love," he soothed, as his hands slid to her shoulders. "Nothing will harm you. I'm here now." He smoothed the hair from her face as he looked down into her terrified expression. He sat down on the bed and pulled her into his embrace. She burrowed against his warmth, clinging to the steadfast anchor as the room's precarious spinning began to subside.

"There were so many of them. I tried to fight them..." her voice trailed off, muffled against his chest.

"It was only a dream, Æstrid. It's over now." He told her with a comforting laugh. She smelled strongly of the honey wine they had shared. Veleif had seen better men than he, laid waste after indulging in five or six cups of the stuff. Clearly the woman had no experience with the potency of the brew and he didn't envy her the pain she would suffer at first light.

"I think speaking of your brother and drinking too much wine is a bad combination for you," he admonished lightly.

"I no longer wish to sleep." she whimpered miserably. Veleif felt her tears against his naked chest as she unburied her head.

"Nothing can hurt you here, Æstrid, not even your dreams." He lifted her gently placed her back on the bed. His fierce warrior princess, drunken and vulnerable looked small and frightened. She trembled uncontrollably despite his reassurances and Veleif released a sigh of resignation.

He stretched out beside her and covered them both in pelts, tucking the edges securely around her shoulders. She was too intoxicated and exhausted to protest and nestled tightly against him. Somewhere in the distance Æstrid felt lips graze the top of her head, and heard hazy, lulling heartbeats drone in her ear.

Veleif stared up at the ceiling and cursed the irony.

Never, ever could he have imagined sharing Æstrid's bed for the first time would entail the maid snoring drunkenly in the crook of his arms. The gods were truly testing him when they'd placed Æstrid Karisson in his charge.

# Chapter Fifteen

Æstrid's eyes flew open and she shot up in bed with a start. Rueful of her quick movements, she choked back the bile that surged in her throat. She closed her eyes and took a deep, calming breath. Curse this pounding in her head, curse her sour stomach, and curse all wine *and* winemakers; and for good measure, curse their offspring, too.

What had happened? Wine and dreams and *Veleif?* Had Veleif been in her room? A stirring recollection of dread warred with her lingering nausea. She'd been lying in his naked arms.

Æstrid looked down and released a sigh of relief. Her clothes were still intact. Stepping gingerly from the bed, Æstrid steadied herself against the back of a chair. Every muscle and bone cried out in agony, echoing the throbbing pain in her temples. With a sigh and a groan, she squinted at the blasphemous jug and her stomach flipped at the thought. Æstrid gritted her teeth against the pain. There was only one cure, one nauseating remedy to allay this sickness. More wine.

Not bothering with the cup, Æstrid tipped back the jug and gulped down a deep, satisfying sip. Curse Kollsveinholdt's wine and her predicament, she thought darkly. It wasn't until she felt the warmth crawl along her veins and the everlasting thrumming in her head cease, did she sigh in pleasure as the nausea abated.

Vivid recollections of last evening's memories began to return. Had Veleif held her tenderly after waking from her nightmare, or was that a dream? No, she was certain he was there, but for how long? And more importantly, *why* was he there?

The answers to her questions would have to wait. Taking another fortifying sip, Æstrid vowed she'd swallow enough of this wicked brew to see her through this day and no more. Taming the snarls from her hair and plaiting it into a heavy braid, Æstrid finished with bracing cold water on her face. It was time to face the day and whatever it would bring.

Standing in the middle of the bustling kitchen, Æstrid was still at odds if Veleif's presence had been real, or was merely a part of her dream. As the day was drawing toward the evening meal, she was no closer to determining the truth when Asa repeated her question for the third time. The woman faced her with hands on hips, frowning as she waited for the answer.

"My lady, are you well?" Asa asked, eyeing her suspiciously.

"Yes why?" Æstrid said hastily and tested another roasted potato. The woman may have concern for her distracted behavior, but none would be able to find fault with her food.

"You seem very troubled today. Are you sick?" Asa frowned impatiently. Without waiting for an answer, she pressed a hand to Æstrid's forehead.

"I'm not ill, Asa," Æstrid ducked away, masking her annoyance. She couldn't unburden her thoughts to Asa without the risk of every wagging tongue would whisper their own versions that Veleif had slept in her bed.

As Æstrid waved the boys to carry out the first trenchers of the evening meal, Asa still spied her skeptically. With Berra taking the recent days to rest, Asa assumed command of the kitchen and she was no less militant in her responsibility. The woman was astute, but unfortunately, today wasn't the day Æstrid wished to be the object of her scrutiny. It had been difficult enough to steal samples of the honeyed wine to see this day through.

"I'm fine, Asa," she fibbed. "If you have any concerns, it should be for these pies. Pray we've made enough to satisfy Arnor's great appetite."

Æstrid's steps turned leaden when she reached the great hall. Her mouth felt like parchment, her muscles were screaming for rest, and she drew upon every strength to quell the nausea that threatened. Veleif's eyes twinkled mischievously when his gaze locked on her. His face split into a roguish grin.

She shot Veleif a heated glare. She'd readied her excuses to simply retire, but the unscrupulous warlord had reappeared and seemed to take great humor in her misery. Everything last night *had* been a dream. Any tenderness she had imagined from the dark prince was quickly banished to the land of myths. Veleif leaned back casually in his chair and spoke loudly to the men near his hand.

"I'm thinking tonight we hold a drinking contest. Let's see how the men of Kollsveinholdt can hold their spirits! What say you Æstrid?"

Æstrid visibly paled.

"If her skill with a horn is anything like her skill with an axe, I'll not challenge her," Irik roared. Arnor and Thorliek joined the jocularity as Veleif gave her a smug smile.

"I'll decline. Respectfully," Æstrid said, as she slipped quietly into her chair.

"The gods be praised! I'd couldn't bear the thought of having our meals suffer because Æstrid was too sick from drink," Arnor confessed. Æstrid tossed Veleif a smirk, wanting nothing more than to wipe that smug look from his face.

"My lady, I swear this is by far the finest food you've given us so far," Arnor boomed across the hall. Echoing chants of praise followed his lead. The big Viking licked his fingers appreciatively and smiled at her as he reached for another small pie of potato and onion in its flaky crust.

"I'm uncertain what pleases me more, Arnor," she laughed, "cooking the food or seeing you consume it with such delight."

"May you never tire of seeking that answer, my lady," Thorliek beamed as he plopped another of the small pies into his mouth.

"Bring the wine, Nar." Æstrid beckoned to the boy. He rushed forward, but stopped as Veleif waved the boy away. Æstrid turned to him with a frown.

"Am I to die of thirst?"

"No wine for you tonight. Milk or ale. No wine," he informed her between mouthfuls of the flaky pies. He chewed dispassionately and fixed her with an icy challenge.

Æstrid's scowl deepened. She countered his stare with one as fierce as her own.

"Milk or ale?" she parroted, incredulous. "Do you think I'm a mere babe that I would drink milk with supper? Come Nar, I'll have wine," she called out.

The boy rushed forward and Veleif halted him with his hand. He leaned back in his chair and wiped his mouth. His eyes wandered deliberately down to her waist, then travelled back up.

"No Æstrid, you are certainly no child. But. No. Wine," he said tersely.

His empathetic manner last night, whether it had been real or imagined had vanished, and the boorish mountain of stubborn masculinity had returned. The pain in her temples began to throb and Æstrid beckoned once again to Nar.

"Bring me the wine, Nar," she commanded patiently, never taking her eyes from Veleif. The boy stepped forward quickly, but halted mid-stride as Veleif glared him down.

Æstrid clenched her fist, stifling the urge to slap him.

Thorliek leaned forward and glanced between them curiously. Even Arnor paused from consuming his meal. Irik nudged his elbow and smiled. They hadn't witnessed a good argument between the pair in days, and it appeared tonight they weren't going to be disappointed. Æstrid turned and squared off to Veleif.

"Wine. Nar," she ordered stubbornly. The boy stepped forward, but bounced to a halt as Veleif growled. Confusion reigned on Nar's face, who appeared to be in the midst of a strange dance, stopping and starting at the pair's commands.

"Boy, if you serve the lady anything but milk or ale, you'll not see another winter!" Veleif threatened.

Nar blanched.

Æstrid jerked her head toward the boy and flashed him a smile of encouragement.

"He didn't mean that, Nar," she reassured.

"I damned well did!" Veleif thundered. "Ale!" He pointed a finger at Nar and half-rose from his chair. "Ale! You will bring ale!" he shouted.

Nar stumbled backward several hasty steps, then broke into a run toward the kitchen. Undeterred by his outburst, Æstrid gave him an imperious glare.

"I do not wish to drink ale," she hissed between clenched teeth. Arnor gulped from his own horn heartily, utterly amused at the pair.

"You will drink what I wish you to drink," Veleif slammed his fist on the table causing several heads to turn their way.

Chittering laughter broke out across the hall, accompanied by the tinkling sounds of hacksilver exchanging hands. Seeing Æstrid and Veleif at odds usually proved highly entertaining; and lucrative, depending on the wager.

Æstrid stood up quickly, seething from his outburst. Loud sighs of joy and sorrow, mixed with the clinking sounds of more silver changing hands.

Arnor beckoned to Nar. The boy inched forward and Arnor bent to whisper in his ear. The boy nodded eagerly and hastened from the hall.

"It seems, *Kollsvein*, you relish in breaking the peace broken between us. Irik, Arnor, Thorliek," she nodded to the men, not bothering to spare Veleif a glance.

Æstrid hurried from the hall and ran up the stairs to her chamber. Still raging with anger, she grabbed the fur cloak and folded it around her.

Nausea be damned.

All of a sudden, the massive hall of Kollsveinholdt, was not large enough to contain them both.

Æstrid stalked past the curious eyes following her departure from the hall, and closed the great doors behind her.

"So how goes your wooing, Veleif? I'm no expert, but shouldn't the lady prefer your warm company to that of a frigid night?" Arnor threw back his head and laughed.

Not even Æstrid's heavenly salmon could soften the taunts from the table. Without preamble, the fish soured to ashes in his mouth. Veleif no longer had an appetite.

"The lady is so stubborn she refuses to see past her own care." Veleif shoved the plate of salmon away.

"Perhaps you should take her to the cave?" Thorliek prodded. "That would surely soften the maid's heart." The comment earned a frown and Veleif pushed back from the table.

Nar appeared as if by magic at Veleif's side. The boy held Veleif's fur cloak and proudly presented them with a beaming smile.

"What is this?"

The big Viking met his inquiry with a casual shrug.

"I figured you'd want to give chase. I was saving you some time."

"Best hurry though," Irik laughed, "the longer she keeps company with the night air, the longer it may take to thaw her out, my friend."

Veleif skewered the table with a glower.

"Stop. Helping."

### 

Æstrid's anger melted quickly as the beauty of the night unfolded. The air was crisp and dry and the winds had abated to a gentle stir. A full moon's light shone upon the snow, leaving everything at Kollsveinholdt draped in glistening white blankets. Dark outlines of the stone houses stood just beneath the lacy, black branches, all covered with the brilliant snow, and the hum of the distant ocean murmured like an enchanted lullaby.

But it was the night sky that truly took her breath away. Brilliant vapors of riotous color danced in glowing ribbons of green and blue, and gold and purple. Æstrid stood mesmerized as her white fur cloak became awash in color. The hues stretched and swooned against the thousands of twinkling stars and Æstrid ventured slowly out beneath the wondrous canopy of light.

She stared up at the awe and majesty of the display, so much more vivid than could be seen at her home in Karissonholdt. Her arms stretched wide, as the god's night colors flowed over her, washing away every bitter ill of the day. She was instantly light and carefree, forgotten was Veleif's ire, or the constricted pain in her head. The world was perfect and beautiful. Her heart soared in joyous contentment, and without a care in the world, she twirled around in the snow and giggled as the night's magic washed over her like a healing balm.

Veleif muttered to himself as he pulled on his hand coverings with hasty jerks. Æstrid had appeared almost green and queasy when he'd first seen her this evening. Fool that he'd been, he'd sought to tease her as he would his men when they'd consumed too much drink. He should have coddled the maid. Taken her upstairs and ensured her comfort, but he'd needled her instead. Perhaps he'd been around the company of his men too long?

He flexed his fingers and paused to marvel at how the fine wool warmed quickly to his body's heat. He made a mental tally to thank Rafa for the gift, but Rafa wasn't the object of his quest right now.

Half tugging on his great fur cloak, Veleif's boots crunched down the wide steps of Kollsveinholdt. The vision above him made him stop. With his mouth agape, he absently fastened his cloak and turned in a slow, full circle, staring at the inexplicable beauty of the night sky. He'd seen these mystics before, many times; but tonight, the colors were shimmering in a glory that rivaled any he'd witnessed before.

Pinks and purple hues ascended to gold as the vapors danced and teased his senses. The crisp night air filled his lungs and cleared his head. As he stood, slowly turning beneath the majesty of the god's painted lights, Veleif smiled.

The magic of the display wasn't lost on him. His heart lifted with joy as if some enchantment had whisked away every burden he carried. The knots of lust that had tensed his muscles in painful bonds these weeks past, dissolved; and for a moment, he almost forgot what had brought him outside. He marveled at the wondrous colors with the delight of a child, but when a shooting star broke his trance, Veleif murmured a quick prayer of thanks to Odin for the sign.

It *was* Æstrid, he grinned wider. She was his sign, and given as a divine blessing no less. He'd find Æstrid and share this mystical night of dreams with her.

Veleif scanned the steps, looking for fresh prints in the moonlit snow. Spying a set accompanied by what was certain to be the sweep of her cloak, Veleif moved deeper into the village.

"Æstrid!" he called from between the shadows. Her head whipped around and she ducked between two cottages, thinking he had not seen her. "Æstrid?" he called again softly, following the hasty tracks.

She waited until the crunching sound of his footsteps grew near. Æstrid reached down and cupped a handful of fresh snow. Veleif emerged between the cottages and paused in the moonlight. With hands braced on his hips, he couldn't help but take another long glance at the marvel above.

Æstrid stifled a giggle. The fierce prince of Kollsveinholdt had just made himself an easy target.

"Æstrid?" he called out again, impatient for her reply. And reply she did.

*Slam!* The ball of snow caught Veleif full in the face. As he sputtered the wet missile from his face, he was met with the sound of tinkling, female laughter

"You wench!" he bellowed with a smile, and cocked his head to track her movements. Veleif stepped lightly in the narrow space between the stone fronts, stealthily moving forward. He rounded the corner and jumped out to grab his certain quarry, but s*lam!* another ball of snow pelted him square in the face. Veleif jumped back, stunned she had been able to tag him a second time. He brushed and spat the wet pellet from his nose and mouth.

"I warn you, wench," he growled low, certain she could hear. "This a game you will not win."

As he stooped to cup a ball between his palms, *slam!* Another ball caught him full on his backside. Damn if she didn't throw as well as any lad. He spun around and caught her shadowed silhouette flitting beyond the corner of the cottage.

Just as he drew his arm back to throw, another ball caught him square in the face. Snow soaked his beard and ran down his neck inside his tunic. With his arm still poised, *slam!* another pelted him before he could brush away the last.

Æstrid was doubled over in laughter watching his plight. She bobbed away easily, as Veleif hurled a ball at her head. Seeing her paused, Veleif grabbed another handful and rushed her. Anticipating she would duck to the right, Veleif hurled his ball left.

His aim was true and it caught her on the side of the head. Æstrid squealed and sputtered as she ran, brushing away the snow from her hair, and scrambled to form another ball.

Veleif caught her around the stomach and tackled her face down into a drift. Both of them burst into gales of laughter as her arms and legs flailed helplessly. Veleif pulled her up and turned her toward him. She was panting for breath, and her eyes sparkled with laughter in the moonlight as he trapped her squirming limbs beneath his own. With a handful of snow poised above her face, Veleif favored her with a teasing grin.

"You wouldn't," she gasped in mock outrage.

"Wouldn't I?" He arched a brow.

"You don't play fair, Veleif," she laughed breathlessly, as she pushed hard against his unmoving chest.

"And you were warned this was a game you would not win." He tossed aside the snow and slipped his hand beneath her cloak. Æstrid slapped playfully at his hand with a giggle as Veleif leaned close, his mouth hovered just above hers. "To the victor my lady, go the spoils," he whispered.

The tip of his nose was cold as it grazed her cheek, but his lips were soft and oh, so warm. Veleif's mouth moved over hers, his tongue insistent as he coaxed her open, reveling in the silken honey of her mouth.

She attempted to wrench away at first, but it was a weak, half-hearted effort. Æstrid returned his kiss with abandon, and a deep, male groan rumbled low in his chest as he slanted his head and deepened the kiss. Her moans of pleasure sang like music in his ears as Veleif felt her yield and soften. His hand coaxed her closer as he drifted lower, rounding her hip.

When Veleif finally released her lips, she stared up at him. Her lips were still dewy in the moonlight, begging to be kissed again. He edged toward her, but Æstrid heaved against him and broke their embrace.

"Have you gone mad, Veleif?" she whispered breathlessly, as she found her feet and shook the snow from her cloak.

"I'm most assuredly mad, Æstrid. Mad for the most enchanting wench I've ever battled in the snow." Veleif rolled to his back, laughing with his arms flung wide.

"I don't even like you!" Æstrid panted. She tried to stifle her own giggles seeing the mighty prince of Kollsveinholdt rolling around in the snow like a child.

"Are you certain of that, Æstrid?" He rolled to his side and propped up lazily on one elbow. His eyes gleamed with a feral light and his devilish grin made her heart skip. She turned away from him, thankful the night hid her heated face. She exhaled slowly and placed a hand to calm her pounding heart.

"The only thing I'm certain of is you should stay down there on the frozen ground. It will serve to cool your ardor," she hid her smile.

"Not even a swim in the ocean could help me right now, love. Do you know how beautiful you are in this light of the full moon?" His smile deepened and Æstrid's breath caught again.

"Then I shall return to the keep and take myself out of this moonlight," she taunted.

"Not yet, Æstrid." He rose to his feet, still chuckling and brushed the snow from his cloak and trousers. "There is something I wish to show you first."

"I have no wish to see anything else from you, Veleif. If you won't escort me back, I can find my way alone." Æstrid cocked a brow at him and sniffed.

"You're not going to be stubborn because of one kiss are you? Or are you afraid?" His eyes glittered with humor as he took her elbow.

"Should I be afraid, Veleif?" She favored him with a smug look.

"Never with me, but you should be wary," he chuckled and tossed a small bit of snow in her face. Æstrid gasped at the shock of the cold and went to hurl him backward, but Veleif danced away in laughter. She gave chase, but Veleif darted left, then right, ducking her attempts.

Veleif cut easily through the powdery drifts, laughter trailing in his wake. Æstrid laughed again as she hurled another ball of snow squarely on his back. He paused and bent over, clutching his stomach as he caught his breath. He raised a hand in protest.

"I yield, Æstrid," he snickered between breaths, "please a truce for now. I'm afraid this icy slope is not meant for such rough play."

Æstrid stepped closer to him and looked down the trail. It was bad enough to navigate in the gray light of day, the steps were downright treacherous. Their frolicking play had brought them perilously close to the edge of the cliff, but thankfully, Veleif retained enough sense to be wary.

"Surely we're not going down there? At this hour?" she objected breathlessly, stamping the snow from her boots.

"You said you weren't afraid," he parried. His finger flicked the tip of her nose in a teasing challenge.

"No, and neither am I foolish," she gestured, cautiously.

"Trust me, Æstrid." Veleif's eyes bore into hers. The sounds of the sea rose behind him and his eyes favored that raw, reserved look once more. He was pure confidence and power, and in the space of those three simple words, Æstrid would have let him lead her straight into the churning depths of the sea, and trusted him to keep her safe.

She placed her small hand in his larger one, as a shy smile crossed her lips. He clasped it tightly and smiled back at her.

"Don't worry, my precious vixen. I won't let you fall."

# Chapter Sixteen

Æstrid instantly doubted his sanity, as well as her own. More than once she thanked the gods for sureness of his feet as she slid and slipped on the ice. Veleif pulled her close and circled her waist, leading her with trustworthy steps down the icy trail. They hadn't ventured down a third of the path when Æstrid clung to him so closely in desperation, their venture slowed to almost no progress at all.

"You said you weren't frightened," Veleif pointed out, as his lips twisted in mirth.

"I'm not frightened," Æstrid denied, as her nails sunk deeper into his waist. His body was hard and warm beneath her hands. She told herself the cold was the reason she clung to him tightly, not the threat of breaking their necks on the icy path.

"Good. Then you won't mind if I do this." He placed a quick kiss on her nose, and before she could object, Veleif scooped her up easily in his arms. Æstrid bit her lower lip to keep from crying out and buried her head against his chest.

The low rumble of his laughter thrummed against her cheek, and her arms crept up around his neck. Veleif navigated the rest of the path swiftly as she studied his profile. He glanced at her once causing her pulse to sprint, but his mood was light and infectious, and beneath the magic of the drifting colors of the sky, it seemed anything and everything was possible.

She'd never regarded him this closely for this long before and realized, she was no less affected by his presence than she had been with their first encounter. He was, undoubtedly, a man without equal.

The ominous sounds of the ocean grew louder as they neared the frozen shore. Great blocks of ice cracked on the dark waves, yet Veleif's steps remained secure. And the strength with which he carried her on their perilous trek, cocooned her in a haven of protection. For the first time in her life, she felt safe.

"We'll keep your feet drier if I carry you inside the cave, Æstrid." His lips brushed her ear as he spoke. Æstrid was so overcome by the warmth of his embrace and the murmur of his words, she could only nod. Her eyes focused on the curve of his lips and her body shivered not from cold, but from the memory of the kiss he'd stolen earlier.

The faint moonlight and the fading rays of color glowed behind them when they reached the entrance of the cave. His face had all but disappeared in the blackness of the space and Veleif stared down at her wordlessly. Her brow knitted briefly as he seemed reluctant to release her.

The only sound was the recurring roar of the black void of ocean, as it churned with plates of ice. Loud rushes and gentle sways glowed as white as the whitecaps, as they tumbled and split along the shore. His silhouette poised above her and beneath her palm she could feel the steady rhythm of his heart.

"Veleif?" Æstrid whispered. "What is the great mystery you wanted to show me?"

She felt him smile in the dark as he slowly released her, sliding her body down the length of his until her feet gingerly touched the ground. One hand pulled her waist to him and the other snaked up through the coils of her hair. Oh merciful Odin, was he going to kiss her again?

His mouth descended upon hers, gently this time, as he tempted her lips to part. His hand pressed closer in her hair as he kissed her slowly, completely, leisurely. He explored her mouth until soft moans escaped her. It was a kiss of treasure, of respect. As if beyond her will, Æstrid's hands crept up inside his cloak, squeezing the granite expanse of his shoulders.

Veleif slanted his lips again, taking her mouth in languorous, velvety strokes, as his hand travelled down her back. He pulled her closer until she felt the hard length of him pressing against the softness of her belly beneath her gown. Æstrid was drowning, as sure as if she stepped into the untamed currents of the sea beyond. But this was not a frigid current that seized her, this was something warm and wild.

Lifting her beyond the ability to think or reason, she clung to him harder, unable to explain how she could react like this. With Veleif, of all men, who tormented her at every turn and made her blood boil. Veleif, who was now kissing her so thoroughly, her entire world was hurled from a chasm of confusion into a deep pool of liquid desire.

She was gasping for breath when he finally broke their kiss. Æstrid clung to his shoulders, certain if she let go, her legs would give out beneath her. He pulled her close and wrapped his arms around her tightly. His lips buried in her hair as he whispered something unintelligible. It seemed forever as he held her there, until the world stopped spinning and righted itself again. She couldn't form a single word, and was thankful it was he who broke their silence.

"I'll start a fire," he whispered softly.

She nodded dumbly, still in the aftermath of a stupor from his kiss. She stumbled a half-step as he moved away, and could only wonder at the tearing void she felt at the loss of his contact. Æstrid hugged her arms around her chest to still her shivering. She couldn't determine if it was the sudden chill, or the repercussions from being branded from that kiss. Unless she was mistaken, his message was disturbingly clear – he'd marked her as mine.

Veleif rustled about as he sought out the tinder and quickly set small kindling to flame within one of the great pits of the cave. Adding more wood, the fire quickly jumped to a blaze, and he regarded her in wary silence.

She was nervous and touched her lips absently, as she neared the welcoming light. Æstrid kept a cautious distance between them and turned to see the hull of the longship come into view behind her.

The progress was astounding, as most of the hull was covered with long boards, taking the shape of the boat. It had been little more than a skeleton when she'd seen it only a week before.

"It is an extraordinary ship, Veleif," she breathed in wonder.

"It will easily carry two score men with room to spare," he smiled proudly.

For some reason her heart sank. Voyages at sea were perilous and lengthy. When the ship was completed, undoubtedly, he'd be gone for months before he returned. Did the thought of his absence disturb her? Or was it the fact if he left without her, her own journey home would be delayed? Æstrid shook her head to chase the thoughts. Veleif mistook her light frown for curiosity.

"Is this what you wanted me to see? Your ship?" She moved toward the structure and ran her hand over the boards in admiration. His eyes followed her every movement and Æstrid blushed under his scrutiny.

"No, but you'll have to wait a moment. Stay here until I call you," he smiled mischievously.

Her heart lurched at his teasing expression. He picked up a glowing stick from the fire, and using it as a makeshift torch, hurried toward the back of the ship. Æstrid watched the small, reflective glow move along the length of the boat then disappear completely.

"Veleif! I don't wish to wait!" she called out impatiently. The shadows loomed off the cave's height above her, as Veleif lit the fire pit on the other side of the ship. He refrained from an answer and Æstrid swore she heard the tinkling sound of tiny bells, echoing in the dark recesses of the cave. What in the god's name was he keeping from her?

"Veleif, please!" Æstrid stole along the path she'd seen him take. Stepping gingerly in the faint light, she neared the hull of the ship.

"Patience, Æstrid," he called out laughing amid more jingling sounds. Just as she crept carefully, rounding the back of the hull, she cried out startled, as Veleif almost toppled into her. Two strong hands closed upon on her forearms to steady her fright.

"My lady, have you always been so willful? Or is it just with me?" He asked with a mocking frown.

"Oh no, it is not just you, Veleif. My father had much to say on the subject," she giggled.

"No doubt just before he put you across his knee," Veleif laughed and grasped her hand. Giving him a playful slap to the shoulder, Æstrid tried to peer around him, with every bit of bouncing excitement as Nar was wont to do. The curiosity was killing her.

"What are you hiding, Veleif?" Æstrid grinned.

"Not hiding, Æstrid," he said cheerfully. They rounded the back of the boat. In the light of the newly lit fire, was a wonder Æstrid could never have imagined, and a gasp of amazement escaped her as she rushed toward the marvels.

Five small ships were artfully arranged in front of the fire. Beautifully made and painted, the vessels looked exactly like the longboat behind her, but so much smaller. The fronts and backs curved upward to points decorated with dragon's heads, and the miniature ships stood on wooden legs, with carved bows beneath.

Æstrid stretched out her hand in wonder, as a look of astonishment crossed her face. The miniature ships were painted brightly in blue and red. Tiny rows of silver bells encircled the necks, attesting to the musical sounds she'd thought she'd heard.

Veleif watched her closely as she ran a tentative finger along the carved edges. She walked between them, and around them, as her face alternated between admiration and curiosity. He crossed his arms in front of him and beamed with pride.

"By the gods, what on earth? I've never seen anything like this. What are they?" she breathed.

"Your cribs, Æstrid," Veleif smiled.

"Cribs! I've never seen… I never thought… they're extraordinary!" She moved around each of them again, her lips parted in astonishment. "You didn't tell me anything. When I asked you about the cribs, you said you would think about it."

"And so I did think about it." He waved a hand at the beds. "I will not see my people put their babes in simple mangers, Æstrid. I've decided all new babes born here will receive one like these." He placed his hand on one of the tiny ships and moved it, showing her how it rocked. "You see, it moves side to side, like the ocean. I swear the babes of Kollsveinholdt will have their sea legs before they can walk." He chuckled again seeing her pleasure.

Æstrid shook her head in disbelief and rocked one nearest her. The sound of the bells tinkled across the silence between them. Her eyes misted with emotion, yet she couldn't fathom the reasons why. Had she come to care for these people in such a short time? Or was it that Veleif had taken her suggestion so deeply to heart, he had created these wonders?

She swallowed hard and blinked several times and looked over at Veleif who regarded her hopefully. He was a man as unpredictable as the seas – blowing hard and rough one moment, and calm and tender in the next. Æstrid gave him a soft smile.

"You will have to defend your kingdom, Veleif. Every newborn here will grow up considering himself royalty with beds such as these." Veleif laughed loudly at her jest and moved closer to her side.

"They please you then?"

"Yes. But I cannot imagine why my opinion should be important. I'm… just a guest here as you said," Æstrid shrugged shyly.

"These were your idea," Veleif said proudly, and twined her fingers with his. Æstrid shook her head, her eyes wandering over the extraordinary creations.

"Veleif, *these* were not my idea. Few men could hardly dream up such invention, let alone make them." She rocked one closest to her and smiled at the sound of the bells. "Asa, Gudney, and Skur will be beside themselves. Berra and Ingulfrid will be too stunned for words. And how you managed to complete them so quickly…" her voice trailed off in wonder.

"Everyone helped build them, Æstrid. No task is difficult with many hands to help. Though I admit it was Arnor's idea to add the bells." They both laughed at the admission.

"You are a mysterious man, Veleif," Æstrid murmured and shook her head, unable to take her gaze from the beautiful works in front of her. She peered at him askance, her voice barely above a whisper. "A complicated one too, I think."

"Complicated?" His brows drew together as he looked at her. "That is how I would describe you Æstrid, not me."

"Me?" she countered defensively.

"Yes," he nodded. "What else do you call a woman who runs from a hall because I deny her wine one moment and is pelting me with snow the next?"

Æstrid shrugged her shoulder dismissively then stepped away with a pouted look. "Why *did* you do that, Veleif? You think to control me in some twisted way? Or are you just boorish?"

"No, Æstrid. I was merely trying to spare you another restless night." He ran a hand across his beard with a frustrated sigh. "When you drink wine in the evenings, you suffer bad dreams. Nightmares even. I know." He thumbed his chest. "I hear you crying out from your chamber. I only sought to spare you from those demons, Æstrid, to ensure a peaceful night's rest for us both."

"You could have told me. Instead of being such a... an arrogant devil," she replied innocently. Veleif exhaled an aggravated groan.

"Would you have everyone at the table know your secrets? Besides, you leave me no choice with your brazen squabbling," Veleif frowned, "at some point, Æstrid, or by the graces of the god's own power, or perhaps if some enchantment freezes the ocean to solid ice; you will accept a simple request of mine, and stop fighting me at every turn."

"Then it was true... you came to me in my bed... it was not a dream..." she blushed and turned away. His voice turned rough and deep.

"I told you nothing can harm you here, Æstrid. Now come to me." His voice turned rough and deep. Though his words were hushed, the import of the meaning thundered over her in a deafening wave of emotion. She turned and looked at him and Veleif held out a hand.

"Is that a command, my lord? Or a simple request?" she whispered.

"Consider it a simple request if you come, Æstrid – a command if you do not." A smiled tugged at the corner of his lips. Æstrid stood uncertain and silent. Despite everything that passed between them, he'd remained honorable and trusting. This was Veleif. The man who wasn't used to having his orders betrayed, yet here he stood, surrounded by evidence of his compassionate spirit.

Her heart pounded, as his eyes encouraged her, desired her. He was proud, stalwartly male; calling across the chasm of uncertainty, drawing out the woman within to find safe harbors within his considerate protection. Æstrid realized suddenly she didn't want to be anywhere but here. Not simply existing in the house of a hardhearted father; but living, in a home surrounded by people of compassion and happiness, and maybe, even love.

The comprehension of this truth struck her like lightning. It could be some spell, or some lingering effects of the night's magic lights they'd shared, but she prayed to Odin she didn't misinterpret the possibility of these promises in Veleif's gaze. Lost in wordless admission, Æstrid swayed toward him and placed her hand in his.

"And this, Veleif? Is this to ensure my restful sleep?" she prompted. Veleif parted her cloak with his hands and drew her close to the heat of his body.

"Not if it's done properly, my lady," he grinned.

"Who needs sleep," Æstrid mumbled as his lips brushed gently across hers. He bent her backward over his arm, and parted her mouth with a teasing tongue, making her moan as she clung to his shoulders.

Veleif moved his mouth over hers with relentless purpose, suddenly urgent and demanding. On and on he kissed her breathless until she feared she would collapse. If she thought his earlier kiss had left her dizzy, this one brought her close to faint. Æstrid pushed against his shoulders, thinking to steady her careening world, but her effort was futile. He held her locked against him and deepened the kiss.

Somehow, he glided her cloak from her shoulders and spread it behind them on the ground. Shedding his own cloak and tossing it with hers, he nipped the corners of her mouth gently, coaxing soft sighs from her parted lips. Her arms clung to the breadth of his shoulders, threading upward into his hair, as he returned to her mouth once more. Just as her knees gave way, Veleif caught her hard against him and lifted her in his arms.

He knelt, lowering her gently down to the furs. His lips buried against the delicate column of her throat until he was drunk with the heady scent of her. His teeth grazed the tip of her ear in feather light touches sending shivers of pleasure trembling through her. An echoing tremor coursed through him as he felt her response, wrenching a low groan of primal hunger deep within his chest. She answered the forcefulness of his desire with her own, lifting and sinking at the same time in the swirling eddy of desire.

Æstrid gasped as his fingers touched the bare skin of her thigh, gently stroking her silken limb. Her body, hidden beneath the folds of her dress, now bared to him against the furs like a rare treasure. His palm moved over her with tantalizing strokes in unhurried circles, pressing her bottom until she could feel the fullness of the arousal he held in check. Æstrid finally tore her lips from his.

"Veleif, please I cannot… I cannot do this." Æstrid pushed against his shoulders in soft cries of protest.

"And what do you think *this* may be, my love?" he whispered huskily just above her lips. Cradling her head beneath his arm, Veleif moved until their bodies touched, every inch of his hard muscle fit tightly against her soft, feminine curves.

Æstrid trembled at his heated touch, caressing her bottom, her hip and the flat of her belly. She shoved a palm against the hard plane of his chest in protest.

"Please Veleif, I am… I do not know a man…" Æstrid whispered.

Veleif smiled before his lips took hers once again, deep and slow he kissed her as his hand guided her leg firmly around his waist. He was all but nestled between the warmth of her thighs. Soft moans formed deep in her chest as her body cleaved to his warmth. When he lifted his lips from hers at an unhurried pace, his eyes locked into her dreamy gaze.

"I'll not take you, Æstrid… not this night." His voice was graveled with desire. His fingers reached up to cup her face and she stilled beneath the intensity of his vivid gaze. Veleif's words were thick and hoarse with promise. "But we are not going back to the keep until I see you gone with pleasure. Not until I hear you cry out with it and watch you come apart in my arms."

His hand moved to the inside of her thigh, stoking her softly as tight tendrils of flame seemed to coil deep within. The blue depths gleamed in the soft light of the fire, as he kissed the corners of her mouth. Æstrid could feel his smile against her lips. When his hand cupped her hot center a loud moan escaped her throat.

Slowly, ever so slowly her dress was raised, baring her completely before him as he grazed his lips along her collarbone. His mouth moved lower, hot and wet, running luscious trails around her breasts. Veleif levered himself above her, needed to see her perfect breasts, bathed in the golden glow of the fire.

The sight left him breathless and he fought to hold all logic or reason. Her body lay before him, quivering and wanting, trusting, in spite of the raw passion he's aroused. And Veleif wanted her, in every way a man could want a woman, a warrior king could want a queen.

He wanted to take her, keep her, brand her to him and make her his. And he knew, as the fierce possessiveness gripped him, this maelstrom of desire was sheer madness.

He balanced on the knife edge of control, cursing the cumbersome barrier of his clothes, and thankful they held him in check. He had to stop before this tenuous trust he'd built between them was rent beyond repair. He had to stop before he shattered the vow he'd foolishly uttered.

Æstrid sank her hands into his hair, pulling him closer, tighter to her. His tunic and the hide breeches he wore rubbed against her bare skin as it seemed they touched everywhere from neck to toe. Yet her nakedness brushing against his clothing only seemed to fuel her to greater heights of wanton lust.

Poised just above her, Veleif's gaze seemed to worship the luscious bounty beneath him. He bent his dark head to the ivory mounds, suckling, groaning, unable to stop until her nipples were hardened peaks, wet and glistening in the light of the fire. His hands skimmed over the creamy arc of her waist, the curve of her hip. Then his gaze dipped lower, grazing his tongue in a fiery trail over her belly, sending every nerve ending to bursting with rivulets of pleasure along her spine. His hand cupped her bottom, lifting her hips as his heated words fogged her brain.

"Æstrid, my sweet, sweet, Æstrid." His breath came hot above the damp triangle of curls between her legs. He would never be sated until he tasted her.

His lips hovered above the apex of her thighs and with gentle words he encouraged her to part her legs. Then his hot tongue parted her, drawing slowly over her slick folds until her hips rose up to meet his mouth. He gripped her harder, and moved upon her, ever so slightly, circling her with the barest flick of his tongue. She tried to arch again into his mouth, to deepen the loving pleasure, but he held her tight as he stroked her with feather light touches.

Her hips undulated against him in passionate proof of her response. The cries broke unbidden from her lips, leaving her panting and hoarse. His name became a desperate moan as he taunted and teased, tasted with his mouth. He continued to play with his tongue and lips, as her fists coiled into his dark hair.

Æstrid cried out as she hovered on the pinnacle of reason, her body arched like a bow, until Veleif pushed deep with his tongue, pulling her to him at the same time. The world inside the cave echoed with her screams of exaltation, leaving Æstrid weak and trembling with the power of it all.

Her cries tortured the rigid ache he held in check. As her splintered breathing returned in small gasps, Veleif promised he would have her. Soon. He'd have her body meld with his, surrendered somewhere between savage and sweet, he would make her his.

He took her in his arms again, holding her close, stroking her hair, caressing her body as the shuddering within her began to subside. His voice was rough and ragged as Æstrid sought to put to words what had just passed between them. He traced a fingertip along the rim of her mouth and held her eyes in tender solemnity.

"Don't seek to describe this, my love, just savor the moment. And know I could watch you come apart a hundred times and never tire of such a sight."

Æstrid gazed up at Veleif, marveling at what he'd just done. He lay on one elbow propped above her, his hand moved leisurely over her ribcage, his eyes intense with hunger as ventured lower to stroke the curve between her waist and hip.

"Do you know what it means when a man of Kollsveinholdt brings pleasure to a woman in that manner?" he asked softly.

Æstrid cocked a languid brow and shook her head absently waiting for his answer.

"They are betrothed," he murmured, with a slight twitch of his lips.

"Betrothed?" Æstrid burst into laughter as Veleif frowned slightly at her mirth. Still chuckling, her hand caressed his face, as she smoothed the furrow in his brow with her thumb.

"Of all your talents, Veleif Kollsvein, I never expected wit to be among them."

# Chapter Seventeen

Æstrid groaned awake and flung a bent elbow across her eyes in disgrace. What madness had seized her last night? She, the proud daughter of Gunnalf Karisson, princess and heir to all the lands and coffers of Karissonholdt, had behaved like nothing more than a brazen harlot. With Veleif no less! Had there been some enchantment in the tide of colors that flooded last evening's sky?

Her gut tightened. She envisioned her father's rage if he ever became privy to her bold, wanton behavior. She could see Gunnalf's broad face turning purple beneath his pate of red hair, his arms floundering to the heavens as he cursed and ranted. *A Kollsvein!*

A deep sigh of shame escaped her as the details replayed in her mind. Veleif's kisses stealing her breathless, his hands roaming over her body in abandon, and she, lying naked upon the fur as he pleasured her... Æstrid squeezed her eyes tightly shut.

She'd never be able to face him today. Never.

She rolled to her side and turned her gaze wistfully out to the sea. It was snowing again, but the churning waves beyond the solitary window shaped an idea quickly in her mind. An illness! She'd plead a sour stomach or a throbbing head. She could stay snuggled deep beneath the furs in her bed until tomorrow; and gather her wits and her courage. A space of distance was what she needed.

A timid knock at the door interrupted her thoughts, and Æstrid buried herself deeper into the furs, feigning sleep. With one eye half open, she saw Rafa and Thorgrima peek around the portal, then tiptoe into her chamber. Their arms were laden with fabrics and a tray of strange vessels.

She loosened another groan.

"Good morrow, Æstrid." They bowed and blushed, both grinning ear to ear. Æstrid coughed and sniffed, in preparation for her ruse.

The women seemed oblivious as they bustled about, laying out fresh garments, stoking the fire, and arranging the room to greet the day. Æstrid raised up on her elbow and rubbed the sleep from her eyes.

"We're here to attend you," Thorgrima beamed happily.

"I... I'm not well," Æstrid coughed and flung herself backward on the bed.

"Nonsense! Today is Winter Solstice and my prince sent you these gifts," Rafa chortled undeterred, and scurried to her side, pulling her upright. Æstrid tried to duck away as Rafa's hand found her brow, pressing along her forehead.

"No fever here," Rafa announced with a flourish.

"And you are expressly forbidden to oversee the kitchens today." Thorgrima called out over her shoulder, making a show of pouring scented oil into the basin.

"Forbidden?" Æstrid asked suspiciously and sat up in bed. Rafa exchanged a worried glance with Thorgrima and cleared her throat.

"My lady, please. Today is a day for feasting and much celebration."

"Then my assistance is most certainly needed," Æstrid argued, and swung her legs to the floor. She stopped and looked suspiciously at both women. "How was this kept from me?"

"Veleif has been most insistent you enjoy the fruits of Kollsveinholdt's festivities today, not labor in the kitchens," Rafa rushed to explain.

"A day you'll want to remember fondly," Thorgrima chirped, and received a sharp nudge from Rafa.

"Pray what do I have to celebrate? I'm far from my home and miss my people. It is only this cursed winter that keeps me here." Æstrid sighed and clutched the furs about her shoulders. The women traded another nervous glimpse.

"My lady, perhaps in time you will come to realize fortune's true purpose on this fated journey. But I, for one, would be distraught to see this day turned to one of hatred. Now please, let us attend you and see you fit for the occasion, because despite the circumstance, aren't you allowed at least one day of happiness?" Rafa encouraged.

Æstrid sighed and perched upright on the edge of the bed.

"You're not going to leave are you?"

"No we are not." Rafa shook her head slightly, an infuriating smile still pasted on her face.

"Your instructions were quite clear, weren't they?" Æstrid canted her head to the side.

"Yes they were," Thorgrima nodded.

"And if I refuse?" Æstrid wondered.

"Arnor awaits without, my lady," Thorgrima whispered shyly.

"I believe he was hoping the task of dressing you would fall to him," Rafa giggled. Æstrid exhaled loudly in resignation as she crossed to the hearth.

"Alright. I cannot fight you both." She extended her arms dramatically to her sides and tilted her head back, letting the pelt fall unheeded to the floor. "I'm at your mercy."

Rafa opened the door and a stream of servants bustled in behind her. They hauled the copper tray near the hearth, carried buckets of steaming water, and were armed with piles of fresh linens and woven garlands of fragrant pine and holly. It appeared Veleif had commandeered half of Kollsveinholdt to see to her needs. As quickly as they entered and deposited their wares, Rafa and Thorgrima ushered them all out again.

Æstrid let the women attend her, secretly enjoying the lavish attention, and the fragrant scent of lavender added to the water helped bolster her courage. Rafa rubbed more of the scented oil into her skin until she gleamed, and Thorgrima pulled out a linen shift woven so fine, Æstrid marveled at the softness and the sheen of the fine fabric. It skimmed her body, showing off the deep neckline, and hem was worked with complex patterns of light blue threads. It was a garment fit for royalty.

"It's beautiful," Æstrid breathed in awe, twirling in delight.

"Just one of the gifts from Veleif, my lady. And this as well." Thorgrima spread out the blue overdress, presenting it before her. The long trailing sleeves had touches of white fur, and Æstrid gasped. The garment itself was breathtaking, but the fabric shimmered in the light as it was embroidered all over with fine silver threads. The intricate needlework was heavy at the borders of the sleeves and the hem. Æstrid had never seen, or even imagined a garment equal to it before.

When Æstrid slipped on the overdress, she could barely hold still in excitement, as Rafa combed her hair until it shone like silk. Instead of her usual braid, she pinned the mass up at her temples with clips of fine silver and twisted it into soft curls down her back. Thorgrima added a crown of white winterberries atop her curls.

The women prodded and chatted easily about the grand feast being prepared below, and Æstrid joined their gaiety. She was dressed as a queen, or a goddess even; and gathering strength from the influential clothes she wore, there was nothing she couldn't face today. Even Veleif.

Thorgrima knelt and slipped her feet into soft boots made from gray rabbit fur, and laced them up to her knees. Rafa draped a long length of snow-white fox about her shoulders and Æstrid stroked the silky fur. They both stepped back, and with wide smiles and glowing eyes, the women finally pronounced her complete.

Rafa held up a polished silvered disc and Æstrid squealed when she saw her reflection. What stared back at her was not the wild, untamed girl adventuring through the hills and forests with her brother; but a woman, strong, serene and beautiful.

Arnor waited impatiently in the hallway, shuffling nervously back and forth. When the door opened and the big Viking entered the chamber, he halted mid-stride, his mouth agape. Æstrid giggled at seeing his thus, and whirled before him. His gaze quickly changed to one of deep admiration and he inclined his head.

"I swear by the gods, Kollsveinholdt has never seen a fairer maiden. You honor this house, Æstrid," Arnor confessed.

"Such formalities, Arnor? It is only because of the finery I wear," she laughed, and slapped his beefy forearm.

"Ah, but you forget, Æstrid, I've seen you clad in a potato sack. You were no less regal then, than you are now." His eyes twinkled mischievously as he nestled her hand in the crook of his elbow.

"And you, Arnor," she mused, as her hand swept the full length of his deep blue tunic and black trousers. A broad, black leather belt gleamed about his thick waist, holding daggers worked with intricate silver. His shoulders were draped in short cape of black and red furs, fastened at his neck with heavy silver chain and intricate clasps. His hair and beard were painstakingly groomed.

"I'm certain no women of Kollsveinholdt could escape your fine looks. Or your silvered tongue," she added. Arnor's head roared back in laughter.

"It is my honor to escort you below, Æstrid. But first, there is something here that seems amiss," he teased, and wagged a finger in her direction. The corners of his bushy moustache lifted as he smiled and reached inside his tunic. All three women gasped as he withdrew an exquisite bracelet.

It was wide and heavy, a cuff of pure, gleaming silver. The carvings on the bracelet were painstakingly worked, and in the center lay a dragon's head, with twin blue stones for eyes, winking back at her. Æstrid shook her head mildly as he reached for her arm to put it on.

"I can't accept it, Arnor. It is too rich a gift."

"Would that it was from me, but it is not. I am merely the bearer of the gift," he explained as he slid the cuff onto her wrist. "If you want to protest, you'll have to plead your case with Veleif," he chuckled. Æstrid frowned lightly as her fingertip traced over the patterns of the cuff.

"It seems I'm unfamiliar with the customs here, Arnor. At my home, the solstice celebration doesn't include the exchange of gifts as elaborate as these. Sweetmeats and cakes perhaps..." her voice trailed.

"I don't assume to know the man's mind, though I know him better than most," Arnor shrugged.

"Would that be a blessing or a curse, Arnor?" Æstrid teased.

"Depends on the direction of the winds, my lady," Arnor countered with a smile.

The sounds from the great hall grew louder as they drew near. Hearty laughter and song rose to greet them as they descended the stairs.

When Arnor appeared in the wide entrance with Æstrid at his side, a diminishing hush fell over the crowd and all eyes turned upon them. Æstrid blushed at the attention and Arnor gave her hand a gentle squeeze of encouragement. It seemed everyone at Kollsveinholdt had dressed in their finest for the solstice celebration.

The women glittered, adorned with silver and copper torques, and necklaces of beads and finely wrought chains. Rings and bracelets sparkled atop their swirling skirts and pinafores of soft, embroidered wools. It was such a gleaming display of treasure, Gunnalf himself would have swooned. The men wore their finest linens, wools and hides, rich furs, polished cuffs and shining hilts from their daggers and swords were on display.

Even the great hall was dressed for the celebration. Every candlestand and sconce was lit, promising to chase any remnants of shadows from the darkened corners. Hundreds upon hundreds of candles graced the center of every tabletop, where they stood amid carefully laid boughs of pine and holly. The blazing hearths were draped with garlands of pine woven with white winterberries.

The mingling scents of roasting meats, fresh yeasty breads, fish and oysters, honey wine and ale wafted around them and made Æstrid's mouth water. The air was fragrant with fresh pine needles strewn about the floor, and the drifting aromas of precious spices, cinnamon, cloves and cardamom, all made an indelible stamp upon her senses. Æstrid had never experienced such a display of festivity before and the very air of the hall was charged with merriment and good cheer.

Æstrid exchanged greetings with the smiling faces as Arnor led her forward into the room, and the rising din of the celebration returned. Veleif was standing in front of the roaring hearth surrounded by a half dozen of his men. His drinking horn paused halfway to his lips when his eyes fell upon her.

He was garbed in colors similar to her; a soft, white linen shirt and blue tunic embroidered heavily with silver. The dark hide breeches encased his powerful legs, and black, fur boots were laced up past his knees. Around his broad shoulders a thick, white wolf pelt was fastened to his shoulders with a large silver clasp fashioned in the shape of a dragon's head. She didn't miss the silver torque around his throat, with twin dragon heads resting at the base of his neck. Its design matched the cuff which adorned her wrist.

When their gazes locked, she felt her breath hitch. His blue eyes were vivid, intense, and his face was arrestingly handsome as he smiled at her in admiration. Even standing among his men, Veleif Kollsvein was a man apart. He was a dark, magnificent warrior and her imagination skittered, bringing a heated flush to her cheeks. Merely standing in his company made her feel delicate, protected and oh, so feminine. The cavernous hall seemed to shrink around them, as he drew her hand from Arnor and raised it to his lips.

"My lady Karisson," he purred warmly, "you look more beautiful than I could have ever imagined." His eyes flared as her nearness inveigled all pretense of hiding his passion. It didn't matter now. All of Kollsveinholdt would soon bear witness to this duplicitous deed at hand, and the lady herself would know soon enough. If he was going to be cursed by the night's end, he may as well enjoy the precious strands of merriment for as long as his favor would hold.

"My lord, Kollsvein," Æstrid blushed, and bowed politely to greet the others. As she turned back to Veleif to thank him for his extravagant gifts, a horn was pressed into her hand. When she opened her mouth to speak, Thorliek discreetly signaled to a small group nearby. Several drums began to pound, drowning the hall in pulsating rhythms. Two other men raised their flutes and began piping a merry tune.

Shouts and clapping scattered through the throng as several men broke away from their feasting. With horns and goblets in hand, they pulled their women to the center of the hall, swinging them round, swirling and lifting them high, in time with the music.

Æstrid watched and giggled at the revelry. When she raised the drinking horn to her lips, her head snapped back in surprise, as she shot Veleif a puzzled glance.

"Wine?" Æstrid leaned in to gain his ear. "You serve me wine after all your thundering about me drinking it?"

"Something tells me you won't be sleeping tonight," Veleif shouted above the music and smiled wryly. Before Æstrid could reply, Irik pulled her hand and coaxed her to dance. Whisking her away to join the merriment, Arnor rescued her horn as it sloshed over his hand.

Æstrid's eyes shone bright with laughter as Irik spun her among the others. Veleif sipped the honeyed mead and watched the woman whose fate he held in delicate balance. His mind wandered to thoughts of Tofa, her loyal and passive nature. While he knew Æstrid would be no less faithful to a worthy cause, the maid was anything but passive. She was fire and defiance and disparity all wrapped up in the most tempting curves he'd ever touched.

He sipped his wine deeply, knowing no amount of flattery, persuasion or reason was going to sway her this night. Æstrid wasn't going to accept any of this willingly. She was going to challenge his claim, resist, and fight him as fiercely as any enemy he'd ever faced – and she would be formidable, but so would he.

Veleif smiled as Arnor shouldered Irik away from Æstrid's side, lifting her high in the air and twirling her about. Despite his size, the huge Viking managed to lead her through the dance, skipping gracefully among the crowd. She was beautiful and breathless with the exertion. Her face was flushed beneath the fall of her hair, and her eyes sparkled in testament to her gaiety.

Veleif's hand tightened on his horn. He had no intention of losing this combat. For not only was he battling for their future, but the very future of both their kingdoms. Her delicacies be damned, he was resolved to this deceptive quest. Tonight Kollsveinholdt would have its heir.

"Everything is in place, Veleif. We just await your word," Thorliek smiled, and looked at Æstrid proudly. The lady was graceful, beautiful and had a temperament to keep Veleif Kollsvein entertained long into his twilight years. He couldn't have predicted a better match, but turned and frowned at Veleif's silence.

"Veleif?" Thorliek prompted nervously.

"I heard you, Thorliek," Veleif snapped, instantly regretting his brusque tone. He ran his hand over his beard to steady his patience. "When I place my torque about her neck, you can begin. But first, let us enjoy this celebration. There is no reason not to eat and drink our fill before one goes to war."

A giggling Nar skipped in front of them, and Thorliek snatched a jug from the boy's bewildered hand. He filled Veleif's horn to the rim with the honey wine.

"As you wish, Veleif. For the god's only know what strength you'll need for later."

Æstrid swiped the horn from Arnor's hand and laughing at the giant's astonished expression, took a hearty drink. The revelry consumed her as Oresti, then Blotha, then Irik again, came to claim her hand for another dance. It wasn't until several partners later, when she almost collided with Veleif, did she realize she had not yet eaten.

Blushing and breathless, Æstrid's eyes were glowing with mirth and wine, as she fanned her face with her hand. Veleif reached out to steady her and her color deepened.

"My apologies, Veleif. I haven't even thanked you as yet. I was told you are responsible for these beautiful gifts." She swayed a bit as she smoothed her hands along the white fox pelts. She swore his gaze softened, and even paused a bit overlong at her breasts before he found her eyes again. An unfathomable surge of warmth coursed through her.

"Seeing you in those garments is thanks enough, Æstrid," Veleif laughed, and flashed a heart-stopping smile. "But come, sweet wench, I think it's time you had some food with your wine." He laced his fingers with hers and pulled her along beside him. She peered up into his face as he pulled out a chair next to his on the dais.

A long, wooden trencher was set before them piled high with roasted meats and fish. Æstrid frowned in confusion as a large, silver drinking bowl was placed between them. The piece was a breathtaking piece of craftsmanship, with twin, curling dragons forming the handles on either side. A serving boy filled the vessel with honey mead, as Veleif carved off the choicest bits of roasted meat and placed them nearest her on the trencher.

"I have never witnessed such a grand celebration to welcome the winter solstice before, Veleif. And although I'm not familiar with your customs, I confess I am enjoying the way you mark the occasion at Kollsveinholdt."

"No matter what the future holds, Æstrid, I hope you remember this day fondly. Now eat before you're too flown with wine to remember it at all." He chuckled and gestured with his chin as his shoulder brushed against hers.

"Do I get to drink from this? Or is it all for you?" Æstrid giggled, and ran her finger along the rim of the drinking bowl. Veleif captured her hand in his and nipped her fingertip, then kissed it before trapping it firmly on the table.

"You're already flown with wine, aren't you?" Veleif admonished teasingly, a hint of a smile tugged about the corners of his lips.

"And you, are being your normal overbearing self." Æstrid arched an accusing brow as she giggled and slipped her hand from beneath his.

"Perhaps, Æstrid, but never without good cause," Veleif muttered half to himself. He gave her a sidelong glance as he chewed his meat thoughtfully. Æstrid missed his remark as she laughed at some jest from Arnor's passing.

The wine and ale flowed by the caskful. Æstrid giggled and laughed throughout the meal and her spirits soared at the joyous sights and sounds of the hall. She sipped thoughtlessly from her wine as Veleif and his men entertained her with wild tales and jests. The mercurial prince was behaving every inch a considerate suitor, and she warmed and blushed under his attention. He anticipated her every need, and shot warning glances to his men when he deemed their jokes too bawdy for her delicate company.

Seeing her liberally imbibed, Veleif knew the time was at hand. He certainly didn't want her drunk, but only intoxicated enough to soften the shock of the task ahead. Veleif leaned in close, inhaling the sweet smell of her skin, and pressed his thigh along the length of hers.

"Soon the men will bring in a great log which will burn in our hall for the next twelve days. Thorliek will light candles upon it and invoke the blessings. But while this is a day to mark feasting and celebration, Æstrid, it is also a day of gifts." Veleif reached inside his tunic and pulled out a silver torque, similar to the one he wore. It was intricately worked with scrolls and dragons heads adorning the ends. Fine stones were set for the eyes, sparkling like small flashes of blue fire under the glow of the candlelight.

"It would please me for you to wear this," Veleif whispered warmly. Æstrid gasped at the extravagance of the piece.

"Veleif, I cannot accept it. You've already given me so much," Æstrid protested and shook her head.

"You wouldn't insult me on this happy day, Æstrid. You'll wear it," he said with finality that brooked no argument. Æstrid shivered as his hands brushed her hair aside and he settled the torque around her neck with infinite care.

His thumbs brushed the base of her throat sensually as his gaze turned unreadable. He seemed reluctant to release her and for a panicked moment, Æstrid thought he was going to kiss her, right here in front of everyone. The heat lanced through her where his touch had been, and she swallowed nervously before she met his eyes.

As if all the commotion of the hall fell away, there was only the unmistakable draw of awareness. Veleif so completely and thoroughly male, calling to some unknown place deep within, drawing and awakening on a feminine cord she hadn't known existed. Primal and forbidden, yet mysteriously correct as she bloomed beneath his attentive manners and solitary focus. The scent of him filled her nostrils, and the sensual curve of his lips seemed to cry out for a taste. She shifted nervously in her chair and cleared her throat to break the intensity of the feelings.

"I-I'm sorry, Veleif. I have nothing to give you in return," she smiled tremulously.

"Then you will join me and together we will bless this celebration. That will be your gift," he said, giving her hand a squeeze.

"I'll agree, my lord. But tomorrow, I promise to hate you again," she teased, and sipped more wine. Veleif threw his head back and roared with laughter.

"I vow Æstrid, you'll hate me before the dawn arises."

Thorliek had been watching the couple closely and seeing Æstrid don the necklace, he nodded to the guards near the entrance to the hall. The great wooden doors were swung open and a rush of arctic air swirled into the room.

A dozen men hurried outside and moments later, they heaved and strained against the ropes, pulling in a massive log so wide, a child of four would not clear its depth. Æstrid's eyes went wide at the sight, as she could only imagine how many days it had taken to carve this giant beneath the axe.

The doors closed as the men pressed forward to the main hearth, their heavy burden in tow. The merriment pressed to a higher crescendo, as garlands of pine boughs and berries were tossed in its path. More people joined the dancing and many a head was tossed back with wine and ale, including Veleif, who also seemed to be in high spirits. Æstrid was not unaffected by the gaiety and even tossed an errant garland into the throng, as the log journeyed past their table.

The dancers parted, still high in their revelry as the log was dragged to the center of the stone hearth, a dozen paces in front of the blazing fire. Rafa pressed forward with a tray of fat candles as Thorliek nodded to Veleif over the heads of the crowded throng.

"Go around to the front of the table, Æstrid, and wait for me there," Veleif directed, pulling her to her feet. "The time had come to say our blessing."

As Æstrid moved to the other side, her gaze followed the journey of a torch, passed hand over hand from the great hearth to Thorliek. Veleif reached her side and bent to her ear.

"We'll carry the bowl together, Æstrid." He placed his hand on one side of the ceremonial vessel and she mimicked his lead. Together, they descended the three steps onto the stone floor of the hall amid the song and dancing, with garlands flying wildly about them.

Æstrid's face was flushed with excitement and her eyes were bright with gaiety. The high spirits of the crowd was infectious, and she couldn't help but feel honored and proud to help the people of Kollsveinholdt mark the beginning of the winter solstice. By the time they crossed the short distance to Thorliek, both she and Veleif were draped in dozens of garlands of holly and berries.

Thorliek raised his arms dramatically and the merriment slowly quieted. Her heart beat nervously as every hand in the great hall commenced to a uniform pounding on the wooden tables. The people who were standing, stomped in time on the floor. *Thump, thump, thump*, pause. *Thump, thump, thump*, pause. Without a clue of what was expected, Æstrid stole a look up at Veleif who nodded to her with encouragement.

"Do not worry, Æstrid, I'll guide you," he whispered from the corner of his mouth, seeking to allay her nervousness.

Thorliek lit the first candle with his torch and the rhythmic pounding continued. *Thump, thump, thump*, pause. *Thump, thump, thump*, pause. He placed the candle on the log, and his voice rang out in a chant across the great hall.

"As witness to the tree of light and life, a blessing for this season. To all who come before this hearth today, we are bound as brothers, as family. A drink to your health." Thorliek nodded to Veleif, signaling him to guide the bowl to his lips. Veleif drank deeply, then held it up for Æstrid to follow suit.

The *thump, thump, thump*, continued to vibrate throughout the hall as Æstrid sipped from the bowl. Her eyes went wide as she took a deep swallow. This was honeyed mead, but a great deal stronger than any she'd tasted before. Veleif held the bowl firmly, not letting her escape until she had swallowed three good draughts of the stuff.

Stifling a cough against the strength of the brew, Veleif gave her an approving wink as Thorliek continued his chant. He lit the second candle and placed it on the other end of the log.

"Oh moon of silver, sun of gold, gentle lady and lord so bold. Guide us ever, failing never, and lead us in the ways of old. A drink of praise in love we bring, we share and sing on this winter solstice night." Veleif sipped again and passed her the bowl to partake of the potent wine. Another three sips and Æstrid swayed slightly, holding on to Veleif's forearm for support.

"This is the strangest solstice blessing I've ever witnessed," Æstrid whispered from the side of her mouth.

"Just keep drinking with me, Æstrid. It's about to get stranger," Veleif replied in a hushed whisper, as he kept his eyes on Thorliek. The elder cast a quick glance to Veleif, who encouraged him with a barely perceptible nod. The candle flames danced upon the log and began to swim a bit before her. Thorliek lit the third and fourth candles. The rhythmic pounding from the tables grew louder.

"Stranger?" Æstrid squeaked.

"Yes. Stranger," Veleif frowned and tipped the bowl to her lips without pause. Æstrid sputtered and wiped her mouth.

"I don't think we were supposed to drink yet, Veleif," Æstrid remarked.

"Oh, I don't think it can hurt," Veleif muttered sardonically, and took a healthy swig. Thorliek flashed them a disapproving glare, adding to Æstrid's confusion.

"Hail night and daughters of night. Hail lord of darkness, and lord of light. Gaze on us with gracious eyes and award us victory within our sights. Drink to the gods and goddesses, gentle brothers, and king of might." Thorliek's voice rang clear and he nodded again to them.

Veleif drank from the bowl and Æstrid frowned at the curious toast. She drank deeply as he held it to her mouth, welcoming the warmth flowing through her. The wine was sweet now, not at all as strong as it had been before. They held the bowl between them and Æstrid contemplated the contents.

"It is a most curious wine, Veleif. I've never tasted its equal," she mused.

"Reserved for the most sacred of occasions, Æstrid." Veleif leveled her with a serious gaze. Thorliek lit the fifth and sixth candles. The crowd's thrumming beats increased to an impossible noise. Æstrid felt her pulse beat in syncopated rhythm with the pounding fists and feet.

"Is this a sacred occasion, Veleif? Then I'm honored you chose to share it with me," she tittered from the wine's effects and leaned close against him.

"If you remember nothing else, Æstrid, mark my words carefully. There is no other I wish to be at my side tonight." His voice was low, almost a growl as Æstrid frowned up at him. He looked almost angry as a scowl crossed his face. Looking around the room, she had to strain to hear as Thorliek called out, his arms spread wide.

"I hallow this bowl of mead to gods and goddesses high and holy. Aesir and Vanir, first known in the north. Frigga and Odin, Thor and Sif, Freya and Freyr, Balder and Nanna, Disir and Alfar. Bless this hospitality to all who cross this threshold in the name of the season, and bless this wedded union."

Veleif sipped quickly and shoved the bowl against her lips. She frowned at him and swallowed in abject confusion as riotous cheers erupted in the hall. Thorliek's words echoed in a foggy chamber of her mind and an icy question of dread needled to the forefront of her awareness.

*What wedded union?*

Æstrid spun about amid the whirling chaos and confusion, grasping at anything resembling truth. Thorliek quickly snatched the bowl from Veleif, and knelt before them.

"My king, my queen," his voice mouthed in whisper.

The shock of Thorliek's words sobered her like a frigid gale.

*My king? My queen? Did they… did they just get married?* Too stunned to speak, Veleif's arms came around her as the dawning became terrifyingly real.

"Hail, Veleif, king of Kollsveinholdt! Hail Æstrid, queen of Kollsveinholdt!" A thousand voices echoed throughout the hall. Æstrid shrank back in horror, opening her mouth to scream. Before she could issue any sound, Veleif pulled her hard against him and covered her lips quickly, bending her backward in a bone-crushing kiss.

The music began anew and the hall broke into even greater pandemonium. A swarm of people crushed toward the pair, showering them with well wishes and congratulations.

Æstrid beat upon his chest with her fists, squirming and thrashing, trying to tear away. Veleif trapped her tighter in an iron grip and took her screams into his mouth, ignoring the press of bodies surrounding them.

One hand yanked into her heavy curls, keeping her immobile, and his other pinned her against the hard planes of his chest. Æstrid tried to bite her way free, but even that effort was useless as his hand jerked painfully, making her wince in retreat. Veleif finally pulled back, releasing her mouth, but kept her restrained within the circle of his arms.

"Good tidings, *wife*," he whispered just above her throbbing lips. Opposing expressions of distress and joy seemed to war on his face, but Æstrid was too enraged at the moment to contemplate their meaning. A scream tore from her throat as she struggled in earnest against his embrace. She managed to wrench an arm free and struck out as quick as lightning, but Veleif deflected her wrist before she could meet her mark.

"I'm not your wife!" she snarled caustically, trying to twist free.

Her reaction to the deception was predictable, but Veleif knew this exposed argument would get them nowhere. It was best to remove her to somewhere private; before her rage, and his patience, quickly came to an end. Besides, in the midst of this audience, it was crucial they knew, *she knew*, Veleif Kollsvein was not a man to be denied his claim.

A low, male growl sounded in his throat as Veleif tossed her high in the air and caught her quickly over his shoulder. Her breath drove from her in a *whoof!* when her stomach slammed hard into his shoulder. His arm restrained her kicking legs, as the singing and dancing merrymakers opened a path for him to quit the hall.

Someone pressed a horn into his hand and Veleif paused to toss back the ale. Hearty laughter surrounded them as the men clapped him soundly on his unencumbered shoulder. Æstrid screamed and beat on his back with her fists. She raised her eyes and locked a murderous gaze upon Thorliek.

"Unholy traitor!" she shrieked and twisted, pointing at the old man with an accusing finger. "You bastard son of a whore, Thorliek! How could you do this to me? This, this treachery is not valid!"

"It is most valid, my queen!" Thorliek called out to her, then lifted the dragon bowl to his lips and swallowed a deep drink as he closed his eyes. He raised his gaze to the rafters, his mouth moved in silent prayer. Tears of anger coursed down Æstrid's cheeks as she hurled curses upon them all. Her arms thrashed about wildly as she sought to grab at anything she could to break free of Veleif.

Her hands swept the nearby tables, sending platters, cups and food flying in her wake. Two hounds loped forward and tore into the roasted fowl that skidded to the floor. Grabbing at everything in passing, her fingers sank deep and clenched into Rafa's hair. The woman screamed in pain. Veleif stopped and turned to see the cause, but Æstrid refused to lose her hold, and pulled the yelping Rafa unwillingly behind them.

"Hold, Veleif. It would seem your bride prefers a different companion on her wedding night," Blotha laughed heartily. He pried her fingers loose from Rafa's tangled locks.

Æstrid slapped at his hands furiously, and Rafa stumbled free, scrambling on the ground to avoid her raking grasp. Blotha's rumbling laughter broke from deep in his chest as he bore the brunt of her attack. Æstrid screeched in helpless frustration as Veleif laughed and accepted another cup of ale. So far, his new wife was behaving even better than he thought. At least, he had the foresight to remove any weapons from the hall.

"You liar! You traitorous bastard! I hate you!" she sobbed and beat on his back. The faces of the men and women, the food, the tables, all began to swim in watery candlelight as they moved to the end of the great hall.

Veleif shouldered past Arnor on the stairs. The big Viking was well into his cups of celebration as he swayed against the wall. Seeing Veleif's wiggling burden, his hand reached to the coil on his belt.

"Do you need my whip, Veleif?" Arnor slurred. Æstrid gasped in shock.

"No, good friend. She'll be whispering entreaties upon my lips by morn." Veleif gave her a hearty whack upon her bottom and Æstrid yelped and kicked out in pain.

"YOU Arnor! I thought *you* a friend!" she shrieked at him as they moved past. "I shall never, *ever* forgive this slight and I will *never* cook for you again!"

Arnor tossed back his head in hearty guffaws as Veleif carried her up the narrowing hall. Æstrid's flailing hands seized a torch from its rung which she flung hard in Arnor's direction.

"Burn in hell!" she shouted. The torch showered sparks against the stones and Arnor laughed as he stomped them out easily beneath his great boot.

They crossed into the landing and Æstrid's struggles renewed. Veleif hefted her up again adjusting his grip. The wench was more slippery than a salmon in spring.

"You need some patience, my eager wife. We'll share a bed soon enough." His chest rumbled with a vigorous chuckle as his arm tightened around her thighs. Æstrid spit her hair from her mouth and shouted anew.

"I am not your wife! And I'll not share your bed! I'd rather lie with the devil himself, you puss-riddled excuse of a dog!"

Undaunted, Veleif moved up the stairs to his chamber.

"Ah my love, your endearments are sweet upon my ears. Pray you'll always speak your heart," he growled and shoved open the door.

"You diseased, black-hearted whelp. I'll NOT go in there with you." Her hands clutched the door frame and her feet kicked furiously as she halted his progress. Veleif turned his head and saw her white-knuckled grip on the wood. He wrenched his shoulder forward to tear her hands free.

Æstrid let loose a blood-curdling scream.

# Chapter Eighteen

Veleif kicked the door closed behind him, and dropped her unceremoniously to the floor. Æstrid scrambled up to her feet and backed away from him, her eyes sparkling with anger and panic. She quickly took stock of the room. A table, heavily-laden with trenchers of food and jugs of wine, additional candlestands set the room aglow with dozens and dozens of blazing tallows; and the heavens help her, Veleif's massive bed, which bore downy linens, were turned back invitingly with extra furs piled high at one end.

The chamber had been painstakingly tended to see to a bride's comfort, including the chair she had used in her own chamber. It now rested beside his near the hearth. Of course not a single weapon, neither an axe, nor a humble arrow, was to be found within the dreamy setting. After learning her skills with the axe, the bastard probably ordered the room cleared of any kind of weaponry for his own protection.

Veleif latched the door behind him and turned, sweeping his gaze from her head to her toes. Æstrid's hair cascaded wildly about her shoulders. Somewhere in their flight, she'd lost the wreath upon her head. Her mouth was parted and her breasts were heaving beneath her gown. Every muscle in her body was tense and ready to spring if he pressed her.

There would be no reasoning with his wife in this moment, and her posture certainly did not hold a drop of willingness.

*His wife.*

The very knowledge this fiery temptation was his wife, sent his body twisting in knots. He needed to see her skin flushed from his passionate caress, not from her unbridled anger. And he longed to hear welcoming cries of ecstasy tumbling from her luscious mouth – not the hurling curses she was expending so generously at the moment.

But if he intended to breach her defenses on this wedding night, first he needed her temper to cool while he formulated the best approach to this seduction.

Would he wear her down with a patient siege? Or attack headlong with overpowering force? Knowing the depth of this woman's anger and the intensity of his raging needs, the tactics of this campaign would probably entail a bit of both.

"You're a liar, Veleif Kollsvein. You never had any intention of returning me home," Æstrid accused with a sneer. She backed her way across the room to the table newly located for the wedded couple. Keeping Veleif in her sights, if there was any weapon to be had, it would be found there.

"I've been nothing more than a pretty prisoner, marked with your traitorous gifts," she seethed, "well no more!" Æstrid all but ripped the bracelet from her arm and hurled it at him. As her hands reached for the torque, his eyes narrowed dangerous. Unblinking.

"Æstrid Karisson Kollsvein," Veleif said slowly, marking each word. "Do not dare remove that. Ever." The threat behind his deliberate words was so genuine, a shiver of fear pierced her cloak of anger.

"Do not call me that! That is not my name!" Æstrid snapped. She was no match for him physically, but she could slow him down a pace. If only she could find a weapon...

"It is your name. Unless you prefer hellish vixen," Veleif retorted, as he sat down in his large black chair and rubbed his brow as if it pained him. "Besides, it pleases me to see you so attired," he waved his hand indifferently as he unlaced his boots.

"Pleases you? Pleases *you?*" she uttered a short, nervous laugh, as she paused her search for a weapon. Her ire bubbled as she whirled on him. "I'd rather wear a sack than a stitch of what you've given me."

With a snarl, she shrugged the dress over her head and shoved the thing angrily to the ground. Kicking the heap toward him, Veleif eyed her, stifling the sudden amusement that threatened. If Æstrid truly had any idea how his fingers ached to peel away the remaining layers of her clothing, and then haul her to bed – she wouldn't be standing before him, clad only in the shimmering linen shift that molded to her splendid curves.

Æstrid gasped seeing the hunger flare in Veleif's eyes. He sat upright and patient, like a predator bearing down on his mark. Æstrid inwardly cursed her vehement temper. It was a foolish error on her part – vulnerably clad, alone in this chamber with a man who sincerely believed to be her husband. She inched her way along the table, her hand covertly searching behind her for something, anything she could use to fend him off.

"As to my being a liar? I told you I would return you in the spring, *if* you wished to go," Veleif continued, as he kicked his boots aside. His leveled gaze followed her every step. "I think once your bruised pride is mended—"

"Bruised pride?" she interrupted, and stamped toward him, incredulous. How dare he accuse her of something so petty, when it was *his* treachery at hand? "You think this is about my pride? You surround yourself with so many lies, Kollsvein, I doubt even you know the truth."

"The truth, my lady wife, is our marriage ensures peace between our people," Veleif ground out.

"We have no marriage, you black-hearted brute! And there will be no peace. Not from me, not from my people, and certainly not from my father! I agreed to none of this, you devil's swine."

Veleif peered thoughtfully into the fire, and for a moment, Æstrid imagined a look of deep hurt crossed his face. He granted her some flexibility for the shock she'd just suffered, but her curses were wearing thin. The threads of his patience were stretched as taut as his trousers, and he already calculated the path to victory.

This was not going to be an enchanted wedding night between blissful lovers. This was going to be war. He sighed and thought to reason with her once more.

"And what of our sons, Æstrid? Where will their allegiances lie?" he smiled sardonically and unfastened the clasp at his throat.

"We'll have no sons!" she screeched in outrage.

"You'll give me a houseful of sons," he threatened between clenched teeth. "They'll rule the most powerful kingdom of the North Seas, and willing or not Æstrid, tonight you'll have no doubts you are my wife in every way." Veleif waved toward the dragon bed as he stood. He tossed the wolf pelt over the back of his chair, and in one fluid movement, stalked toward her.

Every inch the towering warrior, Veleif's nostrils flared as his eyes turned stormy in a wordless challenge. She made his blood boil and his temper flare. He felt his cock lengthen thinking of the lusty sons this spirited wench would bear him. He craved the release that had built these many weeks, with her always so close, and so damned tempting. Tonight he'd have her, and calm the battle fever racing through his veins.

A tiny yelp escaped her as she matched his steps backward from his unquestionable pursuit. Her eyes widened as Veleif edged forward, stripping away his tunic as he came. The powerful muscles of his arms bunched and rippled as he balled his shirt to the floor. Wearing only his trousers, the slabs of bare, bronzed muscle contrasted sharply to the silver torque at his throat and the cuffs at his wrists. They made him appear all the more forbidding.

Æstrid swallowed hard at the sight of his nakedness and remembered the night he'd bedded Rafa and Thorgrima. He was powerful and passionate, and undeniably male. The spiraling fear threatened to be her undoing as she saw his hands reach for the belt holding his trousers.

"Veleif!" she warned, stealing a look over her shoulder to gauge the distance to the table. If she could reach it and find something to defend herself, then she would spirit away to lock herself in her chamber.

"I am not your wife," she insisted, raising her hands to ward him off.

Undeterred, Veleif kept moving toward her, using his wide shoulders and his half-naked presence to guide her path. He was directing her where he wanted, cornering her like tender prey. Æstrid backed into the table. Her hand scrambled behind her, searching in earnest for a weapon.

Veleif paused, suddenly sensing the enormity of her fear. While he fully intended to take advantage of their wedding night, what she needed right now wasn't his passion, but his assurance.

"You are my wife, Æstrid," Veleif purred softly. Thinking to breach her defenses by catching her off-guard, he drew a deep breath and gentled his tone. "But let us put that fact aside for the moment. I've said before, I'm not your enemy."

He inched slowly toward the table, eyeing the jug of wine, instead of her. She moved away toward the far left, keeping as much of table between them as possible. Finally! She almost breathed a sigh of relief as her hand clutched over a short knife. Veleif casually poured two goblets and looked at her.

"Will you share some wine with me?" He extended a cup. Her mind raced as she looked into his molten eyes, too incredulous at first to speak. If Æstrid wasn't so mixed with biting anger and cringing terror, she would have burst into laughter at his attempt.

"Share wine? With you?" Her violet eyes narrowed as she gave a nervous laugh. Veleif shrugged and tossed back the contents. He slowly stalked around the table and Æstrid moved the opposite way, matching his movement step for step. His eyes roamed over her like a caress.

"Your beauty is the stuff of future legend, Æstrid. It is well we rescued you from the cursed Picts."

"Rescued? Only to become a prisoner within your heathen walls!" she wailed and waved her free arm at him.

"I've kept you safe." He looked at her evenly and set the cup aside as he moved closer. "I'll protect you with my life, Æstrid."

She backed away until there was nothing left but the stone wall behind her. Veleif closed the distance between them, but didn't touch her. Instead, his naked shoulders became a barricade. His arms braced the wall on either side of her head, caging her in. The warm, manly scent of him enveloped her senses with something evocative and dangerous.

It pricked her conscience Veleif spoke with such conviction. For a fleeting moment she allowed herself to believe the sincerity of his pledge. Threads of tension stretched tight in her belly as her heart hammered wildly in her chest.

This man had the power to melt her resolve with his touch. And if he kissed her... oh, if he kissed her, her body wouldn't care one whit about his betrayal. His lips could twist her blazing anger into savage passion as quick as a strike of lightning, and the certainty of this fact troubled her.

"Protect me with your life? You'll do well to remember that when you're dangling on the end of my father's sword," Æstrid mocked.

"That day will never come. Your father is many things, but he can be a man of reason. Unlike his daughter, Gunnalf is one to take advantage of his circumstance." Veleif smiled, dark and taunting. Æstrid gasped in outrage.

"You insult me and my family in the same breath. I've never witnessed such arrogance, Kollsvein," Æstrid noted stiffly.

"Not arrogance, Æstrid. Truth," he whispered.

"Truth? You don't know the meaning of the word," Æstrid challenged.

"Think of the advantages you'll have as queen. Think of what Kollsveinholdt brings to your people."

"Thus speaks the mad ravings of a lunatic mind," Æstrid sniffed dismissively. She had to get past him and quit this chamber, but she was no match for him when he stood this close.

"Mad? Yes, my fiery bride. You could drive a lesser man to madness," Veleif's voice dipped low. His breath was hot on her shoulder as his eyes smoldered, seeming to brand her as he spoke. "But the simple truth is when your father learns of our marriage, he'll be thinking about the gain of his herds and ships, and the increase to his wealth."

"Ah! So the truth is out. You thought to take me as your bride to increase your own holdings, Kollsvein." Æstrid's temper spiked sharply as sparks of suspicion flared in her eyes. Her fingers tightened on the knife, and by sheer will she stayed her hand from stabbing him at the affront.

Veleif's lips pressed into a thin line of frustration. He fortified his resolve against simply crushing her in his embrace and carrying her to their bed. The very air between them crackled with raw power. They were two warrior souls, ready to lunge and fight, and his body was screaming from the heavy pressure, needing to find release inside her.

"If I'd so desired I'd have taken Gunnalf's lands long ago," he said tightly. His fingers flexed against the stone as his patience balanced precariously on the precipice of his endurance.

"Then why didn't you?" Æstrid hissed, as she raised her chin.

"Because nothing at Karissonholdt held my interest. Until I saw you," Veleif confessed. Gushing heat sizzled across her skin at his admission. His words were delivered with such sincerity, she almost believed him. He was not only a consummate seducer; his deceit was as boundless as the sea.

"You lie!" Æstrid spat as if she just tasted something foul.

"Think about yourself for once, my lady. Enjoy what my wealth and power can bring you and I'll lay the entire north at your feet. There will be no more cowering in the shadows of your sire, for you or anyone who serves him."

"Forgive me, Kollsvein, but aren't the merits of a husband supposed to be decided upon *before* the marriage?" Æstrid argued. Veleif broke into a wide smile.

"Now is not the time to discuss politics and plans... I have something else in mind. Something more in keeping between a man and a woman..." Veleif drawled leisurely.

She ached to wipe the grin from his face, and dismiss the flash of fire that kindled between them.

"Given a choice, Kollsvein, what makes you think I would chose you?" Æstrid spat bitterly. She felt a surge of triumph as his smile faded and the muscles in his jaw flexed with tension.

"Because what you stir in me is too powerful to be one-sided. Will you deny I stir the same in you?" He gave her a penetrating stare.

"The only thing you stir in me, Kollsvein, is fury," Æstrid quipped.

"The fury of passion perhaps, and yes, your eyes do speak of passion."

"Betrayer," she hurled.

"Bewitched," he countered.

"Deceiver!"

"Devoted."

"Enough!" Æstrid barked. "I will not participate in your mockery." She darted beneath his arm to gain some distance between them, but Veleif's hand snaked out around her waist and he snatched her hard against his chest.

"Veleif," she gasped as the breath left her body with the impact of his embrace. A space of heartbeats passed between them as glittering eyes roamed her face. He appeared to be searching for words and Æstrid never imagined seeing such a look cross the face – he was almost… tender.

"Accuse my methods, Æstrid, for I am guilty and not proud of such ways. But you know the import our union will bring, to your people as well as mine. The fact remains there is passion between us, and that is a luxury among people of our rank."

"I don't want you," she lied.

"You do," he breathed, as his lips found her shoulder. The heat of his bare skin seared through the thinness of her gown, as her raging anger snapped to raging desire. His scent was intoxicating and his voice hypnotic. He was too close, too warm, too… male! She needed distance before all was lost to her body's traitorous response. Æstrid gripped the knife tighter, poised to strike, but he released her abruptly and took a step back. She trembled from the loss of his heat and the confusion raging within her breast as Veleif extended his hand to her.

"Come my *queen*," he said tightly, "a duty most dreaded is best put behind you."

"I have no duty to you, or your devil's lust," she choked out. His eyes narrowed and a smile crooked his lips.

"Yes, your loveliness bewitches a man, Æstrid, until he fair burns with it. If such yearning makes me a devil, then you are most certainly the devil's bride."

"Then burn, my lord devil! Return to the pits of hell from whence you came!" Æstrid darted to the bed and heaved the heavy candle stand laden with a dozen tallows. The wax and flame swelled instantly to a blazing wave.

A curse tore from Veleif's throat as the pelts began to smolder and the fine linens spiked into flames.

Veleif dove for the bed in horror, snatching coverings to smother the fire and coughing against the repelling smoke. Æstrid leapt upon his side and plunged the knife toward his neck. Veleif turned and raised his arm in defense, but not before her blade glanced a long gash across his shoulder.

"You bloodthirsty witch!" He jerked the blade from her hand before she could slash again. Æstrid's knee came up and caught him near the groin as he turned to subdue her.

With a cry of anger, she surged forward and did the only thing she could think of. She butted him on the chin with her forehead. Hard. It was a foolish move, she knew, as she momentarily stunned herself from the pain that shot through her skull. Veleif staggered back from the blow, more surprised than hurt that she'd dazed him.

"By Odin's hand, woman, if it's a fight you wanted..." Veleif growled, his jaw tight with fury. The pause afforded her a precious second to escape, but Æstrid couldn't resist a taunt.

"If I'd wanted a fight, I'd have engaged Berra. A pregnant woman would undoubtedly be more of a challenge." Æstrid rushed past him, but he was larger, faster, and if the rage that glittered in his eyes was any indication – he was much, much angrier.

By all that was holy, Veleif restrained himself from breaking her in two. He charged her like a ram headlong into his rival. Iron-thewed arms snatched about her thighs as Veleif lifted her mid-air. With one quick swoop and a spin, she landed on the bed. Veleif lunged forward before she could flee, and pinned her body beneath his muscled form.

Veleif half-rose and roared as he held the knife above her head. Æstrid screamed, expecting it to be her last, but he drove the knife into her sleeve, straight through the feathered ticks, trapping her arm beneath the blade.

"Tomorrow I'll give you a proper beating for that attempt," he promised hoarsely.

"Take your hands from me, you filthy cur!" She pushed and twisted. Æstrid choked beneath him, gasping for breath as his weight crushed her. The putrid smells of burnt hair mixed with the metallic taste of the blood pouring from his wound, pinched her nostrils from the assault.

"I warned you before, my daring *wife*. You'll need a bigger blade than that to bring me down."

"I'm not your wife." Æstrid sobbed.

"You are my wife!" He growled above her. His face moved inches from hers, his eyes had gone dark like the sea and sparkled with danger. "I'd have no tender bride to be wooed with honeyed words. You're a warrior's queen, Æstrid. It is correct our mating take place upon a bed of fire and blood."

She started to curse him but he smothered her mouth with his, forcing her lips apart, as he thrust his knee between her thighs. Æstrid lurched beneath him, her fingers of her free hand clawed helplessly at his back. Crimson spatters flecked her face. She shoved at his shoulder, only to have her hand skid off, leaving behind a bloody smear. Veleif caught the floundering member in an iron-like grip and pinned her arm above her head.

Curtained behind the dark fall of his hair, their bodies strained and molded, testing for dominance. Veleif's patience was at an end. Like a ship caught on storm-filled seas, he was tossed into the drowning depths of hot desire. He took her lips with abandon, putting everything he was into the message. Dark. Dominant. Powerful. He was war and a sanctuary. A conqueror and defeated, yielding to the frenzied fire snaking through his blood, and tripping voluntarily into the surging whirlpool of no return.

Æstrid didn't know when the denial fled, she could only answer the devouring summons with equally furious demands. He was wild and exotic. Taking. Demanding. Awakening her to a passion so chaotic, the world tilted at the sinful rightness of the moment. Her mouth touched and tasted, lost in the exquisite intensity of his claiming.

Veleif's pressure on her hand lessened, guiding it upward around his neck. Her nails dug into the hard muscle of his shoulder. Æstrid cleaved to him without restraint, explored his skin as her hand wound up into his hair, and pulled him tighter as he swallowed her urgent cries of bliss.

Veleif broke the kiss long enough to search face. His hellish warrior, who had professed her hatred had vanished – replaced with the challenging woman whose eyes were glazed bright with passion. She mewled in protest as a chasm of air wafted between them, and pulled his head down urgently, needing him to take her lips once more.

"I cannot be gentle, Æstrid." Veleif's voice was thick with promise as his eyes all but devoured her.

"Neither can I," she replied harshly. With a surge of strength, she pushed against him with such force, her gown, still staked to the bed, ripped free from her shoulder. Æstrid tumbled with him as he rolled to his back. Veleif pulled the knife that had pinned her sleeve, and hurled it across the room where it landed with a clang in the back of the hearth. Her body splayed on top of his, as her lips curled back with heated lust.

"Do this quickly, Veleif. Before I change my mind," she demanded.

"Quickly, and not so quickly," Veleif rasped and gave her a tight nod. His hand yanked her skirts above her waist. Her violet eyes went wide and a gasp of surprise escaped her, as the soft hide of his breeches pressed against the naked flesh of her thighs. He wound a hand in the tangle of her hair and drew her down to him as his eyes flared to a fervent height. Æstrid met his passion with equal insistence – hot, open-mouthed, and needy for him to end this torment.

Her fingers flexed and tightened, tracing indelible paths along the slabs of muscle across his chest, his sides. Her breath came fast and ragged as Veleif moved heated lips down the slim column of her throat. His hand kneaded and splayed her bottom, urging her down as he surged upward, coaxing her movement against the pressing heat of his manhood into her soft belly.

In one fluid movement, his arms tightened and he rolled them both until she was beneath him once more. His tongue traced her swollen lips before he plunged in again, mimicking his movement with the thrust of his hips.

He freed himself of the encumbrance of his trousers then boldly plunged a finger into her. Æstrid cried out and arched her hips against his questing hand. Veleif moaned deep and male, finding her wet and hot, clenching on his invading hand. His eyes flamed to a fervent height.

With a deep growl in his throat he grabbed the neck of her gown between his teeth and tore it to her waist. Her breasts, bathed in the flickering light, gleamed before him, full and taunting mounds framed by the remnants of her dress.

His mouth dipped, hot and searing against her, laving, tugging, teasing, undaunted in his quest to taste her flesh. Æstrid's thighs tightened around his waist, her inner muscles squeezing, aching for more as she yanked his dark head toward her. He drove another finger inside her and a blistering heat of sheer pleasure rippled across her body as he stroked her intimately, building her desire with aching pressure.

His breath fanned the flames along her skin as he drove her ever higher. She wanted him desperately, drowning in need for whatever this was that he awakened; wanton passion dying and soaring in scorching collision, blotting out the need for anything else but Veleif.

"It's your husband who spills your virgin blood, Æstrid, none other," he rasped thickly against her ear. His arm folded tightly around her in a merciless grip as his lips licked and traced a hot trail against her throat. His fingers slid slowly from her and just as Æstrid moaned in protest, he hooked his hand beneath one knee and drove into her in one vicious thrust.

Æstrid screamed as the white hot pain exploded in her loins. She cursed and swore as tears poured from her eyes thinking Veleif had certainly split her in two. He stayed buried deep within her, holding himself immobile until the muscles on his arms bunched and his skin was slick with sweat. His lips brushed feather light kisses all over her face, her nose, her eyelids, tasting the salt of her tears.

Every heartbeat, every breath seemed to fuel the blinding ache between her thighs. She looked up at him, her eyes clouded with hurt. Veleif cupped her face with hands and tenderly stroked her cheeks with his thumbs. His lips were a breath from hers as he wiped a tear from the corner of her eye. Æstrid frowned in confusion through her watered vision, as Veleif regarded her with an unmistakably compassionate gaze.

"Would that I could spare you this part, love, but trust me, it only happens once," Veleif whispered gently. His eyes glittered molten silver in the firelight, and the truth of the moment washed over her in profound clarity. Where she had before only seen the ruthless barbarian, she now glimpsed the core of the man, considerate, protective and right now, all hers. Her fists carefully eased the grip in his hair as slowly, very slowly, her breath returned.

"Quickly, and not so quickly," Æstrid breathed, suddenly understanding what he'd meant. Veleif murmured intelligible words as he nipped the corners of her lips and the sobering pain began to take flight again on the upward surge of desire.

Her hands roamed over him in awe of this closeness, this intimacy. His kisses returned, as Veleif explored her mouth with unhurried sensuality, banking the fires of the heat between them. Every inch of their bodies touched and slowly he began to move his hips inside her. Æstrid cried out again not with pain, but with the excruciating pleasure that bloomed within. The powerful muscles flexed and thrust, making her moan at the building friction until she thought she could die from the pleasure.

Veleif's control was rapidly failing. He thrust into her again and again, no longer mindful of his lady's pain as the drive to take her consumed him. Withdrawing and driving until the sweat ran down the sides of his face and splashed in droplets upon her skin. His body arched and a cry tore from his throat as drove into her with one last shuddering thrust. He stayed buried inside her, relishing in the final spasms dissipating within the heat of her core as his hands ran over her body in long, soothing strokes. Æstrid shook and trembled beneath his touch, marveling at what just passed between them. Their breath returning to a normal pace and the crackling of the hearth were the only sounds unfurling between them in the silence.

Veleif smoothed her hair from her face, memorizing every detail of her expression, and regarded her in wonder. If their first time with coupling had been so tumultuous and consuming, what would their next one be? Or the next? His fierce, warrior bride. *His.* With her hair tumbled wildly about her shoulders and her eyes glazed with passion's play.

Without a pause, he felt the blood surge to his shaft again, but when he looked down at her quaking thighs, now smeared with blood, he sobered. Gently easing from her, he schooled his ardor, knowing what she needed right now wasn't more lovemaking.

Her eyes followed him as he left the bed, and he couldn't help but smile at the vision she made. Her silky limbs stretched out languidly along the chaos of their bed of blood and smoldering pelts.

A goddess, who'd surely claimed him and made his own strength magnify with the depths of her passion.

Veleif crossed to the basin and washed his head and neck, gently sponging the blood from his shoulder and between his legs. Wetting a clean linen, he returned to the bed and held it out to her. "Seems we both bled this night, my lady."

Her eyes flared as she snatched the cloth from his hand. "How dare you mock me," she glared up at him. Veleif casually braced his arm on the bed, leaning close to her. His smile widened at her irritation.

"And so my hellion returns," he chuckled and traced a finger along her bare shoulder. "I'd never mock you, wife. I only wish to see to your comfort."

Veleif turned away to pour a heavy cup of wine. He returned to her side and she snatched a thick pelt around her nakedness.

"Drink. It will ease some of your pain," he told her gently. She was silently grateful as she took the cup and swallowed back a heavy draught of wine. Veleif pulled the ruined pelts from the bed and cast them aside to join her bloodied dress on the floor. Then he slid into the bed and gathered her firmly against his chest.

"There is one sure way to keep your temper at bay," he mused, as he tucked a pelt securely around her shoulder.

"And what is that?" Æstrid asked.

His bare leg wrapped around hers trapping her beneath him. He traced a finger along her cheek, his voice was warm and rich, and his breath smelled of sweet wine.

"I should make love to you day and night. It seems to only way to see the shrew sufficiently quelled," he whispered and placed a lingering kiss upon her temple. Æstrid met him with teasing eyes of her own and placed tentative hand on his chest.

"Perhaps I'd demand it. If for no other reason than to see the devil within you flee," she countered. He kissed her deeply and Æstrid felt her limbs relax, letting the drowsy feeling claim her.

"I still hate you, Veleif," she yawned sleepily.

"I know you do," he smiled and covered her hand with his. His broad hand rested at the curve of her waist and Veleif began to stroke her hip in hypnotic rhythm. Exhaustion finally claimed her and she drifted off into the warmth beside him.

Veleif let his eyes wander over the patterns in the ceiling as his thoughts eased over every detail of the day. Æstrid lay soft and warm beside him and he couldn't help but wonder at the fierce passion that lay beneath her surface.

A deep pang of guilt plagued him how they'd tricked her to the altar, but then again, she would have never agreed to their union of her own accord. He thought of Halfdan's journey and prayed the man arrived safely at Gunnar's stronghold and delivered the news. With Halfdan's return home, surely Æstrid would soften even further with her father's blessings — if that was to be Gunnalf's reply.

A tiny smile of pride crossed his lips when he thought of what just happened. Never once did she exhibit a coward's way or plead or beg for mercy. She'd fought him as fiercely as any warrior, heeded her own passion and left him little doubt she was a worthy queen.

Nothing about this woman was expected or predictable. She'd come into his life unforeseen, so why would he assume marriage with her would take a traditional path?

With the long, bitter winter settling upon them, he'd have many hours to devote to working backward from here. He'd woo his beautiful wife and win her heart.

# Chapter Nineteen

Æstrid woke still cradled within Veleif's firm embrace. The distant roar of the sea crashing upon the rocky shore below, lulled her into full awareness. By all rights she should be horrified at the events of yesterday, but the lingering effects of Veleif's lovemaking, the echoes of his intimate whisperings of promises for their future, cocooned her in a languid peace as she cautiously studied his profile.

In the dreamy, translucent light glowing through the ice-covered windowpanes above them, her eyes roamed the angles of his face, the curve of those sinful lips, and she couldn't resist touching a fingertip to the pulse on his neck. There were worse husbands she was certain, men who would not be so tender, or swear their protection, or be inclined to hold her through the night.

Veleif shifted lightly in his sleep, his bare legs wrapped familiarly with hers. Æstrid pulled her fingers away quickly, lest she wake him and tried to ponder shame. Strangely, she felt none. Perhaps this thing between them, as fierce and tenuous it was, could blossom into something more? Perhaps, Veleif would come to care for her, treasure her... dare she hope, even to love her?

But such a bond would not be forged at the expense of her pride. Or his. While he didn't need to spend his lifetime in atonement for the deed of their wedding, neither would she cower to his every whim. If they were to build their lives together, they would do so as equals.

Æstrid noticed the fire had burned low in the hearth. Loathe to leave the warmth of the bed, Æstrid slid across him, taking a large pelt with her.

She grimaced as her bare foot met the stone floor and hopped from the bed to the nearest pelt. Wrapping the fur tighter to shield the chill, she stealthily crossed to the hearth and laid more wood upon the glowing coals.

A rattle sounded upon the door followed by a light knock. Æstrid whipped around at the sound, only to find Veleif propped up on his side watching her with a wide grin.

Her heart skipped a beat at his good looks and she vaguely thought it was unfair he look so beauteous so early in the day, while she was certainly unkempt.

The knock repeated upon the door.

"Begone!" Veleif bellowed.

"My prince, I've brought food to break the fast." A muffled female reply urged behind the door.

"Leave us!" he shouted again. Æstrid glanced hopelessly toward the door as she heard the footfalls make a hasty retreat. Her fists clutched the pelt tighter around her shoulders. Surely he didn't intend for them to starve.

"Are you not hungry, Veleif?"

"Yes, but not for food. Come Æstrid, let me warm you." He pulled back the furs invitingly as she gasped at the sight of his naked torso in the full light of day. Her brows shot up and she spun away from him throwing a haughty look over her shoulder.

There was no time to waste letting his boorish manners run unchecked. Besides, she was famished.

"I prefer to warm by the fire." Then she paused and spun back to face him. Veleif was just rising from the bed when her question stopped him.

"What am I to you, Veleif?" She looked him square in the eyes and took a step toward him.

"You're my wife, and my queen," he said dryly, and gave her slight frown. Æstrid's smile transformed to one of exaggerated sweetness, and Veleif suddenly became wary of the change in her tone.

"Not your slave, my lord? Or your prisoner?" Her voice cooed like honey and her expression softened as she took another step closer to the bed.

"No. Of course not," he answered gruffly.

"Of course not," she parroted and smiled. Then her face turned harsh. "Well then, my lord, your *queen* prefers to dress in her own chambers. And I will and break the fast below where I'll find the company far more agreeable."

She stalked to the door to unfasten the latch. Just as her fingers touched the locking pin, two strong hands gripped her shoulders. Æstrid squealed as she was pulled against him and he turned her, holding her upper arms with her feet barely grazing the floor. Curse the gods he was fast! She hadn't even heard him cross the room.

"Release your hold!" She wrenched in his arms, but he held her fast.

"You'll quit this room when I give you leave and not before." His eyes were clear and piercing as he smirked, "and when you curb your waspish tongue." A pit of dread curled deep inside her belly.

"You dream, Veleif," she snapped.

"When you yield, my lady." His gaze dropped to her lips and Æstrid gasped. She regained her bravado and steeled herself against him.

"Then this chamber shall be my tomb, for I'll never yield to you, Veleif, you—"

"Careful Æstrid," he interrupted. Veleif spun her around and pushed her ahead of him back to the bed. "I've found a strong palm applied to an errant backside is a most effective cure for a churlish tongue."

Æstrid whirled, her mouth agape. "You threaten to chastise me?"

He leaned close and snarled. "No Æstrid, I'm promising you. To bed. Before I forget my patience, *wife*."

Despite her anger, Æstrid thought the better of taunting him further and slipped in beneath the furs. Veleif climbed in beside her and ran his hands long and leisurely over her body and admired the velvety touch of her silken skin. Just as Æstrid convinced herself to lay passive beside him, he traced a finger between her breasts, raised on one arm and studied her for a long, quiet moment.

"There will come a time, my loving wife, when I'll touch you and you'll beg me to take you." His hand slid along the curve of her hip.

"I'll never beg anything from you." She shivered and gave him a withering look.

"That's almost a challenge. But one for another day," he pressed light kisses on the corners of her mouth. Æstrid turned her head away but he brought her round with his hand. "You don't resist me, you resist yourself. Listen well, love, there is no shame in taking pleasure."

He bent and brushed her lips with tender pressure, then gently deepened, light and soft. He placed his hand beneath her neck and gently coaxed her toward him. His fingertips brushed her jaw with a reverent touch, as his lips kept plucking hers in tiny kisses.

It seemed he moved over every inch of her lips, light as thistledown, stirring her ardor. She felt a strange spark ignite within her breast and suddenly she wanted more. As if Veleif read her thoughts, his lips parted hers slowly and he brushed his tongue gently into her.

Suddenly lost in the embrace and forgetting their clash of wills, a soft sigh escaped her as her hand crept up behind his neck. Veleif deepened his kiss with her acceptance, and though Æstrid could sense his rising need, she also felt the iron will of his restraint, as he held the full torrent of his passion in check.

"You do not play fair, Veleif." Æstrid moaned.

"I told you before my lady wife, I do not," he chuckled softly.

"Don't think to soften me with your kisses, Veleif," she warned and placed a staying hand upon his chest. His eyes glinted like blue ice, hinting at his mischief.

"No, my sweet vixen, I would not dream of plying you with such temptation."

He moved and deepened, exploring the honeyed cavern of her mouth as his hand reached down until he found her hand, and twined her fingers between his own. She returned his gentle squeeze of assurance with her own fingers. She moaned deeper as his mouth grew more insistent, and she arched into him, her breasts pressing against his naked chest until the peaks were rosy and hard. The warmth of his skin melding with hers soon had her heated, as flames of pleasure licked across her body.

What was he doing to her with this kiss, simple as it was? He stilled his passion and her own seemed to rise, awaking mind and body from their cold reserve of disdain. Her whole consciousness flooded with a warm excitement, the feel, the taste, the smell of him, all acute and fusing into pleasurable arousal. And then, he released her mouth and she surprised herself at the soft moan that escaped her, as a tiny agony welled within her at the loss of his lips.

Veleif peered down into her face. Her eyes had darkened with the newfound passion. A languid moan hummed from her throat, and Veleif continued, lest she break from this trance. He raised her hand entwined with his and slowly kissed each lovely fingertip. Veleif coaxed her fingers open and pressed his lips into her palm. His tongue ran in slow circles, deeply, sensuously as Æstrid moaned beneath the touch. He watched her face flush and her breath quickened between her parted lips.

He closed the space between them again, this time finding her mouth welcoming beneath his own. He languorously explored her and she wound her fingers behind his neck, weaving her hand into his hair. She was yielding helplessly to a will greater than her own, and returning his kiss with a passion she had never known she'd possessed.

Veleif released her slowly, seeming to be undisturbed by what had been for her, a shattering experience. Her body turned and lifted partially from the bed, the fur pelt slipping from her unheeded. Her hand suspended in mid-air, as Æstrid paused before reaching for his shoulder.

Seeing her silent plea, Veleif returned to her mouth again, pressing her beneath him as her hand crept up and caressed the hard plane of his shoulder. Her kiss became more demanding with a scalding heat surging across her body from the primal force he'd awakened.

Veleif turned with her, drawing her up to lay across the length of his body. Æstrid stiffened and her head arched back, her hair spilling about his face like a waterfall. She softened against him. Her breasts crushing on his chest as he took her lips again, driving her to another fevered pitch. The warmth began to suffuse between her legs and his hand moved along her hip, gently pressing her closer to his searing manhood. The ache for him began to build as his tongue plundered her defense.

Veleif slowly pressed her hip, his hand moved lower, caressing and splaying her buttocks until she gasped as the tip of him moved inside. His glacial eyes now hooded with desire, he spoke in a slow, measured tones.

"Take your pleasure, Æstrid. Take as much or as little as you want." Her body trembled as she watched his face. She tightened around him and slowly slid down, testing for the ache but none came. Only a spreading tingling of pleasure starting where he lay inside her and rippled outward across her body. Veleif inhaled sharply as she moved lower, testing the width and pressure of him. His eyes half-closed in pleasure and Æstrid trembled uncontrollably at the wondrous sensations coursing through her.

His hand on her hip eased her forward and she gasped at the slick friction between them. Tiny beads of sweat broke out in his forehead and she realized it was taking all the control this powerful warrior possessed to hold himself back. Æstrid looked into his eyes and smiled softly for it was this moment she knew beyond a doubt Veleif was a man who pledged his word.

She lowered onto to him quicker and watched him as a moan escaped his lips. He was halfway inside her now, filling her, stretching her, and her own breathing became more rapid. The pain from the night before, now a distant memory, rapidly dissolved to a burning need for more of him. Her nails dug into his shoulders and she leaned down and nipped his lower lip.

"Take me, Veleif. I cannot." A low groan sounded in his throat as his arms came around her and he thrust up quickly. Æstrid cried out in pleasure as he filled her, withdrew and plunged into her again and again.

He was no longer the fierce Norse king, her sworn and despised enemy. He was simply Veleif, hard and male, pleasuring her, making her moan as he touched a sweet spot deep inside her over and over, propelling her upward through waves of pleasure to a place beyond all reason.

She watched his chest swell and his breathing rapid as his hands moved harder on her in time with his thrusts. Veleif was beyond any control he himself had imposed and the knowledge made her heady, for she knew it was all for her. She'd driven him to this state.

Veleif was groaning with each stroke and her voice matched his own. He thrust upward so hard, his hips lifted from the bed, taking her so deep Æstrid could only throw herself upright and arch backward. A scream of pleasure tore from her lips as a thousand shattering stars burst all over her. Veleif followed soon afterward, shooting hot and deep into her as his hands imprisoned her hips, pulling her down to take his seed.

Æstrid ground down onto him, her eyes glazed and dreamy as soft moans of pleasure interrupted her ragged breathing. Veleif pulled her down to his chest, holding her firm and took her mouth once more. He rolled again, taking her beneath him and Æstrid felt him twitching inside her.

"Lie to me, my little wife, and tell me that I hurt you," Veleif whispered softly in her ear.

"Not... as much." Æstrid replied breathlessly as a heated blush crept to her face. His fingers lazily traced her breastbone as if in awe of the perfection of her skin.

"It's fitting a woman of your fire and spirit should take such pleasures equal to your passion. I promise your nights will be anything but boring." He kissed her neck making her shiver again as he held unmoving inside her. Æstrid pushed at his shoulder until he took his weight from her and levered up on his elbows.

"But it's daylight," she stated. Veleif glanced up toward the windows above the bed as if seeing it for the first time. His lips slowly suffused into a smile.

"Then there will be no secrets between us," Veleif chuckled. He stroked her hair, marveling at the glorious, silky mass that spilled across the bolsters. He took her mouth again and before she could protest, pressed her deeper into the furs.

# Chapter Twenty

Æstrid fell into a rhythm in the cold and bitter weeks of winter at Kollsveinholdt. Gudney and Ingulfrid had delivered healthy, squalling sons soon after the wedding feast, and Æstrid had been present to assist in their births.

The women whispered praise for her labors, as Æstrid gazed into the cherubic faces of each newborn. When she proudly laid them in the cribs Veleif and the other men had built, Æstrid felt a surge of accomplishment bloom in her breast. Here at Kollsveinholdt, she was appreciated and cherished.

She oversaw everyone's comfort and not even the smallest detail escaped her. When Arnor spent two long days and nights tending an orphaned calf, she surprised him one evening with an oversized platter of sweetened breads bathed in honey, for his efforts.

Æstrid and the others chuckled with delight as the great Viking was humbled by her gift. They all agreed, through much mirth and ribbing, they'd never seen such a sight as Arnor relishing each succulent bit with hearty moans and grunts of appreciation.

A few days of brutal winds descended upon them, making it impossible to leave the security of the keep. There would be no shipbuilding or even straying outside, until this latest storm had passed.

Devoid of any work or duty, Veleif saw the opportunity to ensconce himself and his bride in their chamber, and made it explicitly clear not to be disturbed until the temperatures climbed to a bearable height. He instructed Asa to make sure food and drink were left outside the door and he himself would retrieve when he wanted.

In between his bouts of lovemaking, which left Æstrid breathless and content, Veleif would simply lie with her tucked under the crook of his arm.

She reveled in the sound of his deep voice as he spoke to her of Kollsveinholdt, his parents and told her stories of his childhood.

He shared with her tales of their travels and trade, often making her prone to bouts of laughter, usually involving some mishap from Halfdan, where he and Arnor would come to rescue.

He listened patiently as Æstrid shared her own adventures with Leidolf and the life and people of Karissonholdt.

Lying before the fire and quivering at the things he'd just done to her, she traced her fingertips along his sweat-dampened skin.

Æstrid wondered about this man.

He plied her well, softened her with passion's touch and taken her to heights unknown. He had carried her closer to the fire and laid her tenderly upon the furs. As he'd kissed her body from head to toe, he'd paused, lifting her hips to his mouth and sipped her slowly, worshipfully, until his tongue made her body wrack with pleasure. Her cries had echoed about the room as over and over he took her to the hilt of bliss.

Now that her passion was thrice spent, she could only marvel weakly at what he'd done.

She'd seen his many moods, and knew he cared a great deal for those around him. Still, was it possible this man could show her such joys and not feel even the smallest speck of tenderness toward her when they were out of bed? And how long before this man of seemingly insatiable passion would grow tired of her?

Veleif seemed to sense her mind was uneasy.

He curled behind her, and stroked her bared hip leisurely, as they watched the dancing coals in the hearth. His lips buried at her neck just beneath her nape.

"Your mind strays from here. What thoughts plague you, wife?" He kissed her gently.

"Will Rafa and Thorgrima share your bed?"

Veleif looked down at her in surprise. It was a curious question to ask, after he'd just made love to every decadent inch of her.

"Are you a jealous woman, Æstrid?" Veleif frowned.

Icy fingers clenched her heart as Veleif had responded with a denial, but answered her with a question of his own.

"No, I only desire fair warning when you do so, as those nights I would prefer to sleep alone."

"You'll never sleep anywhere but by my side." He moved his fingers over the smooth curve of her shoulder.

"But your women?' she frowned at him over her shoulder.

"My *women?*" he questioned in confusion. A hard rapping on the door broke his retort. Veleif growled low in his throat as he'd left explicit instructions not to be disturbed.

"Does no one in Kollsveinholdt heed my orders?" Without bothering to don his clothes, Veleif tore open the door to vent his wrath upon whoever dared to interrupt. It was fortunate Thorliek sought him out, for anyone else would have cowered beneath his blackened rage.

"Halfdan and Irik have returned. They wait below," Thorliek said, as he swallowed nervously. Veleif's anger softened somewhat and he nodded to the elder. "I'll join you shortly."

Veleif dressed quickly, loathe to have Æstrid leave the chamber but she would not be dissuaded from news of her father. They entered the hall together, and saw Halfdan, Arnor and Thorliek in front of the fire.

Halfdan sat barely upright in a chair, and Irik was stretched prone on the floor. Both men were sodden, bedraggled messes, and Irik lay unmoving.

When they approached, Halfdan rose unsteadily to his feet, and Arnor supported him under his arm.

Æstrid gasped when she saw them and broke away from Veleif.

She huddled close to Irik and placed her ear to his lips. His breath was shallow, but he still lived. Both men's beards and brows were crusted with ice. Their faces were pale and a faint blue tinge circled Irik's mouth.

"Why did you not call me sooner? This man is near death." She hissed angrily as sparkes flew from her eyes.

Arnor shifted uncomfortably under her scrutiny and Thorliek merely shrugged.

"Oh, you men!" Æstrid growled, "I pray I'm never subjected to your tender care! Rafa! Thorgrima!" Æstrid brushed past the group and darted toward the kitchen.

Echoes of clattering dishes and scuffling feet over Æstrid's crisp but muffled tones, rapidly followed her disappearance to the kitchen.

A shivering Halfdan cast a worried glance toward Veleif and Arnor.

"My wife," Veleif stated.

"Your queen," Arnor said at the same time. Both men simply shrugged their shoulders, yet Halfdan couldn't dismiss an ominous sense of foreboding.

A rapid stream of people poured from the kitchen with Æstrid urging them close behind.

Rafa bent to Halfdan's feet and began to unwrap his boots, still cold and stiff with ice. Before he could protest, a steaming mug of wine and herbs was thrust into his hand.

Several pairs of hand pulled and pushed his clothes, and a soft wool blanket was placed about his shoulders, followed by a thick bear pelt. Veleif stood in astonishment witnessing Æstrid's quick attention and brusque directions.

His new bride, it seemed, was born to command.

"Arnor, more pelts. Lay them here in front of the fire. Thorgrima, remove his boots. Nar, fetch more heated wine from Asa. Rafa, bring hot food for Halfdan."

When Arnor laid the pelts in front of the fire, the violet eyes turned up to Veleif. "Veleif, Arnor move him there. Thorgrima, help me remove his clothes."

Halfdan tossed back another mug of hot, herbed wine as Rafa plied his hair and beard with dry linens. He was already feeling the warmth return to his numbing limbs and his vision clearing from the bitter cold. He watched Æstrid and Thorgrima tend to Irik, praying to the gods they would be able to save him.

Veleif's face was deep with worry as Æstrid cradled Irik's head and held a cup of heated wine to his lips. Stripped of his frozen garments, the man's color started to return but he had yet to waken.

He bent to Irik and took the cup from her, forcing the brew down his throat. After managing to get him to swallow, the man finally sputtered and coughed and Veleif favored her with a dazzling smile.

"A wave took him, Veleif, not ten feet from shore. I was only able to grab his arm and pull him behind me until I could gain some ground to the beach," Halfdan croaked weakly. "I carried him up here, though I feared he was already dead."

Irik blinked his eyes open slowly, and stared at Æstrid in dazed confusion. The firelight haloed behind her hair and he failed to recognize the beautiful face in front of him.

"My journey is complete then, for I have surely arrived in Valhalla." His voice was hoarse and raspy, as he spoke in wonder.

Everyone broke out in laughter and even the worried faces who appeared in the hall, softened in smiles of relief.

Veleif squeezed the man's shoulder and Irik turned to him with a jolt.

"Your journey is not complete, Irik. Apologies, my friend, but you're still alive," Veleif informed him.

"Veleif! But who is…" he turned back to Æstrid.

"The lady, Æstrid, Irik. My wife and your queen," Veleif said proudly.

"By the gods," he whispered weakly. "Apologies, my lady."

Æstrid smiled at him and Irik was dazzled yet again.

"You eat and rest, Irik. You'll stay here until your strength returns. Then we'll move you where Thorgrima can see to your care," she said softly.

Thorgrima's face appeared beside Æstrid, and Irik had not remembered her as being so beautiful. The blonde hair seemed to glow around her shoulders and even his weakened state, Irik could not imagine a more fortunate fate.

He grabbed the front of Veleif's tunic in a weakened grip.

"My prince, are you certain this is not Valhalla?"

Everyone laughed again and Halfdan turned to the men.

"The boat?"

"It is secured, Halfdan." Arnor placed a reassuring hand on his shoulder. Halfdan shook his head in disbelief and tried to stand, but Thorliek pressed him back.

"There is a chest aboard. It must be brought at once."

Two men dragged the wooden chest close to Halfdan's feet and all eyes faced him with curiosity. The man's shoulders visibly lowered in relief. "It would seem a cruel jest to sail to Karissonholdt and back, only to be claimed not ten feet from my own shore."

Veleif rose and helped Æstrid to her feet, leaving Irik in Thorgrima's care. She evaded his hand and stood stiffly beside him as she waited tensely for her father's news.

Æstrid wrestled with the sudden tangle of emotions. Veleif was becoming more in her eyes than she wanted to admit. She could not deny her softened heart. Even though his methods of wedding her still chafed, she did not wish her father to wage a war upon him or his people.

She was starting to care for them and despite it all, these days surrounded with warmth and love were among the happiest she ever had.

"What news do you bring from Gunnalf?" Veleif said, with his arms crossed on his chest. Now that his men were assured to survive and sufficiently thawed, he was eager to hear the news.

"Gunnalf Karisson is a most stubborn man," Halfdan frowned, "it was three days we waited before he granted us audience. You were right to send only the two us, however. More men and Gunnalf would have taken it as a threat."

Veleif gestured to Nar indicating to bring him a cup of ale. Halfdan was never good at getting to the point quickly, and if he was interrupted, the man would start his tale from the beginning again.

If he wanted to know if he and Æstrid were united with a blessing, he would have to wait.

Veleif sipped his ale as he listened to Halfdan describe the hall at Karissonholdt, the food, and the women. Finally, he explained with great detail, meeting Gunnalf.

"He is a man as large as Arnor, with a fierce mien and heated temper." Halfdan glanced at Æstrid. "My apologies, my lady, if I offend."

"No need, Halfdan," Æstrid assured him. Her father was an imposing man. Veleif noticed how carefully she schooled her stony countenance as Halfdan had spoken of her home. No doubt Æstrid missed her people.

"Now where was I?" Halfdan stroked his beard in thought.

"A heated temper," Arnor quipped with irritation. He silently wondered how Halfdan did not find his neck run through with a sword at Karissonholdt. The man took over long to tell a story, and it didn't sound like Gunnalf was a man of patience.

"Irik told him of how we found his son and you as well, my lady, about your near sacrifice by the cursed Picts. He presented Gunnalf with the bracelet stolen from the boy's arm as proof and Gunnalf remained silent.

"He could only stare at it for a long time. It was then he asked if his daughter, you, my lady, had been killed as well.

"When Irik and I assured him you were not, he flew into a rage. He pointed a sword to Irik's throat demanding to know what ransom was required.

"When we told him none, that you wanted to unite the tribes without bloodshed between us, the man flew into a greater rage and drove his sword into the ground near Irik's feet.

"He demanded more proof that your offer was true and sliced his palm along the edge of his blade. He made Irik do the same and swear a blood oath that this was no trick. And after they clasped hands as brothers, Gunnalf retreated from the hall, telling us he would give his answer soon.

"Well our quarters improved after that, but Gunnalf remained closeted away. Whispers among the household said he took to his chamber and refused food or drink through the next two nights."

Æstrid was not surprised at this news. Her father sometimes took to meditative bouts when faced with a decision of importance.

Veleif drained his third ale as he listened with half an ear.

Halfdan described the details of Gunnalf's chamber, down to the arrangement of the pelts upon the king's bed, where he and Irik had been summoned on their third night.

Arnor, he observed, was on his fifth ale, and was also placating his strained patience with a mouthful of Æstrid's bread.

"Gunnalf kicked this chest to us. He said it was small payment to the man who avenged the murder of his son. He would be honored to have you accept it, my prince, as dowry to the lady Æstrid.

"He said, and again, apologies my lady. He was sorry he did not have a chest big enough for a dowry that would begin to compensate you, my prince. He said," Halfdan swallowed hard. "He said even if he drained all the silver in Karissonholdt, it would not be enough to put up with a lass of her temperament."

Halfdan looked contrite at the admission, and his color deepened as Arnor sprayed ale at the news.

"The devil you say!" Æstrid fumed.

Veleif rubbed his palm across his face to hide his smile, as Arnor sputtered and wiped his tunic. Halfdan cleared his throat and continued after an encouraging nod from Veleif.

"Gunnalf ensured us he will arrive as soon as the weather breaks and discuss all the details of uniting us to one kingdom with you, in person. He also added…" Halfdan glanced cautiously at Æstrid, and he paled.

"Careful, Halfdan," Æstrid warned. "I'm not above seeing to your recuperation personally."

Halfdan took a fortifying gulp of wine.

"He added you should make haste, Veleif. For now that his son is gone, and his daughter is no longer of his house, he requires a grandchild very soon to assure his bloodline remain intact."

Veleif stood silent for a moment, wondering why Halfdan could not have just said that first, and spared them all unnecessary details. It was Arnor's hand clapping him on the shoulder that broke him from the daze.

Æstrid sat down on a nearby bench, visibly shaken.

Thorliek moved to her side and placed a comforting arm on her shoulder. Though he himself was thrilled at the news and what it meant for them all, Veleif wasn't so certain Æstrid was resolved with her father's blessing.

Arnor opened the chest and Veleif was taken aback at the generous amount of silver it contained. He stepped forward and clasped Halfdan heartily. "My everlasting thanks Halfdan, for the journey you made and on behalf of your queen as well."

"Somehow I do not think she shares your joy, Veleif." Halfdan glanced at Æstrid sitting and staring at her hands folded in her lap.

Æstrid was deep in thought.

Her fate was sealed.

Her father was more concerned with Leidolf's death. He cared nothing for her, but only that his wretched line to be bought and sold for a chest of silver. Both Veleif and her father had brought her to this end.

She was his wife in truth, and while she could be saddled with a husband who could never measure the strength or compassion of Veleif, yet her lack of choice in the matter still chafed her pride.

Besides, the riches of the chest her father had sent, seemed well enough to placate the ruler of Kollsveinholdt.

She finally met his eyes and he could read neither sadness nor joy in them, just an eerie calm that he found most unsettling.

"What say you, Æstrid? This good news of your father's blessing." He spoke across the room.

All eyes turned to her and she stood up and smoothed the front of her gown.

Veleif swallowed preparing for the worst, and cursed. Just as he was gaining ground with his bride, her next words would probably have them at odds for weeks. He was not eager to return to their warring ways.

"Blessing? Is that what it is? I've seen more compassion and joy witnessed between shepherds trading sheep. Please don't ask my opinion of your dealings now, Kollsvein. I am once again, insulted you'd pretend to care."

She turned and left them all staring in bewilderment as she left the hall.

Arnor was the one who dared break the silence, but only when Æstrid was well out of earshot.

"Mayhap it would have been easier to war with Gunnalf," he mused as he regarded his horn of ale.

Veleif shot him a cold stare and snorted.

His mood was sour that the woman he'd come to care for was... hurt. And it was he who'd brought her this pain.

Veleif knew his bride would shun any attempts of comfort and he had a sudden need to release his angst.

Besides, Arnor's jest was ill-timed.

"What say you Arnor? Let us go to hunt."

With one hand gripping his ale, and the other poised inches from his mouth, about to devour Æstrid's infamous bread, Arnor half-shouted. "In this weather?"

"Yes! I fear you've grown soft with all this women's coddling." Veleif snarled and stalked away.

Arnor stuffed a few more loaves in his mouth and spied Halfdan, who was smiling up at Thorgrima's doe-eyed care.

"Women!" Arnor snorted and followed in Veleif's footsteps.

# Chapter Twenty-One

"You fear *I* have gone soft?" Arnor squatted over Veleif, with his great hands splayed upon his thighs, looking down at his prince. Arnor shook his head, frowning at him as Veleif tried to stifle the moans of agony coming from his bleeding thigh.

Not two paces from them, the small black bear lay dead on its side, Veleif's axe still sticking from its chest. Arnor grimaced at the snow, the puddle of red growing larger before his eyes, as he was trying to discern who was bleeding more – Veleif, or the bear.

"Can you stand?" Arnor asked in an impatient tone.

"Don't you think if I could stand, I already would be?" Veleif gritted beneath the pain. The bear had turned to strike in defense and caught Veleif's thigh with its claws before he'd been able to strike it down. It was his own fault, for being too brash, too insistent to attack the quarried prey, too intent on forgetting the look of hurt on Æstrid's face.

Arnor peered closer at the pulsing wound and drew off his belt. As he wrapped it about Veleif's upper thigh and drew it tight he said, "It seems the gods have blessed you, Veleif. If that bear had better aim, I think Gunnalf would be denied his wish for grandchildren."

Despite his waning consciousness, Veleif let loose a string of oaths, including insults to Arnor's immediate and all of the man's previous ancestors. Arnor scowled back and secured the belt tighter, seeing the blood begin to slow.

"My apologies, Veleif, but it will be easier for both of us this way." Arnor balled his fist. The last thing Veleif heard was a great crack of thunder, before his universe burst into a thousand stars.

Arnor wrenched the axe free from the bear's chest and tucked it into Veleif's belt. Then he hauled the man over his shoulder and paused, looking back at the bear. The meat and hide seemed too much to waste, but Arnor knew by the time he returned, wolves would have it all but finished.

With a heaving sigh, he lifted one of the paws and dragged the bear behind him, drudging his way across the snow back to return to the keep.

When Arnor was in sight of the village, he heard a shout and then saw the boy Arnkel, run toward his cottage. Moving forward between the drifts, puffing clouds of breath under his double burden, Arnor pressed on with renewed vigor.

There was no great distance remaining, but Arnor was unsure of the fact that Veleif had not stirred was a good sign or a bad one.

He hadn't hit him very hard.

Within minutes he saw half a dozen men streaming out and running toward him. Arnor breathed a sigh of relief and finally released the bear's paw. He'd make better time now, without dragging the beast behind him.

Oresti and Slothi reached him first. The brothers were the two fastest runners in the village and Arnor was not surprised they reached him well before the others.

"By the gods, Arnor! Is Veleif dead?" Oresti asked seeing the blood covering Arnor's front.

"I don't think so," Arnor shrugged, and spun around so the others could check him.

Slothi's face was deep with worry as he lifted Veleif's head by the hair and peered into his prince's ashen face.

"He yet lives, Arnor, but for how much longer, I know not." Slothi's voice was grim.

"Then you two bring the bear so I may get him to the lady Æstrid quickly," Arnor ordered. Four other men joined the group, and despite their attempts to help carry Veleif to the keep, Arnor would not release him. It took two men to drag the bear, and they could only marvel at Arnor's great strength. The big Viking once again solidified his reputation he was undoubtedly the strongest among them all.

"Oresti, Slothi, run ahead and alert the lady Æstrid her lord's been hurt. But I warn you men, be gentle in telling the news," Arnor boomed. They both swallowed and nodded and dashed toward the keep. Arnor did not envy them to be the first to face Æstrid's wrath.

By the time they reached the entrance, Arnor had regaled the group with a great tale of Veleif's glorious fight with the bear. He felt their tension ease as his story grew wilder with each step.

"Veleif and the beast had stumbled across each other in a fine clearing on the wood. The bear asked Veleif who he was and he proudly announced he was the king of Kollsveinholdt and commander of its ships. The bear scoffed and said he was king of all the wood, from here to the mountains across the sea, and Veleif could not pass without paying his weight in silver as a toll.

"The two kings circled each other, each one bargaining to yield the path. It was only when the bear began to insult Veleif, the negotiations were doomed to end. But our king, being the generous lord he is—and the more intelligent—recognized the bear as no king like him, but simply a coarse and crude renegade of the wood.

"Veleif had offered the bear to leave in peace, but the bear would have none of it, and began insulting our lord more deeply. He swiped at Veleif in the face, hence the darkening bruise on his jaw...

"The creature rose to his hind legs and swore an oath he would come and terrorize our village, stealing all the children from their beds, and make of them a hearty snack. Well, when the foolish bear threatened all of Kollsveinholdt... that was when Veleif's diplomacy ended. The arrogant bear sealed his fate.

"Veleif lifted himself from the ground, in such a rage as I've not witnessed before, and hurled his axe. It flew so swift and true, the bear could not even see it before it cleaved his chest and brought the beast to the ground in one swift blow."

Gasps of awe and praise escaped the men as they listened intently to Arnor's tale.

"But he stood too close, and the bear caught him in the leg with his massive claws, as he tried to reach for Veleif, just before death found him."

The appreciative ah's that flowed through the group had Arnor smiling when he reached the top of the steps. That smile was short lived, as the doors were torn open and he faced Æstrid, her frantic face paled when she saw the rash of blood covering Arnor's tunic.

"By Odin's mercy, Arnor! Tell me he is not dead!" Her eyes went bright with tears and she scurried around him, cradling Veleif's face.

"He lives." Arnor's brows lifted at her reaction. For all his strength and all his years, he still had yet to understand women.

"Take him up to his chamber quickly that we may tend his wounds." She ran ahead of him, barking orders of what was needed—hot water, linens, herbs and wine, medicines they kept in the kitchens.

Everyone in the hall rushed to do her bidding. Arnor smiled widely as her last command from the top of the stairs was to bring a hearty plate of food for Arnor and a cask of ale to wash it all down.

Arnor laid Veleif down upon his great dragon bed, as gently as the man was able. Thorliek, Irik, and Halfdan rushed in as well, along with a press of people carrying items Æstrid had ordered.

She surveyed him quickly and whipped around to Arnor, her hand pulling his short sword from his belt before he could stop her, Æstrid slit the hide on his breeches, cutting them away to fully expose his wound.

Three long, gaping gashes crusted with blood and still seeping brought a gasp from her lips. She barked to the men to give them room so Thorgrima might help her remove the rest of his clothes. Halfdan placed a hand on Arnor's bicep and guided him backward with a nod of respect.

The fire was stoked higher and they soon had Veleif stripped down. Thorliek and Æstrid's heads bent together in deep discussion as Thorgrima, joined by Rafa, cleaned Veleif's wound.

"This is all for naught if we cannot get the bleeding to halt," Thorliek pronounced, worriedly.

"I fear to remove the belt, lest the rest of his blood pump out of him." Æstrid's voice was thick with worry and she bit back the tears that stung the back of her throat. She never imagined seeing Veleif in such a state.

"We could remove his leg and save the man." Thorliek suggested, his voice tinged with sadness.

"No Thorliek. I do not think Veleif would care to lose his leg. I think we will help him fight for it yet, and by Odin's mercy, we save the man as well."

"Already the wound grows dark," Rafa pointed out. "If the infection spreads…"

Æstrid blinked back the tears and wished their words were not true, but she could see the evidence for herself. Her mind raced and she clenched her fists in frustration. She tended her father, her brother and other men of her village, but she had never faced an injury as grave as this.

Then she remembered once, her father's side slashed deep from the cut of a sword, accidentally swung in practice. Maedge, the old woman who taught her the healing arts, had shown her how to heat a knife and effectively cauterize his wound.

Æstrid glanced down at her arms and noticed how quickly they had healed from the stinging salt spray of the ocean, but left hardly a reminding scar from her time with the cursed Picts.

"It is too deep to stitch," Thorgrima said softly.

"His wound will not need stitching." Æstrid said with finality. She explained the process to them and they winced in reluctant agreement, though Rafa was hard-pressed to believe Veleif would survive such treatment.

When Æstrid bathed his wounds in warmed salt water, Veleif moaned and tossed but did not wake from his unconsciousness. It was when she took Veleif's knife and heated the blade to glowing, she ordered Irik, Arnor and Halfdan hold down his shoulders and legs.

"Whatever you do, do not let him move. Your prince may be strong, but you're three against one," she ordered.

All of them exchanged worried glances and Thorliek loosened the belt about Veleif's thigh. The bleeding started again, but was nowhere near the flood they expected. Rafa paced nervously at the far end of the bed, wringing her hands, until Æstrid assured her all would be well. Her words seemed to soothe the men as well, but Æstrid's stomach knotted in turmoil.

She smoothed away the hair from Veleif's forehead and Arnor was puzzled at her tender ministrations. Despite their feuds and battles, he had no doubts the woman loved Veleif beyond her admissions.

"You told me once, my lord, a dreaded duty is best put behind you." She looked up into the faces of his worried men and her heart seemed to rip in two as she touched the first long gash with the heated blade.

Veleif woke from his oblivion as the bellowing scream of pain tore from his throat.

"Hold him!" Æstrid cried as the men struggled to still his thrashing limbs. Their arms bulged and strained as they forced him to the bed, their breath heaving. Even Arnor's great strength could barely hold Veleif back.

His eyes shot open, glazed with pain as she seared the next gash. Tears sprung from her eyes and the stench of his roasted flesh burned her nostrils. The howls of Veleif's anguish choked them all, but before Æstrid sealed the third gash, thankfully Veleif fainted away.

Shaking, Æstrid wiped the blade and set it aside as Thorliek inspected the wounds closely.

"The bleeding has stopped, my lady." Irik placed a steadying hand on her shoulder and Halfdan looked at her with grateful eyes.

"I fear with even my warrior's ways, Æstrid, I could not have done that to him," Halfdan admitted. They watched her smear the leg with a creamy mixture and the women finished wrapping the leg with clean strips of linen bandages.

Æstrid had a skin of snow brought to her and placed it next to his carefully propped leg. She said a silent prayer hoping the cold would ease some of his pain of the burn. Thorliek pronounced there was nothing left for them to do except wait and see how he fared throughout the night.

Arnor left to clean away the blood and refresh his clothes, Irik and Halfdan brought more chairs and were hesitant to leave the chamber. Below in the hall, it seemed everything moved in silence. No one spoke more than was needed and everyone held a breath of apprehension, worried for Veleif's health.

Æstrid smoothed away Veleif's hair again. He was so still and so pale. If only his eyes would open and he would speak. Even to hear him utter a string of oaths would sound like the sweetest music to her ears.

# Chapter Twenty-Two

Two days Æstrid worked tirelessly by his side, changing the bandages on his leg and applying soothing unguents to his wounds she mixed herself. Since Æstrid steadfastly refused to leave Veleif for any reason, Arnor joined her in the evenings to pass the time. Tonight, he regaled her with his tale of Veleif and the bear king.

When he finished telling his account, he peered at Æstrid cautiously over the rim of his horn, waiting to hear her praise for the story. Æstrid leaned forward with her chin propped on her elbow and wore a deep scowl. It was almost enough to make him lose his appetite.

Almost.

"So that is what happened, Arnor?" she asked suspiciously, and raised a brow.

"Yes," he smiled, and wiped his lips with the back of his hand.

"There is one thing that puzzles me about your account," Æstrid mused. Arnor raised his horn again and took what he considered to be a fortifying draught. "The bear king all but mauled Veleif, and we've seen the evidence of such."

"He was most fearsome," Arnor assured her.

"Certainly so. Yet I find it hard to believe the creature would ball his paw into a giant fist and strike him in the face. Surely, he would have kept his claws outstretched and sought to mar him instead?"

"Well… perhaps it did not happen exactly as I said…" Arnor shifted uncomfortably.

"You struck him didn't you?" Æstrid prodded softly, with a slight smile playing about the corners of her lips.

"Only to render him unconscious. To ease his pain while I carried him back. He's lucky I did not break his jaw and tarnish his pretty face," Arnor defended gruffly.

Æstrid touched a dampened cloth to Veleif's jaw and shook her head. She hid her smile as she spoke.

"I understand your reasons, Arnor, but I cannot agree with your methods. And while you surely saved his life, I think you should serve some punishment for striking your prince."

"You jest!" Arnor scoffed.

"No sweet breads for you one week should be punishment enough," Æstrid announced. She heard his gasp of outrage and caught his horrified expression from the corner of her eye. "In fact, no bread for you at all, Arnor. No warm, soft bread, baked fresh and golden from the ovens, spread with honey and berry jam…" her voice trailed off as Arnor's mouth watered.

"I think you are over tired," Arnor grumbled beneath his beard. Nothing disturbed him more than the thought of banishment from the bread now coming from Kollsveinholdt's kitchens. He thought to soften her with an offer of kindness. "Why don't you rest in the adjoining chamber? I'll keep watch over him."

Æstrid chuckled and piled some pelts into Veleif's great black chair that had been pulled to the bedside. She settled in as if to sleep there. "No Arnor, my place is here until he wakes. And don't think to win me over with your feigned concern."

"You and Veleif are well suited. A more stubborn pair I've never seen." Arnor shook his head.

"Now you are the one who jests, Arnor." Æstrid's eyes twinkled at him.

"It is what all of us said when suggesting he take you as wife on winter solstice. Veleif was so immovable at first, I think it took two, no three full casks of ale to bring him around. He wanted to wait until Halfdan and Irik returned with your father's blessing before you wed."

"What?" Æstrid gripped both of the arms of the chair with her hands. "Veleif sent those men to my father?"

"I've said too much," Arnor frowned, then glanced over at her, "and the details I do not remember."

Æstrid twined her fingers together in her lap. "Perhaps… four days without the bread, instead of a week would prompt your memory?"

Arnor shook his head.

"Three?" Æstrid asked sweetly.

"I fear it was so long past, I don't recall the details. But perhaps Veleif is not the tyrant you think he is? And if you look close, you will see he cares for you, beyond the simple protection of your being. A luxury little found in the union between two houses. And I think, you care for him as well."

"You overstate yourself, Arnor."

"Perhaps," Arnor laughed, "but I am not blind. This thing between the two of you, it bodes well for Kollsveinholdt. A united kingdom will need a strong lord, and an equally strong lady to thrive."

"Thank you, Arnor," Æstrid sighed.

"But tell me true, would you stay at my side day and night if I were so injured?"

"Of course," Æstrid answered quickly.

"Then I consider myself fortunate, Æstrid that you care for all of us with equal diligence." Arnor laughed loudly then shook his head again as Æstrid shifted uncomfortably in the chair.

"Sleep and calm your fears. I'll wake you if he stirs."

"Are you always so forthright in your observations?" Æstrid shifted down in the chair and stifled a yawn behind her hand.

"Somehow I think you would have me no other way," Arnor smiled.

"Tell me the story again, Arnor… of Veleif and his defeat of the bear king…" Æstrid's eyes fluttered closed as Arnor's deep voice regaled his tale once again.

### ###

"My lady, Veleif is awakened." Thorgrima shook her shoulder gently. Æstrid pushed her hair from her face and shot up straight in bed. She glanced around and found she was in the adjoining chamber. That treacherous Arnor had more than likely carried her here when she fell asleep.

Æstrid ran into the chamber and found him awake. He looked pale and weak, but his eyes were open and seemed to flare as his gaze swept her from head to toe.

"Where is everyone? Why are you alone?" she demanded frantically and rushed to his side. Veleif took her hand in his and pressed the back of it to his lips. When he looked up at her his piercing eyes were hot and liquid, clearer blue than any sky she had ever seen.

"I sent them all away, Æstrid," he told her, and gently pulled her arm until she sat on the bed next to him. Her hand touched his brow and she found no fever there, in fact upon seeing him closer, his color was much improved. Her pulse beat rapidly as his hand crept up her arm and his fingers rested at the back of her neck.

"I know what you did for me, my lady wife." He studied her lips before he met her eyes again.

"I hardly think you know what any of us did, Veleif. You fainted away."

"Irik and Halfdan told me of your healing. Thorliek and Arnor told me of your courage."

"Ah, such traitors we have amidst these halls." A smile quirked about her lips.

"Yes," he chuckled. "I fear I'll never grow tired of their honest treachery, regaling me tales of your brave care."

His hand pulled her closer and the first touch of his lips were gentle, brushing and pressing against her. Æstrid softly moaned against him and Veleif gently parted her mouth, kissing her with a tenderness she'd not thought him capable.

"If you think to win me with one kiss, Kollsvein, I think your brain is still riddled with fever." She smiled teasingly and placed a hand on his chest.

"Would two win you then?" he whispered huskily, his eyes sparkled with a teasing light.

She crooked her head at him, as if considering the offer, and Veleif didn't wait her answer. He pulled her to him again and kissed her deeply, exploring her mouth with all the depth of a passion-starved lover. When he finally released her, both of her hands had crept up and rested on his shoulders.

"Two is... good," she whispered, as if contemplating judgement.

"Only good? Let's see what endearments can be coaxed from you with three." He took her lips again and pulled her down on top of him. Æstrid protested to be mindful of his leg, but Veleif would not be denied.

His arms half-lifted her until she was tucked in protectively under the crook of his arm. He traced the hollow of her cheek and ran his finger down the line of her neck, gently lower until he traced the line just above her swelling breasts.

"So you care for me then, my lady wife? As I care for you?" Veleif whispered in her ear.

Æstrid's could feel the blush creep all the way to her throat and she snuggled in against the warmth of his embrace.

"Yes. But I wonder if I would recover so quickly if our places were switched and I was in your tender care?" Æstrid pondered, her voice barely above a whisper. She felt Veleif's smile.

His hand moved lower and gently cupped the fullness of her breast. His thumb barely brushed the straining peak, eliciting a sharp intake of breath as she felt it harden and strain against the cloth.

"And you desire me then, my lady wife? As I desire you?" His palm brushed lower, gliding along the side of her ribcage, then slid lower, his fingers splayed against the flat of her belly. His hand moved over and rested on the curve of her hip, lightly pressing her to him.

"You do not play fair," Æstrid rasped. "Your leg ..."

"My leg is not a hindrance." He pressed the hot length of his manhood against her, and his eyes turned dark and stormy. His hand slid to the small of her back, then lower, cupping her buttock to pull her closer. His lips ran along the line of her neck, making her softly moan. Veleif raised up to look at her.

"And you lo—"

The door burst open and Rafa and Thorgrima froze at the sight. The women carried trays of steaming broth, and another piled high with fresh bandages and vessels of Æstrid's herbs and grease to change the dressing.

Æstrid blushed to the roots of her hair, having been caught in such a position. She quickly scrambled to the side of the bed and tugged her gown back into place.

"I'm sorry my lord, my lady," Rafa whispered.

"No, come in." Æstrid beckoned them inside, earning a frown from Veleif.

"Leave us," he growled.

"You'll come in. It's time to change the bandages," Æstrid countered.

Veleif lay back and sighed in resignation. He folded his arms behind his head. Why should he expect the moment to express his love and wrest the same from her, would go smoothly? The gods were surely laughing and he snorted with the humor of it all.

"You didn't have to leave the bed, Æstrid. There is no chance of disturbing their virgin eyes."

"You think this funny?" Æstrid stiffened at his jest. She didn't see the humor. It was the exact thing Thorgrima had said the night he took both the women and had chained *her* to his bed. Besides, the strain of the past days of worry and now the loss of his delicious embrace left her wanting. Peevish.

She ached to melt against his satiny skin until their breath mingled. Moaning between his kisses. Deep. Tender. Wild. And somewhere between the fostering exchanges of passion, Æstrid knew he was on the precipice of uttering those words she yearned to hear.

The feelings of his heart. But Veleif hadn't spoken his pledge, and then again, neither had she.

"I cannot imagine a more pleasant way to wake up from a mauling than to find three attentive women in my chamber," Veleif chuckled, as Thorgrima began unwinding the bandages from his leg.

"We are all delighted to see your health improved," Æstrid smiled, with exaggerated sweetness.

Veleif frowned and for the life of him could not imagine what had changed her mood. Just moments ago he was about to ease into her and slake this craving lust she had awakened. He slipped into a darkening brood.

Veleif growled as Rafa tried to spoon some bone broth to his lips. Jerking the bowl from her hands he half-shouted, "I'm no helpless babe. I'll feed myself."

"Ah, that's more like it." Æstrid smiled with her hands on her hips. "I can pronounce you well on the path to recovery, Veleif. Your mean spirit has returned." She moved to the door and looked back at him. "I suggest you remain abed a few days more. You need time to build the blood you've lost before your strength will return."

"Where are you going?" Veleif shouted from the bed.

"I fear I've neglected much in the past few days, Veleif. Now that you're recovered, I can turn my attentions elsewhere. Perhaps the stables even, where I'm certain I'll find the cows and sheep of sweeter temper than here." Her eyes glared hot at him as she slammed the door behind her. Rafa and Thorgrima exchanged worried glances.

Veleif swore loudly and Æstrid was glad the door was closed, so she couldn't hear the force of his wrath. Veleif struggled to rise, but fell back against the bed. He cursed louder, finding himself too weak to stand on his own.

He'd sent his own men on a precarious mission to secure her father's consent, so she would be more agreeable to this marriage of theirs. He'd risked a ship, gold, even silver to unite them. He'd wooed her, cajoled her, and comforted her. He shared his mind and thoughts, and made her weak with passion's play night after night, only to have her turn jealous of his trusted servants?

No, this wench did not respond to gentle taming.

And she had the gall to call him mean of spirit?

By Odin's hand, he'd show her exactly how mean-spirited he truly was. If needed, he would call upon Arnor to chain her to his bed once more, until she realized how foolish this behavior was.

His only regret, as he looked upon the worried faces of Rafa and Thorgrima, was that he lacked the strength to chain her himself.

This brush with death he'd been dealt, only served to make him want Æstrid more fiercely than anything he'd ever desired.

She was provoking, challenging, and passionate. He had brief glimpses of her softer side, her care, and Veleif wanted all. She stirred him to anger, to righteous unbalance, yet maintained a respect and wit about her.

The anticipation of being with her was exactly like what he felt right before a battle, when faced with an opponent of equal strength.

But it wasn't a sword or a spear he wanted to conquer her with, he wanted all of her – every facet of this maddening woman who had become his wife.

The women finished wrapping his leg and moved to leave the room.

"Stay Rafa. Thorgrima," he commanded gruffly.

They looked at each other, then back at him with curious gazes upon their faces.

"Are you certain? The lady, Æstrid…" Rafa worried.

"Is not likely to soften her mood anytime soon," Veleif groaned, and stretched back on the bolsters. "Tell me of Arnor's tale. I should like to hear it as I rest once more."

# Chapter Twenty-Three

It was fear.

Plain and simple fear gripped Æstrid.

Fear had plagued her when she'd first seen Arnor carrying Veleif. Fear so strong, it had taken every ounce of her will to set a molten blade to him to save his leg. Fear that he would never wake and die there upon the bed. And her fears were realized, when Veleif woke, he spoke no words of love, but merely expressed his lust.

Veleif cared for her, desired her, but the words he shared conveyed nothing of love.

And if he didn't love her, how would he come to love their children? Would he be the brutish father as Gunnalf had been?

Oh, her father cared for her, and for Leidolf, but as possessions. Proof of his progeny. Her heartless sire had never shone one whit of tenderness she and her brother had craved.

"Have you told him about the child yet?" Asa asked her somberly, as she brushed past her in the kitchen. Æstrid's brows arched up and she quickly frowned, but considering Asa's state, she couldn't remain angered long.

"You should be in bed and resting." Æstrid looked down at her swollen belly.

"No I fear I cannot sit still. It is better to be here. Slothi has become most annoying of late. He too, insists I lie idle but I fear I've adopted your obstinate ways." Asa grinned proudly. Æstrid smiled back into her bright, blue eyes. The woman was impossible to argue with.

"Come, I think regarding stubbornness, you are far outmatched," Æstrid insisted. She slipped an arm about her waist. "I'm seeing you home, lest this babe of yours be born here in the kitchens."

Æstrid pulled a woolen shawl about Asa's shoulders and led her outside. She supported her tightly as they walked gingerly across the snow to Asa's cottage, where they were greeted by a worried Slothi.

He took his wife up into his arms and carried her away and Æstrid smiled at the caring attentions of her husband.

"My thanks," Slothi sighed as he returned. He offered her some heated wine to chase the chill from the trek. "How did you not freeze?" His gaze ran over her in a frown.

Æstrid laughed as she sipped the wine and shrugged, chafing her arms in front of their hearth. "I forgot my cloak. I was too concerned with getting Asa here."

They both paused as a soft cry came from the bed. Slothi and Æstrid ran to Asa's side and Æstrid realized she had returned the woman none too soon. She gripped Asa's hand and soothed her, noting with some chagrin, Slothi's face went deathly white.

"Slothi," Æstrid said calmly, "gather every blanket you can find. Then set your largest pot of water on the hearth. When that is done, go seek Berra and bring her here. All will be well Slothi, just go." She patted his arm and turned back to Asa and piled more furs behind her head to make her comfortable.

There was no amount of cajoling to keep Veleif in his bed another evening. Though he dressed in warm leg wrappings, boots and a woolen tunic, he could not pull his trousers on without great pain to his leg. Throwing on a long dark cloak, Veleif made his way slowly to the hall. Despite whatever rumors may be spoken or whispered, Veleif was going to put them all to rest with his appearance. Never would the lord of Kollsveinholdt appear weak or infirmed before his people.

He met the shocked stares of Irik, Halfdan, Arnor and even Thorliek, as he gritted his teeth silently against the pain and took his chair. Æstrid's seat was conspicuously empty and the thought of her rebuff darkened his already blackening mood.

Thorgrima paused with her mouth agape when she saw Veleif at the table, but hurried to fix him a trencher. When she returned, she was rewarded with Veleif's scowl as he called Nar to bring him the crate of bottles of vodka they had traded for in Novgorod. Arnor's brows raised at Veleif's request and he couldn't resist a jibe.

"It would seem your pains are great, Veleif. I've never known a man to drink vodka unless he's near death from a battle wound... or plagued by an irksome wench." Arnor leaned back and laughed so loud the entire table could not help but join the joviality. Veleif scowled at him and called for horns to be brought all around.

"Irksome wench? Ha! I think it is an irksome wench who plagues Halfdan." Veleif pointed and tossed back the vodka in a single gulp. The others followed suit. Halfdan gaped at Veleif in surprise.

"Excuse me, my prince?" Halfdan sputtered.

"No I don't think I will. Do you not see Thorgrima's attentions, Halfdan?" Veleif choked down another draught of vodka and let loose an airy cough, as it burned all the way to his gut. He regarded the empty horn and had to admit, the pain in his leg was already bearable. "You'd have to be blind not to see the way the woman dotes on you." Veleif's voice boomed louder.

"It seems blindness runs rampant among some of us in Kollsveinholdt." Arnor laughed and Veleif swayed lightly toward him, pouring everyone another draught. Veleif slammed his hand on the table and bellowed.

"Thorgrima!"

The woman rushed to the table, looking curiously at Halfdan before she knelt before Veleif. He stood up too quickly and leaned on the table for balance. Perhaps that vodka was stronger than he thought? His hand shot out in her direction.

"You! Thorgrima have served this house long and well. Would you ever disobey the command of your lord?"

"No, Veleif," Thorgrima glanced up him in utter confusion.

"Halfdan?" he shouted down the table where Halfdan sat. The man looked up at him, almost petrified. "I know you obey my orders without question!"

"Yes, Veleif."

"Do you wish to marry this woman? And suffer the agony of matrimony?" Veleif swayed and all brows raised. Only Arnor frowned.

"Er, I... I do not think it would be agony," Halfdan stammered, as Thorgrima blushed.

"HA!" Veleif teetered back into his chair. "You have my blessing if you wish. But bring her to heel quickly, Halfdan." He slapped his palm on the table and muttered almost to himself. "Lest you suffer from want of a woman who does not want you."

Veleif poured a full horn of the wicked vodka and drained it at once.

"You're drunk." Arnor swayed toward him in his chair.

"No more than you, my friend." Veleif gave him a sloppy smile. Then he frowned at the vacant chair beside him. He snapped his head to Nar and waved the boy over, grabbing him by the front of his tunic when the boy was within his grasp.

"My wife, Nar, where is my wife?" he snarled. The boy went wide-eyed, but relaxed as Arnor peeled Veleif's hand away from his shirt front.

"I have not seen her since this morning."

"Fetch her!" Veleif thundered and watched as Arnor poured more vodka for them both. "I'll have no more of these insults in my own hall."

Questioning gazes ran about the tables and soon all eyes turned to Veleif. Murmurs of both concern and mirth travelled among the men and women. They wondered at Veleif's drunken state as much as the lady's absence.

Nar skated to the kitchen and not finding Æstrid there, rounded the hall quickly, taking the steps to the upstairs chambers two at a time. Veleif called for more bottles of vodka to be shared and soon the entire hall was toasting to their lord's good health. When that grew tiresome, they drank to the upcoming wedding of Halfdan and Thorgrima.

Spirits and merriment were running high. It was only when Nar appeared at Veleif's elbow, did his mood descend to a darkening rage.

"What do you mean you cannot find her?" Veleif scowled fiercely at the boy.

"It seems she is nowhere in the keep. But she cannot be far, her cloak was in her chamber," Nar replied, hesitant.

Veleif's mind flashed to an image of Æstrid, poised amid the livestock, surveying the flocks as she vented her discontent among the herd. He tossed back another horn of vodka remembering how she'd said she'd find the stables sweeter than his company. Veleif stood up and rocked back on his heels.

Who was this defiant wench he'd married? He would go to the stables himself! If he found his lady was within, by Odin's hand he'd

226

make certain she stayed there until she begged her release from her 'sweeter' company.

Staggering past his men, Arnor reached out to steady him, but Veleif shrugged him off. Arnor's brows raised as he watched Veleif walk precariously to the door, instead of taking the stairs to his chamber.

"Where are you going, Veleif?"

"To the stables, Arnor," he announced with a flourish, as if it made perfect sense.

Arnor rose on his feet and he shook his head as he stepped gingerly after Veleif. It seemed the stone floor of the hall was listing, like the deck of a boat. Surely he had not consumed enough vodka to lose his senses? Picking up a full bottle of the stuff, Arnor stumbled after Veleif.

"Veleif? Why do we go to the stables at this hour?" Arnor grumbled.

"To retrieve a wife. And she'll be as surly as an untamed beast I'm certain," Veleif laughed.

Arnor glanced back at the table as if he was deep in thought. Then he tucked a second bottle under his arm and growled to the Halfdan, Irik, Thorliek and several others who shared the table.

"What are you doing still sitting there? Veleif goes to battle. It's our duty to lend our swords if need be."

The men scrambled after him, a few bracing the table to steady their walk. It was a curious sight to see Veleif, Arnor, then everyone at the head table stagger from the hall. One by one, the remainder of the merrymakers within followed outside, down the frozen steps of the keep, and cradled more bottles of the precious vodka in their arms.

The whispers of speculation to their destination grew with every pace, as bottles were passed between the men and the women. The noise of the throng awakened several families in the nearby cottages.

As more doors opened and cloaks were donned, the numbers of the retrieval party quickly swelled. Vodka was passed to the newcomers and Taar the tanner, rolled out a large cask of ale.

Arnor's stride caught up to Veleif, and the drunken prince draped an arm around the giant's shoulders. Thankfully he clung to him just in time, as Veleif's feet hit a patch of ice. His boots skidded on the slippery surface and nearly sent the two of them tumbling headlong into the pens just outside the stable.

Pausing and seeming out of breath, Arnor passed the bottle to Veleif who tipped it back and swallowed a long gulp of the icy vodka.

Somewhere in the back of his brain Veleif wondered why the fiery liquid no longer burned, but he could hardly ponder the fact as Arnor interrupted his thoughts, and encouraged him to take another pull.

"If you're going to gather your wife, this is no time to sober up, Veleif," Arnor said. He tipped his own bottle back, then released it with a satisfying ah!

"Sober? I'm plenty sober, old friend. It is you who needs to drink your courage to face my wife," Veleif grinned, then clanked his bottle to Arnor's.

They both took another pull. Veleif bowed his head and shook it then as if to clear his brain. Then he thrust his bottle to Arnor's chest so hard the great Viking let out an audible grunt. Stumbling toward the barn, he paused and turned back to look at Arnor.

Veleif raised his arm and pointed at him with almost an accusing tone.

"She thinks me mean of spirit, Arnor." He half-stumbled, half-limped back to the giant, who shook his head in sympathy.

He snatched the whip coil from Arnor's belt who looked down at him in surprise.

"You'd beat the lady, Veleif?" Arnor frowned, ready to snatch the whip from him if needed.

"Never!" Veleif smiled up at him and patted his chest with a reassuring palm. "It is only for effect."

He turned back to the barn and cracked the whip before the doors. "Æstrid!" Veleif swayed slightly. "Come out here now!"

Gasps of surprise murmured through the crowd, but the only sounds Veleif heard were bleating sheep behind the door.

"Æstrid?" he repeated and leaned his ear closer.

Damn!

The stubborn woman chose to greet him with nothing but silence. Veleif tore open the door and stepped inside.

Without thinking, he cracked the whip again above his head bellowing her name. Sheep began to spill around him through the open door.

Arnor and Halfdan were the first to reach the stable doors, and the crowd rushed forward to calm and capture the frightened sheep.

More torches were lit and more ale was poured, as the chase for the scattering flock ensued.

The chaos outside the barn, brought even more people spilling from their cottages. Inside the barn, Thorliek elbowed forward between the warriors. His arms filled with the lamb he carried as he peered down at Veleif who they found sitting atop a great mound of dung.

"It appears, my prince, your wife is not here," Thorliek laughed.

"Not unless she's grown more legs," Irik roared loudly, as he grasped Veleif's forearm and pulled him from the pile.

"Perhaps we should bathe you before you find her?" Halfdan wrinkled his nose at Veleif. They all laughed and took hearty pulls from the vodka once more. Veleif wiped his mouth on the back of his hand. "Ha! She's the one who said she preferred this sweeter clime."

He strode outside and faced the crowd. His eyebrows raised for a moment, surprised at the numbers of people he faced.

"The first one who can tell me where the lady Æstrid is, I'll match their weight in silver." Veleif shouted out with his hands on his hips.

Murmurs ran through the crowd. Whispers of 'Is my lady safe?' 'Has she been taken?' and 'Nay, I've not seen her' were heard throughout.

Arnkel, Berra's son, a small boy of no more than five, ducked through the wondering crowd. He ran to Veleif pulling his sleeve to get his attention.

"My prince. Asa had a baby."

Veleif looked down and smiled at the boy. The blue eyes that looked up at him were wide with pride as he shared the news. Veleif ruffled the dark hair affectionately. "That is great news. But 'tis late, and you should be in bed, Arnkel."

The boy shook his head no and tugged his sleeve again. "Æstrid, I mean, my lady, Æstrid, she sent for mama. I think, Æstrid, I mean, my lady, is helping them."

Arnor looked down at the boy and appraised him from head to toe. "If the boy speaks true Veleif, you've saved yourself a great deal of silver. It looks like he weighs no more than a wineskin."

Arnkel placed his hand in Veleif's and craned his neck almost completely back to peer up into Arnor's face.

"It is lucky I'm here for you my lord, Veleif. If *he* found your lady, I think it would take all the silver in Kollsveinholdt to pay him."

Everyone within earshot roared with laughter, and Arnor lifted the boy to settle him upon his shoulders. Veleif peered up at Arnkel and smiled, raising his bottle of vodka in toast to the boy.

"You're a bold lad, Arnkel. Soon you'll take Arnor's place and command all the ships of Kollsveinholdt."

The boy's face lit up as he dug his hands into Arnor's hair, clinging to him as they walked with crunching steps to Asa's cottage. The swelling crowd followed behind, until it seemed everyone at Kollsveinholdt had joined.

"It's time you married, Arnor and got yourself some sons." Veleif slightly slurred his words but he was certain Arnor understood.

Arnor laughed loudly and placed a protective arm on Arnkel's leg. "Not I. I have no intention to traipse around on a freezing night, just to bring my woman to heel."

Veleif grunted and halted about thirty paces from Slothi and Asa's cottage. Everyone filled in around him, and torchlight glowed across their expectant faces. Veleif pondered the door and swallowed down more vodka as all eyes of his people were on him.

"It is unseeming I should knock, like some beggar..." he muttered angrily to Arnor. Arnor stroked his beard deep in thought.

"Just call out for her," he reasoned finally.

"Slothi's cottage is built strong. I doubt they would hear you within," Blotha pointed out. He peered over Veleif's shoulder, having wormed his way to the front of the group. More vodka was tipped back and shared, as they debated the best way to breach the cottage.

"Just kick down the door, Veleif. There is no need to wait," Halfdan instructed.

"But that would leave Slothi without a door on this cold night," Irik protested.

"With a newborn babe inside and no door to keep this cold at bay…" Thorliek frowned, and gulped down a draught of vodka from Halfdan's bottle. Halfdan growled and snatched his bottle back from Thorliek.

"Oh you drunken men," Rafa shouted, and threw her hands in the air, glaring at them fiercely.

"If you took this long to invade a village, the enemy would die of old age first," Thorgrima scolded.

"Or expire from boredom," Gudney chuckled and jostled her baby in her arms. The women laughed and Rafa stepped boldly forward and knocked on the door.

"This may work too," Arnor shrugged, as Veleif rocked toward him, now tipping back a fresh horn of ale someone handed him. The men swayed and exchanged enlightened glances as Rafa called out, "Slothi! Slothi are you well?"

"This may work too," Arnor shrugged as Veleif rocked toward him, now tipping back a fresh horn of ale someone handed him.

The anxious gathering held a collective breath as the door opened slowly and the astonished face of Slothi appeared. He glanced about in confusion as the entire population of Kollsveinholdt was in attendance, with Veleif himself standing at their center.

"We bring you tidings, Slothi," Rafa smiled.

"To the birth of your child, Slothi!" Halfdan raised his vodka in toast and tossed back a hearty swallow. Others began shouting their congratulations and toasted as well.

Slothi stepped beyond the door, still confused at the curious gathering. A horn of ale was pressed into his hand and the cheers went up around him. He was met with hard clapping of congratulations upon his back, and in no time at all the merrymaking resumed in earnest.

"What say you Slothi? A boy or a girl?" Thorliek shouted across the throng.

"A son, Thorliek!" Slothi shouted, with a huge smile and the crowd again erupted to share his joy. Veleif slapped Arnor's shoulder and his face broke to a wide grin.

"Come Slothi." He raised his bottle. "Let us drink a toast to your son."

Slothi edged his way to Veleif's side. With arms draped over each other's shoulders, the two men began to drink in earnest to the health of Slothi's newborn son.

# Chapter Twenty-Four

Æstrid held a cup of hot tisane to Asa's lips and waited for her to drink. Berra wrapped the new baby in soft woolens and tucked one of Taar's fur pelts around him to place him at Asa's side.

"He is beautiful." Berra smiled down at her.

"He's so small and perfect," Æstrid observed, as she stroked the babe's tiny hand.

"You will have your own soon, Æstrid," Asa yawned, "and thank you both. I cannot imagine what this would have been with only Slothi to attend me." All three chuckled and Æstrid frowned.

"Where is Slothi? And what is all that noise?" The women fell silent. They had been so engrossed with the baby's care, it was the first time they realized there was a rowdy commotion outside the cottage.

Asa sat up slightly and inclined her head. Berra exchanged a questioning glance with Æstrid. Berra swept from the room and they heard the woman open the door. The sounds outside increased, then lowered again as Berra shut the door and returned to the room. Her blue eyes were wide and sparkling with humor and a smile played about her lips.

"What is it?" Æstrid tensed. Asa looked at her in suspense.

"It would seem the whole of Kollsveinholdt is outside the cottage." Berra laughed.

"What?" both women said in unison.

"Even Veleif is among them," Berra chuckled.

"Veleif? He should be in bed and resting from his injury," Æstrid worried. Asa gazed down in the face of her sleeping son.

"Many hours have passed, Æstrid. I'm thinking no one knew when we left the kitchen…" Asa smiled over to Berra whose grin widened.

"Perhaps Veleif became distraught?" Berra considered.

"Or wants the comfort of his wife?" Asa pondered.

Æstrid snorted.

"If you two think that, you do not know Veleif. He cares not *who* comforts him," Æstrid said stiffly. Both women frowned at her.

"That is not true, Æstrid, I've seen the way he looks upon you," Asa said firmly.

"And what way is that, Asa? Do you think he see me or the ships and flocks of Karissonholdt?" Æstrid snapped defensively. Berra laughed and Asa joined her.

"I'm certain when Veleif gazes in your eyes all he sees are ships, Æstrid," Asa teased.

"And I'm certain when Veleif runs his hands over you, the only thought in his mind are the vast bales of wool that come from Karissonholdt," Berra mocked.

Æstrid prickled at their teasing and stood up. Berra crossed the room and put a hand on Æstrid's shoulder. She shook her head and still giggled. "Æstrid you are so wise and so foolish."

"I think one of you should see what brings the entire village to my door," Asa prodded, and smiled covertly at Berra.

"It should be you, Æstrid" Berra pushed Æstrid to the door and they both heard the sounds of the merrymaking grow louder. She opened the door and shoved Æstrid through without giving her a chance to protest. The door closed quickly behind her.

The scene before her was unexpected to say the least. Æstrid swore every face of Kollsveinholdt was in attendance, including two ewes and a billy goat, who wandered among the throng. The silvered light of the moon washed down upon snow, and the night was lit all around as endless torches bathed hundreds of happy faces in a golden glow.

Just beyond the gathering, she spied Arnor with Berra's son Arnkel, resting upon his shoulders. Next to him stood Veleif, draped happily over Slothi's shoulders as they passed a bottle between them.

Æstrid's brows furrowed and her anger boiled. She knew the extent of his wounds and the fact Veleif was here in celebration instead of resting in bed incensed her. Did the man have no care for himself at all? Or for her?

Her aggravation grew with each step, so much so, Æstrid never even considered the need for a shawl or cloak to stave off the night chill. She moved closer to the group, halting about twenty paces from him with her hands on her hips.

"What in Odin's name do you think you're doing?" she shouted angrily. The crowd grew gradually silent at her outburst. Everyone paused and Veleif looked up at her, somewhat surprised that Æstrid had appeared.

He tried to remember what brought him out to the village this night. Had he been looking for her? Veleif blinked dumbly several times. It took a few moments for her question to register in his brain clouded with vodka. Finally, he formulated his answer.

"My lady, I do believe we are drinking." Veleif smiled with a lopsided grin, and swept his hand wide as he swerved into a deep bow.

Seeing their prince about to fall flat, Arnor and Slothi helped right him. Æstrid's brows raised in astonishment. She'd never seen Veleif in such a state before. Æstrid glowered the tittering crowd's laughter to silence, and inched forward a few steps.

"You should try some vodka, Æstrid. It seems to melt even the coldest of hearts," Veleif laughed. Oresti ventured forward and cautiously pressed a bottle into her hand before he quickly jumped back to the protection of the group.

She wasn't used to having such tender concern over another's wellbeing, any more than she was used to the raging desire that pounded through her. How dare he say her heart was cold when it was he who practically wrenched it from her chest these past days?

Æstrid stared at the bottle in disbelief. She held it to her nose and sniffed it curiously. She quickly stiffened at the pungent smell. She'd never encountered a beverage that could make her eyes water so quickly. Æstrid stifled the tears that threatened, not from the vodka, but Veleif's callous remark. She quickly replaced the emotion with a biting reply.

"Indeed? Then you should drink more heartily, Kollsvein, for I see no evidence vodka has warmed yours."

Veleif stiffened at her scathing remark and several gasps were heard among the crowd. He was drunk, but not drunk enough that he couldn't distinguish an insult. The effect was most sobering and he felt a deep ache creep up again in his thigh.

Veleif peered closely at her as he steadied himself on Slothi's shoulder. Everyone, including himself, seemed content in this celebration. For the life of him, Veleif couldn't think of one reason why Æstrid should look so angry. Wasn't he supposed to be angry with her?

"My prince, you found her." Irik pointed with a bottle dangling from his hand, woefully lacking timing.

"She doesn't appear too happy to be found," Halfdan roared, and everyone joined the mirth.

"Found?" Æstrid asked in bewilderment. Veleif suddenly remembered his reasoning for being here in the first place and teetered precariously. His heavy brows drew together darkly. Arnkel piped up from his perch on top of Arnor's shoulders.

"I thought you said we were here to bring the lady to heel?" The boy inquired honestly. Æstrid was taken aback at the lad's words and her head snapped to Veleif.

"To heel, Veleif?" Her words were spoken low and dangerous. Thorliek and Arnor both groaned, but Veleif was too far gone to recognize the warning in her question. Then her words came at a higher pitch as she circled dangerously closer to Veleif.

"To heel? I see it takes you, your men at arms and even the entire village to think you can accomplish such a feat." Laughter sprinkled across the crowd, although the female chuckles rose a bit louder than male ones.

"Our lady looks so angry I wager our swords would melt before that heated gaze," a male voice snickered above the laughter and everyone broke out into heartier giggles.

Veleif shrugged off Arnor and Slothi's hands and took a step toward her. His face was twisted in a menacing growl and his eyes glittered almost silver in the torchlight.

"You are fortunate you're a woman Æstrid…"

"Fortunate?" she interrupted with a snide laugh, and threw both hands in the air. "I assure you that is an opinion held entirely by yourself!"

"Still that waspish tongue of yours." Veleif swayed, then sputtered in thought. "What keeps you from attending me? You will explain yourself!"

"When you explain why you're not in bed healing your leg," Æstrid shot back.

"Why are you not in the stables?" Veleif roared at her accusingly. All eyes turned to Æstrid.

"Why were you *in* the stables?" Æstrid countered, as heads turned toward Veleif, eagerly waiting his answer.

"Æstrid, I warn you…"

"Warn me from what, Veleif? Your wrath? You have never seen wrath until you see it from a Karisson!"

"You are a Kollsvein!" he stepped toward her.

"I am a Karisson!" she shouted, and thumped her fist on her chest.

"Kollsvein!" he snarled.

"Karisson!" she hissed.

"Æstrid Kollsvein, the sooner you learn some obedience, the happier we both will be."

"Obedience?" Æstrid's voice shrilled up an octave. Arnor and Halfdan both groaned. Thorliek pinched the bridge of his nose as if it pained him.

"If it was obedience you wanted, then the deception is on you, Veleif. I bow nor scrape to no one!"

"Æstrid I am done with these insults of yours!"

"Are you?" she asked, as she raised a curious brow.

"Aye!" he growled at her.

"Well I'm just getting started, Veleif."

"Perhaps we should rescue the drunken fool?" Halfdan whispered inquiringly to Arnor as he took another pull from his vodka.

"The lady said she was just beginning. It would be a shame to not let her finish," Arnor laughed.

"Tell me, Veleif. How have I insulted you? Was it when I made *you* a slave in my house? Or perhaps it was when I *chained you* like a beast to my bed?" Curious murmurs went throughout the crowd and all eyes turned back to Veleif.

"Do you need me to fetch more chain, my lord?" Taar called out laughing. His face crumbled to pure fear as Æstrid screeched and hurled the bottle of vodka at his head. Irik cried out and leapt to catch the flying missile before it could hit Taar who was too stunned to move. Irik palmed the bottle gently as he shook his head.

The crowd cheered as Irik proudly held up the rescued bottle, but quickly quieted to hushed murmurs as Veleif raged on.

"Do not make me the villain with your half-truths, Æstrid. You're lucky all I did was chain you up after you tried to stab me. If it had been anyone else..." Veleif snarled. Gasps of surprise buzzed through the people and all eyes looked to Æstrid.

"Anyone other than the daughter of Gunnalf Karisson you mean! I doubt you'd take pains to trick a maid who could not bring as much into a marriage, Veleif," she accused.

"You think I married you for Karissonholdt? So that is why you remain so willful toward me?"

"Willful? You great blustering fool! Am I willful when I spend hours in the kitchens to make the food better for you and your men? Am I willful when I spend night and day tending your foolish wounds?" Her anger peaked as she waved her arms at him.

"Only to leave your duty to your husband and seek the stables," Veleif shouted.

"Stables? Forget the stables, you drunken fool," Æstrid sneered, as her eyes roved over him. "But then again, maybe I should seek counsel there. Even the most stubborn ram in the stables makes more sense than you."

"Enough!" Veleif raised his hand to stem her words. "I've suffered too much of your biting tongue. You're my wife! It is past time you behave like one."

Æstrid glanced around to the curious faces intent on their exchange and settled back on Veleif.

"I have been a most dutiful wife. Considering I was made a wife against my consent, Kollsvein! And maybe, you spliny bastard, you would have more of a care for me as a wife, if you thought yourself more of a husband."

"More of a husband?" Veleif said, incredulously. "We both know Æstrid, you lack no attention from me as a husband."

"With Æstrid as a wife, I'm surprised Veleif ever leaves his bed," a male voice called out and the crowd roared with laughter. Veleif cast a harsh look toward them as her words echoed back in his delayed brain.

*More of a husband?* Did she not know what she brought out in him? He wanted to protect her, impress her and satisfy her every desire no matter how large or small. Despite the amount of vodka he'd consumed, he noticed something in her was changed. Æstrid had a feral air about her, it was almost a fear; and Veleif suddenly realized the source of her anger.

It was a fear *for* him. By Odin's hand, this seething, beautifully fierce woman who stood in front of him truly did feel for him. It was a paralyzing thought.

"I didn't spend day and night tending you, worrying over you, praying to Odin to keep you safe only to have my work undone by your foolishness. Tell me, Kollsvein, how are you supposed to execute the most basic duty of husband, protecting me, if you can't even use your leg? Did you even consider that?"

Their gazes collided. Veleif's face was half-gilded in the torchlight. His arms were folded across his chest and one hand raised as he stroked his lower lip, pondering her tirade, and his own, thoughtfully. Æstrid shivered beneath his molten gaze, inwardly cursing that her heart could ache beneath his implacable regard.

A collective hush fell over everyone, and the only sound was the intermittent crackle of the torches in the night's gentle wind.

"Well?" Æstrid scowled impatiently, "have you nothing to say, Kollsvein?"

Æstrid caught the hint of a smile behind Veleif's hand and her brows raised in astonishment. Did he actually think her humorous?

"I have plenty to say," Veleif broke out into a deeper grin. "The first of which is you are right."

Æstrid was taken aback at his words but quickly recovered her aplomb. "Now I know you're flown with vodka."

"No, Æstrid, there is not enough vodka left to dull the effect of your stinging speech. However, I appreciate your anger. In fact, I find it most welcoming," Veleif chuckled, and braced his hands on his hips. Then he threw his head back and erupted into hearty laughter.

Arnor, Irik, Thorliek and Halfdan, as well as many others all exchanged shrugs of confusion. A few in the crowd even scratched their heads at Veleif's mirth.

"I hardly see the humor, Kollsvein," Æstrid bristled, her eyes snapping violet.

"Æstrid, as everyone bears witness, it is only your tender care that enables me to even stand. But this anger of yours is more than pride." Veleif stepped to within ten paces of her. His arms crossed again on his chest, and a ghost of a smile still played about his lips.

"Now hold your tongue until I finish," Veleif said gruffly, as Æstrid opened her mouth to speak. "Would that I could take back your brother's death, or what you suffered at the hands of the Pict. Would that I had known you were Viking when you were brought among us. But I did not.

"And while it still pains me to know what you had suffered, I am more surprised by you each day. Captured and forced against your will, you face each challenge with a wealth of courage only surpassed your grace and beauty. Our lives at Kollsveinholdt are better for having you come into it.

"If you do not know the depth of our appreciation for your labors, then the fault is ours, Æstrid, not yours. And your anger is just. Your care and pride are deep and worthy. You'd no sooner see your works undone than the weaver see his cloth unraveled or the brewer see his casks turn sour."

"Veleif, I…" Æstrid took a step toward him but stopped as he held up his hand to halt her progress.

"Let me finish, woman. The first night in the hall when you stabbed Blotha, I saw a warrior's pride reflected in the most dazzling eyes I've ever seen. A woman skilled with axes and fire, all wrapped up in spirit. I saw a woman with a face Odin himself would covet, and a fierce character that matched my own.

"Do you think I am a man who would bend to callous whims and take a bride for mere ships and some cattle? I took you to wife because you're the most beautiful, maddening woman I've ever known. You vex me one moment and make me rage with passion the next. I took you to wife because I love you, Æstrid Karisson."

Æstrid's eyes were bright with tears, as were many women throughout the crowd.

Halfdan sniffed as he took another pull of vodka. Thorliek coughed and wiped his eyes as Arnor shuffled his feet impatiently.

"So look at me, Æstrid and look well. I'll keep you no longer against your will but I would have your answer to a question first. It irks my pride your choice was removed, so I give that to you now. And I'll respect your decision for I love you too much to go against your wishes any longer.

"Æstrid Karisson, will you be my wife?"

Æstrid felt the hot tears pour down her cheeks as she covered her mouth with one hand to stifle the sob that threatened to choke her. It was as if all the people faded away and only Veleif remained.

Veleif who stood before her, tall and proud. Her warrior, her husband who just told her the words she'd longed for.

He loved her.

The emotion ran unchecked, pulsing through her shaking limbs.

"Veleif!" Æstrid cried out and ran into his waiting arms.

He pulled her into a tight embrace and kissed her hair, her nose, and the salty tears from her cheeks. He was holding her until they were only one body, one breath, standing together in a perfect fit, united against any force seen or unseen.

Æstrid could feel his heart beneath her palm, his desire and love all mingled together in his embrace, his kiss. She could feel the hard, heated muscles of his body and knew he must be suffering pain from his wounds, but Veleif uttered not a single sound of protest. His fingers wound into her hair, cradling her head gently. His eyes devoured her as he searched her face once more.

"I love you, Veleif Kollsvein." Her voice came in a throaty whisper.

"Then I am a man who needs nothing more." His mouth plunged down on hers, taking, tempting, pouring himself into her with the heat of love and longing.

When Veleif finally broke their kiss it was only then, they were aware of all of Kollsveinholdt had broken out into laughter and hearty cheers around them.

Veleif pulled her close and spoke softly above her lips.

"So that's a yes then, my lady?" he smiled down at her. Æstrid drank in the teasing gaze and returned her own coy smile.

She covered his hand with hers and guided it down to her belly.

"Yes my lord. For this child conceived between us, I can only think of him made in love." Æstrid watched his face waiting for the full import of her news to sink in.

Veleif stilled and a brief frown crossed his face. Then the dawning came and his expressions ran the full gamut from disbelief to overwhelming happiness. He held her at arm's length and raked her possessively from head to toe. He looked at her hand covering his and met her eyes once more.

"You speak true, Æstrid? You are with child?"

"Yes, Veleif. And he will need a father such as you." She nodded at him her eyes shining bright with tears.

Veleif swept her up and spun her about, laughing as Æstrid squealed within his embrace.

"To the hall everyone!" he shouted. "Tonight we celebrate! Eat and drink for Kollsveinholdt will have its heir."

The crowd surged forward, pressing them with congratulations and good wishes. Skins were tipped and bottles clanked, as the crush of bodies scuttled toward the great hall.

Veleif pulled the wolf skin from his back and tucked it tightly about Æstrid's shoulders. She gasped as he swept her up into his arms and cradled her against his chest.

"Your leg!" Æstrid protested.

"I told you before, was not a hindrance," Veleif whispered huskily and snatched a kiss. His eyes burned with lustful promise. "And I'll prove as much when we reach our chamber." Then he raised a curious brow.

"Why are you not wearing a cloak?" he asked with mock vexation.

"Why are you not wearing trousers?" Æstrid parried, as she nuzzled her lips against his neck.

"Women!" Arnor spat, as he fell into pace beside them.

"Ah yes. To Women. The most desirable and infuriating of creatures, my friend," Veleif laughed, as his eyes sparkled with a devilish light.

242

"May you always find me so, my love," Æstrid teased, as she lifted her mouth to his.

Veleif's embrace tightened before he kissed her once again.

"My fondest wish, my vixen bride."

# Epilogue

*Seven months later, Kollsveinholdt*

Æstrid paced with worry in the bustling hall. Or at least she paced with as much as her swollen girth would allow. A noisy flow of men ebbed and flowed through the door, rivaling the great seas beyond. They needed tending to their cuts and scrapes, more food, more arrows and shields, and much to Æstrid's chagrin – more ale.

It seemed any Viking skirmish, or celebration for that matter, required copious amounts of ale. When finding Kollsveinholdt running low on skins of the amber brew, Æstrid called for jugs and casks to be carried down to the beach.

A large Pict ship had landed not a mile from the keep that morning. Veleif, Arnor and Halfdan led the excited men out to meet the invading party. According to Blotha, who first brought the news, the conflict should have been a simple one. But now it was well past the noon hour, and Æstrid was certain Blotha's reports had been sorely downplayed.

Her hands strayed protectively to her belly. The child had lowered. Sleep these past weeks was impossible, as an air of anxiousness overtook her. She and Veleif spent many an evening laughing happily as the babe kicked in protest, while Veleif would cover her with hot kisses along her ripening shape.

But where was he?

Æstrid had seen nothing of Veleif since he'd rushed from the hall this morning. Donned in full leather armor, he'd merely brushed a quick kiss upon her forehead, and promised to return victorious before the midday meal.

Æstrid paced again as Irik stumbled in. His sword dripped crimson and his hair and beard were matted with blood and sweat. "Ale!" he called and Æstrid rushed to his side. Rafa pressed a horn to his hand, and Irik quaffed heartily before he spoke.

"Veleif! Is he well?" Æstrid shook Irik's shoulders uncaring that half the ale spilled down his bloodied shirtfront.

"Yes, he's well," Irik nodded.

"What is taking so long?" Æstrid demanded, and shook his shoulders roughly.

"My lady, please," Irik winced at her rough treatment. Æstrid gasped as she pulled back her hands which were now covered in blood. She hadn't seen the gash on Irik's arm and hastily wiped her hands on her apron.

"Rafa, get him bandaged," she ordered quickly.

"My lord asks you seek your chamber," Irik panted, as he gulped more ale.

"Are we in danger?" Æstrid stiffened.

"No, but it will take longer than we'd planned. The bloody Picts have come in a dozen boats, not solely the two Blotha spotted this morning."

Æstrid frowned with worry and she twisted her hands nervously. "But that would mean there are hundreds of Picts upon our shore."

Irik laughed. "At least a hundred, my lady. But they are no match for us. Still, it takes a while to cut them down. Veleif sends his apologies for his delay and asks you rest until he returns."

"Apologies for his delay? What rubbish, Irik!" Æstrid stalked past him and pushed angrily through the doors of the hall. Irik moaned and watched her go. He looked up at Rafa who bound his wound tightly with fresh linen.

"He'll skin me alive if anything happens to her."

"Most likely," Rafa agreed, "but I've no doubt you'd lose some skin if you tried to stop her."

Æstrid hurried past the cottages to the open pasture of Kollsveinholdt. She scanned the beach below and continued moving through the grasses to gain a better view. If only she could see Veleif, and assure herself he was all right.

She saw the column of smoke another hundred yards ahead, rising skyward beyond the cliff. Rushing forward to the forest edge, she peered below and the horror made her stop. Irik had been correct. A dozen ships scattered haphazardly along the shore. The tide washed red and bodies were scattered, twisted and broken, as water lapped over their prostate forms.

Three ships were engulfed in flames as more Picts charged the warriors. The sounds of swords and shields rang out, along with cries of death and charge echoed toward her above the rocky clifftop. Æstrid spied Veleif, back to back with Arnor. Both men swung their sword and axes, cutting through the howling savages, sending them reeling backward to their deaths.

Then the pain hit her.

A deep, slicing pain ripped across Æstrid's abdomen causing her to cry out. She stumbled with the agony of it and gripped her stomach.

"No! No! Not now!" she moaned, and staggered toward the trees cursing the blinding pain in her lower belly.

Æstrid panted for strength as she pressed against a tree trunk. She gripped the bark mercilessly and cried out again as another contraction tore through her. A great gush of water rushed between her legs and Æstrid looked down at the sodden mess of leaves cloying to her hem. She was too far away from Kollsveinholdt to return, and too far away to call for help.

"I'm sorry child." Æstrid groaned and hugged her stomach. All the preparations she and Veleif had made were now in vain. She glanced over to the distant keep, thinking of their downy bed, the great hearth in their chamber, and all the women who could attend her. A tear rolled down her cheek as she untied the apron from her shoulders.

With a painful effort, Æstrid spread the apron on a grassy place just beyond the copse of trees. It was almost funny, seeing the cloth upon the ground. Veleif had spent weeks, painstakingly carving and rubbing the wood of their babe's cradle. The tiny longship was so heavily laden with silver, it had taken four men to carry the piece to their chamber. But the cradle would have to wait. The newest Kollsvein's first bed would be a humble cloth in the woods. She stretched and walked a few anguished steps, trying to relieve the aching in her lower back.

"It will be just you and I, my darling. I only hope you don't rob me of enough strength to save us both if wolves should come upon us." She was almost sorry she'd said the words out loud, but another rending contraction robbed her of any coherent thought. Æstrid screamed out again and waited for the pain to pass.

Doubled over and breathing hard, Æstrid stroked her stomach. She'd seen enough babes born at Kollsveinholdt these past months to know this child was anxious to greet her. This was not going to be a long labor, and Æstrid laughed through her tears as she mused out loud. "You'll probably arrive home before your father, tiny Kollsvein."

She screamed again in agony.

Æstrid moved with unbearable pain to lay down near the folded apron. Her breathing was hard and she flung her arms to her sides. She let another hard contraction rife her body, screaming again through the hurt. When it subsided she gazed up at the sky, marveling at the shade of blue. A rare sky to be certain and the distant sun provided some meager warmth. Æstrid grabbed her stomach again, crying out as another hard contraction pierced her. She bit her lip and felt hot tears wash down the sides of her face, sticking into her dampened hair. She murmured up to the sky, closing her eyes in whispered prayer.

"Odin, I'll trade my life for the safety of this babe. Please take mercy and bring him unharmed, despite my foolishness."

Halfdan pulled his blade with a sneer from the last Pict throat he'd slice that day. He made his way over to Veleif and Arnor, both men braced against the rock wall of the cliff, panting and surveying the wreckage of the fight.

The smoke burned Veleif's nostrils as Arnor passed him a skin of fresh ale. He tipped it back, welcoming the cooling brew. Veleif paused to wipe the sweat pouring down his face and passed the skin to Halfdan.

All three men broke into grins. When Arnor's chest shook with a deep rumbling laugh, it spread like a contagion among them. Soon they were all doubled over, awash with laughter and the heightened energy of a victory well fought.

"Take a score of men and put the bodies in the boats," Veleif called out to Oresti. "Burn them all for I doubt the sharks have yet found a taste for Pict." Hearty laughter broke out and more skins were passed.

"We'll make it back in time for dinner," Arnor joked as the bloodied, sweat-streaked men made their way leisurely up the beach.

"Leave it to Arnor to think of his stomach before all else," Halfdan chortled.

"His stomach comes before his cock," Veleif laughed, "it's why he still remains without a wife."

As they reached the top of the path up the cliffside, still joking about Arnor's appetites, Veleif spotted Irik, standing still and alone. His face was solemn. A warning shiver traced his spine as the hair stood up on the back of his neck. His warrior's instinct told him something was terribly amiss.

"What news, Irik?" Veleif halted suddenly.

"The lady, Æstrid," Irik mumbled hesitantly.

"What about her?" Veleif roared, and grabbed Irik by the shirt. Irik's eyes went wide in shock.

"She's not about, my lord," Irik blinked rapidly.

"Not about? Where is she?" Veleif demanded.

"I don't know, my prince. She was anxious for news of you and quit the keep. No one has seen her, but she went that way. I think." Irik pointed to the pasture.

Veleif's face twisted in rage as he shoved Irik backward. "Did you not think to escort her? Carry her back? Lock her in her chamber?"

"I'm sorry, she... she slipped past us," Irik stammered.

The fist came out of nowhere.

Irik lifted himself from the grass and stole a look upward. Arnor rubbed his knuckles while Irik rubbed his jaw.

"If anything has happened to the lady Æstrid, rest assured my friend, there will be very little of you left when Veleif comes to seek his vengeance," Arnor promised. Irik scrambled to his feet to apologize again, but Arnor was already running toward the pasture just behind Halfdan and Veleif.

Panic.

Sheer panic gripped him. Veleif had just spent most of the day in a tiring effort fighting the Pict, but he felt none of it. Odin himself couldn't have stifled the surge of raw power blasting through his limbs. He tried to suppress the images of Æstrid as he ran. She could not be lying somewhere bleeding and broken.

His mind flashed to Tofa and he willed the image away. How cruel was fate that he be given a woman to love this deeply, only to have her taken from him once again?

All three men halted abruptly when they heard the scream. Halfdan put a hand on Veleif's chest and cocked his ear. It came again, a gut-wrenching scream that gripped his heart with an icy fist.

"Over there!" Halfdan cried out.

They sprinted toward the wood.

"By the gods, Æstrid!" Veleif thundered.

She lay just before the woods, her face contorted in pain. Her nails raked deep furrows into the ground beside her.

He flung himself to her side in an instant, cradling her head and smoothing the hair back from her face.

"Veleif," Æstrid panted weakly, then screamed as a long, tortuous contraction took her once more.

"Do something!" Halfdan roared at Arnor as he squatted down to Æstrid's side.

"Me?" Arnor cried, "I only know of killing men, not birthing them."

Æstrid gripped both Veleif and Halfdan's hands and looked up at them as if seeing them for the first time. Their faces were blackened and rivulets of sweat ran down their cheeks and foreheads. Their hair and beards were matted with dirt and blood, and their clothes were filthy and stained. Halfdan even had bits of seaweed sticking into his beard. But the worst was the odors coming from the men.

"By the gods you stink!" Æstrid shouted. Her face twisted in grimace against the offensive assault. She pushed away from them and struggled to half-raise from the ground. Her head wrenched side to side seeking to gulp air that was not filled with their wretched stench. "All of you smell worse than the rotting innards of diseased fish."

Veleif stared down at his wife incredulously. His words came sharper than he intended.

"I'm sorry we didn't have time to bathe and rub scented oils upon our skin before you took your little stroll, Æstrid."

Another excruciating convulsion seized her and Æstrid clutched onto Veleif and Halfdan once more. Arnor chafed nervously as he watched her suffer, and Halfdan tried to pry her bone-crushing grip from his hand.

Veleif watched as she eased her head back again upon the earth and panted for breath. Her suffering tore through him with equal amounts of pity and fear. His own helplessness quickly transformed to anger. He suddenly wished for a hundred Picts to unleash his frustration upon, rather than watch her suffer. His brow creased to a deep frown and he looked to Halfdan and Arnor.

"Take her feet, Arnor. We're carrying her up to the keep," he growled, and bent to lift Æstrid into his arms.

"Don't you touch me!" she snarled.

Her voice was so deep and laced with venom, all three men bolted backward in unison. Her fingers seized Halfdan's and Veleif's shirts in death-like grip so brutally, both men knew they would bear marks of her clutches afterward.

Æstrid screamed through another ripping pain.

"Æstrid, you can't stay here. We're taking you back where you will deliver our babe where it's safe and proper," Veleif commanded sharply.

Disbelief swam over her as the agony momentarily subsided. She was horribly exposed, lying in a field surrounded by three bloodied, stinking warriors; and *he* was going to start ordering her about like one of his men?

"*Proper?* Kollsvein, do you think I care one *whit* about what is proper?" Æstrid hissed. She grabbed Veleif's soiled shirt with both fists and jerked him down until they was nose to nose. "Do you have any clue of what to do right now?"

Veleif swallowed hard and shook his head no.

Æstrid glanced to Halfdan and Arnor, both of whom wore looks of daft simpletons – albeit pale simpletons, as they shook their heads in the negative.

Æstrid groaned in misery.

"If men were this stupid at conception, no woman would have to go through this." She shoved Veleif away.

"Most men are drunk at conception," Halfdan pointed out, earning her glaring stare.

"And most should be drunk at birth. Fetch us some ale, Arnor," Veleif said, and ran a hand through his hair in frustration.

"If you move from that spot, Arnor, I'll get up and run you through with your own sword," Æstrid threatened. Another scream took her as Arnor paled and chafed in helplessness.

"Would there were more Pict invading," he muttered, "I'd rather face a score of ships on my own than bear witness to this."

"Yes," both men agreed in unison as Æstrid calmed again.

"Veleif take off your shirt. We're going to need something to wrap this babe in when he arrives," Æstrid directed.

"This shirt?" Veleif looked down, palming the stained linen that covered him.

"Yes that shirt, you dolt! Between the three of you, it is the least foul." Æstrid's eyes brooked no disobedience as Veleif reached for his shirt hem. Halfdan stayed his hands and unsheathed his short sword from his scabbard.

"No, Veleif, the lady's skirt will do better."

Before anyone could protest, Halfdan sliced Æstrid's skirt to her knees and proudly held up the ripped length of fabric with a toothy grin. Æstrid moaned again in agony.

"Veleif, you're going to have to move between my legs and guide the babe forth. He's not long in coming now." Æstrid panted to the sky, her eyes glazed in pain.

Veleif exchanged worried looks with Halfdan and Arnor.

"You put him in there, it is only fitting you take him out," Arnor shrugged.

"I'll give you your weight in silver if you do this, Arnor," Veleif implored with narrowed eyes.

"Not I, my prince! I'm no midwife," Arnor stiffened, and raised his hands in protest.

"Halfdan?" Veleif urged. The burly Viking's pallor turned ashen behind his dirt-streaked face, as he shook his head in refusal.

"Not for all the silver in Kollsveinholdt, Veleif."

"By the Gods!" Æstrid shrieked. "You bunch of halfwits. How do you keep your heads in battle but lose your brains now?"

Veleif ran a nervous hand across his brow as he knelt between her legs. Arnor lowered his great bulk to Æstrid's left, and Halfdan hunched down on her right. Veleif choked down the fear and the nausea that threatened and drew upon every shred of strength he held within. He suddenly was overcome with a surging wave of calm, and knew someone in this misplaced group needed to keep their senses.

"Give her something to bite down on, you sorry lots," Veleif ordered.

"Halfdan, give her your sword." Arnor nodded with his chin, then grimaced as Æstrid's hand crushed his own.

"Why me?" Halfdan straightened, indignant.

"I saw you fight, man. Your sword will be the cleanest," Arnor said gruffly. Æstrid listened to them all laugh and began hurling curses upon them between her cries of anguish.

"I think you're frightening Arnor with your screams, my lady." Halfdan chanced a look into Æstrid's face now pinched with pain.

"He should be frightened!" Æstrid snapped at him between panting breaths.

"Enough of this!" Veleif barked, "Æstrid this babe is almost here. It is time to push him forth."

"I cannot, Veleif," Æstrid whined weakly.

"You can and you will!" Veleif thundered.

"Don't you take issue with me, Kollsvein!" Æstrid cried out.

"Push, Æstrid!" Veleif ordered roughly.

"I hate you, Veleif," Æstrid sobbed weakly.

Veleif levered himself up between her legs and caressed her face tenderly. "Hate me all you wish, my love. Curse me to hell for all time, but right now, Æstrid do not fight me. Now push!"

Halfdan and Arnor exchanged worried glances.

"Push, my lady. I think your son is anxious to meet his parents," Arnor smiled encouragingly.

"Push, my love. I'm right here with you." Veleif's tone gentled as he smoothed the hair from her face.

Time suspended in that moment and Æstrid's violet eyes met the blue depths of his confident gaze. She saw strength in him and something inside her shifted.

"We'll do this Æstrid, together," Veleif said, with an encouraging nod. She inclined her head in agreement and drew a huge breath.

With a last great cry, Æstrid drew upon every bit of strength she could summon. Her body arched back in pain as the scream tore from her throat. Arnor and Halfdan turned their heads away with breaking hearts as Æstrid's fingers crushed their own.

The babe surged forward.

Another scream and the babe was freed from her womb gushing forth into Veleif's waiting hands. Veleif cradled the warm, bloody baby in his palms, unable to speak as he stared down in wonder. A tiny cry broke his trance and Veleif quickly wrapped his son in Æstrid's tattered dress.

She gazed up at him through her bended knees. The sight of Veleif holding their babe flooded her with unfathomable emotion. Her eyes swarmed with tears, then she felt warm trickles spill down her cheeks.

"Is he... or she?" Æstrid choked, her voice barely above a whisper. Veleif's gaze locked with hers and behind the blood and dirt covering his face, he broke into the most dazzling smile she'd ever seen.

"A son, Æstrid. You've given us a son." He knelt forward and tenderly placed the baby in her waiting arms. Tears and laughter flowed freely now as Æstrid gazed down at her new son for the first time. Halfdan coughed and wiped his eyes. When she looked up at Veleif and seeing the love and wonder radiating from him she shook her head in disbelief.

"He's perfect, Veleif. Completely perfect." Her hand reached out and she stroked the dark hair on her son's head.

"Perfect?" Arnor snorted as he glanced down at the babe and flicked his wrist. "He's covered in blood and... and..." Arnor turned his head quickly and made strangled noises as his shoulders heaved.

Veleif and Halfdan laughed and clapped the great Viking on his back until he regained his composure. The babe cried out lustily and drew his fist to his mouth. His whole body turned red with the effort, and Æstrid placed him against her breast, covering them both the remnants of her skirt.

"He bellows louder than you, Veleif," Halfdan laughed, still wiping his tears. "Though it appears he has Arnor's great appetite."

"I think Arnor's appetite may be abated for a long while," Veleif chuckled.

Arnor pushed himself roughly to his feet and wiped his mouth with the back of his hand. "While I congratulate you both, I can wait a lifetime before seeing that again."

Everyone, including Æstrid, broke out in laughter. Veleif bent close to Æstrid, taking her lips with his own.

"Despite your choice of the strangest birthing chamber in Kollsveinholdt, my beautiful bride, you did well. You did very, very well," Veleif whispered, and cradled her against him.

Æstrid nestled against his broad chest, and glanced up to Halfdan and Arnor, then met his gaze once more.

Surrounded by the warmth and laughter of her filthy warriors, life was glorious. She finally found her voice, laced with sentiment, and rasped between her gasps of laughter.

"Despite the help of Kollsveinholdt's most unkempt midwives, Veleif, for once, I cannot disagree."

# Author's Note & Links

I hope you enjoyed *His Viking Bride* as much as I enjoyed bringing these characters to life for you. I'm often asked, "Why Vikings?"

Being a Florida girl, a story set in the frozen Nordic climates was about as dissimilar from anything familiar as I could get. I was working on developing a Viking vampire character for my novel, *Aftermath of Five*, and came across a Nordic brooch on Pinterest.

Of course, one click led to another, and I was quickly sucked down the rabbit-hole with images of this fascinating culture. It is a civilization and a history, I admit, I knew very little about.

I became so interested in Viking culture; the ships, the trading, the clothes, the architecture, etc., my imagination soared. I found these people had an inventive perseverance despite the harsh conditions in which they lived.

And living in such a climate would make you formidable in all things, hence, Veleif and Æstrid began to take shape in my mind. I think it was the photographs I saw of the Northern Lights that truly inspired me to say, "How about a Viking romance?"

Yet the challenge for this Florida author was setting a romance in snow and ice. What is romantic about freezing winds and churning seas? Other than snuggling?

While sub-zero temperatures, brutal north winds, and living in stone and clay structures provided a real challenge as a backdrop for a romance, I took creative liberty and adjusted the scenes accordingly.

Between you and me, when I began *His Viking Bride*, I banged my head more than a few times and cursed, "What was I thinking? Snow? Ice? I live in the tropics."

While *His Viking Bride* is inspired by research, I have taken creative liberties with the actual facts of the period.

This is not a book that should be taken at face value for historical accuracy, but rather, enjoyed for the fictional tale that it is.

While purists may argue, and rightfully so, my use of potatoes in this book, I am reminded of a comment made regarding one of my all-time favorite movies *The Aventures of Robin Hood*, starring Errol Flynn.

The movie received criticism for one of the final scenes. According to historians, crusaders did not wear their white robes with the red crosses on the front when they returned home. They wore the crosses on the front when they embarked on a crusade, and turned them to the back when they returned home.

However, it would be impossible to identify crusaders on film with crosses on their backs, the decision was made to turn the crosses on the tunics to the front. As Æstrid was endearing herself to the people of Kollsveinholdt, I thought potatoes used as a hand warmer would be much easier (and tastier) than an onion or a leek. I think Arnor would agree!

As the actual history and facts began to unfold during my research, my imagination wandered uncontrollably. I learned one theory of the word 'beserk.' According to this belief, the word stems from Vikings taking beer breaks during skirmishes.

Halfway through a battle, the warriors would remove their shirts, ingest copious amounts of ale, and then resume fighting — hence going "beserk." However, more popular theories actually place the origin of Berserkers (or berserks) as champion Norse warriors who fought in a trance-like fury, due to ale and the use of mind-numbing mushrooms.

Vikings also used horses, not so much in a domesticated capacity, but rather to reach battlegrounds more quickly. They would jump off and then fight on foot.

These facts struck me as outrageously humorous; and humor became the foundation for this novel.

I also searched for a potential alcohol that could be used to drive Veleif to a drunken state for the end scene. Learning that Vikings drank plenty of ale, (mead and wine, were traditionally served for religious events) and milk and water were also popular. Since this was a "special occasion" I settled upon vodka.

While vodka is not quite historically accurate, but Vikings were avid traders and travelers; vodka, created in the regions of modern day Russia and Poland, seemed to be a logical choice.

Regarding the inspiration for the overall story, one of my favorite comedies by Shakespeare is *The Taming of the Shrew*. I've always respected Katherine's headstrong nature and laughingly enjoyed Petruchio's wit in his single-minded quest to tame his bride. *His Viking Bride* is my homage to the bard, and I drew a great deal of inspiration from his work.

I followed a traditional romance structure in this book, but the characters allowed me add in some very non-traditional elements.

Hello? Vikings...

Æstrid and Veleif, two demanding souls, wouldn't have had it any other way.

Besides, what could be more romantic than a moonlit snowball fight under the majesty of the Northern Lights? I'm certain our Vikings ancestors enjoyed their fair share.

I welcome your comments and love to connect. You can find me on Facebook, as well as Instagram, and Twitter @olivianorem.

To stay updated on the latest works, release dates, and specials, please visit my website: www.olivianorem.com.

Thank you so much in support of this book. Indie authors such as myself thrive on feedback. Please take a moment to rate or review this work on Amazon, Goodreads, or wherever else you post your comments.

Ratings and reviews are critical to our craft, and we appreciate your taking the time to share your opinion. Even clicking a few stars makes a huge difference to authors such as myself.

Best Wishes,
Olivia

PS. As an added thank you, I've included a sneak peek of *Lights, Camera, Scotland!* a paranormal, Highlander romance, and the first look from *How to Steal a Highlander*, a time travel romance. Both books coming in Spring, 2018.

# About the Author

Since Olivia is old enough to remember, she devoured books and stories and became enchanted with the worlds the authors created. Imagination, unforgettable characters, and the swoon-worthy, alpha males have made a huge impact on her writing style.

Olivia is known for strong, sassy characters who are always ready with a quip of humor, despite their situations.

Born in the Chicago area, Olivia moved to the sunny shores of the Tampa Bay more years ago then she cares to admit. This award-winning author writes full-time, and enjoys her "C" hobbies: cats, cigars and classic cars.

## Upcoming Titles by Olivia Norem

His Viking Bride, Audiobook, March, 2018

### Fiction:

Outlaws: A Brothers in Justice Novel, Volume Two

Redemption: A Brothers in Justice Novel, Volume Three

Angel's Assassin Trilogy

### Romance:

How to Steal a Highlander

Lights, Camera, Scotland!

### Erotic Romance:

Wicked Wicked Days

Wicked Wicked Wilderness

## Chapter 1

Ian Macfarlane, seventh Earl of Glenross, jolted to a halt and stared at today's tabloid, artfully arranged on his desk. There was no escaping the vivid waters of the tropical beach, or the topless blonde who graced the cover.

The woman had her bronzed thigh skewered around the muscular torso of some male heartthrob-of-the-month; and the publisher had managed to place an obligatory black bar over her nude breasts. But they left her face exposed – as always.

Her head was tossed back, smiling in megawatt pleasure, as her hand clutched some noxious umbrella cocktail. Flavor-of-the-month's face was obscured, buried against her neck. The woman hadn't even bothered with sunglasses, as if she wanted to announce to the world her ridiculous affair, which rocketed her photos all over the cheesy tabloids.

Large, ugly, block type read: Kathe Caught - AGAIN!

Ian skipped the subtitle.

Katherine garnered so much publicity in the past six months, she was the opening segment on every panel show across the United Kingdom. The comedian's were having a field day speculating on who Kathe would hook up with next.

The photo shouldn't have bothered him. Normally, drivel splashed across the pages of a tabloid wouldn't have earned a second glance; but Ian MacFarlane felt his carefully architected composure shatter in the wake of the image.

The topless, laughing blonde, mocking him on the cover of the cheap newsprint, was his wife.

The wife he hadn't seen in almost a year.

Ian calmly extracted the tabloid from his desk and folded the newspaper in half, closing the damning photograph upon itself. Just holding the evidence of Kathe's indiscretions burned his hands. He paused for a tranquil moment, then folded the paper in half again.

Suddenly, without thinking of the consequences to his self-control, a feral growl tore from his throat. Ian ripped the paper into bits and shoved them into the bin beneath his desk.

The destruction didn't soothe the deep, raging ire brewing in his gut. It didn't pacify the proud Scot's temper of a man whose wife was frolicking around the world half-naked, and taunting him with her latest arm candy.

Ian breathed deeply. He needed to mollify his bad humor and lose himself in the sanctuary of his office. He pulled out his chair to begin his day, rote with mind-numbing reports and emails and blurred decisions, when his door burst open.

So much for sanctuary.

"See the morning rags then, brother?" Colin's cheery voice boomed across the space as he entered. The man was grinning from ear to ear and sloppily tossed himself into a chair.

Ian shot him a cold look and ignored the outburst, hoping Colin would take the hint and leave. He turned toward his computer screen with a silent grimace and waited for the icons to load.

Colin clapped his hands and rubbed them together vigorously. The younger man's eyes were sparkling with wicked good humor as he chuckled.

"Just wait 'til you see the sales sheets this morning. I swear every time Kathe makes a front page, sales go up over twenty percent," he chuckled.

Colin jumped from his chair and rushed from the office, only to burst back in again seconds later. Ian bristled at his younger brother's mischief. He may hold the title of Executive Vice President of Operations, but Colin shunned any bit of professionalism at times. Especially when it came to him.

"Almost forgot." He carried a beaker of amber liquid, swirling it proudly in his hand and extended it to a scowling Ian. "Taste it. I think we have the blend perfect now. This is going to make us a fortune."

"Colin? Do ye realize it is nine o'clock in the morning?" Ian tilted back judiciously in his chair and folded his arms across his broad chest.

Colin peered at his older brother with an unspoken 'so what?'

"This whiskey heeds no clock, Ian. Besides, this can't wait. We just need your approval."

As far as Colin could remember, he'd never seen his brother in his office clad in anything but a suit. Ian's custom-tailored shirt was stiff and starched beneath his double Windsor knotted tie.

Everything about him was perfunctorily inflexible, even more so since his separation.

If ever there was a man who needed to relax, it was his brother. Besides, a wee dram of whiskey wasn't about to loosen his buttoned-up problems.

"Come on, humor me," Colin urged.

"I've spent decades humoring ye, Colin." Ian's mouth curled in a frown as he took the beaker with a sigh. It was plain little brother wasn't going to leave him in peace until he tasted the whiskey.

"I've said a'fore, I see no need for this. Ye've no' a care for ye're birthright, Colin," he muttered dryly, as he sniffed the beaker.

Ian's brogue always turned thick when he was perturbed. Colin took it as the usual warning sign of his brother's simmering temper, but he was not dissuaded. Poised on the edge of the chair, he watched Ian hold it up to the light, and regard the color with a practiced eye.

Colin slapped his palms on his thighs and waited for his brother's verdict.

Ian tossed back a sip, let it linger on his tongue, and then swallowed. His eyes closed as he let the flavors expand in his mouth. The oak and peat, the honey and licorice, and there it was.

The elusive ingredient Ian could not name.

In fact, no one from the master distiller or the computer analysis done in Edinburgh, to researching the ancient logs of his family's distillery could discover the ingredient.

Ian inhaled, letting the savory smooth warm him slowly all the way down to his churning gut. He still hadn't let his ire melt away from this morning's glaring tabloid… but this, this was indeed the finest whiskey he'd ever tasted. It was as close to nirvana as could possibly be achieved.

The whiskey was, without a doubt, perfection.

"I'm not approving this," he said flatly, and eyed his younger brother.

"Oh come on Ian!" Colin wailed as he stood and threw his hands in the air. "If ye're not the most stubborn mon in Scotland. It's a blend, brother. A blend. We'll do a limited release. A hundred bottles. With this mixture we'll only use half the Black Stag reserve."

"My answer is no." Ian set the beaker on his desk and turned back to the screen. It was more than a hint of dismissal, he was being rude. And worse, he didn't care.

"Jesus Ian! We're looking at over a quarter of a million pounds here. For a limited run of a hundred bottles. We can have it released for New Year, and I already have Margot's team working up the marketing plan to secure the pre-sales."

Damn! The man wasn't going to go quietly.

Ian took a deep breath and templed his fingers. "We already have a fortune, Colin. I'll not change my mind and I'd advise ye brother, to stop pursing this foolishness. I said nae a year ago and my answer has nae changed."

Colin eyed his brother, unflinching. He fired one last salvo.

"Kathe thought it was a good idea," Colin said quietly.

"Kathe!" Ian thundered and stood abruptly from his chair. His face flushed red. Finally, the infamous Macfarlane temper was about to be unleashed. Maybe, this was the fire Ian needed to launch him from the bitter doldrums of indecision.

"Yes Kathe." Colin rose, took the beaker from the desk and drained the remaining contents in quiet victory. "Unlike you, I speak to her from time to time."

"I forbid you to mention anything about our business to that witch! She didn't give a damn about it before, and she sure as hell doesn't give a damn about it now."

"You're wrong, Ian. She does care. In fact she'll be in Scotland in two days. Something about scouting locations for a new film she's doing, with her producer. A lady from Chicago....um, Tam or Jam or something like that..."

Ian's eyes narrowed to slits at his brother's mirth.

"I've invited them to stay at Cloveshire, of course." Colin shrugged casually, a smile played about his lips.

"You whot? Bloody hell, Colin!" Ian shouted. "Did ye not even think about talking with me first?"

"Of course not! I already knew what your answer would be."

"Get out Colin!" Ian thrust an angry arm toward the door. "Get out before I forget ye're ma brother and we come tae blows."

Colin moved toward the door as his blue eyes danced with mischief. "Oh, I'm leaving. It would hardly be fair anyway." His eyes roamed Ian from head to toe. "That suit is so stiff it would probably restrict ye're right cross."

"I'll show ye restrictions!" Ian growled with rage. With a vicious swipe of his arm, he sent the entire contents from his desk, including his monitor, flying to the floor.

Bespoke suits never impeded a gentlemen's range of motion.

Colin closed the door on the crash and chuckled into the worried face of Maggie, his brother's personal assistant. He gave her a dazzling smile as the woman sighed.

"You put another one of those nasty newspapers on his desk didn't you?"

"Of course I did." Colin brushed away an errant lock of his dark hair from his forehead.

"You're a bloody ass, Colin. Tormenting ye'r pur brother like ye do," Maggie clucked in disapproval. She methodically reached for the phone and dialed the IT department to send up a replacement for the Earl's damaged monitor.

Colin flipped the beaker high in the air and caught in one palm.

"All part of my job, sweet Maggie. I am the second son ye know." Colin laughed heartily as he sauntered down the hall to his own office.

There was no doubt in Colin's mind that Black Stag Special Reserve was going to be released in the New Year.

There was also no doubt in his mind, once he had Ian and Kathe reunited at the castle, the two would definitely reconcile. Or divorce. Though Colin heartily hoped it was the former.

A man living in misery was a horrific thing to witness, and in Ian's case, unnecessary.

His brother just needed a wee bit of intervention, and if the impetus came in the form of a brash kick to his stubborn backside... so be it.

Also by Olivia Norem, a sneak peek
*How to Steal a Highlander*, a time travel romance

Katherine Moira Goldman always delivers.

The only female in the family business, she's worked hard to earn her reputation. A professional with world-class skills – and she has yet to disappoint a client.

However, the expertise of Goldman & Associates doesn't lie within the scope of legitimate commerce, but rather in the underground sphere of stealing priceless treasures and delivering them to the highest bidder.

And business is good.

With too many heists back to back, Katherine lands in Scotland for one quick score, a simple boost of some ancient relics. But what she uncovers is so shocking, she assumes she's suffering jet lag. Or has her imagination finally cracked from stress?

Nothing in the ventures of this notorious thief could prepare her for what she uncovered. A dark, rakish man clad in plaid – talking to her from inside an archaic mirror.

Eight centuries before, Simeon Campbell charmed the wrong woman.

This handsome laird had no idea the bonny lass was a masquerade… a dark witch of unspeakable power. When Simeon refuses the offer to join her in the realm of immortality, he quickly learns there is no wrath like a woman scorned.

Cursed by the witch, this tantalizing Scot is consigned to spend eternity within the bond of her enchantment – lost in time, and nearly bereft of hope. Until he's accidentally released into the care of a cantankerous, yet captivating female, in a century he could never have imagined…

Considering her disguises, and the flair for which this modern lass can pick a lock, he's unsure if she can be trusted.

As the pair plunge into a journey to outfox the jilted witch, devilish danger and tempting desire trail them at every unsuspecting turn. Still, this man of honor is determined to stop at nothing to save the woman he swears to protect.

In order for Simeon destroy the witch's source of power, he is resolved to travel back in time, willing to pay the ultimate price if need be.

But Katherine stubbornly knows better than to clash with an enemy fact to face. If Simeon is determined to defeat the ancient evil at its source, he's going to need help.

He's going to need a thief.

# Chapter 1

*Wild beats my heart to trace your steps,*
*Whose ancestors, in days of yore*
*Thro' hostile ranks and ruin'd gaps*
*Old Scotia's bloody lion bore:*
*Ev'n I, who sing in rustic lore,*
*Haply my sires have left their shed,*
*And fac'd grim Danger's loudest roar,*
*Bold-following where your fathers led!*

Excerpt from *Address to Edinburgh*, Robert Burns

*Boston, Modern Day*

"You're sending me *where?*" Kat thundered.

Several heads snapped in her direction, despite the fact that the Beacon Hill café thrummed noisily with clinking dishes and a lively drone of patrons.

"For god sakes, Katherine, lower your voice." Murray's thin lips pressed in a tight line as he chafed uncomfortably. "Scotland. And don't make me repeat myself."

Kat stiffened. She couldn't resist provoking Murray's social sensibilities at every opportunity, but the admonishment still needled.

"You can't expect me to drop everything and just take off… to… to Scotland?" Kat huffed with a dismissive wave. "My schedule—"

"Your schedule," Murray interrupted, "is my business. I am completely aware of your workload, and you're not dropping anything." Murray smoothed his tie as he lifted his espresso cup. His body pitched forward and he stole a glance left and right before he spoke. He kept his voice low.

"This is for a *very* important client. In Asia," Murray stressed.

Kat snorted. She could see the greedy stacks of yen dancing in his soul-less eyes. "Oh please, Murray," she rankled and rolled her eyes. "They're *all* important."

The man would sell his grandmother's walker and make her limp home if there was a buck to be made.

Despite the shadowed interior of the swanky bistro, Kat longed to pull her sunglasses over her eyes as she willed her brain to fire on all cylinders. She took a healthy swig from her wineglass and let her attention wander around the crowded room.

Day drinking irritated Murray. She'd ordered the Merlot not only for spite, but to soothe the vestiges of last night's Katy Perry concert. Her brother Colin had surprised her yesterday afternoon, flaunting tickets.

Blow off a little steam, he'd said. But blowing off steam Colin-style hadn't simply included a concert. True to form, Colin wheedled invitations to the after party with Katy's entourage at an underground club. They took a deep-dive plunge, headlong into a fifth of Crown Royal, and – if her clogged memory was correct – somewhere she broke up a sunrise fight between her brother and a drag queen at a greasy, all-night diner. The altercation started with something about sausage and grits… not that it mattered now.

Fucking Colin.

The silky liquid slid down easily, and Kat welcomed the restorative balance. A calm washed through her limbs. Neither Murray's shocking announcement, nor keeping pace with an Irish brother, was going to knock her off her game. There were only two other people known in the world who had her skill set, *and* her track record.

She was a professional, damn it. Despite her sour stomach and her body screaming for sleep, Kat wasn't about to lower her perception of authority. She set her glass down carefully and folded her arms on the cool wood.

"I have questions," Kat leveled him with a hard look.

"I expected nothing less," Murray sighed imperiously, and sat a little straighter. The gray, wiry man, who had been an unwanted part of her life for the past twenty years, crossed his bony legs at his bony knees. His familiar pose reminded Kat of a bored monarch, reluctant to hear the pleas of his peasants. An arrogant swipe of his fingers indicated she could proceed with the inquiry.

Whether it was Murray's posturing, or the lingering remnants of a hangover, Kat's patience was thin. Today, of all days, she was in a dark mood and her bullshit meter had reset to zero. Even with the pain throbbing in her head, Murray's urgent summons to meet was plain suspicious.

"You have never sent me in the field before without conducting weeks of preparation and recon. How long have you known about this?"

"I received notification two weeks ago. Irrelevant," Murray dismissed.

"*Two weeks?* And this is the first I'm hearing about it?" Her voice rose an octave. Murray glared at her through his watery eyes.

"I didn't want to distract your attention from the Jameson job. Trust me, Katherine, this is the easiest money you will ever make. Next."

Kat snorted again in a rebellious and unladylike manner. "Since when does Goldman and Associates hop over to Europe for a single acquisition?"

His eyes flickered up to hers and he cleared his throat. "Since this." Murray extracted a brochure from his breast pocket and slid it across the table.

"Relics of the Ancient World?" Kat mused aloud as she trailed a fingertip over the scripted title. The glossy cover was a ménage of coins, weapons of antiquity, and old paintings. By habit and training, she'd already committed the exhibit dates and location to memory.

On page six was a photo of the Fasque Castle Hotel. The castle looked as if it was lifted straight out of a Highland fairytale.

Kat pressed her lips together in a frown. She studied Murray beneath half-lowered lids and thumbed through the pages with feigned interest. She searched for his tells, yet nothing in his body language hinted he was even close to pulling her chain. And Kat knew all of Murray's signals.

If anything, Murray looked... nervous.

"I am is not a double-booking you, Katherine. You will complete your transaction with Mr. Jameson and his bearer bonds on Thursday, and then board a plane for Edinburgh in the evening."

"It's too close. I'm not going," Kat straightened. "You're leaving me no time in between assignments. Why don't you send Colin to—"

"No," Murray interrupted. "You are perfectly suited for this field assignment. Colin will provide the necessary intel and computer support from his office." He leaned back with a disapproving sigh and sipped his espresso.

Kat rolled her eyes at his use of 'field assignment.' Screw propriety and screw the man seated across the table from her who complimented her skills and criticized her in the same breath. After all, he'd summoned her to meet him at this upscale bistro, filled with snooty patrons, and overpriced brew served in gold-rimmed porcelain.

Letting the silence hang between them, He appeared totally inconvenienced as he waited for her to ask details, the calculating prick.

Hell, this was *his* meeting. The man seated across the table from her, in one of Boston's most posh coffee and wine bars, was stoic, dispassionate, and incredibly formal. He was also, (at least according to the State of Massachusetts), her father.

And he was a thoroughly, degenerate bastard.

"So what's the score?" Kat released a bored sigh.

"Six, gold coins. Viking in origin." Murray flipped to the back of the brochure and tapped the page. "And this painting."

"Shit, Murray! I hate lifting fucking paintings!"

"Watch your language, Katherine," Murray warned. He reached for a napkin and broke into a fit of coughing. Kat didn't like the sound. At all. Her brow furrowed in closer scrutiny. Murray did appear a little pastier than usual...

"What's wrong?" Kat put a hand on his arm. Murray brushed it away quickly.

"Just a little chest cold. Colin has all the details for you, schematics, plane tickets, and you're registered as a guest at Fasque Castle. The merchandise is arriving on the tenth of this month. That's three days from now. Crews are scheduled to start setting up the exhibit the following Monday."

"Wait. Colin knew about this?"

Murray arched a brow and Kat knew he wasn't about to divulge any additional information. He would deem it unnecessary to include *feelings* in this discussion. All that mattered to Murray was the job.

Her mind already calculated the plan. She'd rob the merchandise while in storage and reseal the crates. By the time the theft was discovered during setup, she and the goods would be long gone. The ensuing investigation would initially focus on the transit and later the hotel guests.

But Kat wasn't worried. Colin would make certain she was a ghost. She had to admit, going to a Scottish castle sounded more like a vacation rather than work. Now all she needed were the details.

"Okay, sounds like an easy boost. What's my cover?"

"There's a wedding taking place over the weekend. You're one of the guests. You are an American history teacher and a distant cousin to the groom. Colin has the dossier prepared on the family so you can memorize it."

"Great. What did you do this weekend, Kat? Oh went to Scotland, crashed a wedding, stole a few priceless relics..." she drawled.

"Focus, Katherine." Murray frowned, then mumbled something like, "after all I've done for you children—"

Kat tuned out the rest of his diatribe. She'd heard it for years.

"Okay, okay," she interrupted and held up her hand in protest.

"Are you ready for tomorrow night?" Murray was just making conversation now. He knew damned well she was ready.

"Of course I'm ready."

"When you're done, take the limo straight to the airport. You're taking the red-eye to Heathrow and connecting to Edinburgh. From there you'll drive to Fasque Castle. On Monday, you courier the package to a hotel in Zurich. You fly on Tuesday and deliver the package to a safety deposit box. Simple."

"Sure, Murray, easy peasy. And I won't be home next week."

"Why not?" He raised a critical brow.

"Since I'm already in Europe, I think I'll take a little vacay. A little me time. I deserve it don't you think?" she prodded.

"I suppose, Katherine," Murray sighed and coughed again into a napkin. "But I expect you back stateside before the end of the month. And don't even consider beginning your little *vacation*, until you're finished in Zurich."

"Fuck off, Murray. Since when have I ever put anything before work?"

Murray drained his dainty espresso with a deep frown and stood to leave. "I have raised you better than this Katherine Moira Goldman. Language."

Kat watched his retreating back wind through the tables as she toyed with the brochure. Dropping the 'f-bomb' in Murray's presence was a guaranteed way to secure an abrupt departure. Not only did he skip the obligatory kiss to her cheek, the prick hadn't been bothered to cover the tip.

Yet Murray's predictable behavior wasn't the source of her discontent; it was the timing of his message. International locations were not wholly unusual for Goldman & Associates, but she was lifting bearer bonds from a trust fund baby tomorrow night. The job had taken two months to plan. Had he forgotten that?

He just blindsided her with this announcement and she had little to no time to prepare. Two jobs back to back? And why had he looked so worried?

Murray was a planner, and he'd never engaged in any operation that resembled a smash and grab. Kat tossed a five on the table and tucked the brochure in her purse. Either Murray had grossly underestimated the risk, or this Scotland job really was a cake walk.

### 

Simeon paced in agitation within the confines of his cell. He'd been shrouded in darkness for hour upon endless hour, and knew deep in his bones, something was wrong.

Terribly wrong.

His warrior's sense prickled at the hackles of his neck, and had been, ever since his view of the marble table top and the empty room had been obscured.

He'd been mysteriously placed – face down no less – in what he could only assume was a box. Before the darkness had closed around him, he'd caught a glimpse of dozens of white, pillowy objects, and heard the squeaky, crunching sounds as his mirrored container was placed upon it. It was unlike any straw he'd ever seen.

Then complete darkness.

He heard the double sounds of metal clips snapping shut. After that, the distant pounding of nails on wood and Simeon assumed his perpetual prison had just been crated.

Twofold.

A whim of time passed compared to what he had experienced before. The squeak of nails, the snapping of clips, and light broke across the translucent barrier that held him imprisoned within Isobel's cursed hand mirror.

He'd seen the odd faces of bustling men, wearing odder-looking caps, against interior walls that could only be made from his familiar Highland stone. Boxes and crates were stacked around the room and Simeon assumed he was in some sort of a tower. A castle tower.

He pressed his ear against the cool glass and strained to hear their distant speech. Men's voices held the familiar lilt of brogue, but the words they used were different from his own. And on the chance one of them passed in front of his field of vision, Simeon was aghast. They seemed kindred, but their manner of dress was confusing. Not a single man among them wore a linen shirt or was draped in plaid. Bereft of any markings of any clan, they wore breeches still, and long overcoats in a dark, blue hue.

Was he still in Scotia?

Simeon studied the face of one of these curious men who lifted the mirror, and knew the man gazed solely upon his own reflection. Simeon caught a glimpse of a glove covering his fingertips, but it was thin and white, not at all like the hide gloves he was used to wearing.

The man was as strangely dressed as the others, in a dark blue shirt with buttons of unknown origin that glinted in the light. He wore no waistcoat, nor was his shirt decorated with any adornment except a white patch of fabric upon his breast.

The patch had peculiar red letters and spelled: 'S-A-M-O-H-T'.

Simeon squinted and mouthed the unfamiliar markings, but quickly determined he was seeing the reflection.

Thomas, he repeated aloud. While he was unacquainted with the Thomas clan, the knowledge almost made him giddy. He was seeing something remotely human in more sunrises than he could remember.

"Thomas!" he bellowed.

But the man had not heard him. No one ever heard him except Isobel, and he hadn't seen her in at least a century, by his guess. The view of the room was quickly obscured as the man set the mirror face-down on a black velvet cloth spread out on a wooden table.

That had been two days ago.

More darkness engulfed him and he listened in wistful silence. There was only the sound of shuffling feet, the unfamiliar lilt of brogue and the distant pounding of hammers on wood...

For Simeon, an impatience settled in. He wanted to see the man in the Thomas garb. He wanted to be lifted from the darkened cloth. He wanted to view the stone walls, count the crates and enjoy respite from this infernal shroud.

But the noises ceased and Simeon was left in abject solitude once more.

Darkness.

Nothing stirred except the sound of his own breath. Simeon pressed his back against the wall and slid down until he was lowered upon the floor. He rested his forearm on a bent knee and rubbed his forehead on his bicep. Inhaling deep and releasing it slowly, he clung to the one thing that had kept him from losing his sanity in this interminable prison.

Hope.

# Chapter 2

*O Thou, in whom we live and move,*
*Who made the sea and shore,*
*Thy goodness constantly we prove,*
*And, grateful, would adore;*
*And, if it please Thee, Power above!*
*Still grant us with such store*
*The friend we trust, the fair we love,*
*And we desire no more.*
*From A Poet's Grace, Robert Burns*

Weddings sucked.

Kat mentally slapped her forehead and cursed. She'd made two classic mistakes.

First, she was posing as a married woman using the flimsiest of acceptable excuses as to why she had arrived without her husband. And second, she attended the wedding as a blonde. The novelty of a singular, golden-haired American wasn't lost on the braw lads attending the festivities.

Music and laughter swirled between the romance perfuming the air, thicker than the roses and spicy lilies that dripped *everywhere* in the bride's signature shade of bubblegum pink. Kat even teared up as the couple pledged their vows of eternal love against the sweeping vistas of Fasque Castle while bagpipes played their haunting melodies in the distance.

Unfortunately, in this love-charged atmosphere she had attracted the attention of one rather zealous admirer…

Brice, was handsome and polite. The man zeroed in on Kat, (or Heather as the name she'd assumed for the event) as his target for a romantic weekend, and simply wouldn't be dissuaded from his single-minded pursuit. It was Kat's first up-close and personal taste with the notorious trait of Scottish stubbornness.

If she hadn't been on an ulterior pursuit, she probably would have dallied in a weekend of hedonistic pleasure. After all, she wasn't attached to anyone, and a girl did have needs… and those needs were crying to be fed at a rampant pace. Between watching the dewy-eyed bride with her attentive groom, both glowing with happiness, and the heartfelt sentiments pouring from the guests, Kat was almost caught up in the allure of the perfect event.

Being one of the world's most successful thieves wasn't exactly conducive to relationships. And intimacy, beyond quick, sexual relief, was strictly discouraged. Lord knows what details might be whispered to a lover. What a boyfriend might learn during a hand-held walk in the moonlight, or suspicions raised because of her prolonged disappearances?

The Goldman rules, which had been drilled into her since childhood, didn't allow for sharing personal details beyond small talk.

Kat had lovers here and there, but she never allowed anyone to know her. The real her. She'd never experience the kind of love she was witnessing tonight at Fasque Castle.

A sharp tang of regret stabbed her chest. She had a front row seat at true love's stage, and all she saw was a reflection of her loneliness. There was no denying it.

Weddings sucked.

Kat needed to focus. Love and romance be damned, she had a job to do. Besides, she had Brice, who was stuck to her side with all the wanted pleasure of gum on a shoe.

Burying the remorse, Kat smiled inwardly and drew upon one of the tenets Murray drilled into them as children: *'When harvesting the cabbage if find yourself with unwanted company… Make him your mark.'*

Simeon waited, tense and vigilant with his face and fingers pressed against the glass window of his prison. There was an inexplicable draw of celebration in the air, he was certain. As certain as he heard the faint chords of pipes...

At last, his indistinct imaginings were realized. Muffled footsteps approached, followed by a heavier set. Simeon craned his neck and held his breath. There it was again. He straightened as he caught the unmistakable resonance of a female voice, followed by a dainty laugh. Then the muted baritone of a male reply.

Simeon punched his fist on the glass with a curse of frustration. He startled upright as feminine tones pierced the darkness.

"Did you hear that?"

A quiet pause and Simeon listened too. The stillness stretched like a warm ache and he felt his chest constrict in false hope.

Silence.

He kicked the translucent door in annoyance, knowing for the ten-thousandth time the glass would hold. But it felt good to release some anger.

It felt good to *feel*.

"That? Did you hear that?" the female repeated.

Simeon's breath caught in his throat. His body tensed. She'd heard him. Saints be praised, the lass heard him. Could it truly be after these quiet centuries someone had actually *heard* him? The joy rendered him almost light-headed, until he realized the voice belonged to no Scottish lass.

What disguise had Isobel assumed now?

"'Tis no' but the sound of my heart, lass." The male voice replied low and husky.

Another feminine chuckle.

Simeon rolled his eyes.

Doubly cursed to solitude and when he finally *heard* another human, what greeted him? A rutting fool!

*Who had Isobel coerced to this chamber?*

"Enough of ye'r tiresome games, ye bluidy witch! Speak the words!" Simeon bellowed and punctuated his angry speech with another hard knock to the mirror.

As Simeon's fist connected with the glass, Brice unknowingly dropped a crate lid with a bang. The sound muffled the punch Kat had heard before.

Kat froze.

Goose bumps spread along her bare arms. It was bad enough this horny Scot had followed her into the tower, but now he was *swearing* at her? She was *so* going to enjoy setting him up to take the blame for the disappearance of these artifacts.

"Did you just call me a bitch?" Kat stiffened.

Her "date" had been arranging some tarps and sheeting into a makeshift bed among the crates. Brice spun around and peered at her sardonically.

"Nay, lass. I would ne'er call you such thing." Brice inched forward. Kat backed up a few steps until her bottom came in contact with a table, preventing any further retreat.

"Stay right there," she breathed huskily. She turned her back to Brice and made a slow show of unzipping her dress.

"Where the hell else would I be goin'?" Simeon ground out impatiently. He leaned his forehead against the glass.

Kat darted a sharp look at Brice. "You're pretty weak at this seduction thing aren't you?" she accused, then rotated away and turned her attention to her shoes.

Simeon jolted upright at the affront. *Weak?* After all this time, locked away under her cursed spell, the bitch dared call *him* weak!

Brice frowned in confusion and jammed his hands in his pockets. "Och! I doona like these games ye Americans play," he muttered, and spun on his heel.

Brice suddenly felt the need for another drink. His brother was right. American women could be downright rude.

"'Twas no' weakness that had ye whimperin' in my bed so hot with lust, it turned ye into a crazed, possessive shrew." Simeon huffed.

"Whoa, buddy. I think you're mixing me up with someone else. Hot with lust? Oh please," Kat retorted to Brice's retreating back.

Damn! She did not need him to leave right now.

"Are ye drunk woman?" Brice frowned over his shoulder.

Simeon frowned.

Isobel didn't get drunk.

What the hell was happening? Unless the voice who could hear him was nae Isobel, but someone else...

Kat hurried across the stone floor in little skipping motions impeded by her tight dress.

"Brice, wait."

"Who the bluidy hell is Brice?" Simeon roared as he kicked the mirror again.

Kat halted. She glanced left. Then right. Then she spun full circle. Someone was here, and it sure wasn't Brice. A cold tremor of dread shivered down her spine, and Kat did not shiver.

*What the hell was going on?*

"All right, you sick bastard. Why don't you just come out and play, huh?" Kat's eyes darted around the dim tower room, as she deftly unzipped the lower portion of her dress. She slipped out of her shoes, fists raised in a defensive stance.

She was ready for this intruder.

"Come out?" Simeon shouted incredulous. His voice curled low and menacing. "I'll twist yer wee neck 'til ye cannae breathe yer mockery."

"Oh, so you want to strangle me, huh?" Kat taunted. Her senses tripped to full alert in anticipation of a blindsided attack.

She took slow, deliberate steps to secure a vantage point. Kat felt the cool press of ancient stone against her back. Her breath hitched as an angry tone permeated the quiet of the tower once more.

"Isobel! Speak the words and face me true, ye bluidy coward," Simeon growled low and dangerous.

The voice sounded irregular, diminutive even, like it was… covered. Or trapped.

Maybe the acoustics of the room were playing tricks on her?

And who was Isobel?

Kat inched along the wall, poised for combat. She edged toward the table and glanced at the object on the black velvet. It looked like a hand mirror, but the silver work was so unusual she allowed herself a momentary distraction.

The mirror was about eight inches long with an oval top that curved downward into a twisted, spiral handle. A barely-pink stone was set into the base of the handle. Between the silver talons that held it in place, the stone glimmered, cut in such a manner, it almost looked… prismatic.

Sparkling blue sapphires, pink prism stones, and rough cut diamonds were scattered amid the markings. The engravings were intricate scrolls and patterns that appeared to be some sort of ancient language.

Kat was well versed in Hieroglyphics, Sanskrit, and had a rudimentary knowledge of Celtic rune markings; but this mirror was unlike anything she'd ever seen.

Her brother Ian would go wild for this mirror.

She scanned a cautionary eye on the stacked crates, and the objects piled on the tables. Everything was catalogued and ready to be carried into the exhibit on Monday.

Whoever had been watching her, had now gone silent.

The inlaid stones winked at her in the dim light. At least eleventh century she guessed, perhaps even earlier. If it was a mirror on the other side, the thing could come in handy to move stealthily among the stacks of crates in a low crouch. She could peek around corners and catch her would-be assailant unaware.

Kat closed her fingers around the handle. A raw surge of pure electricity shot up her arm. Faint blue light began to glow along the markings, illuminating the darkness of the room. Kat released it abruptly and the light faded.

What the heck just happened?

With a wary glance to the shadows, Kat touched her finger to the mirror. The light intensified, powering up to vivid blue.

What was this thing?

Kat picked up the mirror again. Tingling charges shot up her arm and she couldn't stifle a groan of pain. Keeping one eye on the room and one eye on the glass what she saw next in the crackled silver was *not* her reflection.

It was a man.

A man with wild dark hair around his face and the hint of tartan slung over one shoulder. Why on earth would someone put a portrait behind a glass and put it in a mirror? In all her familiarity with antiques, Kat had never seen such an oddity. Not only was the mirror baffling, but why would someone paint a portrait of such an angry face?

"Ye're no' Isobel!" His eyes widened in pure astonishment.

"What the fuck?" Kat sprung back in shock. She dropped the mirror on the velvet as if she'd been burned.

That was *not* possible.

This was *not* happening.

Did she just see a *living man* behind the silvered glass? Who *spoke?* Who had... *expressions?*

Was this real or was this jet lag?

*Severe* jet lag.

Was this stress?

Is this what happened when your mind finally cracked? You started imagining things were real? Animated? She'd read somewhere once about delusional people who saw people on television coming out of the screen and believing they were real.

Kat struggled for air, almost wishing she could shed the constricting dress and adopt a yoga pose.

*"I'm not crazy, I'm not crazy,"* she panted.

Center, breathe deep. Exhale, good. Center, breathe deep.

*"I'm not crazy."* Exhale.

Was her mind playing an anxiety-strained trick on her, or was this extraordinary?

"Who are ye, lass?" the voice demanded.

Kat flinched as his question was punctuated by an echoing slap of his hand against the mirror. "Answer me woman," the man growled again, "I ken ye see me."

It spoke again.

Wait, it *spoke* again. And did it just call her *woman?*

Kat crept forward and leaned over the table. Poised with her hands on the edge as she inspected the oddity closer.

The man was mesmerizing.

Kat tried to look away, tried to keep a trained eye at the room, but it was impossible. Silky black hair fell about his face and shoulders. A face that was sharp with chiseled features. The hard angle of his jaw was dusted with trace of a dark shadow. He had high cheekbones a supermodel would be envious of and a straight, firm nose, leading down to lips full of with sensual promise.

He was quite simply, the essence of raw male magnificence, yet dangerously savage at the same time.

His eyes were hypnotic – piercing blue so light, they were icy. Glacial eyes filled with mocking and curiosity. His sinful gaze raked over her, pausing too long on the shadow of cleavage in her blue gown.

Typical.

Kat rolled her eyes but couldn't stifle an involuntary shiver.

"I ken ye see me, just as I see ye." His eyes narrowed as he pointed an accusatory finger. "Ye hear me too. What's yer name, lass?"

It took her a moment to register exactly what she heard through the thick brogue of his musical accent. Her mind translated his words slowly, as they made sense about half a minute after he spoke them.

This image, this... this man in the mirror... it, he, or whatever this thing was, definitely spoke.

"What?" Kat pointed a shaky finger at the mirror.

"Yer name, lass. What are ye called, ye ken?" he growled impatiently. Heavy brows drew together in a scowl.

"My... my name?" Kat stammered, trying to recover from the shock. A man. In a mirror. Was asking her questions. This was so not possible.

"Aye, are ye simple then?" A massive hand waved in front of his face.

Kat frowned at the mirror in confusion. She paused another long moment, then leaned closer.

"Wait a second. Did you just ask me if I'm stupid?"

The man shot her an imperious glance.

This exchange was beyond humorous.

Katherine Moira Goldman was talking to an ancient relic; and it, or he, or whatever it was, was giving her attitude.

"Listen up, buddy. Until I know who or *what* you are, it wouldn't hurt to be a little nicer. It's not like kind of thing happens to me every day. You *ken*?"

Simeon ran an impatient hand over his shadowed jaw and exhaled his frustration. Nicer? He simply wanted to know her name so he *could* be bluidy nice. Then he could sway her to say the words to release him from this infernal prison.

The endless passage of time in hellish solitude, devoid of sights or conversations would have driven a lesser man to madness.

Simeon had no want for food, or sleep or lust; even the need to relieve himself had been removed from his existence. In this place, he simply *was*.

The interminable wonder if he would ever have any desire for anything mortal as his cell stripped him of everything a man was... had been answered tonight.

The lack of these simple cravings, he'd pondered long ago and then forgotten. Forgotten until a few moments ago, when this mysteriously bonny lass, who spoke strangely, had not only heard *and* seen him, but stirred a rising lust so powerful, he cursed and welcomed the barbarian within.

So may God forgive him if he was anxious to the point of rudeness.

Simeon gathered his shredded patience and made a second attempt. This time, he tried a rakish approach.

After all, women had always adored him.

He'd never known one not to succumb to his slow smile or seductive speeches. If he had seen correctly, and he was certain he had, this lass on the other side of the mirror had trembled when his gaze rested upon her bonny breasts.

Still, it appeared as if no matter how many centuries had passed one fact remained resistant to change – the bonnier the woman, the more cantankerous they were.

"My apologies, lass." Simeon's head bowed in a respectful nod. He leaned a casual arm above his head on the glass, and rested his forehead there. "As unbelievable as this may be, 'twas a witch's curse hae imprisoned me here long ago. I'm as startled as ye, for it's been more years than I can count I've nae heard nae seen another person.

"My name is Simeon Campbell, lass, and ye'd honor me deeply to know who ye are as well."

Made in the USA
Columbia, SC
03 August 2018